Out of Mind

STELLA CAMERON

Out of Mind

A
Court of Angels
Novel

MIRA®

ISBN-13: 978-1-61664-053-8

OUT OF MIND

Printed in U.S.A.

In loving memory of
Suzanne Simmons Guntrum,
the sister I wish had been my own.

Prologue

Two hundred pink, spun sugar pigs.

Billy Baker ripped off the top copy of the order and put it with the others on a counter behind him.

The bell still jingled a little on the bakery shop door. Willow Millet had just closed it behind her as she left. Working on her catering jobs—the unusual stuff of course, because that was his specialty—never bored him.

It was almost time to shut the place for the night. He bent over to slide a tray of napoleons from one of the glass cases.

The bell jangled again and the door slammed.

Billy popped up, smiling, always ready to serve a customer. "Hey!"

The shop was empty.

Someone had changed their mind about coming in. Shrugging, he looked down at the confections he had to get put away for the night. Many of them would go for half price in the morning.

Click.

The neon open sign in the window went out and the chain that turned it on and off swung a little. He hadn't touched it.

A sharp sliding sound made him jump. A snap followed and he jumped again. And felt slightly sick.

The long bolt on the door had slid down and seated in its hole in the floor. A sliver of shadow in the rim of light along the jamb showed him the door was locked.

Billy's rubber-soled shoes squished on the linoleum when he could finally make a move to go around the counter and see who was playing tricks on him.

A needle-sharp prick into the flesh between his eyebrows stopped him where he was. He muttered, "Ouch," and touched the spot. It left a tiny speck of blood on his finger.

Bees?

Not in his shop.

But there it was, a buzzing sound. Where... "Damn!" The thing jabbed him again, and again and again on his forehead.

Each time he swiped at his face, more blood smeared his skin.

His heart sped up.

This was stupid. He was panicking over a bee. And the thing was so small he couldn't even see it.

A jab to his neck all but buckled his knees. It was a sharp, throbbing bite.

Every breath he took got shorter.

He broke out in a sweat. Another poke stung the soft tissue beneath his left eyebrow. His ear was the next target.

Whirling, he flung up his arms, beat the air, blinked while the left eye began to swell. "Get out! Go! Fucking bees!"

"Simone!" He yelled for the girl who did the light, late-day cleanup in the kitchen. "Simone."

She didn't come.

Thwack. A hard thing smacked the back of his head. He spun around, but there was nothing to see.

He wanted out of the shop and headed for the door to the kitchens. A broad wing, with spines he could see inside its transparent gray skin, slapped Billy's face, knocking him backward behind the cases.

Then the poking came in a flurry, thrust knifelike points into his face and neck, his scalp, in rapid succession.

Not a bee, a bird. A bird with a bloated body, wings like spined webs, and no eyes.

Billy got to his feet and reached for the broom. A blow to his head made him giddy and the handle fell from his grasp.

Again, there was no sign of the bird.

The lights went out. It wasn't dark in the shop yet, just dim. Bile rose in his throat. He had never seen such a creature before and now he couldn't tell where it had gone. But he could still hear its buzzing noise, or its whirring. The wings set up a roaring and a great current of air swept over the room.

Louder and louder it roared.

From behind the case, rising, came a swift surge of darkness and two black and shining globes. Eyes that must have been shut before they bored into Billy. Talons sprang out, and the beak snapped, shooting out a long, black tongue each time it opened.

And the eyes came straight at Billy, straight at his face, eye to eye.

He opened his mouth to shout again, but a deep, dull pain flowered in the middle of his back. Gasping, clutching at the end of the nearest display case, he saw his cell phone on the counter and reached for it. His fingers slipped on the glass.

He stumbled, gagging.

The tips of two sets of talons embedded in his face, fleetingly.

Back came the bulging eyes and this time they didn't stop. They collided with his face, and the foul-smelling tongue swiped across his mouth. The beak emitted a harsh, howling caw.

Billy grabbed at his neck and jaw, he pounded a fist into his chest, clawed at the racking pain.

His heart?

Blackness spread from the edges of his vision.

It was done.

1

Willow walked quickly along Chartres Street.

Her breathing grew shallower, and the space between her shoulder blades prickled.

Don't look back. Keep going.

Jazz blared from bars and clubs. People spilling from doorways onto New Orleans's crowded sidewalks jostled her in the throng. They danced, raised their plastic cups of booze and wiggled the way they never would at home. Colored metallic beads draped necks and more strands were thrown from flower-laden balconies overhead. Laughter and shouting all but drowned out the noise of passing vehicles.

Another French Quarter evening was tuning up.

Her new enemy clawed at the pit of her stomach: panic. Until a few days ago she had been a completely in-charge, take-on-the-world woman. Then she had become convinced she was being followed.

Whenever she left her flat in the Court of Angels behind her family's antiques shop, J. Clive Millet on Royal Street, someone watched her every move. They were waiting for the right moment to grab her—she was certain of it.

Don't run.

Sweat stung her eyes, turned her palms slick, and her heart beat so hard and fast she couldn't swallow.

If she didn't prefer to ignore the paranormal talents she had in common with the rest of the Millet family, she could come right into the open and ask some or at least one of them for advice. But how *could* she ask Uncle Pascal, her brother, Sykes; her sister Marley; or even one of her other sisters in London if they would help? Despite some recent slips, she continued to insist she was "normal," and so were they.

Willow suspected her family watched her more closely these days, which meant they had figured out that she was stressed. Keeping anything from them for long was impossible. She felt the smallest twinge of guilt for enjoying the comfort that gave her.

Why was she only feeling someone shadowing her rather than actually seeing a face? That was one of her talents—she saw the face of a negative human force, sometimes a long time before meeting the person.

This time she couldn't pick up any image.

Darn it that she was burdened with the Millet mystique. She saw the looks she got. Every New Orleans native knew about the family, which she didn't think helped her business, Mean 'n Green Concierge, all things domestic, nothing too large or too small. She only mentioned her concierge services in ads she placed for personal assistant services.

The sun was lower, a red ball that seemed to pulse in a purpling haze. And there was no air—just tight, wet pressure. Willow had grown up in the city and loved it, but heat did add to the sense of doom she felt.

Even the scent of flowers cascading from the scroll-work of black iron galleries was too sweet. That didn't make any sense. Willow loved to smell scented petunias and jasmine, and the rich floral brew that almost overcame the aroma of hot grit and used booze. Not today.

She cut a left onto St. Louis Street. Usually she rode her green-and-white scooter with its little equipment trailer around town, but since she'd only been going to discuss an order with Billy Baker, the specialty baker she used, she'd decided to walk instead.

Being on the scooter would feel safer—even more so when she got her new helmet with large, rearview mirrors.

Two blocks and she turned right onto Royal Street. A cop listened distractedly to a ranting drunk and his gesticulating buddies. For an instant Willow considered asking to talk to the cop, but what would she say?

She didn't run, but she did speed up.

Her hair lifted a little on one side, as if blown by a breeze, only there wasn't one. Softness brushed her neck, then something tiny and sharp.

A scream erupted; she couldn't stop it. Willow stood still, forced the sound from her lips and then spun around, searching in every direction. Nothing. There was nothing but people, people everywhere. She touched her neck but there was zero to feel.

She got stares, and more space to herself on the sidewalk.

The shop sign, J. Clive Antiques, shone gold against black paint and she did run the final yards until she could get inside. The doorbell jangled, and she jumped, despite expecting the sound. She closed herself inside and bowed her head while she marched purposefully toward French doors leading out into the Court of Angels at the back of the shop. Her flat was there among those belonging to other family members. She wanted to get to her private place and lock herself in.

"There you are, Willow."

Uncle Pascal. Current family head since Willow's father had abdicated his responsibilities—more than twenty years earlier—in favor of running after family secrets in various parts of the world, Uncle Pascal had a penchant for stating the obvious.

"Here I am," Willow said and thought, *and here I go,* as she carried on past gleaming old furniture, glittering glass and finely glowing paintings, toward her goal: the back door.

"I've been waiting for you," Uncle said, moving into her path. "I say little about you continuing with this silly, mundane business of yours when you should be honing your natural skills, but I do expect you to check in with me more regularly than you do."

"Sorry, but I do make sure you see me in the mornings."

She dodged to one side.

So did Uncle Pascal—the same side. "I want to talk to you about your future," he said.

She looked at him, big, muscular, shaven-headed and handsome…and really irritated right now.

"Futures take care of themselves if we let them," she said, instantly wishing she hadn't said anything at all. "I mean—"

"I know what you mean. You have buried your head in the sand and you continue to pretend you can avoid who and what you are. We all know what you are, Willow. And now you are needed to play an active part in the very serious situation we're all facing in New Orleans."

Very serious situation? Do you know exactly what's been happening to me?

What she must not do was lead the potential witness, her uncle. If he knew something that would impact her, let him spell it out on his own.

"You don't intend to come clean with me, do you?" Uncle Pascal said. "Despite everything, you'll go on pretending everything is what you call, *normal*."

She raised her chin. "What makes you so sure it's not?"

"We have our ways, and we already know it's not," he said, his brows drawn ominously downward over a pair of the very green eyes common to all Millets, except her brother, Sykes, which was a great concern to some members of the family. "But this delivery proves we aren't the only ones aware of a threat."

He went behind the shiny mahogany counter and hauled an open cardboard box on top.

"Who are *we*, Uncle?"

He scrubbed at his bald scalp. If he didn't shave it, there would be a thick head of red hair, but for reasons they all tried to ignore, he had first shaved it when he took Antoine's place as head of the Millets. Uncle Pascal didn't want the job, or so he said, and since the red hair was one of the major attributes that qualified him, he chose to get rid of it in defiance.

"Who?" Willow repeated, growing angry at the thought of the others huddling together to discuss her—

invading her privacy, as usual. "Have you been in my head again? You know it's against the rules unless you ask permission to enter my mind."

"Rules?" Pascal said, his brows elevated now. "What rules? You don't believe in the Millet rules, or anything about the paranormal talents with which we are all blessed—so why would you care or acknowledge the rules? Or are you finally accepting them?"

She closed her mouth and crossed her arms. There would be no winning an argument with Uncle Pascal.

"Even if we didn't know something unusual is going on with you, this would make sure we suspected as much."

He lifted a crash helmet from the box. White with Mean 'n Green's lime-green insignia that looked a bit like the wings on the Greek Hermes's heels, it was the twin of the one she already used, apart from rather large rearview cycling mirrors mounted on either side.

Willow gaped. "You opened my stuff!"

"It wasn't shut. It was delivered by a messenger from the place where you bought it. I thought it was something for the shop. Aren't these mirrors interesting?"

"For safety," she said, glowering. No way would she admit she wanted eyes in the back of her head these days and mirrors were the next best thing.

"And what about this?" He placed a smaller, oblong box beside the bigger one. "I suppose this is for safety, too."

"That's my business." She scrambled to excuse that second box. "It's something I'm going to give Marley and Gray for their kitchen." Her sister Marley and Gray Fisher were recently married, or Bonded as the Millets preferred to call it. There had also been an actual wedding to please Gray's dad, Gus, who was one of Willow's favorite customers.

"I know what's in this," Uncle said.

She snatched it away and turned it over. It was un-opened. "No, you don't. You're trying to trick me into telling you."

"Why do you think I need to open a box to know what's inside?" he said. "Don't you think a Beretta PX4 Storm is a bit overkill for a first handgun?"

2

Ben Fortune also saw the gun inside the package and couldn't imagine Willow being able to hold the thing steady. This was a very small woman. He knew well that she was strong, but could she hit what she wanted to hit with the weapon?

He saw Willow's back stiffen. That didn't have to be because she had sensed him behind her, standing near a Napoleonic desk he had been examining when she hurried into the shop. But given the long pause after Pascal announced the gun, he didn't think she was reacting to that. She should have responded to her uncle by now.

Odds were that she did sense Ben. His own fault since he should have made sure that was not possible until he wanted it to be. From Pascal's behavior he must have assumed Ben would mask his presence until he was alone with Willow. Pascal had promised to leave them once he'd had his say with his niece.

Too bad one glimpse of her and Ben had forgotten to do what should come naturally—reveal only what he must until he found out exactly how the land lay with the woman formerly pledged to become his lifelong Bonded partner.

That was a pledge he had never given up on, regardless of how Willow thought she could call all the shots. Despite sending him away—for good, she had insisted—she must have expected him back eventually.

Ben smiled slightly. A few experiments, really touching experiments, would prove if they still had what it took to send each other into pain and ecstasy at the same time. They had never actually made love—Willow had seen to that—but the foreplay was explosive, unforgettable. He heated up from the inside out thinking about those incendiary sensations. That electric, erotic pain between two of their kind was considered proof of preordained Bonding with a Millet. Somewhere in the mists of that family's founding, a brilliant elder must have thought such intense feelings would test the loyalty of a male's prospective mate and protect their women's honor.

Apparently, the founder responsible for the concept had not taken into account that irresistible stimulation could become addictive.

There would be a test between Ben and Willow, but he had no doubt the compulsion would be as strong as ever.

He hadn't seen her in two years since she told him they weren't meant for each other. After that she wouldn't see or speak to him.

Ben had left New Orleans, and ran the family business—a very successful club, Fortunes, and other enterprises around the city—from his retreat on the island of Kauai.

"You can see inside closed packages?" Willow said to Pascal.

"That surprises you?"

She muttered something, but she wasn't concentrating on her uncle. Instead Ben could see her struggle not to turn around. Her shoulder blades pressed together, then released, as if she were trying to relax.

Well, if the way he reacted simply to the sight of her was any indication of things to follow, he'd better not miss any vitamins.

"Hey, Willow, remember me?" he asked her through channels he attempted to open between their minds.

He'd lost his marbles, not that she had ever responded to his mind contacts in the past. That would have put the lie to her insistence that she had no paranormal powers.

"What are you doing here?" she responded, gripping the counter with both hands.

His turn to stiffen. The muscles in his back and thighs turned rock hard. Damn, this was great, she'd forgotten to cover up.

"What do you think? You and I have unfinished business. It's been unfinished for too long. And you need me now—you need all of us."

"Sykes got you here, didn't he? He could have talked to me about it first. You two have always shut me out."

"You decided to shut us out, Willow. You and I could always be as close as you wanted to be. The decisions on that were yours, remember?"

"I didn't ask you to come. I— Oh, darn it."

He felt her cut him off. It was gratifying to know he could cause her to break rules she'd made for herself in her teens when Willow had decided she would be "normal."

"You're upset and trying not to need anyone. Don't shut me out." It was worth another try to establish an intimate connection with her.

Willow didn't respond, but she did give in and look over her shoulder. And now his knees snapped into locked position. Those fabulous, brilliant green Millet eyes searched for him. The curly hair was as outrageously red as ever, the skin as pale and freckled, the features as unexpectedly sophisticated and irresistible. Then there was the small, totally sexy body....

Their eyes met.

Hers grew wider and took on a bright sheen. Ben knew it meant she was fighting tears. Willow prided herself on being in control. For her to lose it showed him just how much he'd shocked her.

She faced him and crossed her arms under her breasts. At least the familiar white shirt with its ugly Mean 'n Green insignia was made to fit her these days, rather than falling from her shoulders to the knees of her white jeans, like an oversize painter's smock.

What had he hoped? That after all this time she wouldn't have the same power to reach out and grab him in places he'd as soon control? *Thank you, Sykes, for dragging me here to suffer some more. I hope Willow knows what a concerned brother she's got.*

"Willow, let's finish here," Uncle Pascal said.

She felt his tap on her shoulder but ignored it. Ben was here and she'd already done the unthinkable, responded to his poking at her mind. She could pretend she hadn't done it, but what good would that do? He'd only wonder how much more she was trying to hide about herself.

"Hi, Ben," she said, relieved her voice sounded steady. "What brings you to New Orleans? I thought you were an island-dweller now."

"I am an island-dweller. I'm also a native of New

Orleans and I love the place." He seemed about to say more but settled his lips together.

There was no sight that could do to her what Ben could, just standing there, weight on one long leg, black hair pulled back into a tail at his nape, dark blue eyes deceptively sleepy-looking…. She was staring at him.

"You okay?" Ben asked. "You seem unsettled."

He had always been the king of smart comments. "Surprised to see you is all," she said. His dark shirt fitted tight over his wide chest and toned belly, and disappeared beneath the waist of jeans washed enough times to hold a shadow pattern that accentuated the slim and the not-so slim bits of him.

Willow had known Ben all her life. He was seven years older than she, and as they grew up he had treated her like a kid sister. She thought about how all that had changed. Kind of coincided with him "noticing" her. Willow had watched him grow tall, fill out and become a big, hard man with more psi powers than was healthy. But then she had realized he was watching her leave girlhood behind and, evidently, something about her pleased him—a lot.

The misery she had felt knowing she wasn't what he needed in a Bonded partner started an ache she had hoped never to feel again once it lost its sharp edge. But she was experiencing that longing now. He was too much for her, too strong, too skilled, too flamboyant, too much of a free spirit. Her suspicion that this was true had been confirmed by his sister, Poppy, who was very close to Ben. Poppy had been upset, tearful, but she had made herself warn Willow of the dangers in becoming Ben's permanent mate.

At least she'd had the sense to end things between them before they put a seal on their fate and she shriveled up, bit by bit, while she watched him become bored with her. He would still have been stuck with the agreement—but even if he tried to hide it, Willow would have felt his dissatisfaction.

"Why are you here?" she said sharply.

"I already told you," he said, without glancing at Pascal, who would quickly figure out that there had been a silent communication between Willow and Ben.

"You didn't say what you've been told about me," she said to Ben. Her gaze shifted sideways for an instant as she analyzed whether she'd made another reference to their personal communication.

Ben didn't want to trick her into anything. "Sykes said he's been worried about you. When I got here, Pascal told me the same thing, and I'm thinking the rest of the family will have similar stories."

She spread her hands. "Worried? Why?"

"Because you're worried." He needn't kid himself that she'd be easy to break down. "To quote someone near and dear to you, you're even more fractured than usual. You've been very quiet and you never go anywhere other than work."

She frowned, but her eyes were brighter than ever. "And that's different from what I usually do? I work hard and when I get home, I'm tired."

"And you sent for a crash helmet with two rearview mirrors," Pascal put in. The man had done a good job of fading into the background behind the counter where he sat on a high stool.

Willow shook her head. "I'm safety minded. I'm

going to have all my staff wear similar gear—just as soon as I've made sure it works well."

"Most people who ride motorcycles or scooters, or whatever, rely on handlebar mirrors. Cyclists have a mirror on one side on a helmet and it's about a quarter the size of those."

"Most cyclists don't need to see anything but oncoming traffic and what's around when they want to make a turn," she snapped back, and turned red.

Ben saw her moisten her lips and his belly contracted. He would have to contain himself. "Whereas you think you have to see all around, traffic, pedestrians and anything else that might be a hazard?"

"Yes," she said. "Now, if you'll excuse me."

Excuse her so she could run away and hide, the way she'd been hiding from him all this time? "No," he told her. "I'm not excusing you. Not unless you take me with you. Now I've come all this way, the least you can do is talk to me. I should have made you talk to me before I left. I see that now."

She blinked rapidly. Her lungs felt compressed. Did he really intend to trap her like this? To force her to go through all the misery again? For an instant she closed her eyes. His arms around her would feel so good. Of course she knew the other sensations that would go with the comfort—unless things had completely changed between them.

Willow looked at him.

"There's only one way to find out if we're still pledged, Willow."

"You don't know anything, Ben. You don't know why it could never work between us."

"Tell me why, then. Or let me hold you. What could be more natural than two old friends embracing?"

"You're rushing me again," she told him. *"You rushed me all the time. Even when others said I was wrong for you."*

She put a hand over her mouth.

"Others?" He had always suspected interference. *"What others? We were the only ones who mattered. We still are."*

"No. That's history." She collected herself visibly. "It's good to see you, Ben, even if I am a bit prickly. Some things never change." Willow forced a chuckle. "I do have to see to some business right now, but I'll get in touch with you and we'll have dinner or something. For old times' sake."

And that little speech was for Pascal's sake and to get Ben off her back. "Fine," Ben said. "Great. Do you know where to find me?"

She shuffled her feet in white tennis shoes with lime-green flashes down the sides. "Um, at Fortunes?"

"No. Poppy runs the place now—with Liam's and Ethan's support when she needs it. I'm still the financial man, but I don't want to tread on their toes." Liam, a history professor, and Ethan, a lawyer, were his brothers and Poppy, his only sister. "Sykes says he's completely tied up in his studio working on a mammoth piece of sculpture so he's letting me use his flat here."

Her face tightened and she breathed rapidly through her mouth. "Here?" She croaked out the word.

Ben didn't miss the wicked smile on Pascal's face. Pascal had encouraged a match between Ben and Willow. Part of what Ben intended to do in New Orleans was find out who had interfered in and ruined something that had promised to be fantastic. He should not have waited so long, but he had kept hoping she would ask him to come back.

"Willow, the people who won't settle for anything less than your safety think you're being threatened. They're not sure by what, only that it's happening—or you think it is."

"I'm not imagining things," she said heatedly. "Oh, leave me alone, please."

A mad scuffle accompanied Winnie, Willow's sister Marley's Boston terrier, downstairs from the regions where Marley worked on restorations. The dog clamped a vast, yellowing plastic bone between her teeth. She positioned her shiny black-and-white body in front of the shop door and wiggled in apparent anticipation.

Ben glanced up the stairs, expecting to see Marley, but there was no sign of her.

The doorbell jangled wildly and a tall, commanding man came into the shop. He took off a gray silk fedora. Tie askew at the open neck of a very white shirt, every inch of him screamed confidence, and the glittering smile—or grimace—turned his dark face into a demonically exotic vision no one would ignore. Ben had not had much to do with Nat Archer, but the detective was not someone easily forgotten.

Winnie gave a sigh of ecstasy, abandoned her bone and rolled onto her back in front of Nat. Ben decided the dog had known the man was coming.

"Hi, Pascal," Nat said, "Willow. I'm pressed for time but I wanted to come myself." He looked sideways at Ben. "Ben Fortune. It's been a long time. I heard you were in Hawaii." He rubbed Winnie's round, pink and splotchy tummy.

"Yeah," Ben said. "I'm visiting—sort of."

"Is Gray here?"

Ben remembered that Marley's husband, Gray Fisher, had been a New Orleans Police Department homicide detective before turning to full-time journalism. Gray was Nat's former partner.

"He's on a story, Nat," Pascal said.

Marley trotted downstairs in a large, paint-stained apron. "What's up?" she asked the policeman.

"Could be what we were worried about has started again. I don't have a lot of evidence, but something's happened and there are similarities to what we went through a while back."

"Well, we knew it wasn't likely to be all over," Marley said. "Those creatures, or whatever they are, intend to take over this town. Or that's the way I read it. So does Gray."

"Me, too," Nat said. "But don't think we're getting any support from NOPD—they're too afraid to admit they could have a rogue paranormal force bent on invading New Orleans. They're afraid for themselves and terrified about how they'd cope with mass panic in the populace if rumor got out. Or some of them are."

Ben ground his teeth together to stop himself from begging for an explanation of all this "code." *Rogue paranormal force? Invading New Orleans? Mass Panic?* Sykes hadn't finished explaining the whole story.

Willow swallowed and stared at Marley. One of her three sisters, Marley's eyes were forest-green, darker than Willow's, and her hair slightly less neon although just as curly.

"Marley," Willow said, "you'd better give Gray a call." Marley had gotten herself involved with a dangerous life-form they knew only as Bolivar, an Embran, and she'd come close to being killed. That had been about four months ago and Willow was suddenly convinced they were about to suffer another confrontation with these things they understood so little about, other than that they had an inexplicable vendetta against the Millets.

"I'm not going to jump to conclusions," Marley said. "Or should I?" She looked at Nat.

"This isn't the place to talk about this. What if customers come in?" Uncle Pascal said.

Nat locked the door and reversed the open sign. He turned to Ben again. "How much do you know about everything?"

"If we're talking about the same thing," Ben said, "only what Sykes has told me in the last few days. Not a whole lot, and nothing about renegade paranormal forces from—wherever." His voice got low. "Sounds like all the families might need to be involved, though."

There were a number of strong psi families in the city. They didn't live in each other's pockets, but they came together when they were needed. Mostly they were polite, but kept their distance from each other since there was a history of some explosive confrontations.

"The police need to be involved, too," Nat said. "We already are. Or those of us who can't make ourselves dismiss the idea are."

"Are you still homicide?" Ben said. His only exposure to Nat Archer had been at Fortunes during an investigation.

"Sure he is," Marley said quickly. "Homicide at

NOPD. He was our lifeline while… We've been through interesting times, Ben. For a while it looked as if some of us weren't going to make it. There was this…thing… that could morph from a human into a monster and it got me—just about. Nat doesn't have a lot of support from his department—"

"None, except from my partner, Bucky Fist, and a few bright cops who can't forget what they've seen," Nat put in. "Gray and I knew we weren't finished with these interlopers. We didn't kid ourselves they'd give up because we stopped 'em once. Marley almost got killed, and a number of other women did die," he finished, staring at Ben. "Now I need a few words with Willow."

"Why?" Marley's voice rose. "Should I track down Gray?"

Nat shook his head, no. "Not now. I've got to make this short and get back."

"Back to where?" Willow asked. She felt cold.

"*Is* it the Embran again?" Marley asked in a low, intense voice.

"Could be." Nat looked at her hard and she took a deep breath. "We shouldn't get ahead of ourselves. But—" He made a visible decision not to say any more on the subject.

Marley nodded, but her face was rigid.

"How long have you been here in the shop—this afternoon?" Nat asked Willow.

She shrugged. "Half an hour at the most."

"Thirty-seven minutes," Pascal said helpfully.

Nat thought about that. "How long did it take you to get here—from wherever you've been?"

Ben heard Willow swallow. "I don't know. Not long."

"Let's quit the twenty questions," Ben said, putting himself between Willow and Nat Archer. "Just spit out what you want."

"I'm here because the Millets are good friends of mine," Nat said. "I didn't want to send an officer in an obvious car. If I don't ask Willow these questions, someone else will. At this point I'm asking off-the-record and hoping I can head off any involvement for her in the future."

Willow's heart missed a beat. She stepped from behind Ben. "I went to discuss some orders with one of my bakers. He does the best spun sugar fancies in town. Billy Baker. That's his real name. Baker Baker—that's his shop. It's on—"

"Chartres," Nat finished for her. "You came straight here?"

She ran her tongue over the roof of her mouth. "Yes. And I hurried so it could only have taken minutes. What is it, Nat?"

"Bucky Fist's over there now. Billy died—apparently about the same time you were there."

Willow heard Marley gasp and Winnie rushed past to lean on her mistress's leg.

"That can't be," Willow whispered. "He was fine when I left."

"Was anyone else there with you?"

She paused before saying, "No. How did Billy die?" she said, horrified that the vital man she'd been with so recently had supposedly died—the moment she left his shop. "He was alive when I left him. Really, he was. He was laughing about having to make two hundred sugar pigs."

"I believe you," Nat said, not referencing the pigs. He gave another engaging smile all around. "The woman who found Billy saw you leave the shop, Willow. You're pretty hard to miss. And everyone around here knows who you are."

Ben wanted to punch the guy out—even if he was smiling. Willow hated being identified as "one of those strange Millets" everywhere she went.

"Looks like he had a heart attack," Nat said.

"That's not acceptable," Pascal said in his customary formal manner. "Why are you here if he had a heart attack?"

"It was more than just a heart attack. Billy had a bunch of tiny puncture wounds on his face, neck and head. I wouldn't have been called in and I wouldn't be here if it was a natural death." He glanced at Marley. "Doesn't have to be connected, but some of us know it isn't the first time we've had a corpse with wounds that don't make sense—at first."

Willow's hand went to her neck.

Nat's cell beeped and he answered, "Archer." He listened for a long time then said, "Yes, sir," and hung up.

"What?" Willow said, seeing the fury on Nat's face.

"Carry on, folks," Nat said. "Message from above. I've got to back off this case."

3

This was too much.

Another Embran was in town. He didn't know where exactly the new specimen had set himself up, or what forms he could change into, but another one of them was in New Orleans and thanks to the last efforts of the creatures from deep in the earth, this one would be better prepared to carry out his plan.

If he succeeded, would his kind pour from below, like battalions of fantastic monsters, to overrun the city? Jude Millet knew the answer, but asking himself the question again gave at least a tiny suggestion that it might be impossible.

They would never succeed. He pushed back the tails of his black coat and planted his fists on his hips. A humming grew within his brain and he gave a grim frown. His force, the power of his gifts, trembled at the prospect of confrontation to the death.

Fuming, Jude paced the attic in the building that housed J. Clive Millet. All he had been granted were a few months of peace since the last giant upheaval, and he didn't appreciate this fresh intrusion. He wanted, no, needed much more time to consider how to deal with several disparate issues: First, doing what he could to help his family cut off the Embran attempts to destroy them. Second, guiding the Millets and other psi families involved toward finding what he knew as the Harmony, an object purported to contain a treasure they must protect. Also, he longed to help settle the Millet division over who was or was not suitable to be head of the family.

And he must also be sure that New Orleans, and the powerful psychic families who lived there, most in anonymity, continued to thrive. The less talented families, or perhaps the younger ones—in centuries—faced a smaller risk than the prime ones, the Millets, or the Fortunes, or even the Montrachets, but if any of them went down, all would suffer.

He had had his suspicions that the present generation of Millets had not done what was needed to be certain their work with the Embran was finished.

But he had not expected a fresh onslaught so quickly.

This time would be more difficult.

This time there was no willing go-between with that world down there. Or none that he knew of.

With a breathy sigh that filled the attic, he drew himself up to his full height and pointed at the gauzelike web separating him from the "real world." Even the term made him smile. What did these newcomers know of reality?

The curtain fell away and he walked, albeit unwillingly, to look down from the single gabled window on Royal Street floors below. The last of the sun had mercifully bled away, leaving only wisps of purple amid the murky gray of the encroaching evening.

There were times when his ability to hear whatever he

wished to hear could be a damnable nuisance. Today, especially late in the afternoon, he had given in to a premonition that he needed to listen in to his descendants. The games they played! Sykes bringing young Ben Fortune back to New Orleans—not that Jude might not have done the same thing himself. It seemed that the problem child, Willow, had attracted attention from a malevolent force—little doubt about what that force might be—and her brother, Sykes—also Jude's favorite—was using the occasion to play matchmaker.

Jude wholly approved of a match between Ben Fortune and Willow, as long as that young woman was ready to accept her own talents—and those of her family.

But there would be time enough to deal with that after Ben helped to make sure Willow didn't manage to stumble into serious or worse trouble. Jude had felt her rushing through the streets, and he had heard her exclamation when she felt something odd. Small, sharp tapping on her neck.

And now some baker was dead, supposedly of a heart attack, but with small puncture wounds on his head.

Ah, yes, signs of Embran were simple to recognize once one knew what to look for.

Sykes had been down in the shop, too. He knew he should not use invisibility to hang around spying on his own family, but couldn't seem to suppress his natural love of mischief.

Jude sighed. The red-haired issue must be dealt with quickly. Sykes, dark-haired and blue-eyed, should be running J. Clive Millet and looking out for the family since his ineffectual father, Antoine, refused to do so. Pascal didn't want the job, or said he didn't, but was too responsible to walk away.

Sykes's talents were, as he'd heard some young whippersnapper say, "awesome," and Jude was immensely proud of the one who was, unfortunately, suffering because of Jude's own mistakes.

His eventual plan was to put all that right. And he hoped it didn't take another three hundred years, which was the length of time he had been working on the problem so far.

Several centuries ago, after losing the love of his life to a mysterious death, Jude had married a woman Embran, in Bruges, Belgium. Of course he hadn't known she was Embran or that she intended to use him to further her own evil plans. The Millet family had suffered unspeakably. He had been tricked by the creature's beauty and charm—her kindness to him in his time of grief—and had no idea of her true nature or form until she managed to have his entire clan chased from Belgium by those she had caused to suspect the Millets of witchcraft.

That had started the entire superstition about dark-haired, blue-eyed males being a curse. All the Millets were born redheaded and with green eyes. Then Jude had come along and when they could no longer try to pass him off as a changeling, he was branded a mutant with hair as black as night and eyes the blue of deep water over a reef.

That was why, since Antoine Millet had shirked his duties in favor of supposedly going in search of a cure for the curse, his brother, Pascal, had taken over as Millet-in-Chief while dark-haired, blue-eyed Sykes was kept on the sidelines.

"They are all so stupid," Jude said into the silence. "While they fuss about minutiae, enemies threaten their

existence and the existence of every psychically empow-
ered family in New Orleans, together with the poor mere
humans who get in the way."

He opened a door in an ancient dresser and slid out a
painting he made himself look at occasionally, just to
sharpen his determination. It showed him as a man of
twenty-nine, his hair long and black as it still was, apart
from some gray streaks, with the sweet-faced blonde
woman who should have become his wife. On her lap
was what they had jokingly called "their first child," a
dog she had adored.

Once more he recalled the pain of losing her, and his
unspeakable mistake in turning to someone else so
quickly. He sometimes allowed himself a little quarter
because his nemesis had, in fact, been red-haired and that
had been part of what fooled him into marrying her.

"Never be fooled again," he told himself. "And make
sure none of the ones for whom you care are fooled."

There must be a way to move actively among his people
without them suspecting his presence. This time he could
rely on no one but himself to keep the flow of information coming so that he could direct matters as necessary.

They didn't know it downstairs, but their enemy was
already among them and Jude expected this one to make
the last one look like a toy for a child to cuddle. Death
was in the air, again, and a plan to reduce New Orleans
to the earthly stronghold of the Embran.

There was much he didn't yet know, but he would find
out—with some help from an emissary.

He gazed down on the gathering waves of people in
the streets and considered how he should choose his col-
laborator.

But of course! Jude laughed and braced his weight on either side of the window. Of course. He had the perfect solution to his dilemma.

4

Willow opened the French doors to the courtyard behind the shop. She glanced back at Ben. He smiled at her, but Willow hurried outside—unsmiling—and shut the door again.

"Give her a few minutes," Pascal said, putting the box containing Willow's new helmet into Ben's arms.

Marley smothered a snigger and Ben narrowed his eyes at her.

"I'll take the gun, too," he said.

"She shouldn't have a gun," Pascal said promptly.

"Come on, Winnie," Marley said, her expression innocent. "Time to leave great male minds to work out what's best for the little woman."

Marley glanced past Ben and raised one fine, red brow. "Some things never change," she said. "Are you ever going to grow up, Sykes?"

Ben grinned. Sykes Millet, a formidable paranormal force, used his ability to be invisible judiciously—except when he wanted to tease sister Marley. He never tired of sneaking up and letting her see him when others couldn't, something he didn't do with anyone else.

"Don't smirk at me like that," Marley said. She

crossed her arms. "If you've got something useful to suggest, show yourself so we can all swoon over you."

A heavy hand landed on Ben's shoulder and he looked into Sykes's brilliant blue eyes. "How long have you been here?" Ben asked.

"I was worried about Willow. Something's definitely going on. I caught up with her in the street and came here with her—more or less."

Pascal shrugged as if he was out of patience. "Really, Sykes. Why not meet your sister out there like any normal man and walk with her back to the shop? Why all this silly showing off?"

"Normal?" Sykes said with a wicked grin. "If you don't know the reason for my caution, I'll tell you. I was trying to see if there was something around that shouldn't be there. With me walking along beside her in clear sight, I doubt there would be anything to see."

"Was there?" Marley, Pascal and Ben asked together.

Sykes sat down and stretched out his tall body on an old fainting couch with gilded legs shaped like fish standing on their heads. He put his hands behind his neck. "Depends on what you mean by *was*." Sykes appeared all shadows and angles; his eyebrows flared and he managed to look as if he belonged on the eighteenth-century couch, even if it was much too short for him.

A Renaissance man with muscles like steel, whip-fast reflexes and hands honed to weapons by years of chiseling stone, Sykes had made a name for himself as a sculptor.

Marley sighed, but Winnie trotted over to plant her front feet on Sykes's ribs and lick his dramatic face.

"No more evasive answers," Pascal said shortly.

"When Willow's hair moved away from her neck out there and she felt a sensation on her neck, *was* there anything there if I couldn't see it? It made her scream."

Ben's jaw tightened and he turned to look down on his old friend. "I saw her touch her neck just now. Why? You know, don't you?"

Sykes got up and paced. "You're the one who's going to find out what she felt, Ben. She may tell you. With the rest of us she won't admit there's anything in the world that's not what she calls 'normal.' Her hair moved, or was moved. And she felt something. I thought I saw a separate shadow, but I couldn't be sure. So was there something?"

Ben thought about it. "Didn't you say that after Marley and Gray came together and Willow accidentally let everyone know she can see hidden events and feelings, past and present, you thought she was ready to join the fold?"

"Sykes is an optimist," Marley said. She sat on the stairs and Ben was struck afresh by the appeal of the Millet women. "Willow has powers none of us had guessed at. She could see how Gray had suffered in the past, and how it affected him, but she only slipped up and let us know because she felt badly for Gray."

Ben screwed up his eyes. "An advanced power, I should think. And rare. Where is Gray, did you say?"

"His office is still at his dad's cottage in Faubourg Marigny. He's either over there or out on the job. He'll be back a bit later."

"I may need him," Ben said. He wasn't above confronting Willow with solid evidence of how "normal" she was. "I'll be seeing you."

Ben gave Sykes a look that warned him to not follow him as he went after Willow. As powerful as Sykes was, he wasn't the only one who could be around without others knowing it. The difference was that Ben used invisibility to travel to other locations, often returning without anyone being aware he had ever left. And in truly extreme situations he could manipulate time—which was a skill he had never told anyone about. It was dangerous and carried more responsibility than anyone could take lightly, but Ben was schooled in keeping the changes minuscule and returning time to its rightful place once he'd carried out what had to be done.

He held out his hand for the package containing the gun. Pascal grimaced, but handed it over.

"Good luck," Sykes said with a sympathetic shrug. "I think it's time for me to get back to work."

"Thanks," Ben said, going out into the Court of Angels.

Alone among the lush ferns bobbing over cobblestones, the tough, shiny leaves of gardenias and the stone angels—some not very angelic-looking—Ben collected himself.

This courtyard had intrigued him since he was a boy. The atmosphere was like no other place. Ben had seen and felt things here that he had never felt anywhere else.

Subtle things he had only mentioned to Sykes, whose experiences among the shadowed stone faces and occasional gargoyle poking from a door lintel were different from Ben's, but no less intense.

Today he did not experience anything remarkable.

He wanted to see Willow on his own. He wanted her to at least give him a little opening into her life again, but if they couldn't accept every aspect of one another, the incredible emotional and sexual power she wielded over him wouldn't be enough.

Would it?

The patterns thrown by leaves shivered on red brick walls around all sides of the courtyard.

There it was, gentle laughter, almost giggling, so faint he strained to hear it. Automatically, he stared from stone figure to stone figure. They weren't laughing.

Green-painted metal staircases zigzagged upward between randomly placed windows, stopping with a landing at each floor. The Millets' flats faced him on each side, including Sykes's, which was where Ben would live while he was back in New Orleans…unless Willow kicked him out….

He glanced up at Willow's flat and barely pulled himself together enough not to jump. She stood at the open front door, leaning on the jamb, arms crossed.

It was definitely giggling he heard, and it saturated his senses.

To smile or not to smile?

Ben fashioned a restrained upward tilt at the corners of his mouth and strode to jog up the steps and meet the woman he wanted.

"Hey, Willow," he said, arriving in front of her and keeping his demeanor more-or-less solemn. That wasn't hard. He suddenly felt solemn…and insecure? Ben Fortune didn't go in for feeling insecure very easily.

"Hey, Ben."

The giggles faded into gusty titters that slithered away. He had always intended to do more research on the Court of Angels, but never got around to it.

"I brought your helmet up," he said, feeling lame.

"Thanks." She reached for the box, but he made no attempt to give it to her.

This was the first time since his return that he had stood so close to Willow. She really was a little woman. All the women in her family were small. He recalled his sister, Poppy, reminding him before he left for Kauai that he should "Look for a woman you won't crush." Poppy was tall and almost too beautiful. She had always been his friend, but in the past two years he had come to truly admire her.

"You've got my gun, too. How did you manage to get it from Uncle Pascal?"

"By letting him know you're mature enough to make your own decisions." Not completely true, but Marley had just about said that and Ben hadn't disagreed.

"Thanks for that." She smiled a little, but immediately bowed her face in the way he remembered so well. Willow talked a tough story, but she had a shy streak a mile wide.

"Are you going to invite me in?"

A frown came and went quickly. "Of course. Come in. I don't suppose Winnie followed you out, did she?" She peered around him and down into the courtyard. "She likes to come up when Marley works late and Gray is gone."

"Too much going on for her to concentrate today, I think," Ben said, sensing Willow's disappointment.

Willow shook her head as if the dog didn't matter to her. "Gray doesn't get back early most nights. He's at his dad's working. His dad is Gus Fisher—we look after his cottage and make sure everything gets done over there. Gus loves Winnie, too. Winnie likes to ride over to Gus's in my trailer."

He was no closer to going inside her flat. "Dogs and

trailers match," he said. "Not as much as dogs and pickups, though. I'll have to take you to Kauai one day and you'll see how every pickup has its dog in the back, or several dogs."

She gave him a quizzical look, but at least she didn't protest that she'd never be going to Kauai, or not with him.

Yet.

"Gray and Marley live here, then?" he said.

She nodded. "Yes. They like it here. Gray's all over the place with what he does and it's convenient for Marley to be close to work."

"Marley looks happy."

She smiled broadly. "They both are. They can't keep their hands off each other." She laughed at that.

Ben felt a spear of jealousy. "I've missed you," he said. Everyone said he was fearless—this was a time to prove it.

Willow's white, freckled skin turned pink. She had thick, auburn eyelashes that spread shadows across her shining eyes.

"Is it okay if I say that? Friends are supposed to care about each other."

"It's okay," she said and walked into the flat, leaving him to follow her. "It's dinnertime. Are you hungry?"

He barely stopped himself from saying he wasn't. "Getting there," he said. "I got in late yesterday and slept. Then caught up with Sykes. I think I forgot to eat."

"Oh." Her expression suggested she had not expected him to take her up on a vague offer of a meal. "Well, you're in luck. It's gumbo here tonight. I cooked a whole mess of it yesterday and it's always better on the second day."

He closed his eyes and made sounds of ecstasy. "Gumbo? When you live in the land of pork and poi, good as it is, gumbo sounds exotic. I'd love some, but there's no hurry."

That got him another look. He could see her thinking that he sounded as if he was settling in. If he were sneakier, he'd tune in and listen to exactly what she was thinking. That was generally against his principles unless absolutely necessary.

But he wasn't ruling out running the risk if he had to.

"Let's go in the living room," Willow said. "It's tidy for once."

"It's always tidy," he reminded her.

Her expression flickered as she must have remembered how much time they had spent there together in the past, but she used turning off the television to cover any awkwardness.

"Do you still like background noise if you're alone?" he asked, and winced.

"Why don't I take the boxes from you?" she said, facing him again.

He'd as good as asked her if she was lonely. She used to use the television to fill up time when he was away from New Orleans.

She didn't answer him.

"Can we see what you've got here?" He put the packages on the floor and sat on the edge of a well-worn blue armchair. But he stopped in the act of removing the helmet from the box. "Am I being too pushy? Taking too much for granted?"

She took a bit too long to shake her head, no. "Look at it. It's state-of-the-art and should be really safe."

Once she had got to the flat she must have immediately changed her clothes. She looked fresh and curvy in a yellow cotton dress that skimmed her body.

It was far too long since he had touched her.

Ben concentrated on the helmet. "Wow. Are you sure it's not too heavy?"

"Why would it be too heavy?"

Looking straight at her and making no attempt at laughing anything off, he said, "Because although you're strong, you're small. I like to think of any equipment you use being the right weight for you." He looked from her face to her sandaled feet—bare and smooth, just as her legs were. "It wouldn't help much if I put you in a bulletproof vest that made it impossible for you to run, would it? You'd need one in your own size."

"Bulletproof?" She frowned and all traces of the blush disappeared. Her hand touched her neck again.

"Just an example," he said. An unfortunate one, given that she was so jumpy lately. "Do you have a rash?" he asked suddenly.

Willow's lips parted and her eyes grew bigger and an even brighter green. "What kind of question is that?" She checked her arms and legs.

"That was clumsy," he said. "It was your neck I had in mind. You rub it as if you think there's something there."

Instantly, her right hand slid beneath her hair and she backed away.

"What is it?" he said, getting up. "What's going on, Willow? Sykes knows there's something happening. They all do and now I do. Would you fill me in, please? Sykes only touched on what he suspected."

She shuddered and Ben caught hold of her shoulders.

Her hands came up, but she didn't try to push him away.

Nothing had changed. He closed his eyes and dug his fingers into her flesh. Never before, and not since Willow, had he felt the searing jolt of pain and pleasure that immobilized him when they first touched.

"When I left I actually hoped I'd forget this," he whispered. "What a fool I was."

"I'll never forget it," she said. "We shouldn't—"

"Don't say it. It may be true, but don't say it. I can't stand hearing you send me away again."

"I had to."

"Why?" He pulled her closer. "You never told me why."

"We aren't meant for each other."

"My God," he said, shaking with the effort of not taking her into his arms. "How can you say that?"

"Everyone said…" She turned her face away again, but slowly looked back at him.

"*Everyone* said what?"

"Nothing. I'm not what you need. Leave it at that."

There was no decision; he just brought his mouth down on hers, hard and demanding. And she held still, her fingers resting on his chest. The web of raw sensation spun around them. He had never understood it. Only the Millets had this mystical Bonding element—he could vouch for that with certainty.

Her mouth grew warmer and softened under his. Gasping, she stood on tiptoe and slid her hands up to his shoulders.

Their lips parted, and their tongues entwined. He vaguely heard her moans and his own ragged breathing.

The slide of her fingers up his neck to rest on his jaw left a trail of heat. Her body bent into his and Ben's pelvis jerked against her, hard. He felt the pulsing, the throbbing in his groin. Willow had to feel his erection.

"Willow," he said. "I'm breaking apart."

Her breath came in sobs and she shook so hard he clutched her to him, smoothed her back, rocked them together. He smoothed his hands up to the sides of her breasts.

"We can't," she said brokenly. "We can't let this happen, Ben. You know it."

They grew still but hung on to each other.

"I had to do that," Ben said. "I had to find out if anything had changed. It hasn't. Are you still going to say you're not what I need?"

When Willow didn't answer, he sat down again and rested his face in his hands.

"Don't," she said.

"Don't what?"

"I don't know. Feel bad, I guess. You'll meet the right woman, just give it time."

He didn't understand what point she was trying to make, unless… "Tell me you don't feel anything for me and I'll help with any business that needs taking care of here and get out of New Orleans again."

"Don't ask me questions like that," she said. "Look, we haven't seen each other in a long time. It's a shock. We're reacting to that."

"That was some hello, Willow." Parts of him kept right on reacting to her. "Do you still say there's nothing out of the ordinary—or not normal, as you call it—about you?"

"Yes," she said emphatically. "I've started to admit that the rest of you have some sort of weird traits, but I don't have them."

"You," he said, "are either a liar or you're in denial. Down there in the shop, when you didn't expect me to contact you, you responded. You're telepathic—at the very least."

At first he didn't think she'd answer him at all. Then she took a deep breath and said, "Whatever you say. Do you still want to eat?"

He swallowed the "no" that wanted to snap out and said, "You bet."

"Fine. Come and help then. I've still got a job to do tonight."

"Tonight?" He looked pointedly at her dress. "Dressed like that? And at night?"

"Yes, like this. I'm going to help a customer host a party. His wife can't be there until later. It's a casual party—pool party." She patted her hip. "I've got my swimsuit on already."

5

Willow and Ben didn't share gumbo that night.

After she'd told him to go and find someone who wanted him to run her life, he had left. Now she felt irritable and disappointed.

But she couldn't let him march back in and take over. Could she?

She couldn't get over that kiss, that he had started it and she had let him. And enjoyed it.

That's probably all we could ever have in common—amazing sexual attraction. Willow sighed.

"What's your problem?" Pascal said when she went into the shop again, new helmet in place, to let them know she was on her way to a job. "And Ben? What did you do to him? He hardly said a word when he came through on his way out."

"I've got to get to that job," she said, avoiding his questions. "I'm helping out at a party."

"You're angry, too," Pascal said.

"No," Willow said. "I'm not. And I'm only letting you know I'm leaving because everyone's so upset at the moment."

"But you're not upset?"

"No. Bye."

"Where are you going?"

She wanted to say she didn't owe him a schedule. Instead, she said, "Uptown. Right off St. Charles Avenue. Near Bordeaux Street. The people's name is Brandt, Val and Cleo. They're very well-known in New Orleans—socialites."

"I never heard of them," Pascal said.

Willow planted a kiss on his cheek. "You only hang out with old money, Uncle. The Brandts don't even have one important generation behind them, so they aren't your kind." She gave a mock shudder.

He shook his head. "Probably vulgar. And you shouldn't be waiting on them, either."

She laughed. "I run a housekeeping and all things domestic business. I should be picky about who I work for? 'We are Mean 'n Green—you need it, we get it, or do it or fix it.'"

"Of course you can't be calling me a snob—nothing could be further from the truth." He shook his head. "So why is Ben mad at you?"

"He doesn't have any right to be mad at me," she snapped. "I'm nothing to him."

"Is that a fact?" Pascal looked at the stairs to see his trainer, Anthony, coming down with a tall, green drink in a frosted glass.

"I can hear you getting excited from three stories up," Anthony said. No one looked better in a muscle shirt, than blond, tanned Anthony. "You know how bad it is for your blood pressure, Pascal. Sit down and drink this. It'll settle your nerves."

Pascal grimaced and Willow took advantage of the

moment to slip back into the courtyard and make her way through to the storeroom where she kept her scooter and trailer. Her office was in the Warehouse District, and the other vehicles were parked there, but she couldn't see herself wasting money on something frivolous to drive to and fro—or wasting an opportunity to advertise Mean 'n Green on the trailer at all times.

Ben hovered nearby, trying to feel guilty. He failed. If Willow wouldn't look after herself, he'd just have to do it for her. That was what Sykes wanted him in New Orleans for anyway. The only puzzle was why Sykes didn't do the job himself.

Stand-in hostess for some man's pool party? Was she insane? She couldn't really think all the guy wanted was for her to stand around offering canapés.

Willow swung open two heavy green doors to a crowded space where bicycles and her scooter, complete with trailer, were stored in front of boxes stacked to the rafters.

He could follow her at a distance, but why bother when he would rather be as near to her as possible?

Ben settled his presence into her trailer and grinned at the odd expression on her face when she noticed a change in the balance of her "wheels."

She looked cute in her little yellow dress, brown sandals, and wearing the green-and-white crash helmet complete with oversize rearview mirrors. Her skirt hiked way above her knees—something else he enjoyed.

The kiss had been enough proof for him. He wanted Willow more than ever.

This was the first close-up look he'd had of the scooter. It was well equipped enough to satisfy a long-distance motorcyclist, complete with GPS, a mount into which she slid a cell phone before adjusting an earpiece beneath her helmet, and a radar scanner.

The scanner made him grin. He wondered about the top speed on a scooter pulling a trailer—even a very small trailer.

With obvious increased effort, she wheeled the scooter into the passageway between the shop and one wing of the Millets' flats. He did feel a bit bad about the way she had to strain, but he wasn't happy with her at the moment.

Willow hoped she wasn't developing a problem with the scooter. Steering or something. The company's small truck had cost a fortune in repairs lately and she needed to pad the bank account again.

Sometimes Willow thought it would be faster to walk shorter distances than try to maneuver through city traffic with the scooter. Unfortunately, she wasn't able to carry everything she needed in her arms.

She set off for St. Charles Avenue.

Honking on all sides. Vendors with carts on all sides. Screaming people on all sides. Usually when she was out here, she felt more alive than she did anywhere else. This evening she was steaming and everything annoyed her. Steaming, and so sad she kept blinking back tears.

The only really important thing to worry about was that Billy Baker was dead. After the abrupt way Nat Archer left, she didn't know if there was something she should be doing. Nat said he'd been told to back away from the case.

When she reached St. Charles Avenue it wasn't so busy. Willow could feel grit spitting against her bare legs. She should have taken the time to put an overall on top of her dress. Riding around like this had to look wacky and it wasn't comfortable.

The scooter was giving all kinds of signals suggesting it found the trailer too heavy. She had made the mistake of overloading it before.

Billy's death was unbelievable. His excitement over his own business rubbed off on her. He could make her grin with his ideas for whimsical sweets.

That should be past tense now. Willow sniffed and her eyes burned.

Too bad she had to do this job tonight. She was concerned about money right now. Business hadn't been so great lately. If it had, she wouldn't have agreed to do this job for the Brandts—she didn't like the uncertainty of it. Cleo Brandt had told her to get there at eight to have time to talk to her husband, Val, before guests arrived. A pool party starting so late didn't make sense to Willow.

The Millets had their *rules*. Willow grimaced; she also had rules and the main one was that she was completely independent. She had to be vigilant because finance wasn't her strength.

Her cell rang and she turned it on. "Willow here." She wished she didn't have to be connected to all callers at all times, but she did.

"Zinnia's pissed," a male voice said and she frowned. "It's Chris. I didn't want to bother you so I tried Zinnia at home and you should have heard that bitch."

Chris was one of Willow's three supervisors. Zinnia ran the office.

"You know she doesn't work when she's not being

paid," Willow said, checking her mirrors. They really gave her a great all-around view. "What's the problem?"

"I dunno."

She winced. Chris was good at his job, but there were definite gaps in his communication skills. "Okay, Chris, why are you trying to reach one of us?"

"We're not catering the Brandt job, are we?" Chris said.

"No," she said, competing with a lot of noise at Chris's end.

That was something she had not told Ben. Her job tonight was to play the hostess and nothing more. Not even hand out canapés as he snidely mentioned. Cleo Brandt had called at the last minute and sounded embarrassed when she said Willow didn't need to worry about anything but making sure the evening went smoothly. In other words, Mean 'n Green hadn't gotten the most lucrative parts of the event.

"Why wouldn't they want us to do everything?" Chris asked.

Willow's patience thinned. "I don't know the answer to that. You know we're picking up all the business we can right now. We can't be picky."

Chris was quiet for a few moments, then he said, "No. I just don't like it if I think you're being taken advantage of, boss."

She smiled. "Thanks. We'll try to watch each other's backs. But that wasn't why you called."

"There's that yellow tape stuff everywhere," Chris said. "The whole place is off-limits unless you're a cop or something."

The Brandt job receded from Willow's mind. "What place?"

"Where I've been watering the inside plants tonight. I took a break to get some dinner. I was only gone forty-five minutes or so, and when I got back, everything was nuts. I want to know if I should go under the tape and finish the job. I still got to fertilize. I've got a key."

"Are you talking about the dance hall on South Rampart? Where the woman lives upstairs?"

"Surry Green. She's some sort of actress. Complains about the music all the time like she didn't know she was renting over a dance hall. We do her shopping and take care of her plants. She's got hundreds of them. You can't move for the palms in there."

"There's crime scene tape all around, you said?"

"Yeah."

"The dance hall is taped off?"

"That's what I said. Must be trouble in there. Cop cars all over the place."

"You left in the middle of a job to get dinner?"

"I knew you'd say somethin' about that," Chris said. "She was all in a twist because she had a date. I asked if she'd rather I went in after she left and she said, yes, to give her some time. Should I go up the side stairs anyway? She'll be apoplectic if she gets home and I haven't finished."

"*No.* The plants can wait. Call her later and explain."

"Gotcha."

Willow smacked off the phone. There had been occasions when Chris had taken duty too far. At least he'd called and given her a chance to stop him this time.

The cell rang again.

"Hey, Chris," Willow said. "What's up now?"

"Something bad, I think. One of those coroner's vans

is here. Just a minute." He spoke to someone in the background then said, "Let me find out what they're saying now. I'll call you back."

Willow moaned with frustration, then felt the rig swing awkwardly behind her and collide with the curb. She looked over her shoulder and slammed on the brakes. The trailer teetered toward the sidewalk.

"I hate this whole day," she yelled, jumping clear.

Ben jumped, too, just in time to stop the almost stationary death trap from finishing up on its side.

He had to make this look good.

Willow tore off her helmet and prepared to watch a total disaster. At least no one was going to get hurt. Would the bank give her a loan if she explained her run of bad luck?

She let her arms fall to her sides.

The trailer, still balanced on two wheels, rocked back and forth in a "shall I fall over or not?" way. Her load of supplies must have shifted, although it had never happened before.

An urge to help right things wasn't a good idea, she knew that.

The trailer stopped, stood completely unmoving on those two wheels, then dropped, quite slowly, to settle on all four again.

Willow stared, her heart beating too fast. The phone was ringing again, but it took her so long to make herself move that it stopped.

Finally, she rushed to the scooter, just in time to answer Chris once more.

"Surry Green's been murdered," he said. "Remember when those singers got whacked?"

She closed her eyes. Chris watched too many crime shows. "Yes," she said faintly. "It was almost four months ago." How could she forget when Marley had gotten caught up in the case and almost died? "You're telling me that since you left to have dinner she's been murdered, the cops know about it already and they're all over it?"

"That's it. Folks around here are saying this is another weird one. Spike through the heart, someone says. Like they kill vampires."

"Chris," she said tiredly, "remind them the only vampires in this town are in books."

6

Dr. Blades, what seemed like seven emaciated feet of him, slouched against a refrigeration bank in the morgue.

"Hey, Doc," Nat said, walking into the Medical Examiner's lair with Gray Fisher—Marley's husband—at his heels. "Nice of you to ask us over."

"I asked *you* over," Blades said, giving Gray the evil eye. "If you want him here, it's up to you."

"Gray was in on the dragon case," Nat said, damned if he'd sound defensive. "He may not be a cop anymore, but he thinks like one and it was his wife who came close to ending up as one more of the dragon's tasty treats."

"That thing wasn't a dragon," Blades said of the monster that had been responsible for the deaths of at least ten women. "It just had some Komodo traits."

"You never saw it," Nat said.

"I didn't have to, I saw the bites," Blades reminded him defensively.

"Not a dragon," Blades said, giving Nat the kind of hard stare that told him Blades probably didn't believe his own words, but he wasn't going to admit that. "That's the official word on the subject. You'd better accept it."

"Yeah," Nat said slowly, seeing Blades with a slightly fresh eye. The man was no more convinced that New Orleans wasn't host to a rogue paranormal force than Nat was.

Gray was checking his watch, again. Nat figured his former partner didn't like being late returning to the Court of Angels where the most important person in his life hung out, Marley Millet Fisher.

"I keep dead-ending on some questions I've asked," Blades said, glancing at Gray as if he wished he would leave—or disappear. "The man and woman who were the dragon's—I mean the pair who were there when the last lot went down. Your people got them. Where are they? No one's saying anything about them, or not to me."

"Eric and Sidney Fournier?" Nat said cautiously. The brother and sister were a thorn in his side. They had some kind of weird connection to the Embran Dragon, as Nat and those who believed New Orleans was under insidious attack called "the thing."

Blades watched Nat and Nat felt Gray waiting for him to continue, too. "They were bound over," he told them.

"So they're in jail," Blades said. The deep, purplish hollows beneath his cheekbones didn't get more reassuring to look at. Neither did his dome of a head and pale eyes with no eyelashes. The lack of eyelashes went with the lack of eyebrows.

Nat cleared his throat. "In fact, they're not in jail."

"Where are they?" Gray asked. He and Blades had never gotten along, and he said as little as possible in the doctor's presence.

"Well—" Nat pursed his lips and blew out in a

tuneless whistle "—I've been told not to ask more questions about that. But I don't think they're in custody anymore."

"What?" Gray said explosively. "Don't you think you should have shared that with me? We've got people to look out for. How can those two crazies be on the loose?"

Gray stepped back and Nat saw the instant when Gray's attention shifted elsewhere. Gray, Nat could tell by the shuttered distance in his eyes, had mentally checked out of the morgue and the conversation going on there, at least for now.

"How did that happen?" Blades asked. Actual concern replaced his usually impassive expression. "I didn't hear about it."

Nat shook his head. "I said I don't *think* the Fourniers are in custody. I didn't get a definite answer."

"Because they think they can keep the lid on this," Blades said. He looked ruffled, not something Nat remembered witnessing before. "The fools, they're shoving their heads in the sand. This is going to make things harder."

"Why?" Gray said, returning to the conversation. "What kind of burr got stuck under your saddle? You didn't get us over here to discuss—"

"I didn't get *you* over here at all," Blades said.

Nat cleared his throat. "You said there was something interesting you wanted to show me, Dr. Blades," he said and winced when he heard Gray mutter what sounded like *"Dr. Death,"* under his breath. The last time Gray called the man that it had been out loud and had caused antagonism between them that had lasted for years and still continued.

Blades must have heard, too, but he set his jaw and ignored Gray. "We got a body in this afternoon. Heart attack."

Nat's own heart quickened. "You mean Billy Baker?"

"How did you know?" Blades's frown bunched his hairless brow over his eyes.

"I was called in before they decided it was a heart attack," Nat said.

"It *was* a heart attack."

A rap on the doorjamb got their attention. "Excuse me," Ben Fortune said. "I was told I'd find you here."

It wasn't easy for Nat to cover his surprise.

"Who are you?" Blades said.

"This is Ben Fortune," Gray said, his eyes wide and innocent. "Sykes must have sent you over, Ben. I guess he couldn't get here himself."

"Right," Ben said.

With any luck Blades wouldn't figure out that neither Sykes nor Ben should know anything about this meeting, but Nat wasn't fooled. He had just run into Gray on the street when Blades's call came in. They had come straight here. Nat decided the dormant psychic ability Gray was rumored to have rekindled since he met his wife, Marley, was real. He had contacted Ben telepathically and got him here.

Nat had witnessed too much evidence of psychic abilities to dismiss their existence and both the Millet and the Fortune families—and who knew what others?—were legendary for their mystical gifts.

Blades didn't shake the hand Ben offered.

"This isn't a social gathering," Blades said. "Archer, this is something very serious."

"I'll vouch for Ben," he said, imagining a scene where he was stripped of his weapon and badge for flouting his superiors. "He's an old friend with some experience around cases like this." Once they were out of here, he'd have to nail Ben and Gray to find out what their deal was.

"Like what?" Blades's face would have fitted right in on Mount Rushmore.

"Cases where we may be dealing with supernatural elements."

"Did I say anything about that?"

"You're going to," Gray said, making Nat wince.

"Shut the door," Blades said in a monotone. "I've got something to show you."

"Surprise," Gray muttered.

Blades let his eyes close momentarily. Beside Ben and Gray, big men who exuded vitality, the doctor resembled a wraith.

Following the ME, Nat went with Gray through another door into a smaller room where a covered body lay on a steel table.

Ben shut the outer door, caught up and immediately covered his nose. Gray and Nat did the same thing, but Blades's expression never changed at the odor.

"What are you looking for?" Blades asked Ben, who had looked over his shoulders in both directions as if searching for something.

Ben shrugged, one corner of his mouth turning up. "I thought both bodies might be in here."

"There's only one," Blades said, looking quizzically at Ben. "So far." He pulled gloves from a container on the wall and snapped them on. "How come you were called to a heart attack?" Blades asked Nat.

"One of the officers at the scene thought I'd want to be there," Nat said. "He saw one of the dragon victims."

"And he thought this was another one?" Blades shrugged. "Surprising he'd make the connection."

Nat hadn't missed Ben's remark about two bodies. This wasn't the moment to press him about it, but plenty of explanations would be needed later.

Was there another body? One that raised suspicion? Nat kept his attention on the body, but his back tensed.

The overhead lights flattened everything in the cheerless space. White blended with steel and every surface gave off a glare.

"We're between a rock and a hard place," Blades said, plucking at the sheet. "The powers that be in this town are afraid of something and you know what it is." He gave Nat a significant look. "General panic in the city. People are settling down a bit after the last lot. Short memory is a great healer, but if this new event gets out, it won't take long for connections to be made. Then the rumors will fly."

"Shit," Gray said. "It's happened again, hasn't it?"

"Something has," Blades told him, drawing the cover away from a body. "I'm glad your wife, Marley—isn't that her name? I'm glad she's okay. I know it got close there."

Promptly, Gray said, "Thanks. I appreciate that."

Blades waved a hand. "I think Molyneux and the rest of them will resist admitting this has anything to do with the earlier cases, don't you?"

At first Nat wasn't sure what he was seeing. He went closer and looked down on what had been Billy Baker. He identified the man from what was left of very curly blond hair.

"My God," Gray muttered.

"What did that?" Nat asked, studying livid, exposed flesh that seemed to have bubbled.

"The skin's peeling off," Ben said, closing in. "From the ribs up. It looks like it lifted up in circles around the little red wounds."

"It started up here." Blades indicated the area of the forehead and scalp. "I don't know what caused the wounds yet."

"Maybe you won't now," Ben said. "Won't the missing skin make it harder?"

"We'll see," Blades responded shortly. "The technicians said the skin was all there when they bagged him. It didn't drop off in the bag, it just disappeared. I thought you'd want to know there were what looked like puncture wounds, Archer. Nothing like the ragged messes we've seen before, but still punctures."

Nat glanced away from the table. "Maybe they've been practicing," he said, "and developed more finesse."

He added, "So what did he really die of?"

"Heart attack," Blades said, sounding annoyed. "Scared to death I should think. He must have seen whatever was coming and died before it could kill him."

7

Val Brandt behaved as if he didn't know or particularly care to know most of the people at his own party. Handsome in a muscular, glossy, self-assured way, his charm was undeniable. But the smiles he aimed in all directions were not the kind that made people feel warm, or they wouldn't if most people weren't a little or a lot drunk.

Every inch of the Brandts' classically sumptuous home was incredibly beautiful. *Rich* was the word that came to Willow's mind. Nothing had been spared in putting together the best of everything.

Willow had spent almost two hours at Val's side and still wasn't sure why she was needed. The guests used the house and grounds, including a large oval pool and white-washed, purple-wisteria-loaded cabana, as if they lived there.

Food and drinks loaded every surface in a honey-colored granite, blond wood and stainless steel kitchen where the visitors wandered in and out, helping themselves. More tables were set out in front of the cabana. Servers worked on refills, but Willow hadn't seen any sign of a recognizable catering company. Supplies had already been there when she arrived.

"So, what d'you think?" Val said.

They stood in the foyer beside a table bearing a huge arrangement of tropical flowers. The front door stood open and a constant stream of arrivals and departures laughed its way past.

"Of the house?" Willow felt out of her depth and it annoyed her. She wasn't usually intimidated.

"The whole place," Val said, his blue eyes bright in a tanned face that made his blond hair almost surfer-white. "Chloe will be back before long I'm sure, and she'll expect me to have entertained you." He smiled widely. "You're going to love Chloe. Everyone does."

"I'm sure, but I came to do a job," she reminded him. "It's nice of you to want me to be comfortable, though." In fact, she'd done very little other than repeatedly explain to those who didn't know Val Brandt that she was not Val's wife.

Willow reminded herself of the fall-off in her business and how much she needed one or two new and lucrative clients.

Val surprised her by slipping a hand beneath her elbow. He wasn't a tall man, but she still looked up at him. The big smile had gone, replaced by the slight drawing together of his eyebrows and a serious intensity in his eyes.

"Let's go back out to the gardens," he said. "I'd like us to talk about what Chloe and I have in mind. First I wanted to watch you with people. See how you coped."

"Really?"

Being watched, for any reason, was at the bottom of her welcome list. Lately she had a creepy feeling that eyes were trained on her whenever she was away from her office or flat.

She folded her hand around the cell phone in her pocket. Chris hadn't called back and she wished he would, even if it could be inconvenient here. It hadn't sailed past her that twice in one day a Mean 'n Green employee had been present at a death scene. That wasn't a fact she wanted to get around.

"You fit in real well, Willow, real well," Val said. He paused for a long kiss on the lips from a blonde in a green bikini.

They arrived outside the back of the house on the raised, white stone terrace again. Torches had been lit among beds of shrubs. A combo played mellow jazz that blended with the scent of warm flowers—and hot, perfumed skin. The night was cooling down, but a residue of humidity clung to the air.

Willow couldn't miss the sexy cavorting in and around the pool, but behaved as if she hadn't noticed a thing. She needn't have bothered to put the swimsuit on under her dress since nothing would get her to take off any clothing here.

"You can see what our problem is, can't you?" Val said.

Blank, Willow looked around.

"I see you do. We like the social life. Having the place filled with friends makes us happy. We pride ourselves on supporting the arts, and occasions like this are meant for those people to network. But we've had a bad time getting good help. For tonight Chloe hired some casual help we've used before and had everything delivered early, but we wanted to see you take over. Too bad she had to leave. She'll be real pleased with you, real pleased."

Since she hadn't done anything, it was on Willow's mind to ask why, but she resisted. "That's good."

"You've got a great, easy manner. You fit right in and know exactly the right note to strike. You've got a real calming manner, real calming. Most people couldn't walk in here cold and start putting guests at ease. You're a natural. And you look the part. A little arty yourself, maybe, and very easy on the eyes."

This might not be one of the new customers she wanted to take on, Willow thought. Only weeks earlier, Chloe Brandt had contacted her with an offer she wouldn't consider. Chloe wanted her to consider becoming their full-time assistant, and Willow wasn't interested. She was hoping, however, that she might be able to pick up smaller jobs from them.

A tall brunette with a fabulous figure shown off in a low-cut, one-piece white swimsuit, strolled up, tying a length of white chiffon around her hips. "I am so late, Val, honey," she said. "My shoot ran long. Tell me you forgive me. Where's Chloe?"

"Willow, meet Vanity," Val said. "Friend of the family since we were children. She's a model. Chloe had an engagement, darlin'. She should be back anytime."

"Poor Chloe," Vanity said. "I'll look after her when she does come home. She'll be interested in meeting your new friend, Val."

"Willow is a professional," he said rapidly. "And she's very good at what she does."

Vanity, who had lovely Mediterranean features with deep brown eyes and olive skin to complete the package, gave Willow a speculative glance. "I'll take your word for it," she told Val.

"I'm Willow Millet." Some things needed to be made clear and fast. "I own a company that caters to domestic needs. We take care of everything from shopping, cleaning and generally maintaining households and gardens, to large catering jobs and special events. We can also deal with personal assistant work—theater tickets, restaurant reservations—you name it and we can probably do it." Willow considered her network of go-to people her greatest strength.

Vanity looked interested now. "How many regular employees do you have? It's always the casual staff that make me nervous."

"We have a full-time staff of six and several regular part-timers. We employ a large pool of what you call casual workers, but they are all well-vetted and we rarely have to call in first-time employees."

Vanity smiled approvingly. "So you did the catering tonight? The food looks yummy."

"I didn't—"

"Willow also makes sure her events run smoothly," Val interrupted. "She's a natural hostess and you know how often Chloe isn't up to all the noise and fuss. Look around. Everyone's having one hell of a time."

"I shall steal you away from Val and Chloe then," Vanity said. "I have the worst time getting good help."

"We found her so she's ours," Val said, laughing. "We're going to keep her so busy she won't have time for you or anyone else."

Willow grew more uncomfortable by the second. This wasn't her scene. She was happy supervising staff at an event like this, but she realized that she had no interest in playing hostess.

"Millet," Valerie said suddenly, snapping her fingers. "Not *the* Millets? The voodoo ones?"

"Psychic," Willow said reflexively. Darn her carelessness. "That's the story they tell about us, anyway."

"Mmm," Vanity said, giving Willow a piercing look. "But you say it isn't true? All the red-haired, green eyes stuff? You are all red-haired and green-eyed?"

This could get boring. "Actually not. But a number of us are. It's just worked out that way." She forced a little laugh. "The family has a penchant for a certain look in the people they choose as partners."

"You did admit the psychic bit," Vanity said and her dark eyes sparkled with interest.

"I said that's the story about us," Willow told her. "That's all. New Orleans does love its little myths."

Screams from the pool demanded attention. Two men held a streaming beauty aloft while she stripped off the top of her bikini and flung out her arms. Torchlight flickered over her large, white breasts before she kicked free and landed back in the water. A great deal of splashing and screeching followed, and a lot of underwater action. Willow turned hot.

Vanity bent to whisper in Willow's ear. "Women like her embarrass me. How about you?"

"I'm not supposed to have opinions when I'm working," Willow said. "But I agree with you."

A shadow passed over her and she felt as if it slipped away into a group to the right. Willow's skin tightened and she shivered. She looked to see what or who had caught her attention, but couldn't make out anything remarkable.

Her throat tightened, as if a big hand had gripped her there and she dragged in a breath.

A subtle shift in the atmosphere, almost nothing at first, made it hard to concentrate.

Anger?

In every direction she saw apparently gleeful party-goers, yet she felt growing anger around her. A harsh current buffeted her, and she glanced from Val to Vanity, neither of whom registered anything unusual.

"Look after Vanity, will you," Val said to Willow. "I want to run inside and see if there's a message from Chloe. She should be here." He went toward the house.

"You don't need to look after me. I'm not Chloe." Vanity sounded somber enough to make Willow stare at her. Somber, but not angry. "Chloe isn't strong—I don't mean physically—and I watch out for her. I'm like the sister she never had. All of this is something she hates, all the noise and fuss. And she can't stand anything lewd, which is getting harder to avoid these days—particularly with the circles they move in. He's worried because she's late." She nodded after Val's retreating back.

"Oh, dear." She wondered why Val had lied about Chloe liking big parties.

Vanity shook her head. "It's okay. She'll have found somewhere to be alone until she can cope. She has her places."

More parts of swimsuits landed beside the pool. And more guests jumped in, most of them naked before they reached the water.

"And a good time was had by almost all," Vanity said, sounding impatient. "Fortunately, they'll start peeling off before long. Just as soon as they have to crash—or whatever else they have to do. Don't open any closed bedroom doors or look behind bushes."

Willow decided she liked Vanity's commonsense attitude, even if the party was already out of hand and scary. She didn't like the thought of going down the driveway and out to the street in the dark on her own when the time came, but she had parked the scooter out there to avoid getting blocked in.

A man in an orange aloha shirt and relaxed silk shorts confronted Vanity and held out his arms. "There's my best girl," he said. "And they're playing our song."

Vanity smiled and let him dance her away to the area near the combo where couples clung together and swayed in the colored puddles from fairy lights around an awning.

Willow decided she would go into the kitchen and see if she could help freshen up any of the platters. What she really wanted was to be back in her flat, preferably with Winnie curled up beside her if that could be managed. Keeping busy was the next best thing. She nodded and smiled approvingly at a man replenishing jugs of sangria.

A flash of dread wiped away her smile.

Slick, cool awareness opened her mind until she saw everything as if by floodlight. The warning signs of the so-called power she unwillingly shouldered were familiar. Until a few months ago they had come to her rarely, but the frequency was increasing.

"Leave me alone," she whispered fiercely, feeling wild. "Go away." Then she felt ridiculous talking to nothing and no one in particular.

Her eyes met those of an elegant man lounging on the cushions of a wrought-iron chaise. Immediately, she lowered her gaze—to his well-made body clad in dark gray, his long legs and bare feet.

She had to see his face again.

Younger than she'd thought at first, perhaps much younger. In his twenties, but with mature, confident features.

Anger.

Wincing, she barely stopped herself from whirling away. Was it this man who caused the anger that swirled around her? Why would he?

Vibrations, like an intermittent stream of air blasted against a thin rubber membrane, blocked out the voices, the music.

Not just anger, but rage. She felt it more strongly by the moment. And it was all around her, pushing at her, tossing her hair and plastering her skirt to her legs.

Someone touched her and she knew it would be the young man from the chaise. "Are you okay?" he said, inclining his head. Up close he looked a little older, perhaps in his early thirties. His concern showed.

"Fine," she said. "I was thinking about some things I have to get done."

He inclined his head. "It's a party. What do you have to do except enjoy yourself?"

Pretense didn't sit well with her—it always seemed pointless. "I'm an employee," she said pleasantly. "I'm helping out, overseeing things until Mrs. Brandt gets here."

He raised arched brows. "Val Brandt has good taste. Don't hold your breath for Chloe to show up—poor girl hates parties. She may come when just about everyone else has left." He took stock of the surrounding activities. "This isn't her scene. She's quiet—distinguished, I guess you'd say."

"So why have parties like this?" she asked before she could edit herself. "Forget I asked. It's not my business."

"What's your name?" he said. "I'm Preston Moriarty."

"Willow Millet."

"Well, Willow Millet, it is your business if you're supposed to make sure a party is a success. Not that these parties are what you'd call theme affairs, or even guided revels."

"Is it always like this?" Willow asked.

"Not always. The crowd varies."

"But you're often here?"

He dazzled her with a smile. "Uh-huh. I hope you're going to be here often, too. I'd have more to look forward to."

"Why do you come if you don't like it?"

He looked away. "I didn't say that. I'm part of the trappings, the expected hangers-on. Val and Chloe have been very good to me, and they like having me around. There are never enough single men—or so they insist."

"I see," Willow said although she didn't really.

Willow's eyelids slipped shut. Iciness enveloped her, encased her like armor. She felt so cold she wasn't sure she could move, so cold her flesh seemed numb. And through the numbness she felt, very vaguely, a stroking pressure that passed all over her body—repeatedly—before resting heavily on her head. Her neck wobbled.

Once again the exploration of her body began, so intimate she tingled, but she couldn't say a word or try to evade these invisible hands.

"Willow?"

Her eyes wouldn't open. Under her hair and around her neck passed firm pressing fingers. Surely she felt fingers. Her mind wouldn't stay focused. Small, sharp pricks tapped on flesh that felt thick, as if it was anesthetized.

Over her shoulders the fingers passed, down, beneath her arms, then over her breasts. She shuddered. Her nipples peaked and the stimulation speared down between her legs.

The fingers tweaked her nipples and still she stood like a statue, unmoving, but quivering inside. Onward. Whatever this was mapped her body in an openly sexual way. It smoothed her buttocks through the dress, cupped her there, slid around to the front, cupped her mound and delved into the folds where the clitoris felt swollen and intensely aware—ready.

Her legs began to buckle.

"Willow, look at me."

Her eyelids shot open and she looked up at Preston Moriarty. His frown, the narrowing of his eyes made her wonder what he had seen.

"You're trembling all over," he said. "Are you ill?"

Even while she longed to drop to her knees and curl up on the ground, she searched for an excuse. It would have to be *some* excuse.

He pulled her into his arms and stroked her back. "It's okay. Tell me what you need me to do."

She wanted to pull away but hadn't the strength. "An old illness," she muttered. Not so far away from the truth. "There's a residue and sometimes it hits me. That hasn't happened in so long I can't remember the last time." Nothing like it had ever happened, but she could choose to lump it together with the inconvenient reminders of the powers she continually tried to ignore, like insights into the pasts of others with startling visions of terrible suffering they had endured.

"Malaria?" he said. "Something like that?"

"Similar," she said and straightened away from him. "You're so kind. I'm glad you were standing there. I think I could have passed out otherwise. Yuck, that was awful."

He slipped an arm around her. "Would a drink help? Or coffee? Let me take you inside."

Willow didn't want this man holding her. Or any of the strangers who surrounded her.

"I might have known you'd find the prettiest girl out here," Val Brandt said, stopping in front of them. "You have to watch out for Preston, my dear. He wouldn't be good for your reputation."

She gave a short laugh and looked at Preston. The compression of his mouth was anything but a sign of amusement.

"Willow here felt a bit faint," he said. "She should probably sit down."

"I'm fine now," Willow said.

"Excuse us, Preston," Val said. "Willow and I need some time alone."

"Do you now?" With a half smile, Preston walked away, toward the pool, pulling his shirt over his head as he went. He dropped his pants and shorts and stood naked, his back to them, for several seconds.

He picked up his clothes and turned to drop them on a table, looking fully at Willow as he did so.

Preston Moriarty was quite a man.

"Come and take a dip," he called to her. "It would make you feel better."

Two running footsteps and he dived into the pool.

Val rested an arm where Preston's had been. "Come and let's find a quieter place," he said.

Willow started to panic. Being in a strange place with a lot of people she did not know or trust wasn't something she would ever seek out, and with perceptions heightened, and threatening premonitions bombarding her, she grew close to running blindly for the way out.

"You're upset, aren't you?" Val said. "This wasn't the best night to have you come for the first time. Believe me when I say things rarely get like this."

He sounded sincere, but she was not sure she believed him at all.

"I spoke to Chloe and she'll be here in about half an hour. Let's just sit here." He pulled out a chair for her at an empty table. "Sangria?" He picked up a jug that stood there surrounded by glasses and poured.

She didn't accept or refuse, but let him put a drink in front of her and pour one for himself.

"Name your price," he said.

Willow looked at him slowly. "Excuse me?"

Val shrugged. "This is a new venture for me, hiring someone to run our lives around this house. I have no idea what the going rates are and I don't care. We'll pay whatever will make you happy."

Willow gathered herself. "I don't think this is the best time for us to have this discussion," she said. "My company can accommodate most household and entertaining needs. Why don't we make an appointment to talk when your wife can be here to explain exactly what she has in mind."

He ran blunt fingers through the hair that fell repeatedly over his forehead. "I told you she'll be back shortly."

Willow let her eyes wander, not really seeing anything, while she tried to decide what to do. He hadn't threatened her, not at all. In fact, he had been polite and done his best to show her approval. It wasn't his fault she seemed to be having an emotional crisis.

Standing near the combo, holding one of the poles that supported a striped awning, a very familiar, tall, lithe, dark-haired man stared in her direction.

The instant she saw him, her body relaxed. And just as quickly she tensed again and got mad. Ben Fortune was following her around. Who had told him where to find her?

Ben said something to the bass player and strolled toward Willow.

"Are you mad?"

She heard him enter her mind but turned to Val and ignored Ben. "We are pretty busy at the moment," she said. "But we could deal with upkeep of the house—and the grounds, if you need that. Shopping—"

"You don't belong in a place like this. There's danger here. Tell whoever he is you're leaving."

Ben's arrogance infuriated her.

"I think Chloe hopes you'll live in," Val said, his tone concerned. "There's a wonderful, private apartment she's redecorated in the house. Chloe gets her mind set on things. You aren't married, are you?"

"No," she said.

"It's none of his business," Ben told her furiously.

It wasn't, but she could be forgiven for responding automatically to Val's question.

"There's Chloe's car now." Val got up and pointed toward a separate garage beside the house where lights had gone on inside. "She'll be right out."

"Are you going to excuse yourself? Now?"

Willow tasted the sangria. "This is good," she said, frowning and trying to concentrate. "A little orgeat syrup might make it even better."

"I'll make sure I pass that on," Val said, grinning. "You're going to love it here. You'll have complete freedom to take charge of things."

The glass flew from Willow's hand and smashed on the stone terrace.

Val shouted, "Broken glass. Stand back everybody."

"Good heavens," Willow explained. "I'm so sorry."

Of its own volition, the table upended, followed by the three chairs Willow was not sitting in.

She got up and the fourth chair tipped over.

A woman screamed, and another, and men yelled.

A wind whipped across the grounds, bending trees double, roiled across the surface of the pool and turned it into whirling funnels that splashed over the sides and over those who sat or stood nearby.

Someone yelled, "Tornado!"

Willow shut her mind tightly, blocked out anything else Ben might have to say and gritted her teeth. Glances into the areas beyond the front walls proved what she expected—all was calm out there.

The torches blew out, fairy lights failed and lights in the house went off. Yelling and shoving raged around Willow, and she closed her eyes.

It was no wind that swept her from her feet. All she could do was allow herself to be borne away in unyielding arms, her hair tossed across her face, her body racked by the force of speed.

Speech was out of the question.

When she tried to see, thick darkness blocked everything.

She couldn't feel emotion, or react.

Silence came as suddenly as the madness had arrived. She sat on something soft and the air was pleasantly warm. Cautiously, Willow opened her eyes again.

Seated on the couch in her living room, she was alone—except for a small, red-brown dog at her feet.

8

He was in deep shit.

Ben hung out in the courtyard overlooked by the Millets' flats, and the shadowy forms of stone angels. There was nothing to stop him from going up to Sykes's place and tucking himself into bed—other than intense curiosity and a sense of doom about Willow's reaction to her little journey.

She was no fool, and she'd spent enough time around families like theirs to know she'd been snaffled, and who she had been snaffled by.

He smiled slightly. This might not be all bad. First he'd gotten her away from the sleazeballs Uptown, and then he'd created the kind of upheaval bound to get her attention.

Ben wanted Willow's attention, on him. He also wanted to quit waiting for something crazy to start happening. Not that a couple of people dying for peculiar, indefinite reasons wasn't crazy, but that didn't have to be the end of it.

That was the other thing. Those deaths seemed to have something to do with Willow and her company—otherwise why would both events take place around the presence of Willow or one of her employees?

He had gone a bit far at that party.

Could be he should have found another way to protect Willow—and get her attention.

Soft laughter met his thoughts and he looked sharply around the courtyard. Water poured lightly from a fountain in the center, a young angel holding a shell. He couldn't see it clearly, but he remembered it well enough.

As he'd experienced before, the faces of angels and the few gargoyles hiding above lintels had brightened in the darkness, and they all looked at him. He nodded in all directions, acknowledging their presence. And he accepted the strong likelihood that others—he did not know who—were using the figures to focus his concentration on them.

"Friend or foe?" He projected the thought and it was met with titters. He had tried this before and already knew his thoughts reached listeners in the courtyard.

A gentle and fleeting caress passed over his face, and he lowered his eyes. *It could be a mark of friendship,* he thought, *a reassurance.* But there were those entities that would use any subterfuge to find what most unattached spirits wanted: a host.

Ben wasn't available to be anyone's host body.

He would go to bed, but first he owed it to Willow to stop by—probably to apologize, too.

He ran up the steps, making no attempt to be quiet. Pascal slept in apartments above the shop, on the Royal Street side, and with most of the other Millets in London or making themselves scarce, as Sykes was, only Willow would be here.

He gritted his teeth. He'd forgotten Gray and Marley. One look at their darkened flat suggested they were probably not at home—he hoped not.

With the lightest of taps on Willow's front door he wondered if she'd hear him at all. He could see light through the drapes in her sitting room.

But only a few moments passed before she opened the door a crack and peered out. She saw him and scowled. "You've got a nerve."

With an innocent look, he shrugged. "What's the matter? I saw your light on."

"And I saw you at the Brandt place, Ben."

"Did you? Well, I admit I was there, but I didn't think you saw me. You didn't answer when I spoke to you."

"You were on the other side of the pool. How was I supposed to hear you?"

"You know what I mean." He tilted his head to the side. "You heard me contact you exclusively earlier today—in the shop. You answered."

"A fluke," she said, and he heard snuffling.

"Is Winnie with you? I was afraid I might wake Gray and Marley, but I guess they are out."

"I don't know," she said, opening the door a little wider. "Come in. It's time we got some things straight."

She turned away, but not before he saw a small dog with what looked like wiry orange fur. The animal was tucked under Willow's arm where it appeared completely comfortable.

"That's not Winnie," he said.

"You noticed."

"Don't be smart. You've got a new dog."

"Yes," she said. "Marigold. She's a stray I've taken in."

"When?" Ben said.

"When, what?"

"When did you adopt the mutt? I didn't see her when I was here before."

Willow gave him a smirk. "Goes to show how unobservant people can be."

He followed her into the living room, and she sat in a well-worn but comfy-looking blue chair, the dog on her lap.

"D'you like small dogs?" he asked.

"Yes."

Not much of a conversation starter there. "Just a puppy, I guess," he added and dropped to sit on the edge of the couch. "It'll grow."

"I don't care one way or the other. She's mine and I like her however she is."

"You got her from a shelter?" he asked, becoming suspicious about the origins of Marigold.

Willow didn't answer. She lifted the dog and looked into its eyes. "You're beautiful, aren't you? Wait till you meet Winnie. You'll have to put her in her place."

"Did you find it in the street and decide to bring it home? That sounds like something you'd do. Someone could be out there looking for that dog." He looked a little closer. "Probably not, though."

"My dog is very good-looking," Willow said. "And her ego is too good to let her be crushed by your meanness."

"You can't call it Marigold, though," Ben said.

If he could just sit there and look at Willow he'd be a happy man—at least for a little while.

"I can and I'm going to," she said.

"Would you consider Mario?" he asked.

Willow frowned and took a better look at her new pet.

"Oh. I'm only used to girl dogs so I thought… Ben, I don't want you interfering in my life."

"I'm not responsible for your girl dog being a boy dog," he said, deliberately obtuse.

"Don't play games with me."

"I'm not," he said with his best boyish smile. "I'd settle for you accepting me and not treating me as if I've got a disease."

"You know it doesn't work for us to be around each other."

"It used to work perfectly until you had your personality change. Will you call him Mario?"

"My personality has nothing to do with it, never did."

"What, then?"

She swallowed audibly. "Common sense. I got plenty of hints that I wasn't right for you, and I finally figured out I wasn't."

This was the closest she'd come to an explanation for the cold front that had preceded his dismissal. Or her retreat would be nearer the truth. Willow had gradually withdrawn from him until he forced her to say what she wanted from him. Big mistake. "I want you to go and find someone else," she had said. "Please just leave me alone."

He had been too shocked to refuse at the time, and later, when anger set in, he couldn't make himself risk hearing her say it again.

"You can't go on pretending you don't have paranormal powers," he said, hoping for some shock value from the sudden attack. "It's ridiculous. It's not true. And if you ever needed to be able to call on your special talents, it's now when something is out to get you."

The dog squirmed free of her arms and landed on the arm of the chair, where it sat like an intelligent red squirrel with a push face and stubby tail.

Ben tried not to meet its shiny black eyes, which were staring right into his own.

"Why aren't you staying at Fortunes?" Willow said. "Poppy must be furious you're not there. And Ethan and Liam can't be pleased you're in town and hiding out."

"They don't know I'm here—yet."

She blinked slowly, visibly turning over the idea he'd just presented. "You're in New Orleans and your family doesn't know it? You run the businesses, Ben. That's weird. Wait till they find out. I wouldn't want to be in your shoes if Poppy figures you didn't go to see her first."

"Poppy will understand. Anyway, I came to help Sykes." He had come to make sure Willow was all right, but figured she didn't want to hear that. "Did you put the gun in a safe place?"

"It will be within my reach all the time," she said.

"You shouldn't mess with it until you've learned how to use it."

She raised one eyebrow.

Ben puffed up his cheeks. "O-kay, moving right along. Marley and Gray talked to me about you having second sight."

She laced her fingers tightly in her lap.

"You can tell when someone has suffered violence. You know what was done to them and how they've been affected. And you are telepathic. Can you project yourself at all, mentally or physically?"

Her lips pursed.

"It's useful if you can, Willow. You must know that. If you're in a tight spot, you may be able to extricate yourself." Or not, depending on the circumstances and how strong her power was. "I should have pressed you on this years ago. I never understood why you pretended you were…untalented. I guess I always thought I could take care of you so it didn't matter what spin you put on things."

"Arrogant," she muttered.

"Can we continue with this topic?"

Not a word.

"Auras. Anything there? Do you see them, read them?"

She turned her face from him. God, she only made him want her more.

"Travel at all—out of body perhaps, like Marley?"

"Or whatever it was you did to me earlier?" she said, wrinkling her nose. "Snatch people up and transport them against their will?"

He ignored that. "How about created reality? Pretty sophisticated stuff, but useful for creating a diversion under dire circumstances."

Her face became blank again. The dog licked her.

"I enjoyed kissing you earlier."

Willow turned red and looked at her hands.

"You enjoyed it, too. I could feel it."

At least that got her looking at him. "That was a mistake," she said. "A reaction to not seeing each other for a long time."

"So you didn't like it."

Willow wasn't into lies. She chose to be silent again.

"It wasn't anything to do with our separation. That

kiss was automatic. We both wanted it, and there's plenty more where that came from."

With every word spoken, the wiry-haired dog with his sprouting mustache, pointy little ears and fur jutting out over his eyes, watched first Ben's then Willow's face.

"He looks as if he's got an opinion," Ben said, trying a smile on Willow. "If you did pick him up somewhere, you'll have to look for the owners."

The troubled light in her eyes didn't make him feel happy. Damn it, if this dog already had a home, he'd find another mutt for Willow.

"You look stressed," he said.

"I don't need a shrink, thank you."

"How about a brandy?"

"I don't have brandy."

"Coffee? Come on, loosen up. You can't hide your head in the sand, sweetheart."

Her eyes narrowed. "You can hope no one figures out you made the mess with that ministorm of yours in the grounds of the Brandts' house."

He threw up his hands. "How could I have made any mess anywhere? We're all normal, remember?"

"You can put a mug of coffee in the microwave. It's in a pot, but it's cold."

He automatically curled his lips, but turned the expression into a smile. "Sounds great." He hopped out into the hallway and the kitchen before she could change her mind and returned in minutes with two steaming mugs. Willow's was half milk, which he remembered she preferred. He'd also found cookies and brought the whole package with him. Willow didn't cook much unless she got in the mood.

He'd smelled the gumbo while he was in the kitchen and it made his mouth water.

Willow got up and took the tray from him. She put it on a marquetry table and stripped paper and cardboard from the box of cookies. "You didn't bring a plate," she said.

Ben grinned. He liked it that she could forget herself and behave as if they were still just Ben and Willow in the comfortable relationship they'd once had—if regular physical pain and intense sexual frustration could be called comfortable.

It would make his argument easier if he could talk about his visit to the morgue, but that would be revealing his whole hand and he wasn't ready for that.

She gave him his coffee and curled up with hers. The dog sniffed her mug and she offered it to him. To Ben's disgust, the creature lapped with obvious pleasure before Willow drank herself.

"Doesn't that bother you?" he said.

Willow looked confused.

"A dog drinking your coffee, from your cup."

"No, it doesn't," she said and kissed the creature's nose.

Ben could have sworn the dog's eyes crossed.

He decided on a slight fabrication over the body in the morgue. "Gray called me." She didn't have to know how he had called him. "Apparently, he and his old partner, Nat, are still pretty close. They discuss cases."

"I know," Willow said. "I look after Gus's cottage in the Marigny, you know. He's Gray's dad. I wish he was my dad."

That didn't say much for Antoine, her own father, who, with her mother, Leandra, had managed to be absent from their family most of the time since Willow was ten. The older Millets had gone in search of something none of them would discuss, but Ben figured it related to the Millet legend and the fact that Sykes's dark hair and blue eyes were considered a danger to the future of his clan. Too bad none of his own attempts to ferret out more details about this mystery had worked.

He made much of drinking his coffee and eating chocolate cream-filled cookies. He'd never been close with his own parents, but for different reasons. They ran a retreat house, a very select retreat house for advanced paranormals in California. Fortunately for them, money was something Ben understood and made with ease so he ran the family businesses and kept the parents supplied with everything they needed.

"Can I talk about my conversation with Gray?" he asked, deliberately offhand.

"Of course."

"He told me that the autopsy's been done on your baker. He's keeping the coroner scratching his head."

Willow's expression closed, and Ben didn't imagine that tears filled her eyes.

"Hey," he said softly. "It's a shock. I'm sorry you're going through this."

"Billy's dead—he's the one we should be sorry for. What are they saying about what killed him?"

"Heart attack, like Nat thought."

"I'm so sad about it," Willow said.

Now he had to take a calculated risk. Somehow she had to be rattled into taking what was going on seriously, very seriously. "The question is why he had it. His heart wasn't perfect, but he shouldn't have had an attack."

"What does that mean?"

The dog scooted back on the arm of the chair and rested his chin on Willow's shoulder. She looked at him with such obvious affection, Ben felt jealous.

"Blades—he's the medical examiner—said the man was frightened to death. By something he saw coming."

"How could the medical examiner know that?" She sounded short of breath. Her small, high breasts rose and fell rapidly in the thin, yellow dress.

Ben looked elsewhere. "When they found the body, there were little puncture wounds on the forehead."

She looked sick. "Something attacked him? Nat mentioned there were marks, but they didn't sound like anything serious."

"Doesn't look as if we're going to know what scratched him because all the skin peeled off. From the ribs up, the skin is completely gone. There's just raw flesh—"

"Stop it!"

"Sure. Sorry about that. I was thinking out loud."

"I'm not squeamish," Willow said. "But Billy was a friend and he was alive and normal this afternoon."

Absently, her hand went to her neck and she felt around with her fingertips.

"What is it," Ben said. "Does your neck hurt?"

"No!" she said fiercely, dropping her arm.

"How about the woman over the dance hall on South Rampart?" he asked.

She sat up very straight, and her freckles stood out sharply from her pale skin. "Surry Green? How do you know about that? Are they reporting anything about it on the news? What are they saying?"

No way would he mention his ride in her trailer.

"Nat knows about it." Ben felt pretty safe saying so since Archer was bound to have found out by now. "One of your people was there, right? Where the woman died?"

"How do you *know* that?" She sounded desperate. "This has been a horrible day."

"Pretty horrible for two people, anyway," he said, without meaning to sound judgmental.

"You think I don't know that? What are they saying about Chris?"

That was the guy she'd talked to on the phone. "I really don't have any details," he said. "I'm sure they'll all be out by tomorrow. No one said anything about a stake in the heart, though." The risk was worth it if he got a measurable response.

"That was just Chris speculating," she said. "Some idiot said it in the crowd outside the building. Ben, what's going on here?" She skewered him with a green stare like none other he had ever seen.

She knew the answer to her own question. "You know too much."

"I have ways of finding things out, honey," he said. "You can't change that."

"Why don't you find someone else to interfere with?"

"You make that sound vaguely obscene."

She actually snickered. "You know what I mean."

"Obscene was that party you attended earlier," he said. "Things like that aren't suitable for you."

"Why? Am I too pure?"

"Yes."

"I wasn't attending the party, I was talking about a job."

"Which you won't be taking under any circumstances," Ben said. "You don't belong in places like that."

"It's a very nice place, and if I decide the job is worth having, I will take it."

"I saw the guy who got too hot for his clothes. He prefers the way he looks without them. He thought you would, too."

"Don't be silly."

"You didn't look away when he put on his show."

"Did you look away when women were swimming nude in the pool?"

He opened his mouth and closed it again. Sometimes it was best to wait for a better time to push a point.

"Ben," she said quietly, "have you heard any comments about Mean 'n Green showing up at the sites of two sudden deaths today?"

He raised his brows, following her line of thought. "No," he said, glad he could be honest. "Don't worry about that."

Her expression gradually grew horrified. "My scooter," she said. "It's outside the Brandts' house. When they see it there, they're going to ask how I got home."

"It's downstairs in the storeroom," he told her.

"How—"

"It is. That's all that matters. Are you going to cooperate with me? I need to know exactly what's been happening. When did you start feeling as if you were being watched and followed around?"

"I never could keep anything from my meddling family. I figured they knew pretty much what was going on with me, but Sykes didn't need to bring you all the way from Hawaii."

"He knew I'd be mad if he didn't."

She looked at him. "Sykes isn't intimidated by anyone getting mad. He's just interfering."

"Maybe." He shrugged. "Are you going to stop closing me out and let me help you?"

"With what? All I've got are silly premonitions, and—"

"Yeah. Only your premonitions aren't silly. You've felt danger. And two people with some sort of connection to you died today. Stop the pretense, Willow. Do you think I'm not aware of it when you close your mind to me?"

"I'm not in your league." She sounded almost frantic. "I never could be, and it only makes it more obvious when we're around each other."

"Fine, only I'm not leaving. If I have to shadow you day and night, that's what I'll do. I thought you might like to do what you can to help is all."

Willow put down her coffee. "I don't need a shadow."

"Not if the shadow is me, right?"

She jumped to her feet. "I didn't say that."

Ben got up and moved closer. Willow backed away. "Dammit," he said. "Why don't you just give in and admit we need each other? Why don't you stop fighting it? I want you, Willow. I've never stopped thinking about you."

"Do you think this is easy for me? Something happens whenever we get too close."

"You noticed?" He took her by the shoulders. "Willow... Okay, okay." Resting his chin on top of her head, he took deep breaths.

He sat with her on the couch, and she gave one of the sweet smiles that reminded him of how shy she had been when they were first attracted to each other.

"Okay, Ben. We're fine, aren't we? Or we will be?"

Taking her hand to his mouth, he kissed her palm and folded her fingers over it carefully. "I will never give up on us."

The phone rang and Willow jumped. She drew back as if she feared being attacked.

"I'll answer it," Ben said.

"No, I will." She snatched up the receiver and listened, hardly responding to whoever had called.

She hung up and the thing rang again. Willow answered again. "I'm not answering any questions tonight. Leave me alone."

A second passed and she said in a hesitant voice, "Nat. Sorry…yes, someone at the *Times* just called. It was nothing."

Ben held out his hand for the receiver, but Willow motioned him away. "This has been a really long day," she said. "I need some rest or I can't think straight. Not that I know anything helpful anyway… Leave Chris to me. I'll track him down in the morning. He doesn't like to be interrupted at night." She listened some more. "In the morning, Nat. I'll be in your office first thing. That's the best I can do."

She held the phone away, and Ben took it from her fingers to hang up. "What's that all about?"

"I was at Billy Baker's right before he died. Chris was seen going into the flat above the dance hall on South Rampart tonight. Someone gave his name to the cops, but they can't find him to ask him any questions.

"And my scooter was seen outside the home of Val and Cleo Brandt this evening. Apparently, a freaky and very localized storm set down on top of their guests at a pool party there. After all the mayhem, I wasn't there anymore but no one saw me leave. Nat's starting to think there are too many coincidences involving me."

9

Caroline watched numbers light up inside the elevator.

There was time to do this.

She was too excited to sleep anyway, even if it was possible with all the noise in the street outside the hotel. She had intended to explore, but Joan's invitation to a little party in the top-floor suite sounded like the kind of exotic thing Caroline had finally escaped from Idaho to find.

It wasn't even midnight. The ship didn't leave until early tomorrow evening—hours and hours from now. Why not meet some of the other singles cruising to the Caribbean with her? That way she would already have people she knew when she got on board.

After the ship returned to New Orleans, she could hang around and see the city, unless she had met someone who gave her a reason to move on quickly, and a place to move on to.

Take it as it comes. Remember what you told yourself: "This is the first day of the rest of your life."

The hotel was old. Everything in the French Quarter was old, and as strangely foreign as the books said it would be. Foreign, thrilling and dangerous, or so it felt.

The elevator opened at one end of a short hall. Facing her, double doors stood slightly open and the kind of singsong, upbeat music she had heard coming from bars in the area escaped the suite where she was headed.

This wasn't like her, going to parties late at night with people she had never met.

Caroline gave a nervous giggle. Going to any parties at all was unlike her, but she was ready to change all that. Her high-heeled sandals caught at the dark red carpet and she wobbled a bit as she walked. The shoes made her legs look good! Confidence was a big part of the new, adventurous Caroline.

"This is the first day of the rest of your life."

Fiddle music, that's what it sounded like. And she didn't understand the singers' language, but thought it could be French. Her tummy jumped around and she took a big breath.

Glass clinked inside the room. She tapped one of the doors and it swung a little wider open.

A big room with more of the red carpet. Heavy gold drapes were closed over windows on the far side, small couches stood in two groups separated by a long table holding lots of bottles and glasses—and some plates of food. Some of the glasses had been used and the food had been picked over.

The place was empty.

This was the real story of her life. She was too late; the party was over.

Caroline trailed past the table. A glass of wine would be nice, maybe two glasses, or more. She crossed one arm over her middle and lifted an open bottle to look at the label. Not that the label mattered—white wine, she liked that best.

"Hey, where did you come from?" a man said. "Let me pour some of that for you."

Startled, Caroline saw him come into the room and shut the doors behind him. The thud in her chest felt like a punch. All the air rushed out.

He was fantastic. Flamboyant with smooth, foreign flare.

"I didn't hear anyone arrive," he said, smiling at her.

She panicked and put the bottle down. "I'm in the wrong place," she said. "Excuse me."

"No, no." He stepped in her path when she started toward the exit. "If you're on the cruise, you're in the right place. People have been stopping by all evening. You just happened to catch a lull. A rather long lull. Welcome. Giving a party all on your own isn't much fun. I think I've lost everyone. It's hard to compete with everything out there." He indicated the streets.

He could, Caroline decided, compete with anything in her book.

"Do you like wine?" He picked up the bottle she had been looking at. "Or champagne, perhaps? This is supposed to be a celebration. What's a celebration without champagne?"

It wasn't easy to keep looking at his face, his very blue eyes. When you'd spent your life in a nothing town in the Idaho mountains, confrontations with men like this didn't happen.

"Champagne?" he asked.

"Yes," she said. "Thanks."

He took a bottle from an ice bucket, unwound gold foil from its top and pried off the wire. One very strong thumb sent the cork toward the ceiling and they both laughed.

Perfect teeth. Perfect tan. And he looked Scandinavian, like one of those Nordic downhill skiers, only bigger. Big, muscular shoulders and chest. His brown silk shirt lay against those muscles, showing them off all the way over a hard six-pack.

Exotic. That was the second time tonight she had thought that word was the right one. His face was exotic, and his hair, long and blond, shining past his shoulders, sent shivers through Caroline. When he bent a little to pour the champagne into two glasses, his hair slipped forward, shadowing his features. Her knees weakened.

"I'm John," he said. "What's your name?"

She took the glass he pressed into her hand. "Caroline," she said. His fingers remained, touching hers, for lovely seconds. He was so sexy.

"Joan told me to come up," she said in a rush. "She'll be along soon. I'm traveling as a single so I got paired up in a cabin with her. We're sharing a room here, too. I was nervous about it at first—being with a complete stranger—but she's really nice."

"Ah, yes," he said, "Joan. Very nice. Great dancer."

"And she's beautiful. You already know her, then?"

"From a cruise last year. Great opportunity to do a lot of dancing, if that's what you like. No shortage of partners. Let's sit down."

Staring at him, Caroline sat on one of the couches, and he dropped down beside her. She couldn't avoid his eyes, or his mouth or the dimple that dug in beside his mouth when he smiled.

He touched his glass to hers and drank deeply. Caroline followed suit. The cold champagne slid over her tongue and bubbled faintly in her throat. Almost immediately, the flood of warmth, the heady happiness, rushed in. "Good," she said.

"The best," he said, smiling again and ducking his head so that his hair slid to almost completely hide his face. "Why are you traveling alone?"

She hadn't expected the question. "I've never been anywhere much before," she told him. "I've wanted to do something like this for a long time, and I don't have anyone to do it with so I decided to come anyway." She wouldn't tell him it was her plan to keep on going until she found someone to be with, someone who wanted to have fun and thought she was the best thing that ever happened to him.

"Do you like dancing?" John asked.

Caroline sighed. She felt warm all over. "I love dancing more than anything else." She would not tell him most of her partners had been imaginary.

He held out his free hand. "Let me have it then."

She frowned. "What?"

He laughed. "Your dance card. I want to fill it up for the whole cruise."

Finishing her glass of champagne to hide the thrill of anticipation that made her flush, Caroline turned her face away.

"Did I say something wrong already?" he asked softly.

She shook her head. "You're nice is all."

"So are you. Let's have a little more champagne."

He took her glass to the table and came back with refills. Every step he took was smooth, sure. Of course he was a dancer.

He would do other things well, too. Like kiss.

"Did you rent this room?" she asked him and giggled. "It's perfect for parties. All it needs is a dance floor."

"This is my suite," he said. "There are two bedrooms, a small kitchen and several bathrooms. Needing space has always been a problem for me. I don't like feeling hemmed in. That's why I insist on the penthouse suite when I cruise."

She drank some more, considering what he was saying. He had to have money. "Must be expensive," she said, then felt silly. Sophisticated women didn't say things like that, or she thought they didn't without really knowing. "Are you a wanderer, too? I can imagine you liking to be in new places all the time." That sounded better.

"Sometimes. More lately than... Well, yes, I guess I am like that."

"Than what?" she said.

John touched her cheek and she stopped breathing. "I can't imagine a woman who looks like you being alone. Doesn't seem right." He shook his head. "You've put me too much at ease. I'm running off at the mouth. I almost said I didn't want to travel so much when I was married, but that's in the past."

"I'm sorry," she said. Her head felt a bit muzzy, but in a good way.

"So am I. Or I was. You get over things. Are you married?"

"No!" The shock in her tone embarrassed her. "I mean, I wouldn't be here if I was. I've never been married." She had looked after her mother until she died a year ago. The death had not upset Caroline too much. Mother ruled with a heavy hand and that, together with never having enough money, had beaten Caroline into her shell.

She almost laughed aloud. Not enough money? Her mother had lived as if there wasn't any and died nicely off, which meant that Caroline finally had a cushion to work with.

John studied her with his head on one side. "What about your family?"

"I don't have one now my mother's dead." She shrugged. "I don't want sympathy because I'm fine with that. I'm ready to move on."

"Good," he said. "Looking at you, I'd say you're going to find it easy to move on and get what you want. You're going to be fighting off the people who want to be with you."

"Looking at me? What does that mean?"

"I think you know—you're gorgeous." He stood and offered her his hand. When she took it, he pulled her up. "Let me show you the rest of this place. It's quite something in a Victorian kind of way."

The solid beat of her heart seemed faster than usual. Her heel caught again and her foot clicked sideways. "It's the rug," she said, frowning. She wasn't sure she sounded completely sober. Better lay off the champagne.

"Take off your shoes," he said, looking concerned. "I don't want you twisting your ankles before I even get you on a dance floor."

She smiled and did as he suggested.

"You should wear a lot of green. It's good with your hair and eyes."

The years when she should have learned to take compliments had sped away, but it wasn't too late to start. "Thank you."

The kitchen was galley-style and functional. Caroline noted a floral arrangement on the counter. "Flowers in the kitchen," she said. "Nice."

There were flowers all over the suite, expensive arrangements with rich, subtle scents. Flowers stood on a short column just inside the bedroom door and there were more on a table in the window.

Caroline's feet sank into white carpet here, and on the bed, a white-covered duvet had been folded down from white sheets and mounds of pillows.

Draped across the bed, a terry bathrobe gave her the feeling she was in a forbidden place, an intimate place. It wasn't just a feeling that she was there with the most interesting man she had ever met.

He turned away from her and she started when he shut the door.

With his head cocked, he watched her and she couldn't form a word. She finished the second glass of champagne and looked into the empty glass.

"There's more over there," he said, nodding to a cabinet with a loaded tray on top. "I'm still thirsty. How about you?"

Once more he took the glass, opened a fresh bottle and poured. He set the glass down a moment and stood with his back to her.

Her legs locked. He was unbuttoning his shirt. Unbuttoning and stripping it off. She was faced first with his broad, tanned shoulders, and when he turned to bring her a fresh drink, the low light in the room sent a delineating sheen across his chest.

He gave her an apologetic little smile. "Even with air-conditioning it's too humid for me in this city. I get so hot." His eyes flickered to hers again. "How about watching a movie? We could see what's on."

Leaving was the only thing that made sense. This was

much more than she was ready for—not that she was a wilting virgin, but she was not experienced and she certainly shouldn't be responding like this to a man who obviously expected her to spend the night with him.

"You okay?" he said, screwing up his eyes. "What is it?"

A steady hum set up in her head. "Nothing."

"You're pale."

"I'm—" Her mouth was so dry she had to keep swallowing. "I'm fine. I should go… It's time…"

"If that's what you want," he said, disappointment evident in the sudden droop of his mouth.

He wasn't so clear anymore. She could see his blond hair against his shoulders, his face stark in the shadows. Movement took her attention to the hand he rubbed up and down on his chest.

"Now you look hot, too," he said.

She shook her head.

"Yes, you do. Geez, I'm never going to forgive myself if I've made you ill with the champagne. Did you have dinner?"

Caroline couldn't remember. She stared at him, at the way he shrank and expanded, then just expanded.

A god, she thought and wanted to laugh. She couldn't.

She felt the glass leave her hand and John's hands on her shoulders, shaking her slightly. His face was close.

"I—" Her eyes closed.

His mouth on hers sharpened her senses. She opened her eyes again. John kissed her, gripping her arms tightly, half lifting her from the floor. She heard his hard breathing, tasted champagne on his tongue when he kissed her.

She stood there, letting him move her, letting him take off her clothes until she stood before him, naked. He seemed to smile, but she wasn't sure. His touch, firm, almost hard, passed over her body, didn't miss an inch of skin.

Her chin tilted down to her chest because her head was too heavy, and too loud. Lying down was a relief. Stretched out with her eyes closed, things didn't shift around her so much.

But there were noises. Panting. Moaning—grunting. Her body jerked. Vaguely she knew he was having sex with her. Pushing himself inside, filling her up so tightly it stung. If she could have lifted her arms, she would have tried to push him away. He hurt her. The pressure of his weight crushed her breasts and pinned her down.

He spoke, but she didn't understand. But she knew when his mouth covered hers, covered not just her mouth but her nose.

Her chest compressed and compressed. Emptiness rushed in. The air was being sucked out of her—by John.

"John," she tried to cry into his mouth.

The sucking went on.

Her skin prickled. Her mind dimmed.

Drowning?

No, suffocating.

With a huge effort she got her eyes open again and tried to scream. The man spread on top of her was huge. He was John but much bigger and the light in his eyes was fierce, *mad.*

The weight left. He stood beside the bed, bending over her, drawing on her mouth and nose while the world began to turn black for Caroline.

Helpless, paralyzed, she could do nothing to stop this man from inhaling her life. And while he pulled on her insides with the massive drag of his sucking, Caroline got smaller.

She did get smaller, and smaller. She shrank until his mouth drew in her whole head.

A plop and he spat out her head again. She flipped over and landed in something transparent. A loud, loud bang sounded before it got darker. Wherever she was, the way in or out had been closed.

Peering as best she could, her whole vision was filled with a large, almost black eye looking back at her.

Then she knew where she was. Naked, curled in a ball, Caroline lay in the bottom of her own empty champagne glass.

10

"You aren't my father, Ben," Willow said, frustrated that he refused to let her go to see Nat Archer on her own.

Ben watched her face for an uncomfortably long moment. "Glad you noticed."

The precinct house was also on Royal Street and only blocks from the Millet antiques shop.

They had almost reached the black railings around the forecourt that led to Nat's office. Willow stopped walking. She faced Ben with the little red dog she already loved under her arm. "I don't know how you found out when I'd be coming down here. You just showed up when I was leaving my flat. You keep on just showing up. Have you been messing around in my head again? There are basic courtesies to follow—for all the families like us. You know the rules about that."

"I do, but I'm surprised you mention them."

Lightning showers didn't usually start in the morning, but today was an exception. White streaks cracked the heavy gray sky and big raindrops began to fall. The street smelled of damp grit and a suggestion of spilled beer from the night before.

Ben pulled her closer to the coffee shop next to the

precinct house. "Why do you have to try to be such a loner?" he said through his teeth. "You pretend you don't need anyone. Not you, not Miss Independence. Crap. We all need other people."

He didn't get mad easily. Everyone said Ben had a long fuse, and he had almost never gotten angry with Willow. She looked from her white tennis shoes with lime-green flashes and laces, to the open door of the coffee shop. It wasn't much after seven, but a stream of people on their way to work filed in and out. They dragged in. They came out with coffee steam rising past their noses and faint sparks of new hope in their eyes.

"Want some?" Ben angled his head toward the shop.

"I want you to go away and leave me to be an adult. I've got trouble—we both know that—but I'm the only one who can deal with it. And I'm not guilty of anything, so I'm not worried." *Not true.*

"You're right, it isn't true," Ben said. "You're worried out of your mind and I don't blame you."

She frowned at him. "Stay out of my head!"

"I wasn't in there. You were in mine."

Had she been? The thought unnerved her. If she was starting to voluntarily enter his mind, or anyone else's, she was losing her grip on being normal. She *was* normal, dammit. Being around all these so-called paranormal people was getting to her—rubbing off in some irritating ways and all of them imaginary. She would be okay as long as she remembered she only imagined she was psychic sometimes because she was afraid of being so.

"Thinking about it, are you?" Ben said.

If she didn't turn a bit wobbly just looking at him, this wouldn't be so hard. When his blue eyes looked straight into hers and she could see how intensely concerned he was for her, staying mad took a lot of willpower.

Yesterday's kisses still left their imprints on her. She looked at the palm of her hand and sighed. Yes, she really could still feel the imprint of his mouth there. Just giving in and sliding into his arms again would be heaven. It would also be unfair—to him, and to her in the end.

"Thanks for caring about me," she said, softening her voice without meaning to.

"Can't help myself," he told her without a hint of amusement. "For the record. I couldn't sleep last night so I gave up early. I'd already been out for a run and I was back in Sykes's place when I heard your door open. Of course I was going to see what was going on and if I could do anything."

She had noticed the tight black jogging pants—how could she not?—and the lightweight black cotton jacket over a T-shirt. He also wore running shoes.

"You can't do anything, Ben. But thanks. It means a lot that you'd want to help." And it did. What she couldn't afford was to dwell on the sense of loss that only grew worse the longer he was around her. Wanting him but knowing she should not have him was a cruel thing.

He took her by the hand, firmly enough to make sure she couldn't pull away.

Willow caught her breath and stared at him. "Worse," she said, referring to the electric field that formed between their palms and fingers. "I mean, it's even stronger than yesterday."

"Did you think it would go away because I did? You wanted me to leave, Willow, so I did—and I hoped you'd ask me to come back. But no, nothing." His dark blue eyes didn't look at all sleepy in the muzzy morning light.

With the Millets, these hyperreactions between a man and a woman happened only when they were destined to be joined for life, or Bonded as it was known. Willow saw him through tears. She blinked and swallowed and tried to look away. She couldn't.

"Things haven't changed between us," Ben said. "You can't change that and neither can I."

"Of course we can." She made a useless attempt to drag her hand away. "It's all imaginary."

"Didn't you ever love me, Willow?"

This was a nightmare, a nightmare and a dream all mixed up together. "Stop it," she said.

They stood, holding hands, for what felt like minutes before Ben all but pulled her off her feet and into the shop. "Is it still americano with room for cream?" he asked flatly.

Willow nodded. "And yours is americano with no room for cream." Pain had gone from their grip on each other, replaced by tingling warmth.

He grinned slightly. "I take it like a man," he said, and she figured he wasn't only talking about the coffee. "Any luck finding who that dog belongs to?"

"I'm going to call the shelter," she said, her stomach knotting. "And I've put a sign in the shop window. I haven't had a chance to see if I can find any ads looking for a dog. I think he was abandoned. He just showed up in my apartment." She kissed wiry fur on the dog's head.

When Ben didn't answer, she looked up at him, expecting disapproval, but he smiled at her and scratched the dog under the chin. "Don't forget there's plenty of time for someone to come looking for him, but he couldn't have a better home than with you. I'm hoping you get to keep him."

She believed him. "Why do you make it so hard to stay angry with you?" she said and covered her mouth, amazed by what she'd said.

Ben gave a short laugh. "So what's his name?"

"Mario," she said, avoiding meeting his gaze.

"You liked my suggestion," he said, sounding absurdly pleased. "Great."

"Winnie begged her way in around four this morning and decided Mario is her pup. Can you imagine that? I thought she'd hate him on sight."

"Winnie's a one-of-a-kind dog. Does Mario mind being pushed around?"

"She gathered him up and curled herself around him," Willow said. "I think she'd like to have taken him home to Marley and Gray." She laughed. "Poor Marley."

The barista pushed their paper cups across the counter and called Ben's name. Finally their hands parted.

They took the coffee outside and stood under an awning while the rain fell. "I'd better go in there and see Nat," Willow said, indicating the precinct. "When he's through with me, I've got to get to my office and do any damage control necessary. Thanks for the coffee."

He studied her seriously, trying not to be distracted by Mario's penetrating black stare.

"I can't make you let me," he said, "but can I come with you? Nat may kick me out, but I don't think so and it never hurts to let authority see you've got backup. Not that Nat won't treat you well. From some of the things Gray has said about Nat's bosses, he could be under the gun from them and fighting for a way to close this case. It could make him tougher than he'd normally be."

"Well—"

"Both Sykes and Gray asked me to come with you," he said in persuasive tones.

She considered while Mario continued to stare at Ben as if trying to transmit a message. "How did they know I was coming here this morning?" *If you didn't repeat what you heard me say to Nat on the phone last night?*

"Nat told them." At least he hadn't completely lied. Nat told Willow he wanted to see her—at her place or his. Ben had figured that out from listening to her side of the conversation and talked about it with the two men who had more experience dealing with the police than he did. So, in a way, Nat had told them—by a circuitous route.

"Okay. Come with me, but, if Nat behaves as if I'm a kid with parent in tow, please understand that's more than my ego can take."

He nodded. "Okay. And there's nothing wrong with your ego. Let's get this done."

Mario licked her jaw and she cuddled him close. He kept his head tucked into her neck while they entered the precinct house.

Several uniformed cops congregated on the front steps of the building. If they had any interest in Ben and Willow, it didn't show.

Inside, things were quiet, although the duty officer must just have come on because she looked fresh.

"Is Detective Archer in?" Ben asked.

"Surely is," the woman said. "Do you have an appointment?"

"Willow Millet," Willow said. "He's expecting us."

"He's downstairs."

Ben said, "We know the way," although Willow didn't.

He led her through a door and down some steps until they were beneath street level.

"How do you know how to get there?" Willow said.

"Gray said it was in the basement. How hard can it be?"

A corridor took them past mostly empty offices. They could see through mangled metal blinds that few people were at their desks yet.

They arrived at a door that announced Detective Archer, and Ben knocked.

Nat could be seen pacing around inside, and he hurried to open the door. Looking from Willow to Ben, he frowned, but kept whatever he was thinking to himself. "Come on in." He looked at the coffee in their hands.

"Sheesh," Willow said. "I should have brought you some."

"I've already had some," he said, but still he gave her cup a longing look. "Have a seat. Both of you. I don't suppose Gray's started talking about wanting to come back to the department, has he?"

Willow sat in a metal chair in front of Nat's desk. She wouldn't let herself smile at the pathetic hope in Nat's question. It was no secret that Nat missed his old partner. "Not that I've heard," she said. "He's still writing articles—mostly local color. Plenty to write about. But Marley said he's working on a book, too. Fiction, I think. Some sort of mystery. And they're all secretive about it, but Gray has this big project on jazz singers—tied in with all the ones that went missing earlier this year. If I ask about it, all he'll say is that he has 'to be patient,' whatever that means."

"Yeah, he isn't bored with all that yet," Nat said. "Too bad. I don't want you to think I don't appreciate Bucky Fist—he's reliable—but he's ambitious and he'll move up. And I've had two of the best partners ever, Gray and Guy Gautreaux before him. The really good ones don't come along often enough and then they don't stay, dammit."

"I expect Wazoo keeps you up to date on Guy," Ben said. "They're both in Toussaint. Guy's a private eye now, isn't he?"

Nat couldn't have expected the remark, and he didn't look happy. "They are and he is," was all he said.

Willow knew Wazoo was Nat Archer's girlfriend, who lived in Toussaint, not far from St. Martinville and was rumored to have "powers." That's what was said by people who were being kind. Oblique references to ritual and voodoo occasionally came up. Whatever, everyone knew Nat was crazy about her.

"Okay," Nat said. "We've got quite a bit to go through, and you're in the middle of it all, Willow."

"She's not in the middle of anything," Ben said sharply. He was still standing. "Except by coincidence."

"It was actually Willow I asked to see," Nat said, mildly enough. "I'd like her to answer for herself."

Willow was under no illusion that Nat's mild manner wouldn't turn downright nasty if Ben didn't keep his mouth shut.

Ben said, "Sorry," and Willow was relieved.

The office, with its scarred desk and grubby orange carpet, smelled of old nicotine, which must be from other people since Willow had never seen Nat smoke. A whiteboard—scribbled all over—just about covered one sick-green wall and she noted that Nat owned his own watercooler. Very little else in the office was worth noticing.

"Would you like to have a lawyer present?" Nat asked.

She swallowed. "Not unless it gets sticky."

"And you want Ben with you?"

Willow only hesitated a moment. "Yes. This isn't what you call an official interrogation, is it? No recordings or anything?"

"Not even a note, unless there's something I really need to remember straight," Nat said with a reassuring smile that only made Willow raise her guard higher.

A notepad sat on his desk, open to a pristine page and with a pen on top.

"New dog?" Nat said after a long, uncomfortable pause. "It's a fancy breed I should know, isn't it?"

"This is Mario," Willow said and smiled. "He's a mutt." She had yet to try to figure out the ingredients in Mario, but she'd decided he was a small terrier mix.

"Cute," Nat said. "What does Winnie think of it?"

Willow wasn't foolish; she knew when she was being softened up. "She's fine about Mario," she said. "Tell me what happened on South Rampart Street last night. What did Chris say to you?"

Nat picked up a folder and opened it. Inside were papers and a stack of photographs. He gave her the photos. "Anyone you know?"

She looked at the first shot and winced.

"Sorry," Nat said. "If they're too much for you, say so."

"I'm okay." She was grateful Ben didn't say anything. "It's Surry Green," she said, looking at the dead and discolored face revealed by a sheet pulled down beneath the chin. "She lived over the dance hall. What did she die of?"

"I'm waiting for the medical examiner's report. Shouldn't be long. Look at the others."

Willow didn't want to, but she put the first photo on the bottom of the pile and looked at the next one. This time the body was naked and someone had used arrows and notations around the edges.

"Oh, my God," Willow said. "What am I… I'm not sure what I'm seeing."

"A body with the skin stripping off," Nat said dispassionately.

"How could that happen?" she whispered.

"Why does Willow have to look—"

"Don't interfere, Ben," Nat said. "I should have you leave anyway. We don't know how it's happening. Both bodies have tiny red marks on them. It's fair to think whatever made them punctured the skin. Could be the skin started peeling away where the holes are."

"This happened to Billy Baker, too?" Willow's voice felt rusty. "Is it a disease?"

"Not that we know of."

"A sort of Hannibal Lecter thingie, then?" Her heart pounded and she felt sick. "If Billy saw something like that coming at him, why wouldn't he die of a heart attack?"

"Let Ben see that," Nat said. "He's already seen Billy Baker's body."

Ben took the picture and frowned. "There's a lot more exposed flesh here."

"Billy's catching up. Each time Blades checks on him, more skin is gone."

"Should that be happening if he's dead?" Willow asked. "Wouldn't it stop?"

"I think it should. But there's nothing expected about this case." He looked up at her. "Including you, and then one of your employees, being present at the sites of the murders."

She felt Ben shift and gave him a short shake of the head. "When I last saw Billy, he was fine. Chris didn't have anything to do with Surry Green's death. He was out having dinner when all the hullabaloo started."

"How do you know that?"

Her chest felt tight. She shouldn't have to defend herself, but she knew that's what she was here for. "I talked to Chris on the phone. He told me the police tapes were up around the dance hall when he got back from eating."

Ben sat down beside her. *"Be careful. They want to make something out of you being connected to both victims."* He spoke clearly in her mind.

It took Willow an instant to close him out. He had taken her by surprise.

"Where were you last night?" Nat asked.

"Working," she said, getting annoyed. "And being interviewed for a new job."

"At Val and Chloe Brandt's place?"

"You already know the answers, so why ask the questions?"

Nat took several Tootsie Rolls from a blue bowl on his desk and gave them to Willow. "Put those in your pocket for Marley. She loves them."

On autopilot, Willow did as he asked.

"The questions are routine," Nat said.

"You ask me, then you ask someone else to see if our answers match. Isn't that the way it goes?"

"Uh-huh. It was Val Brandt who called in here about

you last night. Evidently there was some sort of minitornado that hit his backyard while you were there. Afterward he couldn't find you. He was really concerned."

"I'd decided to go home," she said, not looking at Ben. "The party had been winding down anyway—before the wind came. I didn't think they needed any added distractions, so I left. I felt in the way. I'll call Mr. Brandt and apologize for worrying him."

"Reports were that what seemed like a tornado set down in those grounds," Nat said. "People were tossed around. Even the water came out of the pool. But you didn't have any difficulty walking away?"

She'd like to shake Ben for his juvenile trick. "No, I didn't. It was a breeze."

"Interesting choice of words," Nat said. "When you talked to Chris, did he tell you his plans?"

Willow thought about it. Mario wriggled free and actually went to Ben to be picked up. Mission accomplished, he sat on Ben's knees, staring into his face.

"Chris hadn't finished watering all the plants in Surry's apartment," Willow said. "He planned to go home after he could get back in there and finish, I think. Chris has been with me a couple of years now. He's good at what he does, conscientious, and I trust him."

Nat didn't comment.

"You know we look after Gray's dad's place—Gus Fisher? Gus thinks the world of Chris. They play cribbage when Gus can trick Chris into it. And Chris has taken Gus to buy coins for his collection. Chris would do anything for him."

"I'm glad Gus thinks so highly of him. Does Chris live alone?"

"What are you getting at?" Ben said. "Why not get to the point?"

Nat narrowed his eyes. "I am getting to the point, Fortune. How are things at that club of yours? I thought you'd decided you didn't want to be hands-on with it anymore."

"The club's great," Ben said tonelessly. "All of our holdings are fine."

"Nat?" Willow said.

Nat took his time looking away from Ben. "Does Chris share his apartment with anyone?"

"No."

"And he lives—" Nat hit a couple of buttons on his keyboard and read the screen "—just around the corner from your business."

"That's right." She wasn't surprised he knew her work address. "He's close to our office. It's convenient for him and me."

"Does he have a girlfriend?"

Willow's mouth was completely dry. She cleared her throat. "I think he dates casually sometimes. There's no one serious as far as I know."

"Who does he pay his rent to?"

"The same agency that rents me my office," Willow said. She felt sick. "Let me give him a call and ask him to come in here."

"We already tried that," Nat said. "And we've been to his apartment. He's not there."

Willow punched in Chris's number and listened to silence then, "The number you dialed is no longer in service." She frowned and tried again. "The number you dialed is—"

Willow hung up. "He always answers. Chris's cell phone is attached to his body all the time."

"What do you know about him? Where does he come from? Family? Former employers?"

"I can check his employment application, but I know there's not much there. Nothing about his family. Look, let's go over to his place and see him. He probably doesn't even know his phone's not working."

"I told you he's not there. Have you ever had him go missing before?"

"No." A bubble of hysteria rose in Willow's throat.

"Give us some time to follow this up," Ben said. "You've blindsided Willow."

"Give *you* time to follow up? You got some kind of law credentials?"

"Shut up, Nat," Willow said. She didn't care how awful it sounded, she wasn't going to let him talk to Ben like that. "You knew before I got here that I wouldn't have the information you need, so why did you let me come like this?"

"To put you on the defensive," Ben said. "So he could see how you reacted."

Nat ignored him. "Chris Parker came out of Surry Green's place and sat in a Mean 'n Green van to watch," he said. "A passerby saw him and reported it to our people.

"What totally throws us is that we think he went back inside after everything was sealed off."

"He broke in?" Willow asked, confused. "Who told you that? The same person who saw Chris in the van?"

"I don't have to give you any more details," Nat said. "I was hoping you'd want to cooperate. We went through some heavy stuff in this town, and a member of your family was involved. Could be there's a connection to this case. If you decide you want to help, let me know. I'm not going anywhere."

Willow stood up and so did Ben.

"Did Chris Parker know Billy Baker?" Nat asked. "Did he have any reason to go to his shop?"

"To pick up baked goods sometimes," Willow said faintly. She looked at her watch. "Chris could be at the office already. The phones don't get switched over from the service for another fifteen minutes or so."

"You might want to look for a new hire," Nat said. "If Chris is still in New Orleans, we can't find him. But we're pretty sure he isn't here. We think he's on the run."

11

Why didn't she cry? Just break down and do what she felt like doing? Ben had grown up with a sister, and female tears didn't bother him. You could comfort a woman in tears; Willow's rigid face all but warned him to back off.

He continued to carry Mario. The dog had a worried look that narrowed his black eyes and made his whiskers quiver. "I never saw a dog settle in so quickly," Ben said, hoping to crack the ice with Willow. "He's worried about you, y'know. He figures you're upset."

Rather than carry on toward the shop, she took an abrupt turn at the next corner and broke into something between speed walking and trotting.

"C'mon, Willow, give me a break and talk to me." He loped along beside her. "What's making you so mad? The deaths, the reputation of your business getting dragged into the case or finding out you've trusted someone you shouldn't have trusted?"

"A, B or C?" she panted, and skidded to a halt. "Isn't that like a man? Everything has to fit into a box. Choose a box, Willow, and we'll sort this little problem right out."

Then she did cry, and Ben was instantly certain he wasn't good at this after all. He pulled her stiff body against his chest and eased her close to the wall, while she clutched at him, sucking in sharp breaths, and he asked himself an old question: why did this pain feel so good?

"Let it all out," he said quietly. "Relax. Let go, Willow."

"R-relax?" Her voice got higher. "Are you relaxed?"

He gave a short laugh. "What do you think? I'm holding you."

Mario seemed ecstatic to be squished between them.

Ben stroked Willow's hair. "Let me take it all on for you. Whatever needs to be done, I'll do. That's what I always wanted, honey, to be there for you."

She rested her forehead on his chest. "Did you ever think that might be part of the problem?"

Caution clicked in and he didn't answer.

"You're larger than life. No one passes you by without staring. Sykes is like that, too, and your brothers. Why is that? Big, powerful men attract people to them when anyone with an ounce of sense ought to run from you."

"This could be good for my ego," he said, avoiding the eyes of passersby. "But somehow I don't think you're complimenting me. What do you want to do next?"

She looked up at him, so forlorn she twisted his heart. "I want to make all of this go away."

"Including me?" he said, knowing it was selfish to ask.

"Ben, when Sykes sent out his SOS, no one had died—at least the two people in question right now hadn't. What exactly did he tell you?"

It surprised him that she hadn't yet pulled away from him. "That you had admitted feeling followed and watched for a couple of weeks. He hadn't identified any obvious threats but he thought you were scared. And he thought I'd want to know. I did and I do. Whatever happens to you, happens to me."

She pursed her lips. "I can't argue with you anymore right now. I've got to find Chris. He didn't have anything to do with the murders, Ben. Believe me. I know him and he's a gentle, free spirit. He's even a bit wacky, but there isn't anything in him that could be cruel."

"You can't really know most people, honey. They only show you what they want you to see."

She looked at him as if he'd turned into a monster. "Do you see bad in everyone? I'm telling you Chris is a good guy. If he isn't around, something's happened to him." Her green eyes turned sharp. "Ben, Chris could be lying dead somewhere."

"With his skin peeling off," Ben murmured.

"How can you say that?" A fresh torrent of tears caught the attention of anyone in the vicinity. "That is just cold."

"Nope. Just a reasonable thought," he said. Damn, but his mouth could have a mind of its own. "You were suggesting Chris could be another victim in the same crime and I agreed. But don't worry. We shouldn't buy trouble before we have to deal with it."

"How long will it be before I see Mean 'n Green all over the news?" She sighed and shook her head. "If I didn't need my business it might not matter, but I do need it."

No, she didn't. She needn't work, ever. Being his

Bonded partner would be a full-time job—he'd make sure of that.

"Why are you so sure you need the business? You could work for your uncle."

"I'm independent and I intend to stay that way. You may not have noticed, but we came out of the dark ages some years ago. I don't need busywork doled out by a male family member."

"Mmm."

"Do you think I could take working with Pascal every day? Do you know me at all?"

The sidewalks were drying under a warming sun. The scent of flowers overtook the aroma of grime again. The mood of the city was rising—too bad Ben couldn't say the same for his own, or Willow's.

Ben rubbed her shoulders, and muscles in his jaw tightened when she arched her back. "I know we're still Bonded," he said. "That isn't something you can change. Sykes has told me it's written in the Millet Book."

"The Millet Book is a myth."

"The rest of your family doesn't think so, and I surely know what I feel whenever I touch you." He massaged the back of her neck with his finger and thumb. "I've missed this." He had even missed the close proximity of crippling sexual frustration. It was like a drug to him, and he didn't think he could dry out again.

She gave a long shiver, then took Mario from his arm. "You should go back to your island," she said. "Thanks for coming with me this morning."

Hurrying, not bothering to check for traffic, Willow crossed the street, going back toward Royal. He winced when she almost walked into a bicyclist with a guitar slung over her back. The woman, wearing neon-striped knee-socks, Doc Martens, a cutoff painter's overall and a lot of tattoos, yelled things ladies might know but didn't say.

Willow started running again.

Following her at an easy pace while keeping the distance between them the same, Ben turned over his options. He couldn't leave as long as there was any question of Willow being in danger, and she was in danger.

She turned to face him, waiting for him to catch up.

"Do you think I can't feel you following me, Benedict Fortune?" she said.

"Whoa, Benedict? Even my mother doesn't call me that."

"You do know what we're doing, don't you?"

"Give me a hint," Ben said.

She scowled at him. "We're waiting for someone else to die. We're waiting for the next corpse with its skin peeling off."

He shrugged. "You always cut to the chase, Willow."

"Are you taking me seriously?"

Sinking his hands into the pockets of his jeans, he said, "I wouldn't dare do anything else—" he wagged a finger at her "—and before you tell me I'm being flip, I absolutely mean that. What I want from you is a little cooperation. Together we can get through this thing and I can keep you safe."

"There you go again. You're going to keep me safe. Who's keeping you safe, Ben?"

"You don't have to worry about that."

Abruptly, she put the dog down at her feet. Her eyes were wide-open and she pressed her lips together.

Ben grabbed Mario up again. "Dogs are unpredictable," he said. "He could decide to run in front of a car. He's got to have a collar and leash."

Willow stared at him, but he didn't think she was seeing anything at all. Both hands went to her neck, beneath her hair, and she shook her head. Then she wrapped one arm around her middle, and he thought she gave a low moan.

Her eyes came into focus and she waved him away.

"What is it, Willow?"

"Nothing."

"Don't give me that. What just happened?"

"Leave me alone." She snatched Mario back and walked backward a few steps before she sidestepped to the nearest wall and leaned on it. "It *is* all about me."

Ben's gut tightened. "Should we get off the street?" He searched around, but saw nothing unusual. Then he deepened his sight to see the others, the ones who drifted among those who were physically present. The others, and there were never many of them at a time, were going about their business without expecting to be seen by people like Ben. They continued to search for a way back from the deaths they had not accepted.

None of them took notice of Willow or approached her. He felt satisfied that these were not part of the puzzle, a good thing since that would be a complication he would rather not deal with, given that he and Sykes Millet were the only ones he knew of who had the deeper sight, the third eye.

"You're doing something," Willow whispered, her attention darting from him to each person who passed.

"Not really. Tell me about your neck and what you feel."

"I can't."

"Why? That's ridiculous."

Willow crossed her arms over Mario. "Okay," she said, keeping her voice very low. "I don't know who, but someone is watching me—all the time. And I get these feelings on my neck. Tap, tap." She drummed the fingernails on one hand against the opposite forearm. "Like that only sharper and creepier. Almost like a stroke with little stings in it. No, not that... I don't know."

He felt a deep anger. He could tell she was telling the truth. But what did it mean? The type of elements that went in for torture—and Willow was being tortured—didn't care about domestic engineering outfits. They didn't care about the businesses of their victims one way or the other. But it looked as if Mean 'n Green had been targeted as a way to discredit Willow.

What made him feel mean was the idea of something touching her.

"Last night at the Brandts I felt fingers on me—on my skin. That never happened before." She turned bright red and rested her cheek on the dog's head. "It was horrible, the worst. An intimate attack and it came while I was talking to people. I couldn't react or they would have thought I was mad. And it wouldn't have changed anything if I suddenly said someone I couldn't see was running fingers all over my body."

Feeling mean turned into feeling murderous. Someone had touched her intimately? It didn't matter how it happened, it happened, and he would find out who was responsible.

"Willow," he said gently. "Let's get you home."

"I can't move," she murmured.

He looked at her closely. "Try," he told her with a reassuring smile that cost him. "Come on—start walking."

"I don't mean I really can't. I'm afraid to. The prickly thing will come back." Again she reached for her neck and he heard her shallow breathing.

Ben deepened his sight again, narrowing his eyes to concentrate on the space around her.

And he tensed.

A small, gray-black, almost transparent thing darted from behind her head. Ben reached for it, but the shadowy object dissolved. He caught sight of its pallid shadow rising against the face of the building behind Willow.

In a whisper of an instant, he put himself on the roof and spread his hands to catch the phantom. Power pulsed through his body. He leaned out, horizontal to the wall where he could see the top of Willow's head far below and people in the street appeared smaller.

This way and that he searched. He could only be away another beat in nontime, or he would be missed.

It, whatever it was, had completely disintegrated. That, or some cloak of complete invisibility had covered it.

He reversed his trajectory, put himself back a fraction later in the instant, and stood with Willow again.

"Ben," she said, and her skin took on a transparent quality. Her forehead looked damp. "I think I'll be next. It's taunting me, but then it will kill me—just like the other two."

Mario barked and Ben jumped. So did Willow. He had never heard the animal bark before. A ferocious attitude turned the little creature into a bundle of struggling legs.

"Cool it," Ben snapped.

"He's feeling something, too," Willow said.

Ben knew that. "Yes," he said. "But nothing will happen to you, Willow. I'm here and I won't let anything happen."

"What if you can't stop it?"

Another surge of power pumped through him. He looked into her eyes. "I will stop it—if something tries to happen."

"Benedict Fortune?"

For the second time today, the second time in perhaps years, Ben heard the ominous sound of his full name. This time, spoken by another female, it was loaded with reproach. "Poppy," he muttered.

"Stop right there, Ben Fortune."

His tall and very beautiful sister, with his brother Liam ambling along behind, approached with heavy footsteps. She noticed Willow, and Ben could have sworn Poppy blushed. But at least she stopped thundering toward him and her expression lost some of its fury.

Liam waggled his fingers at Ben from behind their sister's back. Like Ben and Poppy, Liam was dark-haired and had almost navy blue eyes. The three of them came together, regarding each other with question, although Ben's expression was a cover for guilt. He should have let his family know he was in New Orleans.

12

"We won't open at all until I know where Willow is," Pascal declared. He paced back and forth between a display of Meissen china and cases of Victorian jewelry. "She's not answering her phone, and she always does. How could she have gone without you knowing, Marley?"

The faint tinkle of low-hanging crystal chandeliers usually pleased Marley. This morning it set her teeth on edge. "I don't interfere with Willow's life," she said. "Unlike some, I stick to the rules—completely."

Uncle Pascal had been known to bend those rules and show up in the mind of a family member at the most inconvenient times.

"It's my job to look after all of you," he thundered. "If I have ever seemed to step beyond our written code, it has been to protect one of you." His head shone and he smelled of a subtle aftershave. His energy in the morning exhausted Marley.

"Pascal," Gray said.

Marley looked up at her husband and smothered a grin. His attempt to be serious in the face of Pascal's famous temper was a miserable failure.

"Go on, go on," Pascal said, gesturing with one hand. "What do you want, Gray? But I warn you, it had better be something useful."

"I was only going to mention that it's early and she may not be up."

"Not up? Not up, you say? I told you she didn't answer her phone—not her cell, either—and the office is still switched over to the service. Willow is my most industrious and dependable niece. She is out and about her business first thing. But she doesn't leave without… My dear niece comes to tell me to look after myself every day. Every day—do you hear me? She never leaves without making sure her old uncle is still alive and kicking."

That was too much for Gray. He laughed. Not just a quick chuckle, but a laugh that had him squeezing Marley's arm and doubling over. She couldn't be certain what amused him most: that Willow, whom Pascal constantly told off for not admitting her psychic gifts, was suddenly a saint, or that glowingly healthy and youthful Pascal would feign infirmity.

She had to smile. "Uncle, you're the fittest of the lot of us. You pump iron every day—Anthony sees to that." Pascal's trainer made sure his only client was in perfect shape. "And if you'd ever tell us how old you are, I bet it's not a day over fifty."

"Are you suggesting I look fifty?" Pascal said, glowering.

Translucent, Sykes wafted into Marley's sight. She saw his faintly glowing shadow shape hovering behind Pascal, and she saw her brother's most wicked smile. She tried not to look at him.

"Can we get back to the topic of Willow?" Sykes said, materializing completely.

Marley felt Gray jump, as he inevitably did when Sykes "appeared." Unlike Marley, Gray didn't see Sykes when he was in his coasting state, as he called it.

"I take it we've all seen the news this morning?" Sykes said. "That's why you're all here with the shop door locked and talking about not opening up? It's too early to open anyway."

"It's almost nine and Willow hasn't appeared yet," Pascal said. "She is always here by eight. Something's happened to her."

"How do you know?" Gray said—unwisely, Marley thought.

"I *know*," Pascal said.

"He does," Marley said. And so did she, although she didn't intuit injury to her younger sister.

"He knows," Sykes said. "But you could be fair, Uncle, and admit it was the news that tipped you off."

Sykes was fearless. Marley had always known this, but sometimes she wished he wouldn't bait Uncle Pascal. "I haven't seen the news," she said and looked at Gray. He shook his head, no. Looking at Gray early in the morning when his hair refused to lie down, he hadn't had time to shave and he kept giving her "come back to bed" glances, was almost Marley's favorite thing.

"What news?" Pascal said.

Sykes, his black hair even longer than usual, raised one winged eyebrow. "Why are you and Gray down here, Marley?"

"Pascal asked us to come down," Gray said. He was giving Marley that look again.

"Where's Winnie?" Sykes asked.

"Sulking," Marley said. "She went out in the court-yard early."

"Woke me up," Gray said, although he didn't sound upset about it.

"Willow must have kicked her out earlier than she wanted to leave. So she's grumpy about it. She always goes to Willow early in the morning."

"Yep," Gray said. "But she came back… What time was that?"

"Almost seven," Marley said, putting an arm around his waist. They both shivered.

"So if she was with Willow, that would be when Willow left," Gray said. "Mystery solved. Willow went to work extra early. Now can we go back to bed?"

Marley didn't look at him.

"It's almost nine," Pascal said. "Of course you can't go back to bed. Don't you writers have anything to do?"

"Absolutely," Gray said with an innocent smile.

"I bet she left early," Sykes said. "With pictures of a Mean 'n Green van outside that dance hall where the woman died all over the place, poor Willow's probably been arrested by now."

Marley stared at him. Her connection to Willow was improving steadily as Willow grew more aware of her powers. Marley cast about, trying to pick up a lead on her sister, but found nothing.

"What dance hall?" Gray said.

"The woman lived in an apartment over the dance hall, not *in* the dance hall. It's on South Rampart."

"Willow's got a client there," Marley said. "She's mentioned her…because she's difficult."

Sykes became very still.

"What is it?" Pascal snapped. He rubbed his face. "Sykes?"

"I was looking for Ben," Sykes said.

"I know that," Pascal said. "I thought you might be."

Sykes wagged a long finger. "You're at it again, Uncle, poking around where you shouldn't. I always know, but I let you get on with it as long as you don't interrupt something private."

"You shut me out all the time," Pascal said, raising his chin. "If I get in it's because you've forgotten your guard—not that it lasts long. Where is Ben—I thought he was in your flat?"

"He isn't there now," Sykes said. "Wherever he is, he's totally shut down."

"Mmm," Pascal said, wrinkling his nose. "Willow's gone and Ben's gone. At the same time." He glanced around, obviously not wanting to be the one to suggest Ben and Willow could be together.

"Listen up," Sykes said. "And keep quiet for long enough for me to tell you what's going on with Willow."

He talked rapidly, shushing Pascal's interruptions every few sentences. Marley only became more amazed—and frightened for Willow—as the story expanded.

"Two murders and Willow's being connected to both of them?" Gray said.

"No," Pascal said, shaking his head. "There's a lot going on with Willow, but it's nothing to do with any murders. Willow was in the wrong place at the wrong time yesterday. We already know she left Billy Baker's shop before anything happened to him."

"But she was there right around the time he died," Sykes said. "And her guy, Chris, was seen outside the dead woman's place last night."

"Willow's sure she's being stalked," Marley said.

They fell silent.

"Ben's on dangerous ground with Willow." Sykes made direct contact with Marley without looking at her.

"What do you mean?"

"He's playing with time. He moved her from that party last night and she may not be up to it. It could damage her."

Marley crossed her arms tightly. She was already feeling as if she could be getting the flu. Now her head thumped and goose bumps popped out on her arms and legs. *"I don't understand. Maybe I don't want to. Maybe you're dramatizing."*

"Dramatizing," Sykes said. *"You know I don't mess around when my family's health is at stake. He admitted to me that he moved her last night. Through the same moment, very rapidly. He's intended to tolerate that. What if Willow isn't?"*

Gray had a vacant expression, which meant he knew Marley was communicating with someone else. He probably figured it was Sykes and would wait for her to tell him what she thought necessary. There was no doubt that in Gray she had found her true Bonded partner. He was an incredibly strong man, but also accepting of the elements that made them different from each other.

"Marley?" Sykes prompted.

"We need to find them. Discussing something like this with Willow won't be easy. She's likely to pretend she doesn't believe a word we say."

"As soon as we can, we'll get to Ben first. I think he's avoiding facing up to taking a risk with Willow. Careful, Pascal's trying to get in."

Pascal glared at Marley, and she said, "Anyone got any ideas what the storm in those people's—the Brandts—gardens while Willow was there could have to do with anything?"

A chorus of "No" came back.

"Right," Gray said. "I know my miserable little powers are an embarrassment to the family, but let me try one of them out, huh?" He produced his cell phone and flourished it like a magic prop. Then he punched in a contact.

"Who is he calling?" Pascal said. "I told him Willow isn't answering."

"Neither is Ben," Sykes said, although Marley doubted her brother relied on technology a whole lot.

"Morning, Nat," Gray said, ignoring the questioning looks around him. "This case is expanding fast." He listened for a while. "That's why I called. I wondered if Willow—if they could have come to see you. No, they aren't here yet. How long ago did you see them? They could have stopped for breakfast. Did you call them both in…? Ben just showed up with her and their red dog? They called him Mario? Okay, we'll expect them back then."

He flipped his cell shut.

"Dog?" Sykes said. "What dog?"

Pascal paused in the act of opening a glass case of hair jewelry. "A dog called Mario?" he said. "That doesn't make any sense."

"*Their* red dog, is what Nat said. Called Mario."

13

Willow couldn't help admiring three of the four Fortune siblings in one place. They were striking, all tall, all dark-haired with a tanned gleam to their skin. Ben, Liam and Ethan—the brother who wasn't there— were blue-eyed. Then there was Poppy, whose dark gaze was a knockout and made more so by the shadows her thick lashes cast.

"What's the story, bro?" Liam asked. "I couldn't believe it when I picked up on you here. At first I thought I was slipping, but nope, it was you. Your patterning isn't even close to anyone else's."

"I intend to come home," Ben said, "and visit every-one."

Willow didn't miss the emphasis on the word *visit*. In other words, Ben probably didn't have plans to move from the Court of Angels as long as he was in New Orleans.

She blinked eyes that suddenly stung. The prospect of not seeing him again, for however long, tore at her. But as tempting as it was to encourage him to stay, she would have to let him go—or insist he did.

Ben was a sun in comparison to her tiny light. He had

power she could always feel, strong enough to make her almost fear that strength. And already he was taking over, or trying to take over for her. She would have to find out what had happened moments before his siblings arrived. The sickly tap and slither on her neck had been more insistent this time, but there had been an instant while she stood there, watching Ben watching her, when she had imagined him gone.

Just an instant.

Gone, yet not gone, it happened so fast.

Poppy Fortune touched Willow's arm. "You okay?"

Willow looked up at her. "Not so much right now." She hadn't intended to be quite so truthful, but making things up got exhausting.

"It'll work out," Poppy said.

This wasn't the woman Willow remembered from two years earlier when she and Ben had broken up. Poppy hadn't been sympathetic; in fact, she had been in the forefront, pushing Willow to end the relationship with Ben because *"There's no way you can keep on being what he needs. He's a major psychic talent and you're an afterthought in a psychic family. You're not up to Ben, Willow. Let him go—for his sake if not for yours."*

Poppy's cruel put-down replayed for Willow, word for word, but she said, "Thanks," and nodded. In fact, she didn't know what Poppy meant by "It'll work out."

"You can't let all the stuff about these murders get to you," Poppy said. "We know how big a part coincidence plays in everything. Obviously, you aren't involved in anything. Look at you. Who could think you'd be capable of hurting anyone? Or anything." Her eyes fell to Mario. "Oh, will you look at that dog, Liam! What a little angel."

"He's Mario," Ben said. "And he's a good guy."

Mario actually showed his teeth and they all laughed.

Unfortunately, the mirth was very short-lived. "How do you know about the case—and Willow?" Ben asked. His expression was grim now.

"It's all over the TV and papers," Liam said. "I was glad not to read your name anywhere."

"I don't give a rat's ass where you read my name."

Ben silenced the group again. A muscle twitched at the corner of his eye. He reached for Mario, who went willingly into his arms.

"What just happened?" Poppy said. "We…well, we came this way just to see if we could run into you." She hadn't explained away their arrival at this exact spot and time.

"Nothing just happened," Ben said promptly.

"But you were…" Poppy glanced upward, and Willow followed that glance up the side of the nearest building.

I was right, you did something really weird, Ben. Poppy saw it and so did I—sort of. Willow looked from sister to brother.

"You used remote imaging," Ben said. He held Mario up and peered into his face. "And you used it inappropriately. It's for emergencies, remember?"

"It was an emergency to me," Poppy said quietly. "I was looking for you. Okay, let's not argue. Have you two had breakfast?"

"I have to get to work," Willow said, hearing the lack of civility in her voice. "But it's nice of you to mention it."

"It's been too long since I had a chance to talk to you, Willow," Poppy said. "I've seen you around, but…" She let the sentence trail off.

"We're both busy," Willow said.

Poppy's smile looked genuine. "Another time soon, then?" She sobered. "I should have come to you a long time ago."

Willow felt uncomfortable—and curious.

"I'll go back by the shop with you," Ben told her. "Then I'll run you to your office."

"I've got my scooter."

He gave her a hard look. "I'll run you in today, okay?"

"We were hoping you'd come back with us," Poppy said. "We've got a lot of catching up to do, and Liam and I have an idea we want to run by you. Ethan, too. We could all walk Willow home, Ben. Then you could come with us."

"Poppy—" Liam began.

"Don't worry, sis," Ben said, tight-lipped, but sounding pleasant enough, "You'll probably see more of me than you want to. I've got to do something about getting you married off."

Poppy's mouth fell open. It was still open when Ben led Willow rapidly away.

Liam's laughter followed them.

14

Ben did drive Willow to work. He had pulled her to a halt on the sidewalk, two shops short of Millet's, and opened the passenger door of a black Citroën parked at the curb. "They're all in the shop waiting for us to get back," he said. "You want to walk into that, or get to work?"

Willow didn't ask how he knew what was going on inside a showroom he couldn't see. She accepted that he could and climbed into the car at once, Mario on her lap. "Where did this car come from?" she asked when Ben got behind the wheel. "It wasn't here when we left."

"Of course it was," he said.

Willow pursed her lips and they drove in virtual silence. He didn't even know that with each new and unexplained event, he made her more certain she had to find a way to make him feel good about leaving again.

Mean 'n Green's current offices were in two rooms reached by passing through a recently opened tattoo parlor at the back of a dilapidated terra-cotta-washed building. This morning Willow was glad she had not gotten around to having any kind of sign out for the business yet—that might make it a little harder for the curious to find them.

When Willow got out of Ben's car in the minuscule parking lot, she cringed at the sight of a police car pulling in behind them. She glanced nervously around, expecting the press to have the place staked out. The cruiser was the only potentially hostile object in sight.

"Don't worry," Ben said. "I'm coming with you."

How she wished she could say, "Great." Instead she ducked down to see him and said, "Let me call you if they're here to see me. They may not be, but anyway, we don't want to look as if we're on the defensive and you're my bodyguard."

"Why not?"

"You are so predictable," she hissed. "Now please do what I want for once. Thanks for being with me...." The cop got out of the cruiser and stood in front of the tattoo parlor. "See," Willow continued rapidly, "nothing to worry about anyway. He's here for the tattoo parlor. Happens all the time."

"You mean you work where there's a lot of criminal activity?" Ben said, focusing on the neon sign in the window.

Willow kept her face perfectly straight. "No. Cops get a lot of tattoos."

She shut the passenger door, tucked Mario under her arm, and stood there waving. This was Ben's first visit to the office site she'd moved into less than four months earlier. She intended to stay put until he left so he wouldn't figure out she also had to enter the building via the tattoo parlor.

He looked at her for so long she feared he would insist on waiting her out. She smiled at him and raised one of Mario's front paws.

Ben rolled his eyes, backed up and drove away.

Once he was out of sight, she ran into the building without glancing at the police officer, who remained in front of the building speaking into his collar mike.

"There she is, the woman of the hour," Rock U. hollered when he saw her. He was working over a large black-and-green tattoo on the back of a big kid with matted white dreadlocks.

Unlikely music, the ping of tiny cymbals and rush of water in decidedly Zen mode, floated from large speakers. Pictures flickered on a muted TV high on a wall.

Rock U. subscribed to the open-salon principle. A good thing, since his business was in one room, about eight feet by nine.

"How come you got your name up in lights?" he said, letting each word rise and fall as if he were warming up to sing. "Saw the van right there on the TV. And that uppity Zinnia, she won't even give me a hint of inside info-mation. That girl has an attitude, I tell you. You would think she was manager of a swank hotel, not a cleaning outfit."

As broad as he was long and all muscle, the man was a human billboard displaying many of his specialty tattoos. Like every other day, he wore a black muscle shirt and tight, black leather pants decorated with a heavy key and small tool-loaded chain hanging from a belt loop. He wouldn't tell anyone what the *U* after his first name stood for and the employees at Mean 'n Green had been known to waste time speculating about it. *Unlikely, Unwashed, Unspeakable;* the possibilities went on.

"You got a dog?" Rock U. wrinkled his hooked nose.

"Can't talk," Willow said, breaking into a jog. "But I

love you, Rock U. And it would be so amazing if you thought of a way to delay that cop out there until I've had a chance to talk to Zinnia. I only need a couple of minutes."

Rock U. chuckled. "Just long enough to tell that bitch to keep her mouth shut with the policeman, too? Not just me?"

"Could be," Willow said, her hand already on the battered door leading to Mean 'n Green's salubrious digs. "I'll tell you all about it as soon as I can." *Which will most likely be never.*

She hadn't quite closed the door to Mean 'n Green behind her when she heard the front door open again. Willow figured the cop was on his way and she didn't look back.

The phone buzzed continuously, but Zinnia behaved as if she didn't hear it.

"Listen up." Willow raised her voice to be heard over the racket. "If a cop comes in here, you don't know anything about anything."

"I don't," Zinnia said and blew a gum bubble.

Fabio sniggered. "I don't," he mimicked. The best shopper in town, he sat in one of several chairs behind a long, Formica-topped table Willow's staff shared whenever they were in the office. Fabio worked at a computer—probably doing price comparisons and mapping his day's routes. One of the things the company prided itself on was keeping prices as low as possible.

Willow waited for comments about Mario, but Zinnia and Fabio behaved as if they hadn't noticed him.

"This isn't funny," Willow said when she got no more reactions. "You know we're all over the news."

Zinnia sucked in her gum. "Are we? Can't imagine why." An exotic black woman with a killer figure, Zinnia prided herself on never wasting words.

"Did you hear anything from Chris?" Willow's heart gave an extra thud while she hoped for the right answer.

"No, ma'am," Zinnia said. She answered the phone and spoke into her headset in a voice she managed to make sound recorded. "This is the answering service. The party you're trying to reach will call you back. Please leave a message."

Willow listened to her say the identical words twice more before she said, "Press?" and Zinnia gave a bored nod, yes. This would only get worse.

"Okay," Willow said. "What's your next job, Fabio? Shouldn't you be out shopping for Mrs. Leopold?"

"I surely should. But she canceled."

"She isn't sick, is she?" Willow asked. Agoraphobic Mrs. Leopold never left her house. Mean 'n Green had been buying and delivering everything she needed for a long time, and Willow liked her.

Fabio crossed his darkly tanned arms over his chest and didn't meet Willow's eyes. "As in she's canceled us for good, boss. Says she doesn't need our services any-more."

Willow frowned. "I thought we'd have her forever. She must have found someone else." She thought about it. "You don't think it's money troubles, do you? I wouldn't want to think of her going short of things."

"You go sit in your office, and I'll bring you a nice cup of tea," Zinnia said, silencing the next buzz without answering.

Amazed, Willow whirled to look at the other woman.

"Tea isn't—" She barely stopped herself from saying that making tea wasn't on Zinnia's Agreed-to List, signed only by Zinnia and posted on a corkboard behind her desk.

Willow figured she could use what kindness she could get this morning. "That's so nice of you," she said. "Thank you, Zinnia. You are checking to make sure we're not hanging up on customers?"

Zinnia gave a "what do you think?" look.

Willow went into the second room, her own very small office, which didn't have a door because each time it had opened or closed, the old one scraped her desk. Chris had removed it. When she got around to it, a pocket door would be installed.

"You've got a dog there," Zinnia sang out. "Does he shed?"

So much for kindness. "No, he doesn't. He's Mario. I need a little quiet while I make a phone call."

Squeezing past one side of the desk, she plunked into her beloved wooden captain's chair—this one swiveled and rocked—and brought up the master list of clients on her computer. She clicked on Mrs. Leopold's file, found her number and picked up the phone.

The woman answered in her whispery voice, and Willow asked what had happened to make her cancel their agreement. "If there's something we need to improve or change, I'd really appreciate you being honest with me about it," she added.

The line didn't go dead, but Mrs. Leopold didn't answer the question, either.

"Mrs. Leopold?" Willow prodded. "Would it be okay if I came over and we had a chat?"

"No!" the woman said, sounding frantic. "The locks are being changed right now, so your key won't work. I've already called the police. They know I've been a client of yours, and if anything happens to me, they'll know where to look." This time she did hang up.

"Don't you let that silly thing upset you," Zinnia said. She stood on the other side of Willow's desk, the promised tea steaming in the Spode willow pattern cup and saucer reserved for Zinnia alone. "Put down that phone. And put down that dog, too, while you're at it. You'll get his hairs on your uniform."

Willow looked at the phone blankly, then stared at her office manager. "Why would Mrs. Leopold talk to me as if I were a criminal?"

"Can't think of any reason," Zinnia said, putting the tea in front of Willow, who remembered the phone and did set it down. "And if a cop comes in here anytime soon, I won't be able to think of a reason, either."

"Neither will I," Fabio bellowed, his English heavily accented. "I won't know why the Smiths quit, either." He claimed to be Italian, blond because he was from the north, but the accent sometimes slipped. According to his own reports, he attracted women like mosquitoes to standing water in hot weather.

"Put a sock in it," Zinnia said over her shoulder. "Not another word out of you until the coast is clear. Got that?"

"Yes, ma'am," Fabio said. "I could always lock the door and we'll pretend we aren't here."

"Quiet," Zinnia snapped.

Willow drank some of Zinnia's green ginger tea, breathed in the delicious aroma, then had an insane urge to laugh, until a knock came at that door Fabio had wanted to lock.

"Open it right up," she said. "Don't look guilty, either of you."

Zinnia gave an uncharacteristic wink and sauntered to let in the expected member of the police force.

"Didn't want to scare you by walking in," Rock U. said. He strutted past Zinnia and jerked his head to indicate she should close the door again.

Predictably, it slammed.

"That guy wasn't the sharpest needle in the box," Rock U. said. He had a thing about using the word *needle* frequently. Said it took the sting out of people's fear of them if they were mentioned casually.

"The cop?" Zinnia asked.

Rock U. turned his back on her and addressed only Willow. "Did I imagine it, or was that man who drove you here Benedict Fortune?"

Puzzled, Willow said, "Yes."

"Thought so. He's supposed to be a wizard, isn't he? Word around the Quarter has it you two were an item."

"They surely were," Fabio said. "*Mamma mia,* and what a hot item, if I may say so, boss? The air around you two sizzled—bet it still does. And make that, he *is* a wizard."

Why hadn't she followed Sykes's advice, kept her office door and bought a smaller desk? "Ben's a good friend of mine," she told Rock U. "Cut the gossip, Fabio."

"He's back in town?" Zinnia said, her eyes all but crossed in ecstasy. "That man is a major stud. When he walks down the street, it's like the parting of the Red Sea. All the people get out of his way and stare. Is that black hair still long finger food?"

Willow ignored her. "What did the police want, Rock U.?"

"I could hardly get a word out of him. He told me he'd be parking outside until he's relieved by another cruiser. Then he said he hadn't been told we did tattoos, as well. What else does he think I do?"

"He's watching us," Fabio said. "We are under surveillance." He sounded excited.

"I'm worried about Chris," Willow said. "What if something horrible has happened to him?"

"Probably heard all the fuss and ducked out," Fabio said. "He likes to do his own thing—without an audience."

Without warning, Mario climbed from Willow's lap onto the desk and sat facing the bigger room.

Rock U. frowned at the dog. "He's giving me the evil eye," he said, taking a step backward. "Where d'you get that thing?"

"He's my dog," Willow said shortly. "He's a very good watchdog, and he'll be with me all the time now. With everything going the way it is, I need someone fearlessly loyal around."

"I'm fearlessly loyal," Rock U. said, still eyeing Mario.

Willow heard a low growl, but chose to ignore it.

"The cop made a mistake about tattoos because you won't put a name on your place," Fabio said. "He thinks it's part of the stuff we do."

"I got a sign," Rock U. said, sounding aggrieved. "It lights up and says Tattoos. What else do I need? And you don't have a sign, either. You been here weeks longer than me."

Fabio was enjoying himself too much. "Didn't you ask him why he's sitting out there?" he said.

"What d'you think?" Rock U. asked him. "I asked and he said he was checking around the area. Something about a missing person." Mario got another glare.

Getting up slowly and stretching, Willow's new pet walked across the desk and sat on the very edge—like a sentry.

"Will you stop it!" Willow said. "All of you. Tell me one thing, Zinnia. Did the Smiths say anything about why they were canceling?"

"Said you'd know why, that we all would, and they can't believe *it* of us, but don't have a choice and won't take a chance. That was the whole enchilada."

"I'm going over to the Smiths," Willow said. "Calling Mrs. Leopold first was a mistake. If I just show up at the Smiths, they'll get over any hang-ups they have."

"What hang-ups?" Rock U. asked. When he frowned, heavy brows half covered his eyes.

"What you were talking about when I came in," Willow said, exasperated. "You said we were all over the news."

"Oh, that." His eyebrows shot up again. "I just thought it was pretty good advertising. All I was asking you was how you managed to get the name out in front of news cameras. I was thinking I might try and do the same with mine."

"You don't have a name, remember," Fabio said, sniffing sharply through his slender nose. "It's too expensive to come up with a moniker and get it painted out front."

"Details," Rock U. said. "Now they're talkin' about bats."

Zinnia made an ugly face.

"What about them?" Willow asked.

"They think they're moving into the city—like a plague."

The phone rang and Willow picked it up. "It's Sykes." Her brother used his tough voice. "Ben and I want to pick you up in about an hour."

"Nope," she told him. "I just got here and I'm up to my ears. Bye."

"Just be careful until we get there," Sykes said.

Then Ben came on. "Do not go outside, Willow. Promise me you won't. Go on, say it now."

"Later, you two."

"Say it!" That was as close to shouting as she'd ever heard from Ben.

"Thanks," Willow said in a reasonable voice that cost her control. "I appreciate the warning."

She clicked off and said, "Now. What about these bats? You're kidding, right?"

"He's kidding," Fabio said. "Thinks he's a funny guy."

Rock U. hooked a thumb over his shoulder. "I just heard it on the cop's radio. Reports of bats scaring people. They've been seen—the bats have. Today."

"It's not a good thing to see bats in the daytime," Zinnia said seriously. "Usually means they've got rabies."

Willow shuddered. Her back straightened and a creepy cold climbed her spine. Her brain buzzed.

She touched her forehead, then her neck. "Please give me some time to think," she said. "*Please.* I need to be alone." Could a bat have touched her?

Oh, sure—several times and without her seeing it?

And she didn't think bats went in for the kind of touching she'd felt in the Brandts' garden.

Yet again the phone rang and Willow picked up. "Yes," she said, as evenly as she could.

"Promise me," Ben said. "I've got to deal with something, then I'll be over for you."

"I'm fine, Ben," she said, touched despite her mixed-up feelings. "Thank you for caring. Nothing's changed."

"Promise me."

"I've got people here," she said through her teeth and cut him off again. "Now, folks, give me some space, please."

Dimly, she was aware of shapes moving away from her. Nothing was clear anymore. She propped her elbows, very carefully, on the desk and rested her chin on top.

A quiet click suggested the other three had absented themselves to the tattoo parlor.

The next ring of her phone almost made her cry out. The readout showed Brandt, and she answered, "Mean 'n Green." This would probably be bad, but she could hope it wouldn't be.

"This is Chloe Brandt," a woman's pleasant voice said. "Is this Willow?"

She said, "Yes," with her hand over her eyes. *Wait for it.*

"I'm sure this isn't a good day for you," Chloe Brandt said. "So I won't keep you long. Val told me what a great job you did last night. Thank you, Willow—you saved us."

Slowly, Willow dropped her hand. Her head still felt weird. "I'm glad I could help."

"We have no idea what caused all that bedlam in the garden," Chloe said. "A freak thing is the only answer we can get. It frightened you a lot, didn't it?"

This was Willow's chance to explain her disappearance from the party—if she chose to take it. "I'm not great with storms." It sounded pretty weak.

"Neither am I. Val and I hope you'll give real consideration to working for us. You probably don't have enough time to do all we'd like to have you do—at least at first—but we'll take whatever you can give us."

We're getting more openings by the minute. "We'd better make sure you know what's been happening," she said. "About the two people who have died and the police thinking Mean 'n Green could be involved in some way."

"Yes, but it's ridiculous," Chloe said. "Don't worry about it. The police are desperate for suspects."

Willow agreed to return to the Brandts' home later in the day, but by the time she could sign off with Chloe and turn her phone off completely, she was afraid she might be sick.

She didn't know where it came from, but she welcomed a sudden breeze.

Softly, the curls that always tipped over her brow blew away from her face.

How could she try to explain all of this to anyone? Ben had looked at her so strangely when she told him about part of it. About feeling things. She closed her eyes and recalled standing with him on the sidewalk. He had gone. Only for an instant, but she was convinced he had not been there all the time.

But where had he been, and why?

Or was she imagining everything, including what she

thought was going on with Ben? Was that one more part of some delusion?

The buzzing in her brain gradually shifted, moved outside her head and grew louder. Around and around her it spun. She searched everywhere. There was nothing to see.

Mario came back across the surface of her desk and sat again, this time looking at her. His ears perked up straight.

He was guarding her or warning her.

Delusion.

Strip lighting made the little room bright white, but while Willow sat there, paralyzed by her own confusion, a vaporous puff pressed down on her and spread. Like a deep purple cloud, the thing swelled to fill all the space around her. She couldn't see beyond the thick, bruised atmosphere.

Like clamps, fingers closed on her shoulders. She tried to brush at them, but felt nothing there.

The squeezing moved to her upper arms and started lifting her. She opened her mouth, but couldn't scream. With both hands, she clutched the edge of her desk.

Through the haze she saw someone approaching, a man, a handsome man, tall, with long, dark hair streaked with white. His clothes were from another age, but his face seemed familiar. He didn't look at her, only past her.

Unable to resist the pull, Willow began to rise from her chair. Her thighs banged on the underside of her desk.

"No," she screamed. "Let me go!" Her hands started to slip and her chair rolled back.

The man who approached held a book. This he opened, facing Willow, and he pointed at a page. She read,

The Embran will pursue us until we destroy them all. If we fail, they will destroy us.

On the facing page was an illustration of a dragon, a distorted, incredibly horrifying dragon with rows of bared and pointed teeth, burning red eyes and vast claws jutting from what looked more like human hands covered with scales, than animal feet.

Willow couldn't make a sound.

The man turned the page and pointed. "Listen to them," the man said clearly. Pale and faintly glowing, a beautiful face looked back at Willow and the mouth curved slowly into a smile. With the smile came an overwhelming peace that soothed Willow. She became heavy as if falling asleep. Beneath the picture of the woman was the single word, *Angelus.*

This, Willow thought, was a perfect angel.

The eyes in the picture moved and, like the man's, stared past Willow. Light left those eyes and they darkened with menace.

Willow's body shook, but not because she was afraid. Whatever tried to drag her away trembled and gradually began to let go.

It raised her another inch, and another, while she grew warmer, heavier, and then she dropped, hard, back into her chair.

Mario leaped onto her lap, and she felt his muzzle pressed into her neck.

She looked back at the book, only it wasn't there anymore.

The man in his old-fashioned clothes receded, and when he was gone, the white light from overhead shone brightly again.

15

Ben had almost dragged Willow out of her office. She seemed zombielike at the time and didn't say a word to the staring group they had passed in the tattoo parlor. He told the woman, whom he remembered as someone employed at Mean 'n Green, that he was taking Willow home. With a vacant smile on her face, the woman had only nodded.

They were in luck when the policeman outside seemed to pay no attention to them.

Bringing Willow to Fortunes had been Sykes's idea. Neither of them wanted her back in Royal Street until she had settled down enough to deal with the anger she would face—and the demands Pascal would make. Ben had a feeling Willow could forget trying to hold on to any of her protests about being "normal." They were outrageous anyway.

Also, by now Nat would have had a few not-so-kind words with the laid-back cop outside the tattoo parlor, and the first place he'd go looking for Willow was Millet's.

Sykes hovered nearby. He had shifted irritably from the opposite end of the blue leather couch where Willow sat with Mario at her feet, to the raised bar and Poppy, who hung out there. Preoccupied, Poppy cast anxious glances in Ben's direction.

"Chris has been gone almost twenty-four hours," Willow said faintly.

Ben didn't think it wise to tell her she'd said the same thing a few minutes earlier. "Are you sure he's not the type to take off? Some people aren't into anything heavy—that's why they like to live light and alone."

"He didn't take off," Willow said, and he watched, actually watched her fold inside her own mind. Automatically, he began to follow her, but stopped. He might be able to listen to her thoughts easily as long as she wasn't consciously shutting him out, but when they had been dating, he had promised not to do that—even though she had never actually admitted it could happen.

Expressions flitted across her features. He could swear she was seeing something, and it alternately scared and angered her. All he could do was hope she would share whatever it was, and soon.

Ben kept quiet, although there was enough noise at Fortunes to vibrate the average listener's eardrums.

The club was closed, but a jam session blasted from the stage in bursts. Gabby LaHane, diamonds glinting in heavy gold jewelry, ground out a gritty chorus of "You Held Me Tight," while his fingers drummed rapidly over the piano keys—big, stubby fingers as agile as a breeze through new grass.

"Why are you so sure Chris didn't pack up and leave?" Ben said, shifting to the edge of his own blue-covered chair. The club was just about all blue, including the walls and floor, and eerie, the way the Fortune siblings liked it. "If he didn't, where is he?"

Blinking slowly, Willow looked at him. "There is so much anger," she said. "Everywhere. Anger. Revenge. They want revenge. I don't know why they've taken the others. What do they want them for?"

She wasn't really asking questions of anyone but herself.

He didn't make any sudden moves and shot approaching Sykes a warning glance. If he weren't trying to keep his physical reactions to Willow under control, he would sit by her. The closer he was, the more successful he seemed at keeping her interacting with him.

Ben waited, and so did Sykes, who braced his feet apart and crossed his arms, his eyes unreadable.

"If we don't destroy them, they will destroy us," Willow muttered. "The Embran."

The movement Ben saw from the edge of his vision was Sykes's arms dropping to his sides. The two men met each other's eyes. Ben sensed that Sykes had heard what Willow said and its meaning had shocked him. He padded toward them, as graceful as ever, but giving off waves of antagonism.

"Listen to them," Willow said, very quietly. "They are beautiful, especially when they smile."

"The Embran?"

Willow startled, her eyes coming into focus. But she didn't give him an answer.

"Who is beautiful when they smile?" he pressed.

"I don't know!" Willow spoke so loudly that Sykes came at a run and the dog jumped on her lap. "No, I don't know, I tell you. I want it all to stop. I don't like any of it."

Poppy started to leave the bar, but Sykes looked back and shook his head.

Ben couldn't hold back; he went to sit beside Willow at once and pulled her into his arms. A new reaction, pain, at the bottom of his spine, shot through his pelvis, and he tried to not acknowledge that he was erect. This seemed purely sexual, but his overwhelming feeling was the need to protect Willow. He couldn't bear her to be afraid, and she was deeply afraid now.

Taking the arm of the sofa on Willow's opposite side, Sykes looked into her face. "Take some deep breaths," he told her. "And quit worrying."

"I won't let anything happen to you," Ben said. "Not ever."

She opened her mouth, but her breathing stayed shallow. The hand she closed just above Ben's knee jolted her. It doubled Ben over, and there was nothing he could do to stop himself.

Through waves of excruciatingly perfect pain he heard Sykes's soft laughter and it gave him the strength to straighten up. Gradually he was left with edgy, demanding awareness, and he could hold Willow even closer while he glared at Sykes.

"All over between the two of you, huh?" Sykes said. "It's a good job you found that out before it was too late."

"Quit it," Willow told him. "This isn't a joke."

"I'm sure it's not," Sykes said, struggling for a straight face. "Never having experienced what goes with, er, *it,* myself, I can only guess about that."

What amazed Ben was that Willow didn't try to push him away.

"I never wanted any of this," she said.

"Can you explain exactly what you mean by *this?*" Ben asked. "Who have they taken? You said you don't know why they took them. Was it the Embran who did that?"

She shook her head repeatedly, from side to side. "I don't know anymore. But some have been taken. The Embran, yes, they've started taking people."

"How do you know?"

"I just know." Willow looked sideways at him, and everything she really thought about what might or might not be true about herself, showed in her eyes. "I'm not normal, am I?" she whispered.

"Depends on your interpretation of normal," Sykes said. "Feels normal to me and Ben—and all the other members of our families, and some other families we know about."

"You didn't need me, too," Willow said. "Why did I have to be dragged in?"

"I need you," Ben said quietly, not caring if Sykes heard.

"Something tried to lift me up and take me away," Willow said, still staring at Ben's face. "At my office. I thought it was going to. I couldn't see it or feel it with my hands—only its hold on me and the way I started being dragged out of my chair."

Horror gripped Ben. She couldn't be left alone— ever—not as long as she was vulnerable enough to...to die for someone else's fight.

"Whose fight is it?" he asked Sykes silently.

His old friend raised a brow. They hadn't communicated telepathically since they were kids in school and did it to amuse themselves. *"Willow told you more about the Embran than I thought she knew. I believe there really was a visitation at her office—from someone on our side, probably Jude. He went to save her from whatever was trying to take her away."*

"Yes. But why is she the focus? What she's talking about is a kidnap attempt, but why her? And I think she's getting hints of someone, or more than one, who have already been taken."

"We've got more than that to figure out," Sykes said. *"Someone's dumped a jigsaw puzzle on the floor for us."*

"I never liked jigsaws. Chess is my game." Ben heard Sykes laugh behind his serious face. *"Next time we play I'll bet you the same as usual,"* Ben told him. The last game they played, Sykes won. The record tended to even out, though.

"We'll need to work together with her," Sykes said. *"I'll get Marley on board, too. And Gray. He's coming along nicely."*

"Good idea. They'll jump at the chance—once Marley stops being mad that this isn't all over. She's very protective of Willow."

Ben caught Willow frowning at him. She hugged Mario, who looked smug, yes, smug. The dog had a whole range of annoying expressions.

"What is it?" he asked Willow.

She kept staring at him, then turned in Sykes's direction.

"Watch out or she may hear us," Ben heard Sykes tell him. *"She's giving in to what she is, and her talents are taking over. I want to know how developed her powers are."*

She turned her attention to a glass ball in the middle of the nearest table. Each table in the place had a similar ball. "They're hokey," she said, and he saw her shoulders heave a little. "Crystal balls in a club called Fortunes—awful."

Ben chuckled. "Thank you. They're snow globes with fiber-optic lights." She chose odd times to notice decor. "They've got motion sensors."

Sykes bent to pass a hand over the glass ball near them. Blue light zipped around inside like skinny shards of lightning—and snow whirled.

"Still hokey," she said. "All you need is fake thunder booming overhead."

Ben was tempted, but controlled the urge to oblige.

"You're changing the subject," Sykes said. "Let's get back to what happened at your office. It's easy to gloss over something important, and we need to know it all."

Her face set and she sat even closer to Ben of her own accord. "Okay, I'll say it again," she said in a monotone, a white line forming around her lips. "An attempt was made to kidnap me—I think. I don't know who or what did it. And a man came to show me a book. He was handsome, with white streaks in his long, black hair. His clothes were old-fashioned. And purple smoke filled everything up. Smoke. Haze. A cloud. I don't know. It all sounds stupid."

Ben wouldn't let her jerk free of his arms, which was what she immediately tried to do.

"Back up," he said. "A man with a book and purple smoke? Very normal, Willow—happens to people all the time."

He felt her shudder. "You called before anything happened," she said. "Why did you come rushing over to get me?"

"That can wait. What man? What book?" Sykes had hinted at the things she was talking about.

"I already know," Sykes said. "At least, I think the man could be Jude Millet."

Willow sat up straighter and craned to see her brother. "*That* Jude? The Mentor? The one who reminds us about following the—"

"That one," Sykes said rapidly.

Ben got the impression his friend didn't want all of his family's business aired. That would change once Willow gave in and let Ben back into her life for good. Covertly, he looked at her profile. He had never seen or met another woman who pleased him as Willow did, or one he wanted with even a fraction of the desire he had for her.

She would be his—unless he had somehow hurt her too deeply and without knowing. He would find out what had made her drive him away before and deal with it.

"Jude was the first male Millet born with dark hair and blue eyes," Willow told him, apparently oblivious to Sykes's desire to keep this information to themselves. "He was the one in charge of the family's affairs at the time, in Bruges—that's Belgium."

"I know," Ben said.

"His fiancée had died and he was desolate, so he married another woman—to ease the pain, I suppose. This one ruined the family. Just about. I think she must have had something to do with these Embran people…things, or whatever they are…if they're anything. She was evil, and the people there thought she was a witch. Anyway, because of her, everything fell apart in Belgium and the family had to escape to London, then here to New Orleans. With each move they lost things they treasured.

"That's who Jude was...is. He's our Mentor. He guards the Book of Rules. Our parents are supposedly looking for the book to help them get rid of a curse. I don't understand it when we know it's with Jude. Wherever he is...or..." She looked troubled and confused.

Sykes's expression was blank.

"And it's why Sykes isn't looking after the family instead of Pascal now our parents have taken off," Willow continued, raising her voice to compete with a drum solo. "Sykes is the second male Millet heir—after Jude—with dark hair and blue eyes. Our folks decided to go look for a way to break the curse—that's the dark-haired, blue-eyed curse like Sykes has got—and because Sykes is so cursed, Uncle Pascal had to take over. He never wanted to and he shaved off all his red hair because he was mad at getting saddled with the responsibility for the family and everything else that should still be my dad's. Uncle Pascal's the younger brother, see, and he should never have had to look after things."

"Cursed, are you, Sykes?" Ben said. "I could have told you that before."

"Sure you could." Sykes had the grace to grin. "I guess all this revelation means Willow is welcoming you into the family—just like you'll be welcoming her into yours. I look forward to hearing all your secrets."

"We don't have any," Ben said, attempting complacency. He had no intention of sharing anything secretive about the Fortunes—other than with Willow when the time came.

Unfortunately, Willow didn't show signs of announcing that they were a couple again.

"The man showed me a picture of a dragon—a horrible thing. And a picture of a pale woman's effigy. A stone angel like we have at home. She was beautiful and she smiled at me. Please don't ask how a picture of a stone woman smiles. I don't know. That was before she looked as if she wanted to kill someone.

"If we don't destroy the Embran, they'll destroy us, that's what the man said. And he told me to listen to the woman. He said she was beautiful when she smiled, but I don't know what he meant by any of it."

At the mention of a dragon, Ben had all but stopped listening. "You think that could have been a picture of Marley's dragon? The one who almost killed her?"

"I never saw it," Willow said. "But I think it must have been."

Sykes pulled up a chair of his own and sat in that.

What Sykes had told Ben about Willow was that she could sense or even see old injuries and knew the emotional damage they had done. And some of the time, she knew what others were thinking and feeling, if the contacts were strong. In her case, according to Sykes, *strong* seemed to mean very heightened emotion. Ben began to think there were aspects of Willow that Sykes did not know about.

Willow checked her watch. "I've got an appointment soon," she said, but she didn't meet Ben's eyes.

"What kind of appointment?"

"It's business," she said.

"Where?"

"I'll be just fine now," she told them, making a move to get up. "I can't hide away forever."

"You can if you need to," Sykes said. "And if we make you."

Ben winced and knew he would not have long to wait for the explosion.

"If you make me?" Willow stood up and whirled on both of them. "You don't get to make me do anything."

"You're in danger," Sykes said. "Haven't you figured that out yet?"

"Of course I have."

"No," Ben said. "You're not. Sykes likes his drama. I won't let you be in danger." He meant it. He knew the risks and the concentration he would need to fight off all comers, but this was his intended mate. What he would not tell her was that if she died, so did he. That was one of those secrets the Fortunes pretended they didn't have. They did not outlive their mates, or not for long.

The music swelled to full, hypnotic volume. "Just a Closer Walk with Thee" beat its irresistible patterns around the club. On the stage, the musicians played as if they'd entered a trance and they were many parts that made up one whole.

Ben saw his brothers, Liam and Ethan, walk into the club. They paused, looking his way, but instantly picked up that he didn't want to be disturbed. Carrying on, they went directly to Poppy, who spoke and gestured expansively. All three arranged themselves in a row, elbows on the bar behind them, where they could watch Willow, Sykes and Ben easily.

"It's a zoo here," Ben said. "Next there will be clowns."

"There already are," Sykes told him. "Nasty ones. We're just not seeing them yet, or not clearly."

"We need to talk bats," Ben said, afraid Sykes would say too much for Willow to cope with. So far she was holding up well enough.

"Rock U. mentioned bats," she said, eyes widening. "I thought he was joking."

"Bats have been seen in daylight in the Quarter," Ben told her. "Rock U.?"

"Tattoo parlor guy," she told him. "He said he heard about it on the cruiser radio parked outside our building."

"Did he say anything else?"

"Just that people had been scared by them. Zinnia— my office manager—she said if bats come out in daylight they could be rabid."

"Wish that was all," Sykes muttered. "Some details have leaked out about the condition of the two corpses in the morgue. Blades is ready to take the mouthy culprit apart if he can find him—or her. Now bats have been seen, and the public theory is that they are rabid and that's what's killing people."

"Might be a good thing if they do think that," Ben said. "At least it'll keep them from thinking other things."

He studied Willow, who had fallen silent again. Not so long ago he had seen a shaded being fly from behind her and rise in the air. He had almost gotten close enough to touch the thing—or had he? Could it have been a bat, or what passed as a bat for the locals?

Willow got up. She looked from Sykes to Ben and said, "I need to be alone. There's something I must do."

Ben bit back a protest. She couldn't be left alone, but it looked as if they would have to make her think she had been. With his mind, he told Sykes what he intended to do.

"Are you sure she won't pick up on you?" Sykes said.

Ben gave a short laugh. *"If I can't manage this, we're in big trouble. Talk to Marley, will you? And Pascal, of course. And Gray. If necessary I'll pull in Liam and Ethan—or even Poppy."*

"Not unless we have to," Sykes said. *"We have to be able to control this."*

Their exchange took only an instant, and Willow turned away, heading for the door. She shot them a warning glance over her shoulder.

16

Cabs weren't her thing, but Willow took one back to Royal Street. First, she wanted to get there fast. Second, when Ben and Sykes followed her out of Fortunes, she wanted to be out of sight already.

"Now you know you gotta keep to the center of things?" the cab driver said, starting the same old lecture she'd heard before. "Don't be wandering off the beaten track on your own. Don't matter what time of day it is. Be safe. And if you need a cab—" he shoved a card over his shoulder "—call me."

Holding Mario, she thanked the driver when he stopped a few yards short of Millet's and paid him too much. He tried to give her change but she pressed it back at him.

He took a good look at her then and a pleased smile creased his deeply tanned face. "Guess you don't need my help," he said. "You're one of *them*."

With that, he drove off, and she heard him turn up his radio. Swamp pop pelted the damp and ever-hotter air. Bobi Jackson's "Alligator Woman" started her shoulders rolling.

One of them. The cabby had called her that.

The turmoil Willow felt had not lessened, but she knew what she wanted to do about it. She had a mission, and she had to take control—for the sake of others. Or she would try, just in case the thoughts she had weren't imaginary.

They probably were imaginary, which would be good, because then she could put her *powers* behind her again and go back to being normal.

The sidewalk was thick with the wanderers and the striders. A kid scooted up beside her and cracked his skateboard onto one end, startling Willow. He grinned at her, deftly used a sneaker toe to flip the board into the air and caught it.

All she wanted was to be normal, just plain old normal. Why was that too much to ask?

As quietly as she could, she opened the ornate iron gates to the alley leading to the back of the Court of Angels.

She hugged the wall of the shop and crept forward, trying not to make the gravel crunch under her feet. If Pascal heard her, or any other family member, she would have to face an inquisition. Mario struggled and she put him down. He sat at once and stared up at her.

What would she do if someone came to claim him? The way he'd shown up was strange, but he was part of her life already. She tried to take comfort in not having heard or read a thing about someone looking for a little red dog.

She darted across the alley, skirted the big storeroom where she kept her scooter and the trailer and entered the courtyard, grateful for the cover of palms, lush ferns, and bamboo that exploded from every area. White impatiens, tall but dense rather than leggy, bobbled softly among the dark green fronds. Water trickled like liquid silver from the fountain angel's shell, and she smelled the vanilla scent of creamy clematis climbing railings and scaling over windows.

Deception.

This was a stage set to give a false impression. Why she had never thought of the place that way before, she didn't know. Peace was a facade, and behind that facade, intrigue seethed on every side. And this was exactly where she was supposed to be at this moment.

She had not told Ben or Sykes, but she thought the picture she had been shown of the woman resembled some of the angels in the courtyard.

Willow looked at the ground, listened and opened herself to feel anything that wanted to approach.

Mario trotted forward and disappeared into a bed where lilies unfurled their pointed blooms.

Willow inclined her head to see where Mario had gone—and the faintest shade of pink washed slowly down to color the scene in front of her. Her stomach turned. Pink blended to mauve and she closed her eyes.

She couldn't move, yet movement was all around her.

A strong current, a blast like high wind, buffeted her this way and that. If her feet weren't rooted to the ground, she would fall. She tried to open her eyes, but couldn't.

"Can you hear me?" A man's voice sounded so familiar that she reached out. *"You over there. Can you hear me?"*

Was he talking to her?

"Are you embarrassed because you're naked?" the voice asked. *"I won't look, but you've got to say somethin' to me, girl. Let me know you're alive—if you are*

alive. We don't know how long we've got before someone comes back. We gotta get out of here first."

Willow was too hot. The wind settled to a whirling
stream. Behind her eyelids she saw something small, a
writhing thing she couldn't make out. But she was sure
the voice came from this.

Pale, partly buried in bright yellow granules and
walled off by glass, when the creature stopped twisting
for an instant it became invisible, blended with the
yellow-white of its surroundings.

Of course she knew the voice. "You're Chris," she
said, amazed and not certain whether she spoke aloud.
"Chris? Where are you? Who's with you?" He had not
been talking to her before, after all.

He didn't answer. The tiny shape turned over and
over, like a minuscule shelled shrimp.

"Girl," Chris's voice said again. *"We gotta talk. We
gotta help each other. I'm Chris. What's your name?"*

The next sound Willow heard was a muted crying, so
soft she had to strain to hear it at all.

"Yeah," the Chris voice said. *"Good. You're not
dead—yet. I'd like to cry, too, but there's got to be a way
out of this. Hoo, mama, this is weird. Did you, er...did
you meet someone interesting before you came here?
You know, interesting in a sexy way?"*

The female sound rose to a thin wail.

*"Okay, okay, we won't talk about it right now. But it
was somethin' wasn't it? I couldn't see her, but I could
sure feel her. Geez, no one ever came on to me like that
before. Were you blindfolded, too?"*

"We can't get out," a female voice said. *"We can't
climb the glass. We'd just slip back down."*

"Stay with me," Chris said. *"We'll figure it out."*

"We're going to die." The other one sounded as if she had already given up. Then she said, almost inaudibly, *"I'm Caroline. I don't want to die."*

"No. We won't. If we were going to die, we'd be dead already. We were captured for some reason. I just want us out of here before they get a chance to show us what they think we're good for."

Slowly, Willow's eyes opened. The mauve haze had deepened to a shade of purple she had already seen once today.

Stumbling, parting ferns to step into one of the plantings, she went to the first stone angel she saw and stared into its face. Then she moved on to another, this one tall and very slender, its marble drapery falling in intricate folds.

"Willow, don't be scared," Ben said, so close behind her she reached back convulsively and grabbed at him.

He held her hand firmly, and for what seemed a long time they stood there, both facing the same direction, the skin on her palm and fingers pulsing at his touch.

"I've known there was a presence in this courtyard," he said, keeping his voice low. "You're feeling it, too. What do you see when you look at them?"

She knew he meant the statues. "Nothing. Just…just what they are."

"Ah."

"What does that mean?"

"I'll explain later," he said. "We should go where we can have some privacy."

"I can't leave yet," she told him.

"Because you're trying to find a statue that looks like the woman you saw in your Mentor's book?"

She nodded, moving on to a figure so small she had to crouch to get a close look. This one had the round-cheeked face of a girl child.

Ben steadied her as she stood up again. He slid his free hand under her chin, then wrapped his forearm across her upper chest and pulled her back against him. "We're going to work it out. We were made for this. It's our destiny."

"I've never felt it was mine," she told him. "I'm not strong like you. Whatever these things are that happen to me are shadows beside what you can do." She must be careful not to say too much.

"When people like us work together, we complement each other, Willow. You are a member of an extraordinary family."

"Extraordinarily weird," she muttered.

He chuckled. "We have to work on your attitude, my love."

If she had the willpower, she would separate herself from him. She couldn't do it, didn't want to do it. "Why did you really come back to New Orleans?"

"You needed me," he said promptly. "No other reason."

She eased away and moved on, much more quickly than before, searching out the statues, even checking gargoyles on lintels although she knew their faces from memory and they could never be beautiful.

"Why would that man think the woman was so important? Ben, she did look as if she could be one of our angels."

"I'm sure she did."

"Do you know if Nat's been looking for me?" she said,

her heart slamming against her ribs. "Have you heard anything about Chris?"

She heard the shop doors open and slam shut. Uncertain steps approached, and Willow looked over her shoulder at Marley, who gave them a distracted smile.

"Hey, Marley," Ben said.

She nodded to him.

"Did you hear from Nat again?" Willow asked her sister.

"No. But now you're supposed to be on the run." She smiled impishly, but didn't seem as lively as usual.

"Meaning?" Ben said.

"Willow was sprung from her office by two accomplices and has disappeared. That's the word around, anyway."

He made a face and said, "But Nat didn't call or come here?"

"Nope," Marley said. "I think the media's getting carried away—with a little help from someone called, Rock U.? Tattoo parlor owner with a place near your offices, Willow?"

"Uh-huh."

"Guess I should have gotten over there to see what kind of place you were hanging out in. But I will today, anyway."

Willow frowned but wouldn't allow herself to ask any questions.

"I work for you now," Marley said. "I'm the new indoor plant expert—until Chris gets back. I also plan extraordinary buffet tables and mix one-of-a-kind drinks. That means no two drinks are ever the same. I'm going to be so useful, you'll wonder how you managed without me."

"That's ridiculous," Willow said.

"No," Ben said. "How many people have to tell you to keep yourself safe? Even the cab driver warned you."

Willow snorted. "He didn't mean what you mean. He... How do you know what the cab driver said?" She shook her head fiercely. "Don't bother to say anything. You were there, weren't you? I'm going to have to go over the Millet rules with you."

"She's all *rules, rules, rules* suddenly," Ben told Marley. "Those are Millet rules, not Fortune rules."

"Don't argue about having me with you," Marley said, her dark green eyes skewering Willow. "You would do the same for me. Without you it could have taken forever to find out what Gray had been through—but you could tell, you could actually *see*. Think of yourself as a butterfly coming out of a chrysalis, only you've waited a bit long and you need some help getting unstuck from the sticky stuff. I'm going to help—when Ben's not around, that is."

Willow put her hands on her hips and stepped too far away from Ben for him to touch her. "You've been talking about me," she said. "Discussing me. All of you. I don't like it."

"She doesn't like a lot of things," Ben said. "Especially me."

"I never said that," she snapped back at him. She felt herself blush and added, "You can be a bit pushy, though, Ben."

Marley raised her face to the sky. She watched the cloudless, haze-tinged blue intently, and Willow thought her sister was listening for something. She turned toward the shop and went in.

"I've got a bunch of questions I'd like to ask you," Ben said when they were alone again.

This was the one person she knew who wouldn't push her too hard. He never had. Ben treated her differently from anyone else in their circle—which had made her feel special for a long time, until Poppy pointed out that his deference only meant he didn't think of her as one of them, not completely.

Trying to learn more about the courtyard—if there was more—would wait. "I've got something to tell you, too," she said. "Let's go up."

Without waiting for a response, she started up the steps but turned back when she remembered Mario. He was already running behind her.

Ben stood right where he'd been, staring at her. That stare stopped her. "What is it?" she said.

"Just wondering what it's going to take to get my way with you," he said with a crooked smile. "I mean, to get you to do what I want you to do, of course," he added. Suddenly, he looked exasperated. "I just want you to be sensible."

She set her lips together and carried on to her flat.

On the threshold, she paused.

Ben crowded behind her, moving them both inside, and shut the door again.

"Did you have breakfast?" she asked for something to say.

"It's lunchtime, but I'm not hungry," he said. "I am tired. We haven't had much sleep in the last couple of days."

"I don't think that's going to get better soon," she told him. "I mustn't forget my appointment."

He frowned heavily. "Yeah, you mentioned that. When is it?"

She didn't want to lie to him. "Seven this evening."

His face cleared immediately, and he might as well have come out and told her how relieved he was that seven o'clock was hours away.

"Excuse me," he said and passed her.

Willow followed Ben and didn't say a word when he unplugged the phone in her living room before moving on to the bedroom. Once more he disconnected the phone. "Make sure your cell's off," he said and dealt with his own. He threw it down on her bedside table.

Hesitantly, Willow took out her cell and made sure it wouldn't become a way for someone to reach her until she wanted it to. She hadn't missed what Ben did with his own phone.

"It's warm in here," he said and switched on the overhead fan. He raised his face and said, "Better."

"It'll be cooler in the living room," she said and hoped he didn't hear her swallow.

"Nope. This is the coolest room. This side of the building always is."

"This is my bedroom, Ben."

"I noticed."

What was she supposed to say to that? Walking out would make her feel like a silly kid, but it was what she ought to do.

Ben went around the bed, flipped off his shoes and stretched out on the other side. He patted the mattress beside him and Willow turned hot, then hotter. She radiated heat.

"C'mon," he said softly. "I'm not dangerous. Promise. We've earned some relaxation time."

"And lying on my bed with you beside me is going to make me relaxed?"

"We-ell—you do have a point. But it's up to you to control yourself."

She bit back a smile. He always had the smart comeback. Willow sat carefully on top of her white cotton spread at the very edge of her bed.

"What was happening down in the courtyard?" he asked. "You saw something, didn't you?"

"You know too much," she said. "I keep telling you you're too powerful for me." Willow closed her mouth firmly. That was not what she had intended to say.

His silence unnerved her.

She undid her sneakers and kicked them off, then threw her socks on top. Very carefully, she settled herself in the horizontal position, but as far from Ben as she could get without falling off the bed.

The fan moved a soft breeze across her face. It felt good, or it might if her stomach didn't keep turning over and over and her heart would stop trying to leap out of her chest.

She would wait until he said something.

All she heard was Ben's quiet breathing.

He had said he was tired. More or less. How dare he come into her bedroom, get on her bed and just go to sleep….

Steamed, that's how he made her feel. She rolled her head toward him—and looked directly into Ben's blue-flame eyes. He didn't smile, but he stared back at her and they didn't need to touch for her to tingle all over.

"Do you want to go first?" he asked.

"No. It was a bad idea to say I wanted to talk. There

are things we have to do alone." Like deal with shrimpy little creatures that sounded like people she knew. Telling him about that would *really* make her sound well-balanced.

He reached out and settled his fingertips on her cheek. They both drew in a sharper breath, but Ben's gaze grew so intense Willow felt it branded her.

"Ben, after we left Nat's office this morning, what happened while we were talking on that sidewalk? When I told you about something touching my neck?"

His eyes never left hers. "I listened to you. I believed you."

Gathering her courage she said, "You left, didn't you? Just for…part of an instant? I didn't see it, but I did in a way. Where did you go?"

"I was there." But his mouth set in a hard line, and the way he watched her changed. She had surprised him.

"Are you going to tell me what I saw?"

"Have you accepted that you aren't what you like to call *normal?*"

If she avoided the dreaded question, he might assume she'd meant to say yes, and tell her what she wanted to know.

His fingers brushed from her cheek to her hair and slowly down over her shoulder and along her arm.

Willow tried to keep staring at him but failed. She screwed up her eyes and sucked a breath through her teeth.

"Look," he said, with all kinds of persuasion in that one word, "you *are* normal, but you're gifted. Will you admit you have the gift?"

"The gift?" she muttered. "Why is it called that?"

"Just answer me." The tips of his fingers traced tendons on the back of her hand. Back and forth, back and forth.

"Are you being fair?" she said.

His smile did just what he intended; it made her smile back.

"This isn't about being fair," he told her. "And it's not a joke, not anymore. We've got to circle the wagons, my love, for everyone's sake. I need you to admit what you are and let me know I can trust you to use the talents you have."

"What am I, Ben?"

"You tell me."

"I don't know." She looked at his face again, at his eyes. "Chris is in terrible trouble. He's trapped in sand or something. In a thick glass thing. There's a woman with him."

"At least he's not alone," Ben said, showing no surprise at what she had told him.

"That's not funny."

"It wasn't meant to be. Believe me, two is better than one most of the time. Is this what… In the courtyard, is this what you found out?"

"I heard Chris, then I saw him. Then I heard her, but I didn't see her. I never did see her."

"What would you say that makes you?" he asked quietly.

"Not normal."

"You can do better than that."

"First I feel strong emotion—not mine, someone else's," Willow said. "Sometimes, after that, I see what made them feel the emotion. Fear is the strongest one.

Pain. Sadness. I felt anger and fear everywhere before I heard Chris. Then I knew he was trying to be funny and brave for the woman."

Ben took her hand to his mouth and kissed her knuckles.

"I think I may be clairvoyant," she said softly.

"Tell me something I don't know." His breath was warm on her skin.

"Give me a break. Now I'm admitting it. That isn't easy for me, and it's not easy to admit I've heard what other people are thinking. I've only heard you when you talk to me—without talking." If she was supposed to feel relief at saying all this aloud, it wasn't happening.

He held her hand against his chest. "But you've tried to listen to what I'm thinking?"

She felt the steady beat of his heart. "Yes," she admitted. "I shouldn't have done that."

"You're only human," he said.

"Evidently only barely," she said bitterly. "I've fought this for a long time."

"I know. Now it's time to quit that and start using your strengths."

Willow spread her fingers on his chest. "One of our rules is that we can only use our talents for good. And we're not supposed to listen in to other people without asking permission first. If we don't get it, we don't listen."

"Good stuff," he said. "Unless by breaking a rule you do the right thing. I did leave you when we were walking this morning—just for a nanogap."

"What does that mean?"

He gave an eloquent shrug. "Planck time. Parallel

shift. The shortest measurable length of time, and it appears instantaneous. I passed through a nanogap because I thought I saw the suggestion of a manifestation."

She held her breath and waited.

"I did see it. A wisp of a thing that moved as if it flew. It shot upward—away from you—and I followed, but couldn't grab the thing."

Willow shifted closer to him. "No! I'm glad you didn't touch it. What if it did—you know—what happened to Billy and that woman?"

"All the more reason for me to take it out."

"If it doesn't take you out first," she said. Another wiggle and she was near enough to settle with the top of her head beneath his chin.

They both stopped talking.

Willow pressed her lips to his neck and Ben shuddered along his length. He wrapped her in both of his arms and she rested her head on his shoulder.

"Are you like Marley, then?" Willow asked. "Do you travel out of your body, and that's why I sensed you were gone, but didn't see you go?"

"No. She goes for extended periods—usually many minutes, and only when she's called. I travel of my own will—but very fast, so fast I return with no apparent lapse of time. That's how I brought you back from that house. Through a nanogap. Sykes is concerned about that. In case you lack whatever makes it okay for me. We don't want you harmed."

"It hasn't hurt me."

"No," he said. "Not yet."

She considered that. When she'd realized she had

returned from the Brandts' and was sitting on her own couch again—with a dog she had never seen before at her feet—she hadn't thought to check the time.

"Can you hear what I'm thinking?" she asked.

He shook his head, no. "I often open to you in case you want in, but you've never come or invited me— except by accident, like yesterday."

She loved his grin. "But you'd know if I invited you?" The thought was comforting, mostly because she didn't want him to know everything that crossed her mind.

"Willow, Sykes has told me a great deal. So have Marley and Gray. We may not have much time to set things right."

"What do I do about Chris? If he really is somewhere weird, I need to get him."

"It's not time."

"It *is*. He's scared and stuck."

"But you haven't seen what you can do about it yet. We're waiting, Willow. That's the hardest thing for people like you and me, but there will be a next step. Maybe any minute. Part of becoming what you really are is learning to accept that you will grow stronger, but not immediately. We should think."

What he meant, Willow decided, was that she was supposed to lie there and hope for the next scary happening while Chris kept trying to climb up a sheer wall of glass.

"Relax," Ben said. "That's exactly what I mean. You'll know when it's time to do something—and what that is."

Making fists, she attempted to push away from him. "You said you didn't read my thoughts." He was too strong for her to shift against him.

"You opened your mind to me," he said, sounding aggrieved. "I felt you."

The fan vibrated. Willow didn't want to fight him about anything. "I want you to kiss me," she said.

"This is getting to be hell," Ben said, his voice gravelly. "You sent me away."

"And now you've come back," she pointed out and hiked herself up until she could find his mouth with her own.

He kissed her back. Their lips softened, but the searching was there, too. Kisses weren't enough.

Willow put her arms around his neck and leaned until he rolled onto his back. She combed her fingers through his thick, blue-black hair. He wasn't wearing it tied back.

"Not yet," he whispered, but he let her lead him in another kiss.

When the intense sensitivity was too much, she pulled his shirt out and ran her tongue from his breastbone to the low waist of his jeans, and nipped him there.

She heard him laugh, then, abruptly, he forced her up again and held her where he could see her face. "What are you trying to do to me?" he said.

"Make love to you," she said without hesitation. "Don't you think it's overdue?"

"Why now?"

"You know why. You feel what I do."

He stroked her hair, kissed the end of her nose. "It wouldn't be a good idea."

Willow's cheeks stung. "What do you mean?" Her voice sounded small and lost.

"My love, you know what I mean. Don't you think I want you? Look at me."

When she did, he continued, "I could...I want you, and you know how I'm hurting because I want you. But it's not time yet."

"You thought it was time two years ago."

"I was wrong. If I hadn't been, we would never have parted." He raised her chin. "Have I hurt you? Sweetheart, please don't be hurt—there's something we have to do before we take the steps we want to take."

He wouldn't hear it from her, but he could not have hurt her more if he had struck her. "Okay, Ben. What is it you think we have to do?"

"Commit to each other. For eternity."

"Ben." She watched his face until he frowned, and she thought he had heard her.

"I'm going to take my clothes off. It's too hot in here."

"Is that your way of telling me to get out?"

They would do this—just do it. *"It's my way of telling you not to leave."*

"See how well we communicate?" he said, but conflicting emotions crossed his face. The dominant one was a tight and raging desire that distended the veins in his neck while he pulled away from her and flung his arms over his head.

Willow raised her hips and slid her white jeans down.

Ben's breath came in bursts. She could see the rapid rise and fall of his chest.

The jeans hit the floor.

"This is more than I can control," he said. He rolled toward her, stroking her legs from knee to thigh, pushing his thumb under a leg of her panties and into the hair covering her mound.

Two more fingers followed, slipping down into the

moisture she could not disguise. Her hips jerked upward again, this time because she wanted more of him.

But the instant his fingers met the core of all her sensations, he withdrew his hand and put it over her mouth instead, drowning out her protests.

In one move he sat astride her hips, rocking back and forth, gritting his teeth and sucking up her emotions with his eyes.

"Your jeans," she said.

Ignoring her, Ben started with the bottom button of her shirt and slowly undid the row all the way to the one at the neck. He spread the shirt and she felt his arousal throbbing through his jeans.

His hands covered her breasts in the skimpy, pink lace bra she wore, pushed them together and buried his face in her cleavage. His tongue did magical work, tracing a line just beneath the edges of the bra where her soft flesh swelled, gradually delving a little deeper to curl around a hard nipple.

"It's all fire. Everywhere you touch me burns. There's pain."

"Tell me if it's too much," Ben said. *"But if all pain were like this, people would line up to get some."*

"Don't stop!" Willow cried aloud.

She heard her own thin moan, and wondered at the way her hips pumped up against him. Her reactions had a life of their own.

The muscles in his chest tightened with her touch. She pinched his nipples, and he leaped away, shucking his jeans and briefs.

He penis sprang hard and huge. Willow squirmed, reaching for him.

Standing beside her, Ben shuddered when she held him. He unhooked her bra and pulled it away. He bent to kiss her breasts, to run his tongue in circles, growing ever closer until he took each nipple in his teeth and she writhed.

On her side, she used two hands to guide him between her lips, letting the very edges of her teeth rake him all the way.

A click came from his throat and he swayed forward, tore her panties off and caught her beneath the arms.

Willow rocked her head from side to side. With her eyes squeezed shut, she felt tears run along her temples. Ben moved her as if she were nothing, spread her across the middle of the bed and mounted her. She felt him try to gentle the first thrust, but his restraint broke and they came together as if he were flowing lava filling her up.

Her breasts and belly ached and she didn't want them to stop aching.

Once, twice, he surged into her. Then the climax broke. His and hers. Bursting over them, drawing out a fine sweat that turned their bodies slick, melded their skin into one skin bonded together.

Ben stilled. The only sound was their panting.

She reached down to feel where their bodies were still joined, his strong shaft impaling her just as it was meant to.

Slowly, he slid out, and she held his face, brought it to hers and kissed him, opened their mouths wide, got as far over and into him as her tongue would take her.

His fingers, landing on her unbelievably sensitive clitoris again shocked Willow. She tried to say his name, but he took over the kiss and she couldn't speak.

He was tall.

She wasn't.

Kissing her into oblivion while he worked where she could barely stand to be touched was easy for him. She vaguely felt the rumble of satisfaction in his throat.

He slid fingers up and inside her, drew out and swept to finish what he had started.

Willow struggled beneath him, then fell back, sated, incapable of moving.

He began to kiss her breasts once more, and she spread her arms wide to give herself to him again. The nudge against the entrance to her still-throbbing body opened her eyes.

"Is it okay?" he said. "Again?"

"Again, and again."

17

"I know who you are," he said. "The blindfold is senseless. And it's irritating."

Best ignore him, she thought. Breaking him might take time, but break him, she would.

"My name is One. Say it," she told him. *One* suited her well, for that's what she was, the first one, the most important one. "Say it." This time she raised her voice.

"One."

Sullen. Why must these underlings always become sullen? She knew the answer. He was male and chafed against not being able to control her. But she had brought him with her and he would share in her success.

"You are…" She thought about it. "Servant," she said with satisfaction.

"Damn you—"

"Damn you, *One.*" She cut him off.

"I am no woman's servant."

"You are my Servant for as long as I want to play with you. You are such fun to play with, but I have some lessons to teach you first. I have a purpose to fulfill and I do what I set out to do. Your future depends on my success, but it won't be easy."

Sunlight slanted through a window high in one white wall, slanted across his naked body. She stood before him, glad of her height, and stroked him until he tried to catch her hands.

One laughed and slapped his face.

He bared his teeth, made fists at his sides. He knew better than to strike out at her, even if he didn't quite mask the brief start of what would have been his transmutation. The forked tongue actually flashed from his blackening lips, but he collected himself quickly enough to show only what he wanted humans to see in the two male images he had perfected.

"This is a very important day," she said, lowering her voice to a warm, whispering, soothing hum. "The most important day of your life. Do you want to know why?"

He breathed heavily.

"Because if you don't do exactly as I tell you, it will be your last day."

"I don't have to take this."

"But you do," One said, still all but purring at him. "You made a mistake. You acted on your own. You decided to make your mark by doing something I hadn't told you to do. That was a mistake...Servant."

Power thrilled her—and fear. This man longed to dominate her, but did not dare to as much as try.

"What I did will help us," he said. "It will save time. You need what I brought you."

"You took a risk. I knew nothing about this...Caroline. If you have made a mistake, you'll suffer. I will report you to the Embran Council and their judgment will be swift—and final."

"I made no mistake," he said. "What I did was to help

you. The woman, Caroline, she has no family. No one will look for her. I made sure."

"No one has looked for her yet," she pointed out. "If they do, you will join our research into saving our kind— as a subject."

He laughed and relaxed for the first time since she'd called him in. "I'm not the right makeup, *One.* I don't think I'd serve your purpose."

"We will need host Embrans," she told him. "Didn't you think of that? Hosts to test our findings on. This could be a good thing. If our experiments go well, whatever we implant in you could make you live forever as we all used to. If not…" She let him consider what she had not quite said.

As with his other human manifestation, he was beautiful, an outstanding specimen, one of very few of his kind in their world.

"I have a question for you," he said. "This plan of yours—your *backup* plan. Did you clear it with the Council? All they sent you here for was to make sure the work got done and the Millet specimen they selected is captured and taken to Home Place—by the one who thinks he is here alone to complete the task."

Anger tightened her. "You know better than to question me."

"My only purpose is to serve you, *One.* I live to serve you. My fate depends upon you. It wouldn't help my career if something went wrong because you decided to become the big hero by charting your own course. Is this sexy little sideline you've come up with, this secret collection of shrunken specimens, in keeping with the Council's wishes?"

"You're beginning to bore me." In fact, he caused her to question her own decision, which she would not tolerate. To question was to risk doubt—doubt could cause careless mistakes, or complete disaster.

"Why am I here now?" he asked, but she saw how he braced his feet apart, flexed the heavy muscles in his arms and his thighs, and aimed his hips in her direction.

"That's why," she said, and almost wished she could really purr—like a panther with huge, lethal teeth.

He made sure his subtle movements showed everything off to best advantage. "I'd like to see you," he said, managing to make a simple request sound suggestive.

"I can see you. That's all that matters—I'll make sure everything goes where it needs to go."

He trembled. His color heightened with excitement. "Whatever you want," he said.

"First, what I want you to do—later. You took matters into your own hands. I didn't like that, but you accomplished the task well. I have a list of names with information about where they can be found. There are many names, men and women. Amazing how many loners there are among these humans. All these people with pasts to hide—and they have hidden them well. You will deal with the women. We will gather as many as we can before we must return to the Home Place."

He laughed.

"Make it fast," she told him coldly. "Don't waste time prolonging your own pleasure. The men are mine." She smiled at that.

"This has become a competition," he stated flatly.

"Not for you," she reminded him. "But I will win. I

will accomplish everything our friend was supposed to do for the Council, only so much better, and return to Embran before he even realizes he has failed. They will recall him in shame."

"He thinks he is here alone. You were not supposed to come...One."

"I got permission to watch him and make sure the mistakes of his predecessor are not repeated. It isn't my fault if he thinks he can take his time, enjoy himself among the humans. When he gets back to the Home Place with one of the Millets—if he manages to catch one—we will be well on our way to curing the sickness these creatures caused us. And I will have proved that our plague could have started with the introduction of any human elements, not exclusively a Millet.

"True, the woman who married Jude Millet and then returned to Home Place got there at the same time as the first cases of the Torturous Death. It is likely she introduced the disease through her resumed contacts with her own kind, and they began to die. But I believe that if each Embran were what these creatures call *vaccinated* with the essence of the human, we would become immune to them and be saved. My goal is to find that essence from the human specimens I take back."

"You are brilliant," he said.

"Yes," she agreed. "My way is so much more efficient. We must move quickly."

"I'm ready," he said.

"You are indeed. Have you heard about the *bats* that are attacking the citizens of New Orleans?"

He laughed. "Amazing how many they have seen— and how many people are demanding rabies shots."

"Without seeing these bats, let alone being bitten by them." One snorted.

"Do it." His voice changed at once, sounding not just eager, but demanding.

For her the change was simple. She could accomplish her transmutation at will and smoothly—that was her greatest accomplishment and, added to her enhanced intellect, it made her formidable. Too bad the Council continued to prize man-Embrans above the females of their species.

Lacing her hands across her breasts, she angled her elbows upward, bowed her head and sank into a crouch, grew smaller while thin membranes formed over the bones of her arms, turning them into vibrating black wings. She drew them rapidly through the air, reveling in the beating sound. The folding and reshaping of her transmutation happened rapidly. She had been told how graceful her change appeared. Graceful and potentially deadly.

A moment of discomfort came with the sprouting of short, tight fur all over her newly forming body. Sharp, quill-like hairs dug at her enlarging eyes until they protruded enough to be free. She felt her mouth stretch wide and heard the popping that came with erupting teeth, and fangs she could extend or retract. The slime that dripped from her lips would burn like acid if she willed it. Her size could change, depending upon her needs. At the moment she needed no more than a few inches of girth and less of height. She tucked the fangs away but let her softer teeth remain extended—they were so useful in these moments.

Servant panted with anticipation.

She hovered above the floor, rose to just the right height and set herself spinning. Closer and closer she drew to him until she fastened onto his groin, slid those softer teeth along until they pressed into his tensed body.

Her Servant screamed, shuddered and clutched air. He gave himself to her.

One was nothing but clear mind, and exquisite release.

This was the prize she won for superiority. She could kill, or she could become the giver and receiver of cataclysmic orgasm.

18

"Why are you ignoring me?" Ben asked Willow. He sat in the passenger seat of her van.

"Because I'm pretending you're not here."

He looked at her and put a hand on her thigh.

She batted him away.

"Why would you want to pretend I'm not here?" he said. "It feels so good to be with you."

All he heard from her was a long sigh.

"Doesn't it feel good to you, Willow?"

Another sigh.

"Willow?"

"Too bad you had to spoil the best day I ever had," she said.

She came to a stop at a light. Ben leaned his head back and watched the side of her face. The red light turned her hair the color of smoldering embers and caught the brilliance of her eyes. "You're perfect," he said, and grinned to himself.

"And you're a rat. You're deliberately goading me, Benedict Fortune."

"But we kiss so well. You've got to admit that. We do everything so well together. And if I'm twisted to enjoy the way I feel with you in my arms, then you're twisted, too. You like it just as much as I do."

Ben didn't miss her little smile.

The light turned green, and she drove on in the gathering gray of an early evening turned dramatic by mounds of silver-edged cumulus clouds.

Sirens hollered behind them, and for an instant Ben expected them to be pulled over.

Willow did pull the van over, but only to let a fire truck pass.

She didn't immediately drive on. "You haven't pulled any stunts, have you?" she said. "I wouldn't be amused."

"Stunts?" He tapped her bare shoulder.

"Ministorms aren't likely to hit twice in the same backyard—"

"C'mon—"

"But if I get there and the fire hoses are out, I'll know who wants to stop me from seeing my clients."

He sniffed in deeply. Her hair always smelled like jasmine—his favorite scent. In Kauai he grew jasmine just to remind him of her when he sat on the lanai at night.

Her shoulder felt like silk—all the way to her elbow and back.

"I'm driving, Ben."

"I'd never accuse *you* of being a pyromaniac. Can you even imagine me suggesting you set a fire deliberately?"

"Not if I did it several blocks from the crime scene. We both know I couldn't change anything, anywhere, no matter how hard I tried."

He tilted his face up. Willow didn't know how well

he understood, not only her self-doubts, but her paranormal potential. "Listen, love. Why not give this one a pass and go back to the Court of Angels?" He needed something strong to sell that idea. "We've got to find your angel—the one from the Mentor's book."

"You know it's not there. If it was, we'd have found it—and one of us would remember seeing it, too."

"Not if it's deliberately hidden. Things might look different in this light, too."

"Nice try," she told him, making a left turn. "The way things are going I may have lost half of my clients by tomorrow. The Brandts' business would fill in for a lot of smaller jobs."

"Mario didn't like it when you left him behind."

"He loves being with Winnie. You'd think they'd been together all their lives. Now concentrate and stop trying to get your own way."

"You avoided Pascal when you sneaked out, Willow. He's been waiting to talk to you all day."

"I'll talk to him later. Among other things, he's been trying to get into my mind. That's not allowed."

"Uh-uh," Ben said, hoping he sounding adamantly opposed to such behavior. "He can ask, but he can't come in without your permission. Did he ask?"

She puffed with irritation. "Well, yes."

"So what's the problem? You didn't let him in."

Willow glanced at him quickly. "He never used to try. They've started taking me for granted. They think I've accepted all the…you know, and they intend to draw me into the whole…you know."

"Yeah," he said quietly, feeling smug. "I know all about it."

She rolled her window down a few inches, and warm air rushed into the van. People on their way out for the night hooted and laughed, and a horn played a mournful lament in the distance.

"Do not get out of this van while I'm in the house," she said. "If I need you, I will let you know."

"That's an interesting comment." He leaned to kiss her and felt the softening. He drew back an inch. "How will you do that?"

"Ben!" She sounded as if she were complaining, but her hand ran lightly down his cheek. "Get down out of sight. We're almost there."

"I asked how I'll know if you need me."

She pulled to a stop beside the Brandts' tall front hedges. "If I need you, I will open my mind, Ben, and invite you in."

"That's my girl," he said, and crossed his arms, making himself comfortable. She was giving in, even if slowly.

Willow climbed to the sidewalk and reached back for her briefcase. She popped up and ruffled Ben's long hair, then quickly escaped when he tried to grab her.

From what she could see on her way to the front door, no sign of Ben's mischief remained. The beautiful house glowed warmly in what was left of the disappearing daylight.

She barely touched the bell before the door swept open.

"There you are, Willow. I'm Chloe Brandt." And Chloe Brandt was worth looking at. Not classically beautiful, but a one-of-a-kind woman with sharp features and black hair pulled straight back from a heart-shaped hairline. Large, deep brown eyes didn't quite match the warmth in her voice, but her red lips curved in a naturally sultry smile and there were dimples in her cheeks.

An A-line burgundy shift accentuated memorable breasts and stopped six inches above the knees on fabulous legs.

"Willow Millet." Willow shook hands.

Naturally, an impressive professional floral arrangement graced the central table in the foyer. Their shoes clipped on marble tile all the way to the kitchen Willow remembered a bit too well.

"Is it all right if we talk in here?" Chloe said. "It's my favorite room. Don't they say everyone always gathers in the kitchen?"

"Something like that."

"Are you okay?" Chloe spun around. "You've had a horrible time and it's so unfair."

How could Chloe be certain it was unfair, Willow wondered. "I'm fine," she said. The woman was only trying to be kind.

"Good. Val will be in shortly. He and Preston are talking about enlarging the cabana. Preston…you met him at the party that night, didn't you?"

Willow nodded and had a fleeting memory of the man's smile and his naked body before he jumped into the pool. She felt overheated at once.

"I thought so. Preston makes sure he meets everyone. He doesn't talk about it, but he's an architect, even if he doesn't really practice—he's so determined to publish his novel. But Val likes to get his opinion on things. He'll be coming in for a drink with Val. And they're both such curious creatures, they're bound to want to hang around and listen in to us. Will you be okay with that?"

As if she could refuse. "Absolutely," she said.

This woman didn't look as if she suffered from shyness, as had been suggested. She moved confidently and spoke confidently.

"Chloe?" a female voice called just before the front door slammed shut again. "Where are you, pet? It's Vanity."

Chloe expelled a breath through pursed lips. "In the kitchen," she said, not meeting Willow's eyes. "Vanity's a family friend," she said quietly.

But the emotion Willow felt was too strong for a simple friendship. A complicated pull and push, uncertainty, questions about trust.

"Aha," Vanity said, sweeping into the kitchen wearing a tiny, tight, black tube top, skinny black capris and expanses of smooth skin.

"Hi, Vanity," Chloe said, her smile anxious. "Are you okay?"

Vanity shrugged and pulled in the corners of her mouth. "Yes, sweetie. Thanks for asking." She nodded to Willow. "Nice to see you again after all that furor."

"Val said you had an unpleasant date," Chloe said.

Vanity rolled her eyes. "Awful. It was like eating dinner with an octopus—a horny octopus."

Willow laughed; she couldn't help it. Then she cleared her throat. "Sorry. You're so droll—and I think I may have met the same octopus somewhere."

Both Vanity and Chloe laughed.

"Make us drinks," Chloe told Vanity. "Since you're here, you'll want to sit in on my meeting with Willow and make a nuisance of yourself."

More laughter.

Vanity didn't ask what either of them wanted to drink. She busied herself deciding on a bottle from a cooler as large as the refrigerator. Selection made, she opened the wine and set three glasses of white on the glass kitchen table. She sat down and beckoned.

With each moment, Willow felt less comfortable. They seemed determined to turn her into some sort of superconfidante and family manager. And the family consisted of more than just the Brandts.

She sat beside Vanity and pulled a folder from the briefcase.

Chloe joined them. She brought a wheel of Brie and crackers with her. "To my salvation," she said, raising her glass and nodding to Willow. "The woman who will change my life."

Crystal clinked and Willow took a sip of an incredible Viognier. She said, "Oh, my," and both Chloe and Vanity laughed.

"Can you give me an overview of the services you need?" Willow said. She opened a slim binder and jotted "Brandt" across the top of the first page.

"Everything," Chloe said.

"Oh, can't we just enjoy our wine first?" Vanity said, drinking deeply. "We've got all night for the icky business stuff." She turned aside a piece of the Brie skin, scraped a knife across the cheese and put a thin layer on a cracker.

Awkward, Willow held her hands between her knees and looked at Chloe, who raised one brow. "We can't keep Willow too long," she said. "She's a working girl. Willow, I'd like to turn over the household accounts to you. That'll mean you do all the ordering, arrange deliveries and take a good look at existing household staff. Those you approve of, keep—replace the rest."

Willow made notes and hoped her surprise at the sweeping request didn't show. It had sounded cold. If she did work here, she wouldn't get rid of a soul who wasn't causing major problems.

"There are some suppliers in place," Chloe said, "but if you have people you prefer, feel free. You'll be able to keep up with scheduled events from my daybook. I'll show you later."

Vanity crossed her legs and jiggled a high-heeled black mule from the toes of one foot. "I'm still waiting for the police to figure out what happened the other night when you were here, Willow. I don't buy the minitornado tale."

"Someone made a nice job of tidying up," Willow said, avoiding Vanity's suggestion and looking through the wall of windows at the gardens. "These odd phenomena happen."

She made the mistake of thinking about Ben and felt him entering her mind. *"Nothing to worry about,"* she indicated to him and turned her attention back to the other women.

Val Brandt emerged from behind the cabana with sleek Preston Moriarty in tow. They paused, gesturing first at the pool, then at the cabana, before continuing toward the house.

"They're enjoying themselves," Chloe said with a faint smile. "Boys and their projects. They're easily pleased. I really do want you to take over, Willow. My plan is for you to think of this house as your own. When there's a party, it'll be your party—you'll be the boss, the wife, if you like."

She said it all with a straight and serious face.

"You don't really know me," Willow pointed out.

"Of course she does," Vanity interrupted. "By now she knows almost as much about you as you do. Chloe is excellent at ferreting out all the things you thought nobody knew."

"And I know all this talk about you being involved in the murders is rubbish," Chloe said. "The police don't have any leads. The fact that you've even been mentioned shows they don't have any evidence at all."

Wooden blinds rattled beside an open window.

Willow glanced at them, but they had stopped moving. She made a few more notes.

"Do you have to work, Willow?" Vanity asked.

Willow felt Chloe's disapproval at her friend's question, but she said, "I do. Independence is very important to me. I've always wanted to be able to take care of myself. That's not so easy when you're a member of a very close family."

Vanity's eyelashes fluttered. "Believe me, I know what you mean," she said. "I don't have a close family, but I know all about having to work to maintain one's independence. I always make my plans well in advance. Modeling is for the young, and I don't want to try to hang on doing commercials for wrinkle treatments. I've got a very promising modeling agency."

"Congratulations," Willow said, softening toward Vanity.

"Bring your wine," Chloe said. She got up and left the kitchen with Willow and Vanity behind her. "I don't suppose Val gave you the complete tour."

Without saying much other than which room they

were in, Chloe took them through the house. Each space was flawless. A library and adjoining sitting room brought a grin of delight from Willow. "I could live in these two rooms," she said. "They are so elegant, but cozy at the same time."

"You like them a lot, then?" Chloe said.

"I do."

They wandered through the ground floor, finishing in a long, narrow conservatory on one side of the house. Since it couldn't be seen from the front of the house, Willow had not known it was there.

Vanity insisted they put on smocks before venturing deeper. "Some of the plants have sticky residue," she said.

"Heavenly," Willow said, genuinely charmed by a plethora of shrubs clearly used primarily as a backdrop for dozens and dozens of orchids. A path made from tiny mosaic tiles set in a pattern of interlinking circles ran through the center of raised beds of blooming gardenias. The soil smelled rich.

"It's amazing," Willow said, strolling slowly and stopping frequently to look more closely at a bloom. She glanced anxiously at Chloe. "This is very specialized. Obviously, you already have a very able gardener."

"The conservatory is Vanity's," Chloe said. "She takes care of everything here. There's no room for this sort of thing where she lives, so we gave it to her as a gift."

Surprised, Willow made more admiring sounds. She reached the far end of the glass-and-copper space and stopped again to peer inside an elaborate birdcage that stretched from floor to ceiling across one corner.

All she saw among the beautifully natural enclosure beyond polished brass bars was one small, bright green parakeet and an open-fronted cabinet filled with supplies. "Sweet," she said. "Lucky bird."

"He should have a mate," Chloe remarked.

"Let's go upstairs," Vanity said.

Val and Preston met them in the foyer. Val hugged Willow as if they were old friends. "I gather I didn't make a very good tour guide the first time. Did Chloe show you your rooms yet?"

"What about me?" Vanity said, throwing her arms around him.

Willow was deeply unsettled by Val's question. "I should get back," she said. "My sister has my dog, and I don't like to take advantage."

"What kind of dog?" Preston's dark gray eyes made Willow uncomfortable. "It's so good to see you again, by the way. I was worried when I couldn't find you after our little storm. I'm glad you're okay."

"I'm great," she said. He didn't need to know anything about Mario.

Chloe took her by the hand and rushed her to the wide staircase. She didn't stop hurrying until the two of them were upstairs and she had quickly shown a number of bedrooms and bathrooms. In what she said was her office, a room done in yellows with a floral theme, and a tiny mosaic desk with fragile legs, she snatched up a black leather-bound book with brass corners and tucked it under an arm.

They hurried on to the next door in the corridor.

"This is where we're hoping you'll be comfortable," Chloe said, throwing open a sumptuous sitting room in shades of dark blue, light blue and silver-gray. "The bedroom and bathroom are through here."

Willow felt breathless and trapped, not that she intended to be pressured into doing anything she didn't want to do.

"What do you think?" Chloe asked when they stood in the sitting room again. "I tried to imagine what you might like, but everything can be changed again. You loved the library. We can make this a sitting room and library combined. And if you'd prefer warmer colors, I'll get swatches for you to choose from."

"This is a lovely suite," Willow said neutrally.

Small and blinding, a tiny patch of glaring blue light pricked high up behind Chloe. Willow glanced up, saw it shift inches to the left, then more inches, before it slipped behind the dark blue draperies. She looked over her shoulder, expecting to see someone with a high-powered flashlight. No one was there.

"You have your own entrance," Chloe said, walking to glass doors Willow had mistaken for windows behind the blue draperies. "There are steps that go down to a path that runs past the conservatory. You'll come and go as you please. Of course, whether or not you're here in your off time is up to you. We might as well keep the daybook in here now, since you'll be the one using it. I'll pass invitations to you with a yes or no." She smiled and put the black book on a rosewood table in front of the doors.

"We have a lot to think and talk about," Willow said, still thinking about the bright light. "I'll get back to you soon."

Chloe couldn't hide her disappointment, but she nodded. "That'll be fine. But Val and I are a bit adrift until you can start. He'll be devastated if you don't join us. So will I."

Turning away, Willow headed for the stairs. When she checked behind her, Chloe hadn't followed yet.

Willow hesitated, waiting and wondering if she should go back, but she couldn't discard the possibility that Chloe was trying to manipulate her into a job she wasn't sure she wanted, and not because of the rooms they'd offered her to live in. She wouldn't have to use them at all, or she could set up an office there if she wanted to. The potential job conflicted her. It could be wonderful, and the saving of Mean 'n Green. She would be able to keep all of her staff—something that seemed doubtful with business falling off as it was. But Willow wasn't sure she could feel comfortable around the kind of people the Brandts ran with.

That bright blue light still bothered her. It could have been no more than a reflection off some piece of glass. When she moved, it could have appeared to move, too. Only that hadn't been what it was.

She had the thought that Ben might be up to something and continued on slowly to the head of the stairs. Chloe still didn't follow.

"Do you like it?" Preston asked as she walked down to the main floor where he waited. "Chloe's worked like a demon to get it done quickly."

She didn't trust herself to say anything, but she smiled at them and started back to the kitchen to get her briefcase. Packing her folders away, she noticed how her hands shook. She had no cause to be nervous.

With that thought she picked up the briefcase. It fell open because she had forgotten to close it, and she watched in annoyance as pieces of paper slid all over the floor.

Dammit, she was a basket case. As fast as she could, she gathered everything up, and this time she remembered to close her briefcase properly.

The sliding door to the garden banged open, and Vanity came in with another bottle of the wine they had shared earlier. She wiggled it. "Can't start off with good stuff and expect to enjoy anything less," she said. "It's a good thing Val has a private stash of this in the cabana. What do you think of the rooms Chloe got ready for you?"

"They're beautiful," Willow said, noncommittal.

She left Vanity opening the wine and returned to the foyer.

A cracking sound make her jump. "What was that?" There was another thud.

Val dashed to join Preston and Willow, and they all looked to the staircase.

Chloe had slammed into the railing along the upper corridor. She stared, rocking her head, blinking, as if she couldn't see, not making a sound. She backed off and returned for another collision, harder this time.

Willow screamed and ran for the stairs. Rotating over the railing, Chloe swung, her limbs flailing, to fall onto the stairs themselves.

"Chloe," Val yelled. "Oh, my God."

Vanity came running.

Slowly at first, then gathering speed, Chloe bumped downward, hitting the stair treads and jerking into grotesque angles. Tiny specks of blood sprayed on walls and the stairs.

A yell broke from Val, and he dashed to her, ineffectually trying to stop her from flopping onto the marble tiles.

"Oh, my God," Preston said, striding forward.

Willow gasped. The woman's eyes were stretched wide-open, but they were dying. Willow saw the glazing without going any nearer. Even at a distance, long red welts on Chloe's face and neck were shocking against her white skin. Her head sagged to one side, the face in Willow's direction. More speckles of blood immediately splotched the pale marble.

"Did you hear anything?" Preston said faintly. "Did she scream?"

"No," Willow whispered.

Vanity sobbed, and she shook all over. "Chloe," she said through stretched lips. "What's happened? Chloe?" She heaved as if she would throw up, but gathered herself and looked at Willow. "Get out, now. You shouldn't be here."

"No, stay," Preston shouted. "The police will want to talk to you."

"Leave," Vanity said, moving toward the rest of the group. "For your own sake. Hurry."

19

"What are you doing?" Willow asked, running along the Brandts' front path toward Ben. "Chloe Brandt is dead in there. Get back in the van. We're leaving."

"Dead, how?" Ben looked past her at the house. He should have followed his instincts and "accompanied" her inside, only he expected her to start figuring out if he was around even when she couldn't see him. That could get ugly.

Willow breathed too hard. She gulped and said, "I think someone killed her. It's looks like what happened to Billy Baker and Surry Green—no, not exactly like that. But there's something really weird. I need to get away from here."

"Are you sure that's what you want to do?" Ben took her by the elbow and walked her back to the Brandts' open front door. "Before we got to the end of the block, someone would be telling the police your van was here."

Willow dug her heels in, and they stood there, staring at each other. "What am I thinking?" she said, blinking rapidly, her green eyes horrified. "This is insane of me. Of course I shouldn't be leaving, but..."

"But, what?"

"I— They said I had to get out of there. No excuses, though. I shouldn't have panicked like that."

Sirens howled, growing closer, and Ben led Willow into the front hall of the house. One of the women he had noticed at the party, underdressed in black now, as she had been in white that night, talked into a phone and tapped the toe of one high-heeled sandal. She looked into Ben's eyes and kept on looking.

"You called out to me, you know," he said to Willow under his breath. "Did you know that? That's good. We're making progress."

She slanted him a disbelieving glance. "I just tried to run away from a dead woman who was talking to me ten minutes ago. I'm a heel. You find the strangest times to celebrate little things."

Ben put an arm around her shoulders, managed not to wince and gave her a solid hug. "You're the best. You're also human." Her hand slipped behind his back, and he knew he would walk on broken glass for more chances to hold her.

"I'm going to get hung up here," the woman on the phone said. "You don't need to know why, Carl, and neither do they. Make the calls and tell them we'll get back as soon as we can." She closed her phone.

Ben took in the two men present, one with surfer-blond hair and an athletic build, the other elegant, dark and very well dressed, bending over a female corpse wound into a heap of grotesquely twisted limbs. Both men had been at the party he'd crashed to keep tabs on Willow. He went to look down on the woman's face.

She was a mess, but he was certain he had seen her before. He wasn't sure where. It could have been at

Fortunes. Yes, this woman had known Poppy. They had worked on a charity event together.

"Who are you?" the blond man asked, his voice breaking. "Get away from her. Stop staring—she doesn't like being stared at."

"Are you her husband?" Ben asked.

"Yes. Not that it's any of your business."

"I came to pick up Willow," Ben said. There was scarcely any clear skin to see in the mass of raised and bloody welts that covered the woman's face and neck. "Damn, I'm sorry. The police are arriving now."

"We need an aid car," the blond man shouted. "Get her to the hospital."

Willow's fingers clutched tightly at Ben's. He glanced down at her and frowned at the puzzled expression on her face.

She felt him looking at her. "Are you okay?" she said vaguely. "Don't worry so much."

He let the odd remark go.

"I told you to get out of here," the woman said, looming over Willow. "This is one hell of a nuisance. The police will pounce on you and if we're really unlucky, they'll haul you away on some pretext. They don't have anything to go on that I know of, so you could become their dream come true. You'll be the so-called suspect in custody so the police can keep people calm while the search goes on."

"This is Vanity," Willow said. "And Chloe's husband, Val Brandt, and Preston Moriarty."

Preston looked toward the upper story. "We're going to have to go up there. Whoever did this to Chloe could still be there."

"Wait for the police," Ben said. "We don't want to mess up any evidence."

The sirens arrived outside and car doors slammed.

The foyer felt hushed, but Ben sensed the promise of all hell breaking loose.

"Out now," Vanity said, actually grabbing Willow's wrist. "There's time for you to leave through the back. We're going to need you more than ever. You can't help us if you're locked up. Go! Now!"

Willow jerked her arm away.

"Maybe we should want to keep an eye on Willow," Preston said with the kind of smooth innuendo Ben despised.

"Calm down," Val said. "You're not helping Chloe. Any of you. Willow should be here. The police will think it's funny if she isn't."

"I feel sick," Willow said.

"Breathe deeply through your mouth," Ben told her, although the scent of death already fouled the air.

"The flowers," she said. "Sickening."

Funeral parlor was Ben's last thought before the first wave of uniforms stepped through the door.

"Cynical," Willow murmured. "Bored. Determined. Jaded."

This wasn't the time or place to get excited, but Ben knew he was looking at a woman coming fully into her powers—whether she wanted to or not. He wanted it for her, all of it. And he wanted it for himself. She was picking up emotions and still didn't have enough control to stop herself from singing them out loud.

"NOPD, Sergeant Deneuve," a sergeant in the lead said. "Who's the victim? Who made the call?"

"I did," Preston Moriarty said. "This lady is Chloe Brandt, Val's wife." He indicated Val Brandt, who appeared to have sunk into shock.

The sergeant swiveled his square jaw and thrust it forward while he sized up the rest of them. "You're a Millet," he said flatly, moving his gum from one side of his mouth to the other while he regarded Willow.

"Yes," she said in a firm voice that made Ben grin. "Willow Millet. I'm the one with the Cadillac household engineering firm, Mean 'n Green. You need it, we do it— better than anyone else."

"Uh-huh." The sergeant was a serious man. "The same outfit hanging out around two murder scenes yesterday. And wasn't your family mixed up with the so-called alligator scare?"

"Hey, Sarge." Another policeman shoved his head through the door. "We got press and press and more press. What d'you want to do?"

"Keep 'em back," the sergeant said. "No closer than the other side of the street. And get the tape up. Call for reinforcements for when civilians start arriving."

"We've already got people from around here," the other cop said.

"Do I need to know this?" Sergeant Deneuve said. "You know what to do. Do it."

Two plainclothes detectives walked in, huddled with Deneuve and went carefully upstairs.

Ben could hear excited voices in the street, and the occasional shriek.

The arrival of Dr. Blades wearing green scrubs with a white coat flapping from his thin shoulders meant Willow could put off answering the sergeant about the

Millets' former involvement—only months earlier—with another series of bizarre deaths.

Crime scene personnel straggled in carting equipment, and a photographer started snapping away.

Nat Archer had slouched along behind the medical examiner, exhaustion dragging down every line of his face and body.

"Hey, Nat," Ben said, and got an evil glare for his pains.

Willow let out a soft "Oh." But then she looked away and crossed her arms.

Too bad they couldn't leave now and talk about what was on Willow's mind, and there was plenty.

Blades knelt beside the victim, while another member of the crime scene team undid a large, black bag. Gloves went on before Blades gave Chloe any particular attention. When he did, his facial expression didn't shift, but his sigh was something they all heard.

Uniforms swarmed through the place, following directions to tread lightly, until Nat said loudly, "I want to be first through. If you're not involved right here, make yourselves useful outside until I call you."

Sergeant Deneuve nodded approval and stood observing Blades at work.

Nat's partner, Bucky Fist—stocky, sandy-haired and cheerful—wiped his feet on the front mat. Ben noted this and decided Bucky was either a really nice guy or obsessive-compulsive. Bucky walked in and stood at the ready, close to Nat.

"Is she dead?" Val asked. His lips were colorless and his eyes stared.

Ben felt incredibly sorry for the guy.

"Yes, sir," Dr. Blades said. "It might be a good idea if you went along with Detective Archer here. He'll let you know where we go from here."

"Is the sitting room okay, Val?" Vanity asked.

She took his dull nod for agreement and walked into the closest room, flipping on lamps as she went. Val went with her, but Preston Moriarty hung around until Nat gave him a significant stare and Preston went after his friends.

"Go in there with them, Bucky," Nat said.

Blades examined the dead woman, using forceps to slip smaller specimens into bags an assistant opened for him. "I need to be in my lab," he said. "Fast."

Ben figured that was the man's way of indicating he considered hanging around with anyone but the dead a waste of time.

"Is it the same—"

"No." Blades cut him off and looked up. "Similar but different. Not good news."

Willow moved closer. "Could one of the bats people are talking about do that?"

Blades gave her a bored glance. "Don't tell me you're buying that, too. We apparently have killer bats all over New Orleans."

"People get nervous when they don't understand," Ben said, warning Willow with his eyes to be careful what she said. "They grasp for any explanation."

"Sorry." She came in loud and clear. *"That was a stupid thing to say. He's saying two different things are killing people. Does he mean two different weapons—like knives?"*

"I don't think so." This communication could become very comfortable.

"Can one of you tell me what happened?" Nat said. He had been watching the two of them closely. "Were you both here?"

"Just me," Willow said. "Ben was waiting for me outside. I came for a job interview with…with Chloe. We were upstairs and she was fine when I left her."

Nat cleared his throat.

"I must have been the last one to see her alive," Willow said.

"Last but one," Ben said quickly, wishing she weren't so damnably honest.

Sykes strolled from outside and Blades said, "So much for your people keeping the gawkers out."

Mario edged around the front doorjamb as if he didn't really want to be seen. Trust Sykes to think of bringing the dog, since he gave Willow comfort.

"You remember Sykes Millet, Blades," Nat said. "He's Willow's brother."

"He'd be hard to forget," Blades said, looking from Ben to Sykes. "Bloody gathering of wizards. How many of you are in this town?" He returned to his work.

"That's a good question," Sykes said, his tone amused in Ben's brain. *"Wonder if we could scare up enough for an army."*

"When we've got more time, we'll check it out," Ben told him.

"Behave yourselves." The immediate shocked expression on Willow's face at her own announcement silenced both men.

"Will you show me where you and Mrs. Brandt were upstairs?" Nat asked Willow. If possible, he seemed even more weary.

"Does she need a lawyer?" Ben said.

"I'm not accusing her of anything."

"It could happen, though, right?" Sykes said.

Nat blinked slowly. "Anything could happen."

"We could get Ethan over," Ben said. His younger brother was a lawyer.

"I'll be fine with Nat," Willow said. "All I'm going to do is show him where I was with Chloe." Her voice cracked, and her eyes abruptly filled with tears.

Ben put a hand on either side of her face and wiped away the tears with his thumbs. "Hush," he said quietly, putting his mouth near her ear. "I'm sorry you have to go through this. Maybe it's a good idea to run over things with Nat so we can get you home. Don't answer any questions you don't like, okay?"

She nodded.

"He can't do anything with what you say anyway," Ben told her. "Not without reading your rights and having a lawyer present and all that stuff. This might save dragging things out. Do you want Ethan? I can get him right here."

She gave him a lopsided smile. "I bet you can. It's not necessary. I haven't done anything wrong. And Nat won't do anything to hurt me. Poor Nat," she said and closed her eyes.

Finding out why it was "poor Nat" would have to wait.

"I'll come with you," Ben said. He raised his voice, "Okay if I come, Nat?"

Nat gave a defeated shrug. "You two seem joined at the hip anyway, so why not? Just don't answer questions for her."

Knowing his distraction techniques were futile, Ben attempted to keep Willow from looking at sprays of minute blood spatters on the walls and more blood smeared on banisters, by pretending great interest in paintings higher up.

He felt her go inside herself, and she climbed up the stairs after Nat as if she had closed down her emotions.

She started, and turned back, looking around the foyer. Ben did the same, but couldn't guess what she was look-ing at. She met his eyes.

"Tell me," he said.

Willow shook her head. "I don't know. Everything's happening to me too fast. It's all falling over itself. I think someone here is glad Chloe's dead, but I can't tell who. It's not the same as what I usually feel. It's not…human."

Upstairs, the evidence of Chloe's injuries was not so obvious. It was as if the wounds had really started bleed-ing when she collided with the railings and fell.

Willow went ahead, leading the way to the rooms at the end of the corridor.

She hung back then, but Nat walked in. "There was a strange light," she told Ben. "Do I tell him?"

Ben pulled her against him. "What kind of light?" he asked, very low.

"Bright. Blue. A little spot high up on the wall behind where Chloe was standing." She drew a breath. Despite all she had been through, she was ethereal and com-pletely beautiful to Ben. "Then it slid behind the drapes."

He considered. "Could it have been a flashlight?"

"That's what I thought, but where—"

"Are you two coming in to share your wisdom with

me?" Nat asked, poking his head back out. "I need anything I can get right now. I don't want to scare you, but if my publicity hound of a boss shows up looking for a way to make points with the folks, it isn't going to be pretty. Let's get on, shall we?"

It would be impossible not to see Willow's reluctance to enter the room. She went slowly, looking at only one spot—an area where a modern rosewood desk stood. Ben took in the area rapidly. The drapes she had mentioned must be the dark blue linen ones behind the desk and pulled back from French doors. He automatically looked at the wall. He didn't expect to see any pinpoints of light, and he was right.

Willow launched into an explanation of her last conversation with Chloe and how she had offered her these rooms to live in—or to use as she wished. She gave Ben a questioning glance, and he nodded before she explained about the light.

Nat checked carefully behind the drapes, looked at the doors and said, "They're open. Were they like that before you left the room?"

Willow frowned and said, "I don't know."

Immediately, Nat's attention switched to a leather-bound black book lying open and facedown on the pale blue rug. Nat squatted to take a closer look. He took out a pair of glasses and pushed them on, getting even nearer to the book.

"What?" Ben said.

Nat didn't answer.

"That's the daybook," Willow said. "The Brandts' social calendar is kept in there. Chloe wanted me to take over keeping it up."

"Did she give it to you?"

Willow frowned. "No. She put it on the desk."

"Don't touch it," Nat said. "Don't touch anything. Do you want to say anything else about the book, Willow?"

Ben didn't like the phrasing of the question, but kept quiet.

Willow said no hesitantly. "It couldn't have killed her."

"Why would you make a suggestion like that?" Nat asked.

Ben wanted to tell her to keep quiet.

"There's blood on it," Willow said, as if she were above the scene, looking down. "The brass corners. Someone hit her with them again and again. Jabbed her."

"I can't see blood," Nat pointed out.

Ben could see it, too, but didn't say so. Sykes would see it, or Pascal, Marley.... And now, Willow.

"It's there," she said. "Find who did it, quickly. They've only just started. There'll be more victims."

"This has been too much for Willow," Ben said. "You don't need her here anymore, do you, Nat?"

"Yeah. But I'm not going to make her stay."

Heavy footsteps approached, and Nat's eyes closed slowly. "Keep your mouths shut," he said. "You don't know anything. Don't mention lights, or what you can *feel,* for God's sake."

"Commissioner," Nat said, deference dripping. "Thank you for coming over, sir. This is Commissioner Molyneux," he said to Ben and Willow, waving vaguely.

"Of course," Ben said, hoping he hit the right note. He'd heard plenty about this man from Gray Fisher, who used to work for him.

"You're a Millet," Molyneux said to Willow, by way

of an accusation. Big, on the overweight side, red-faced with small eyes a little too close together, he pronounced *Millet* with the same amount of disdain he might use for *drug trafficker.*

"I am," Willow said. "This is my friend, Ben Fortune."

"Fortunes Club, yes, I know. We've met you and your family before."

Ben didn't remember the occasion.

"I should mention something to you, Ms. Millet," Molyneux said. "I've seen quite a bit of your family in recent months. You haven't made my life easier. Two people died yesterday, and you or your people were in both places. Now we've got another DB downstairs, and here you are again. Wherever you go, ridiculous rumors follow. I'd like that to stop, quickly. If it doesn't, I shall have to consider what your real part is in all this talk of things that go bump in the night."

All expression left Willow's face. "Do they?" she said. "Go bump in the night?"

Molyneux's mouth set in a tight little line. He turned his attention to Nat. "Sergeant Deneuve thinks the woman was attacked up here." He looked around, then at the book lying on the floor.

"She was," Willow said. "I must have been the last to talk to her, and she was fine when I left."

Ben almost groaned aloud.

"Thank you for sharing that with me," Molyneux said. He crossed his arms and worried his bottom lip with a finger and thumb.

Ben met Nat's eyes and shook his head slightly. He waited for the Commissioner to announce that he was having Willow taken into custody.

The man gave a gusty sigh. "This crime scene will be battened down tighter than a puritan's ass, Archer. Everything relating to findings will be on my desk in the morning. You are responsible for knowing where all these…" He waved a hand in the direction of Ben and Willow. "Make sure you can get to them if we need them. Get to it. You've got a long night ahead of you. Don't miss anything. I'm calling a press conference for noon tomorrow.

"I'll talk to Blades on the way out." He looked at his watch. "Get all this sealed off. I'm late for a dinner appointment. Make sure you two are where we can find you," he said as his parting shot to Ben and Willow.

Nat walked Molyneux to the corridor, and Ben could hear low conversation between the two. He felt a draft and turned back to Willow. She had opened the French doors wide and stood outside on a small platform at the top of a flight of stairs. When he approached, she backed down several steps, never taking her eyes from something that held her attention at the top of the doors.

"What do you see?" he asked her, stepping through the door.

She shook her head. "Just checking out an idea. It's nothing. Ben?" She ran to him and put her arms around him, squeezing him until the shivers between them calmed to a steady tingle. "I need you," she said.

He hovered between excitement and fear. "You've got me. We've got each other."

"I just saw something happen," she said, looking up at him, her hair a crimson nimbus in the light from inside.

"It could have been anything," Ben said. "Maybe the door swung open more and—"

"Not that. I saw a woman. It was dark and she was being dragged into a hole. She couldn't cry out, but I saw her struggle. I think it was me."

20

Willow had found Mario outside the upstairs room at the Brandt house and had scarcely let him go since. "Sykes is a teddy bear," she said as she and Ben walked through the few neon lights still on in the Quarter.

"Don't let him hear you say that," Ben said, smiling in the silver-green glow of early, early morning.

"I don't expect him to remember little things," Willow said, kissing the dog's head and smiling at the tickle of his sprouting whiskers against her cheek. "He must have known how much I needed my buddy here."

At Ben's suggestion—to keep them away from the police station—Nat had conducted their interview in a comfortable office at Fortunes. After they had talked for three hours, Nat told Willow to keep herself available and suggested Ben get her home.

"My place or yours?" Ben said with a laugh while they strolled through the barely active streets.

Willow yawned, and clapped a hand over her mouth. "We're exposed out here," she said. "Any second one of these, whatever they are, could attack."

"I think they're more subtle than that," he said. "Sykes suggested we go to his studio. We'd be in the

Quarter, but Molyneux and his gang couldn't find us so easily."

"I've never been to Sykes's studio." Her sculptor brother, who had a solid reputation for his pieces, kept his whereabouts quiet unless he chose to show up on Royal Street.

"Do you know why he's so secretive?" Ben asked.

"I've got a good idea." But she didn't know how much Sykes had explained to Ben.

"Do you really believe in the Millet Curse?" he said.

She paused, watching cut crystals rotate on pieces of fish line in a shop window. Myriad brightly colored spots spun in the semidark recesses.

"I don't know," she said at last. "When I was a kid and my parents first took off, supposedly in search of a way to circumvent the curse, I believed in it then. But that was twenty years ago, and Uncle Pascal is still running a business and family he never wanted to take on in the first place."

"And if your parents didn't have this conviction that the original reason for the Millets running from Bruges was because some poor innocent baby was born with dark hair and blue eyes, rather than the red-green combination, they would be here taking care of things?"

Willow thought about it. "Would they? Or are they free spirits taking advantage of a load of old bunk to shirk their duties?

"Three hundred years ago a Millet with dark hair and blue eyes married a woman who turned out to be a witch—or people said she was. And our family was chased halfway around the world. When do we get to let go of that and get on with our lives?

"I saw Dad a few months back when he heard about Marley and Gray getting together. He came to play the patriarch, and couldn't wait to get away again."

"But the reason Sykes is so private is because he knows he isn't considered up to the task of taking over the family," Ben said thoughtfully. "He's the first dark-haired Millet in direct line to take over since the famous ancestor. Your folks have as good as told him he's dangerous to the rest of you. Don't you wonder how he felt when your father handed the reins to Pascal? That was the same as telling Sykes he'd been disinherited. Bypassed."

Ben could have no way of knowing how often Willow suffered because of this very unfair situation, or how often she and Marley talked about it and tried to figure out how to put things straight. "Uncle Pascal doesn't agree with it," she said. "He's always looking for a way out. I'm grateful Sykes is so strong. But he's not super-human."

With a laugh, Ben said, "Isn't he? I don't think you're right about that. Should I take you to his place and tuck you up?"

The sensation Willow got in her tummy and legs didn't seem the right reaction to being offered comfort from a big brother figure. "I can just go to the Court of Angels."

"We both know that."

"Will Sykes be at his place?"

After too long a pause, Ben said, "No. Not tonight."

"He gave you a key?"

"Uh-huh."

"And told you to take me there for the night?"

"If we wanted to go," Ben said.

"That's a bit obvious, isn't it?"

He looked at her without a suggestion of amusement. "It can be anything we want to make it."

Willow walked on, slowly.

"It's on St. Peter Street," Ben said. "Near Dauphine. Why don't you know that?"

"Sykes never volunteered the information. Things were strained when he found the studio and started spending a lot of time there, so I never asked. We're going the wrong way." She swallowed.

"Yes," Ben said, turning her around. "So we are." He didn't keep the pleasure out of his voice.

He wanted her to himself tonight—but then, he'd wanted that for a long time. What hadn't changed was Willow's own uncertainty about whether they could be happy together for very long.

"I'm going to call Nat first thing and find out if Blades came to any conclusions about Chloe Brandt's wounds. And the cause of death."

"Yes." She wanted to know, but wished she didn't have to think about it constantly.

Even passing drunks were subdued. A man sat on the curb with his feet in the gutter, a bottle hanging between his knees. Stillness blanketed the Quarter, still heat. A storm could be brewing.

"We've got the same issues between us, Ben," Willow said.

"I wish you'd let me in on exactly what they are. It's time we didn't have any issues at all. I'm thinking of getting us both away from here. Start over somewhere. White picket fence, a couple of kids—"

"Don't joke."

"Who's joking? I want to see if you like Kauai, too. My house is on the beach at the most secluded spot in an amazing bay. If I see someone nearby, it's an event."

He turned her left on Dauphine.

"How long would it take you to get bored?" Willow said.

"Go there with me and ask that."

"Maybe I will one day." She glanced up at the side of his face, all angles in the shadows, his hair shining black and tied at the nape. She couldn't imagine a woman who would get bored being with him in a secluded Hawaiian cove.

Power moved with Benedict Fortune, and grace, but most of all, mysticism.

"You're coming into your own fast," he said as if he heard what she thought.

That wasn't beyond possibility. Willow frowned.

Out of the stillness came a current of air. Strong, direct, aimed where it tossed Willow's hair aside. She looked at Ben again, but he hadn't noticed. She took a deep, calming breath and carried on walking without so much as a check in her pace.

This time the uninvited visitor slithered over her skin with a dozen soft caresses.

Willow jolted the length of her body, so hard she ached.

"What?" Ben swung her toward him. "What is it?"

She couldn't speak, only point, at her cheek, her neck—and then low on her stomach.

Ben gathered his forces. Turning all of his energy into his core, he became rigid. A deeper glance around showed him there were fewer of the undead abroad at this time of night—they preferred the perceived challenge of moving among their counterparts in the daylight. Those he saw skimmed along, not quite touching the ground, their eyes fixed on nothing he could see.

There it was, and this time clearer. A winged creature, he thought, and playing some kind of game with him, popping out from behind Willow as if to peer at him, only to dart back.

"Nothing to worry about," he told Willow. He couldn't worry about whether his voice sounded even remotely normal. Keeping her distracted was the aim. Being her strength where she had little was his chosen responsibility.

Her eyes grew larger and she winced, rubbed the middle of her back. This creature wasn't keeping its attention on her neck anymore.

Mario growled and squirmed in her arms. He wriggled until she set him down. Ben saw Willow's dress shift over her thigh and rage twisted at him. She was helpless to stop this sly molestation.

Mario surprised him by closing his teeth on one of Ben's pant legs. He pulled him away a few feet and closer to a boarded-up shop front with a sagging, padlocked gate across the doorway.

Ben walked back to Willow, but the shadowy creature soared straight up from behind her, then swooped. It's absolute lack of sound unnerved Ben.

"You okay?" he asked Willow.

She said "no" so quietly he barely heard her.

"Be very still," he told her. "You're okay."

The thing zipped toward the padlocked gate. It was

fast, but not as fast as Ben. All of his vitality sheathed his center. He shifted, dived sideways and over the gates. He must not take a nanosecond too long.

The last thing he expected was to find himself inside an abandoned shop. The actual front doors were gone and wooden crates had been piled, waist-high, across the entrance. Already he had decided what he must do, and tonight. Going forward, he would have at least one advantage against this will-o'-the-wisp with tiny glittering fangs. It would carry his mark.

The opposition zipped over the crates and Ben followed.

The attack came without warning.

This time there was a noise, a high-pitched sound like a sonic dental drill. Ben threw his hands in front of his face and launched himself through the air, changing direction instant by instant. He focused, using the third eye he reserved for extreme danger. The effect mimicked military night goggles, and he saw a shape move, black with a green outline, diving at him. Only his speed could save him from the thing's bite, and he didn't doubt that with it, bite to kill was the order of the night.

With absolute clarity he understood how inconvenient he was, how important his removal must be to this creature and whoever was behind it. He was certain it didn't act alone.

They wanted Willow.

Ben slammed into a wall covered with empty glass shelves and they shattered. His enhanced sight saw the shards explode, rise like a space shower against a darkened universe and scatter, in slow motion. He held a hand in front of his eyes. Pricks, like delving ice spicules, peppered the side of his face and one arm. He felt fine trickles of warm blood on his skin.

The high buzz screeched from behind him in the stuffy space. Ben whirled, both forearms crossed in front of his face. Eyes, all light but white, colorless, zeroed in on him and shot forward so fast Ben barely resisted blinking. He couldn't afford to blink—any more than he could afford to die with Willow a few yards away and completely vulnerable without him.

As the creature would have collided with him, Ben pitched a scant few inches to the left, and it passed him by. The whining grew louder and now he recognized an angry note. Rage.

This was personal.

Without pause, the wings shot upward, rotated the small fleshy mass hanging below, and came at him again. Blood slid into the corner of his eye, but there was no time to wipe it away.

The whining drone became wild, disjointed, a scream. It came at him again—eyes blazing—and Ben held his position, his head almost touching the ceiling, his body folded and ready to spring.

Ben extended his right forefinger and concentrated on its tip. He saw the minutest pause in the thing's flight, before the wail continued and it came for him again. It was less than an inch away when he feinted to the left and jammed that forefinger into tissue behind one wing. Sickeningly, it dented and fizzed.

He hadn't expected the curdling scream that followed, or the flash of flame that flared, and just as quickly extinguished itself. With a zipping sound, the creature changed visibility. It could be seen with the human eye. Fluid squirted from between the wings, bathing all of it.

One side disappeared from human sight, the other remained visible to anyone. It was the fluid that rendered it impossible to see with normal eyes, and he had burned out part of whatever reservoir stored the stuff. He could hope the damage never healed.

Swooping, the creature repeatedly brought itself to a level trajectory, then fell away again. For one wild beat in time Ben wanted to make pursuit, to attempt to take the enemy down for good. But if he failed and was left too wounded to act, Willow would suffer and he wouldn't allow that.

He heard another sound, a whimpering like a wounded animal—and he smelled burning skin, or fur or flesh.

In one thrust, he returned to Willow.

She stared at him just as she had before he'd left. When he smiled, she smiled back. He waited, expecting her to say she knew he'd been gone. Instead, she reached out and touched his bleeding face, her expression turning to one of horror. "Ben. You're bleeding." She searched in every direction. "What hit you?" She grabbed his right arm and held it up where she could see the wounds there.

"Let's go," he said. "We're not far from Sykes's place."

"Don't you need to be seen by someone?"

"Sure, I need to be seen by you." He felt less flip than he sounded. "A shower will take care of everything."

"Ben. Something really bad just happened. We can't walk away and pretend it didn't. I know you were gone again."

So much for being fast enough to fool her completely this time. "You're too observant." He touched her hair. "Too talented and getting more so by the hour."

She ignored that. "Was it the same as the last time?"

"More or less," he said.

She grabbed him convulsively. "Those wounds could kill you. They've killed before, haven't they? They killed Chloe Brandt."

"Not these. I slammed into some glass shelves. Our ugly buddy never touched me. It tried—but failed."

"But it's still here." She turned in a circle until Ben stopped her.

"It's got something else on its mind right now," he told her. "Like pain. Let's take advantage of that. We need to figure out what we know and what's next—and get some sleep. And we've got to stay out of jail because bars may keep one of us in, but they won't keep that little monster out."

21

Sykes's hideaway, a blue-washed house set in a walled garden and hidden from surrounding buildings by palms and aged shrubs, had one entrance: from an alley beside a faded little hotel.

Willow stuck close to Ben's side, but kept looking over her shoulder all the way to a gate in the wall all but hidden by swathes of red passion creepers. Mario remained draped over her shoulder and growling very faintly.

Neither Ben nor Willow spoke while they made their way through banks of billowing flowers, faintly luminous under the moon, to the gallery surrounding the house. They climbed steps to a front door where flowering vines looked heavy enough to bring down the overhang.

Ben took a key from his pocket and let them in, putting on a table lamp inside the door.

Minimalist. Sparse furnishings, but all beautiful original pieces, and she noticed most were eighteenth-century French.

Willow looked around, into a sitting room, up a flight of stairs to the left and back into gloom in the farther recesses. Panicky fluttering took over her stomach. "I don't feel safe anywhere," she said. "Sorry, Ben, that just said itself. I don't think I'll sleep again as long as I'm waiting for that thing to come after me. We don't know when or where it'll show up. It is me it wants, isn't it? Everyone who has died is somehow connected to me. And Chris is missing because of me. I don't know where to go from here."

"Go where you're already going," he said. "Face it head-on. I think most of what you say is correct, but it's also more complicated. It has to be."

He took her by the hand and they held on tightly, their arms shaking with the power of it. "So I face it, but I can't stop it?"

"I can," Ben said. "I did tonight, and I will again if I have to. I won't let anything hurt you. You aren't alone, and you're not going to be. Not at all until this is over. Right now Sykes and Gray are out there working. Pascal, too. Marley's been doing whatever she does in that workroom of hers and she's not talking, which Gray says is a good sign. He says it's also a good sign that she's eating chocolate with both hands because it means she's really into the project."

"I don't want her traveling out of her body looking for dangerous creatures," Willow said. "Not now."

She felt Ben's close attention and raised her brows at him. "What? Why shouldn't Marley use her power when it's needed?"

Willow frowned. "I don't know, but I don't think it's a good idea. Where's Sykes's studio?"

"On the other side of the house. I've never been invited to see it. It was added on. There are skylights but no windows—or so Sykes tells me."

She shrugged. "Mr. Mystery never disappoints. I'm told his pieces are sold before they're finished, but I don't even know what he makes—I mean, I don't know if he chops bowls of fruit out of wormy wood or chisels the gigantic stone stuff with titles like *Doomed* on them that they put outside buildings."

"Neither do I," Ben said.

Mario gave her a lick and wriggled. Willow recognized the signal that he wanted to explore on his own and set him down. He rushed up the stairs at once.

"I know more about you than you know about me," Ben announced, looking over her head.

The sudden announcement surprised Willow, but she collected herself fast. "That's true." Why pass up a good opportunity? "I always thought you'd tell me what you want me to know if you were ever ready."

He looked into the sitting room with her trailing behind him. "When you've got questions, ask. I'll try to answer. I'm a pretty simple man."

Willow laughed aloud but controlled herself when Ben gave her the evil eye.

"I don't want to stay on the ground floor," Willow said. "I feel safer higher up."

Ben didn't comment and she appreciated that. Rather he retraced his steps and climbed the stairs. "I haven't been up here, but Sykes said to use whatever we wanted."

She felt herself turn a bit pink. "Some protective brother he is. Tossing my virtue to the wind. Or he would have been…" She let the words trail off.

"Not to the wind, just to an old friend he trusts and knows you're already Bonded with."

The dread word, *Bonded.* How could she be certain

Bonding really existed or that it was, as the family insisted, permanent?

"Because we were Bonded and nothing's changed," Ben said, undeterred by the slowing of her feet. "It's a Millet thing, not a Fortune thing, but I've accepted it because I can feel it. And so can you."

"Maybe we only imagine it." She didn't really care that he was letting himself read her mind. If she ever did care, she would tell him.

"You can say that after today?"

She really couldn't and was glad.

"You're not concentrating or you'd know you keep letting me into your mind." He glanced back at her and reached the top of the stairs. "You're asking me to come in. You're communicating directly with me. I don't imagine what I feel for you, Willow."

The first room on the right, a bedroom with no frills, did have a red silk love seat at the bottom of a simple iron bed covered with a plain white spread.

"This could be Sykes's room," Willow said, knowing her brother's simple taste, combined with his flair for the dramatic. "He would be the one to choose white every-thing for his bedroom—almost everything."

"Must be his. He said there's only one bed in the house."

She looked dubiously at that bed. Did Ben expect her to sleep in it?

"I thought you would," he said. "I'll keep watch so you won't have to worry."

"I guess I really am an open book to you," she said. And he was right, as long as he was with her, she felt safe. "Ben, you are human, y'know."

He pulled his long-sleeved black T-shirt over his head and gave her a piercing look. "We both know that."

"You aren't like other men, but you can be hurt. If you couldn't, you wouldn't have blood on you now."

"True."

She was making a hash of this. "I couldn't handle it if something happened to you."

He paused, then tossed the shirt on the bottom of the bed. His torso and arms were long and lean, the muscle well developed. As he was right now, he seemed invincible.

"Why did you send me away?" he asked.

"I can't talk about that."

"I don't want to think about living without you, Willow." He undid his buckle and whipped the belt from his jeans. "Don't duck this—give me an answer. I've earned it."

"I don't want to mistake a habit for something more," she said. "You've always been around—all my life."

"When you were a little kid I thought you were a nuisance," he said with a grin. "That changed."

She nodded and bit her lip.

"What happened today wouldn't have happened out of habit, would it? It was all new—still is. I want you. I've never wanted anyone the way I want you. Something like this doesn't strike twice."

He was offering himself on a platter. An amazing man who could have his choice of women, and he wanted her. That made them equal but for one thing: Willow's questions were growing deeper.

"I can't deny that I've got so-called powers anymore," she said. "How do you feel about that?"

He grinned. "It's the greatest."

"Why?"

"Because you're coming into your own, and you aren't fighting it anymore. You've got a lot to add to the picture. You and I are going to make some team."

"Go shower," she told him. If she kept pushing in this direction, she would only manage to persuade herself that he wouldn't want her if she was normal.

With a long look, he headed for the bathroom, but paused on the way. "Would you feel better if you came in with me?"

"Depends what you mean by 'feel better.' I think I'll hover near the door."

"I'll leave it open." Even with his back to her he radiated smugness.

Willow heard the shower go on and stood close to the door, where steam soon started to creep out.

For the first time in hours she thought about Mean 'n Green. She couldn't abandon the people who depended on her—for services or for their livings.

She looked in a mirror on one wall, not that she could do much to improve herself when her purse was downstairs—and she wasn't going down there alone. Her hair shone as brilliantly red and curly as usual, but her eyes were underscored with dark shadows. "Glad I looked," she muttered.

This was ridiculous. She was held captive by something she had never seen.

But she had seen what it was capable of. Ben told her he got the cuts from glass, and she assumed he told her the truth, otherwise he'd be worrying about his future. But she didn't like to think that protecting her had caused him to collide with glass.

She thought of all those who were ranging around trying to keep her safe. What kind of danger was she exposing them to?

Willow's anxiety embarrassed her so she stood where Ben wouldn't see her when he got out of the shower. The water droned on. Evidently, he was addicted to long showers.

The room canted to one side.

Willow stumbled, grabbed a chest of drawers and saw its drawers fly open. Lamps shot from tables and smashed. The lowered slat blinds rattled and swung.

She looked toward the bathroom. Steam billowed, thicker, from the partly open door, and the sound of splashing water grew louder.

A rumble, deep beneath her, brought a bubble of fear to her throat.

Earthquake?

No, she'd never been in an earthquake.

The house was collapsing.

Without warning, Marley appeared in the doorway to the bedroom.

Willow took a step toward her, but Marley held up a warning hand. Her pale face twisted as if with pain, and Willow could see waves of tremors passing through her body.

"Marley?"

Marley shook her head, no, pleading with her eyes. She slipped inside the room. The blue smock she wore was one she used for her refinishing work, splotched with varnish and paint. Her feet were bare.

The edges of Willow's vision turned fuzzy, faded to gray. A pale green and glaring light illuminated Marley.

Willow moved toward her sister, feet dragging, each step threatening to tear her farther away. She tried to shout for Ben, but any sound choked in her throat.

She was awake.

She was conscious.

This was real.

The wall behind Marley disappeared, replaced by the entrance to a hole. The light she made shivered against the edges of the hole, but everything beyond was black.

A sound started far away and approached, gathering volume until a boom vibrated through Willow's body. Marley tilted her head on one side, and she cried tears that swept to wet her smock. Her hands turned this way and that in begging motions.

Once more Willow attempted to reach out, but cringed away, horrified at the eruption of a huge head from the dark tunnel behind Marley. An enormous, beaked head, no visible eyes, and a beard of misshapen fat hanging beneath its beak.

The head undulated from side to side, the great beak opening slowly to reveal a thick tongue while vast shoulders squeezed through and a wing that seemed to fill the room shot free and gave a swinging flap.

The rush of air upended Willow. She fell, scrambling away, and finally screaming.

Creaking, shaking, the house trembled on its foundation, and Willow cried, "Marley," while she hid her eyes.

At once a force scooped her from the floor and threw her against a wet wall. It held her there, trapped, unmoved by her flailing fists and feet.

"I'm coming," she yelled, using her nails to strike out until a talon took hold of both wrists and squeezed them until the bones ground together. "Don't hurt her. Please." She yanked and tugged but her wrists wouldn't move.

"Be still." A voice near her ear sent pain through her head.

"What do you want?" she cried.

"Just be still."

Panting, she stopped twisting her wrists, stopped bucking her body and pumping her feet.

Slowly, completely terrified, she opened her eyes.

Water from Ben's body soaked her dress.

22

Her wrists would be bruised. Ben hated that he'd caused that. If he hadn't stopped her, she could have clawed his face until he couldn't see to help her.

"Willow?"

Limp, she sagged in his arms, her head dropped back. Her skin glistened with sweat.

He shook her. "Willow, talk to me. It's Ben. I'm here."

Willow came up through layers of darkness, gathering anger, gathering strength, and screamed. She tossed, trying to get free. "Marley," she called, tears clogging her throat. "Wait for me, Marley."

Ben shook her harder. He dared not put her down because he knew she would run. "Look at me." He let her legs slide down and held the hair at the back of her head. *"Look at me, Willow."*

Her eyes opened, as if from troubled sleep, and she blinked at him. Slowly the focus cleared. Ben didn't slacken his grip. She would regain control, and he could only guess what she might do next.

"Did something attack you?" he said, trying to see her skin without attracting her attention too much. "Tell me, for God's sake."

It was Ben who held Willow against his naked body. Water dripped from his hair, over his shoulders and chest.

She pushed at him. "I've got to go. Please, Ben, don't stop me. They've got Marley. It's got Marley. Over there." She tried to twist and see behind her.

"The house shook and everything broke," she said, pleading with him to understand. "Glass everywhere. It was an earthquake, then that, that— It came. It wants me, not Marley. I have to go."

"Talk to me," Ben said. "Slow down. What did you see?"

In a rain of hands and feet, butting him with her head, Willow battered him. He grabbed one of her wrists and she bit his hand. Her strength was abnormal, crazy.

Closing his hands around her waist, he held her at arm's length, but she jumped and crashed both feet into his diaphragm, shoving herself beyond his arm's reach, and shot from his grasp.

She landed on the floor and scrambled.

Ben caught a foot, but she rotated her entire body, launched through the door and stumbled to the top of the stairs.

"Don't come nearer," she said, pointing both first fingers at him. "Stand there." Her eyes, the pupils hugely dilated, raked around.

"Calm down—"

"*Shut up.* Don't tell me anything. It happened. Everything fell over and broke. There was a hole and Marley was in front of it. It was a raptor coming for her. One of its wings was…" She wanted to see her sister's face.

There was no hole, no tunnel, no bearded, beaked head—and no Marley.

Willow buried her head in her hands and backed away. "It took her," she sobbed. "What have I done? She's gone. Marley!"

Ben had barely an instant to stop Willow from careening backward down the steep flight of stairs. He threw himself at her, wrapped her in his arms and groaned aloud when they fell onto the edges of the steps.

With Willow on top of him, he ducked his head into her shoulder and cushioned her. His muscle and bone thumped on hard treads, banged downward until he slewed sideways and stopped.

Willow trembled. She couldn't keep still. When she opened her eyes again, Ben's head rested against a stair and his eyes were closed. He breathed through his mouth.

But he held her so tightly her ribs felt bruised.

She put a hand either side of his face.

Ben didn't open his eyes.

"I'm sorry," she whispered.

He didn't answer.

Willow kissed his neck, kissed the pulse that beat heavily there. She touched his face again and again, ran her fingers through his hair. "Ben?"

She could see into the bedroom. The lamps stood where they always had been, and they weren't broken. Nothing looked different from when they'd first gone into the room.

"Ben, look at me, please." She wiggled, then held completely still when his grip tightened even more.

"I saw it. It took Marley away. Please, help me."

"I'm going to," he murmured. "Just give me a little time, okay?"

"But Marley—"

"Nothing's been broken. There hasn't been an earthquake."

She couldn't budge a millimeter in his arms. "I felt it and saw it. Broken glass."

"Do you see any broken glass now?"

She went limp. "What's happening to me, Ben? I'm not doing all this to myself, am I?"

"No. You're getting a crash course in being what you truly are, is all."

"But Marley—"

"If something had happened to Marley, I'd know," he told her. "Sykes would have contacted me." His head ached, but not so much that he didn't feel the throbbing at every point where her body met his. "But let's call them."

"I hallucinated," she mumbled. "They'd think I was mad if I phoned them."

"You are not mad," he said.

"We should get up," Willow said. An ache started between her legs and contracted muscles in every direction. Her cotton wraparound dress was wet against her skin. Her damp bra scraped nipples already burning from Ben's touch.

She wasn't only wet on the outside.

"Willow, I won't let you run from me again," Ben said. There was nothing light about what he said, or how he said it. He had put her on notice.

"I...I can't breathe," she said. "I *feel* everywhere. It's you, it's touching you."

"We'd better get used to it," he said. "You've marked me, Willow, and I'll stay marked. I want to."

"When they talk about pleasure and pain, this is what they mean, isn't it?"

He gave a short laugh and eased to sit up on a stair with her hugged in his lap. "I doubt it, my love. This isn't anything earthly."

"Ben…"

"Yes."

"Nothing. I keep making you suffer, but you don't go away."

"Get used to it. You're my drug, Willow."

"Let's go to bed," she said. "Let's take what time we can before it all starts again."

He couldn't think of anything more appealing, but he didn't fool himself that their troubles had really paused. They could choose to make themselves a little hiatus, though.

Her knuckles brushed his contracting belly. "You'd better not punch me, warrior woman," he said.

With her eyes lowered, she pulled the tie on her damp cotton dress undone. She opened the front and shrugged her free arm loose.

Then she looked up at him. "My dress is wet."

Ben kissed her, taking his time, smoothing her hair away from her face. He stroked her from neck to back, down her spine to her waist, up her arm, into the dips beneath her collarbones and over the soft rise of her breasts above her bra.

She sighed and shuddered, moaned at the electrical responses they both absorbed.

And he tucked the ends of his fingers under the edge of the bra to catch the very edge of a nipple. He played there, taking his time, changed his grip and pressed his hand flat over her ribs, her belly, and came to rest over the tops of her thighs where they met her body, and her warm little mound.

Willow turned in his arms, tried to get even closer. The skin he didn't touch clamored; the skin he did touch pulsed.

"You seem pretty comfortable sitting on a naked man's lap," Ben said into her ear, running the tip of his tongue around the folds. "It can't be too comfortable."

She tapped him lightly. "If you're looking for compliments, you've got them. You are a hard man."

They didn't laugh.

Ben got her up the stairs and into the bedroom without dropping her, and stood her on the floor by the white-covered bed.

He stood back just far enough that she could see all of him. His drying hair had begun to shine again. A faint sheen threw shadows beneath his cheekbones— and in dips beneath muscles that flexed with the slightest move he made.

The heat Willow felt had nothing to do with embarrassment. Need set up a steady beat, just beneath her skin, into every tissue, every sinew.

She wanted him again, so strongly.

Ben flipped the other shoulder of her dress and it fell to the floor. Once more he embraced her. She was so much shorter, but he hiked her up and held her so he could fit their bodies where they belonged. Her pelvis tipped into him and he gritted his teeth.

Willow eased her bra straps down and undid the front fastener. "I have to feel all of you," she said, her voice a husky whisper.

He felt her, too. Muscles in his legs shook from the effort of holding back.

A heartbeat and she stood before him, naked.

She lay across the bed, her arms stretched above her head.

He made very sure she wouldn't read anything in his mind unless he wanted her to. Looking down on her, he admitted that in many ways he was merely a man, a man with the luck to have found a woman who turned lovemaking into a mystical adventure.

With his knee, he parted her thighs. Lowering himself, he supported his weight on his elbows and kissed every part of her he could reach. By the time he licked each nipple and took it between his teeth, she writhed and begged for him to stop teasing her.

"You think you're the only one I'm teasing?" he said. She knew she wasn't.

Slipping his hands up the undersides of her arms, he laced their fingers together. At the same time he slid the tip of his penis back and forth over the slippery flesh between her folds.

Willow rocked her hips, called out to him, and he said her name over and over.

Like hot surf crashing over her, the release began and brought her arching up from the bed.

Ben felt her breaking apart and glided into her. She was so tight and he knew he was adding to the physical extremes she already confronted. He kept his elbows pressed into the mattress on either side of her, withdrew slowly, sucking air through his teeth and trying to swallow his own groans. He feared she might be sore from earlier.

"Let go," Willow said. "I want you now." She bit his shoulder, wrapped her legs around his waist and moved. She moved him in and out of her with the power of her beautiful, strong legs.

"I'll always want you," Ben told her.

Ben heard their cries, heard his name on Willow's lips and hers on his own.

The night was black, red, thrashing, hot wet skin fused to hot, wet skin, and his only thought was that he wanted them to share what she felt now forever.

23

Ben had woken up to find Willow sitting on the edge of the bed. Try as he might, he had not managed to lure her back between the sheets with him.

In the heat and passion of the night Willow had accepted his certainty that her sister was safe. With the cool of early morning, she wanted to see Marley for herself.

With Mario gamboling beside, they had jogged through the quiet city to get to Royal Street, and Ben had done what he had to do to get a meaningful kiss before they went into the Court of Angels. He hauled Willow off her feet and persuaded her with his mouth that she should wind herself as close to him as she could and give everything she had to the effort.

"It wasn't enough," he had whispered to her, referring to their repeated lovemaking earlier. "There will have to be more, and soon."

Her great, sleepy green eyes had turned a darker shade before she nipped his bottom lip and he set her down.

They tiptoed through the side gates, leaving them ajar to avoid more noise, and made their way into the courtyard. Willow put her finger to her lips and pushed Ben into the cover of an oleander bush. She picked Mario up and put him into Ben's arms. "Give me time to make sure Marley's there," she whispered. "If she is, I need to talk to her. As soon as I'm inside…well, whatever you decide to do, look after Mario."

She walked a few steps and glanced back. "When I'm finished I'll check Sykes's flat to see if you're there keeping the bed warm." She hovered again. "I wish Nat would let us know they've found Chris."

Ben flared his nostrils and nodded. He stepped deeper into the shade of the bush. With exaggerated care, Willow climbed the green-painted iron steps to Gray and Marley's flat and tapped lightly on the door.

He fantasized that the Fishers might not be at home and Willow would be in bed with him, where she belonged, within minutes.

Wearing a long pink robe and with her titian hair mussed into a madly curly mop, Marley opened the door—peered out at Willow, then pulled her inside and closed the door again.

So much for getting Willow back as soon as he'd like. He leaned against the wall, one foot crossed over the opposite ankle, and contemplated the lengthy shower they had taken together at one point—Willow's idea. He turned up a corner of his mouth. The girl had a fertile imagination.

Mario gave one of his "down" wriggles and was soon trotting from planting bed to planting bed, angel to griffon, on his major pleasure in life: reestablishing territory.

Five in the morning was not Ben's favorite time to be abroad, but as he grew more awake he began to enjoy the piquant snap of cool air.

His phone vibrated in his jeans pocket and he worked it out. His sister, Poppy, was calling. "Yes," he said, keeping his voice low. "It's a bit early, sis."

"I need to talk to you, Ben. It's way overdue."

Ben glanced toward the Fishers' flat. "We'll do it. Just not right now, okay?"

"Is Willow with you?"

He frowned. "You sure you meant to ask me that?"

Her sigh whistled on the phone. "Maybe not. Not that way."

"If you want to talk, talk. I've got a few minutes but if I have to go I'll call you later."

She was silent.

"It's not that I mean to rush you, Poppy. Stuff's happening."

"Dangerous stuff?"

His sister had an unnerving history of knowing when Ben hit rocky roads. "It could be dangerous," he told her. Lying wouldn't put her off. "But under control."

"Let's be straight with each other. The Millets just went through some weird stuff. The police tried to cover it up, but we've all known."

"Who is we all?"

"The obvious ones. Montrachets, Fortunes—all the families."

All the paranormal families in New Orleans. Of course the underground they shared was quietly humming—and gearing up for a potential all-out attack by a hostile force.

"Now there's this new flare-up with Willow," Poppy said.

"Where are Liam and Ethan?"

Another silence followed before Poppy said, "What is it? Aren't I up to dealing with this as well as they are? I used to be good enough to confide in, Ben."

"Oh, God, not now with the equality phobia. It was just a question. I'm going to want to talk to all of you."

"I haven't seen them this morning," Polly said stiffly. "But I'm available now."

"Okay." He had to navigate these waters with care. "I'm in the middle of something. As soon as I'm free, I'll get in touch with you—could be a bit later. That okay?"

Poppy didn't answer immediately, then said, "You didn't say if Willow is with you. I want to talk to her, too."

Ben didn't like the sound of that. "Willow isn't here. When I see her I'll give her the message."

"I'll wait to hear from you." Poppy didn't sound happy.

When he hung up, he looked around for Mario and up at Gray and Marley's flat. The door was still closed and there was no sign of Mario.

The courtyard seemed especially green this early in the day. A subtle breeze quivered through the leaves and flowers, ferns resembled lacy swords and the sound from the fountain was like a thin stream of finely crushed ice.

Ben started an anticlockwise circuit of the many stone sculptures. He had the thought that at some time the Millet children might have made a game of knowing exactly how many there were and hunting for them— maybe racing to see who could be first to find all of them.

He located four very quickly. One of those was so old the face had worn smooth, but the stone had a pink tint that wind and weather had polished to a sheen. Willow had tried to sketch a duplicate of the picture in the book she believed she had seen at her office so he knew what he was looking for.

She had seen it. He wasn't dealing with someone who might fool around and make up stories, not anymore. She never had, but neither had she shared visions or other phenomena. And that brought him to last night's bizarre drama. He hoped Marley would be able to talk Willow through what that had meant. Their talents were closer to each other's than his were to either of them.

Changing sound slightly, the water fell as if it were individual small chunks rather than crushed ice. Each one plinked. Ben turned to the fountain, where the water looked the same as ever—except for a phosphorescence that emerged from the base of the fountain in fragile puffs the color of cloudy, blue-green crème de menthe.

He worked his way toward a corner of the courtyard where the foliage was dense. Three figures, no more than six inches high, surprised him. He hadn't noticed them before.

When he crouched to study them, he found they resembled pointed-eared fairies rather than angels.

Not an elegant angel among them, but they made him think that he had no idea of the dimension of the figure they were looking for.

Keeping an eye on the Fishers' front door, Ben continued on. He was halfway around the courtyard when he encountered Mario tucked behind an appealing griffon even more red than the dog himself. "Hey, buddy," Ben said. "Think you've found a brother there?"

Mario sat up, sentry-straight, his whiskers twitching back and forth.

"I see why she likes you," Ben said, bending over to scratch the dog between his ears. Mario's front feet danced on the soil, and Ben could just about feel the little critter's agitation.

"Come on," Ben said. "Let's finish up. At least I've got a few new candidates to report."

His phone vibrated again. Feeling irritable, he answered, but not before seeing Nat Archer's contact. "Nat," he said. "What's up?"

"It's a frickin' nightmare," Nat said darkly. "Willow's not answering. D'you know where she is?"

"I might."

"Obstructing—"

"Okay, I know where she is and she isn't going anywhere. What's on your mind?"

"Has Chris contacted her?"

Mario ran a circle around the griffon and sat behind it again. Ben frowned. "No, he hasn't, and she's worried sick about him."

"If anything was normal here I wouldn't be spilling my guts to you. But Bucky and I don't have a support system, other than a couple of cops they'd probably certify if they found out what they believe. We've got a new weird case, possibly two.

"A woman name of Caroline Benet came to New Orleans to get on a cruise to the Caribbean. She checked into a hotel overnight so she'd be here in plenty of time. That's it. End of story. Her baggage is gone, she's gone, her bed was never slept in. She never got on the ship. They didn't even realize it at first. Somehow she was checked in for boarding and the baggage put in her cabin—only that was forty-eight hours ago and if she isn't overboard, she never got on in the first place."

Ben rubbed at the bridge of his nose. "And that ties in with our issues how?"

"Damned if I know for sure. No one remembers seeing her get on the ship. The hotel does say she checked in for sure, but not out. She's gone off the face of the earth and from reports we're getting we could have a similar story about a female dealer at Harrah's. Someone called in to say she was sick. Twenty-four hours ago. She's not at her apartment, not anywhere we can find out about. Lives a quiet life. No family or significant other. Oh, and the Benet woman doesn't have any family, either."

"I still don't see any connection."

Nat cleared his throat. "We found something."

Ben waited, and he didn't feel so hot.

"Did Sykes tell you about the eggs the Embran use to restore themselves—sort of? They eat them—including the young inside—to slow their own deterioration."

"Huh?"

"It appears that the Embran who have visited earth—we know of only a few for sure over a lot of years. But they bring the eggs of some of their young—that's the young Embrans who are hatched from eggs—"

"Whoa—gimme a minute here. Eggs?"

"Dammit, Ben. This isn't easy. Just believe what I'm telling you and have Sykes and Marley—and Gray—explain it to you. Embran eat the egg, including the young inside. End of story. It makes them stronger for a while.

"Look, I'll go slow. Apparently, the Embran bring a supply of the eggs with them when they come—the eggs they're all born inside wherever they come from. They keep them handy all the time. I guess they have a selection system, and some eggs get to hatch, others are used to give the mature Embran an infusion of strength. So they believe. The dragon that attacked Marley tried eating some to stop himself from falling apart. Either it doesn't work or it was too late."

"Okay," Ben said slowly. "That sounds crazy and sick."

"Forensics came up with unidentifiable fragments at the Baker and the Green murder scenes, and now at Chloe Brandt's."

"Yes," Ben said, striving to sound patient.

"Now we've got more of the same from a reception room at the hotel where Caroline Benet checked in, and in Chris's apartment. They match the stuff the dragon left behind."

"Oh, my God," Ben said, looking skyward. "You mean we could have the first real connection?"

"Same thing with the woman from Harrah's. Only now we know for sure what the fragments are—we think. Minutely crushed bone—not human."

Ben slumped into a crouch again. "That's useful."

"They think it's birdlike, or small animal of some kind. Probably crumbs that fell from Embran eggs." Nat let out a long sigh. "Will you listen to me? Sounds as if I've lost it."

"Sounds perfectly reasonable to me," Ben said.

"It would."

"Isn't there a bird of some kind that crushes bones?" Ben said, speaking his thoughts aloud without meaning to.

"Yeah," Nat said. "What do they call those?"

"I don't know… Ossifrage! Bone crushers. They let the bones fall to crush them, so they can get at the marrow." Willow had called what she thought she had seen a raptor. A big birdlike creature. He wished he knew how much he could trust her vision.

"Shit," Nat said with a lot of feeling. "First bats, now birds of prey. One word and we'll clear this city of everything but the gangs. We gotta keep this under wraps."

"Shouldn't be hard until the first little kid gets snatched."

"Cut out your tongue," Nat exploded. "I'm waiting for Blades's report on Chloe Brandt. Molyneux will have to know about it—don't know what else to tell him. All he does is hold press conferences and order me to keep my mouth shut. He'd fire me if he wasn't afraid I'd start singing all over."

"Are you safe?" Ben asked.

"Meaning?"

"How badly does Molyneux want to keep you quiet?"

Nat laughed humorlessly. "Badly. But he's a man beyond his Peter Principle. He's thick enough to think he can control me."

"I hope he keeps thinking that."

"Me, too. Wait for my next call." Nat rang off.

While Nat finished his call, Mario had been hard at work digging, and he was an accomplished digger. A hole at the back of the griffon was deep enough to show that as much of the stone piece was set beneath the earth as above.

Ben scraped away more dirt, expecting to find a dog bone. No luck with that.

He wiped the back of a forearm across his eyes. Dogs dug holes—didn't mean a thing. Ben got up and parted a stand of bamboo.

Mario went back to excavating the griffon.

"You can't take it home," Ben told him. "You'd get mud on the rugs."

The dog only grew more determined.

Ben stood back and watched while earth sprayed between Mario's back legs.

With a single, muted bark, Mario plunked his bottom on the ground, tail still wagging, and gave Ben a doggy grin.

"Very nice hole." He gave Mario's shoulders a good rub and got pants of ecstasy for his efforts.

"Okay, Sherlock, let's move on." He skirted the bamboo and gave a sleek angel a cursory glance. He had seen her before and wouldn't call her beautiful.

His little buddy hadn't caught up, and when Ben looked for him, Mario sat where he'd been left, in front of the deep hole he had dug by the griffon.

He whined.

Ben narrowed his eyes and went closer. He got down on his knees to explore.

Excellent eyesight was one of his blessings. All he saw here was the dirty base of the griffon and a hole he had better fill in.

Mario started jumping, all four feet leaving the ground at one time.

"Settle down," Ben said. "You'll get us attention we don't want."

He brushed soil from the griffon's base, admiring the way the sculptor had curled the creature's lion tail tidily around its feet.

Competing with a wet, black and snuffling nose, Ben felt along the stone, noting that it was smoother than he would have expected.

Apparently impatient, Mario tried to help by scratching, and catching Ben's fingers in the process.

"Hey, hey," Ben said, wincing but laughing at the same time. "Ease up. I'll look it over carefully, okay? But I don't think you hid your treasure here."

The nails on his right middle and ring finger slid into a crevice no wider than those nails themselves. He dug at it and mashed both nails for his efforts.

A small section of the stone dropped down and back, revealing a little black space behind. With his hands on his thighs, Ben regarded the tiny concealed space.

Mario wasn't nearly as calm. He ran back and forth, stuffed his nose into the opening, looked at Ben with eyes that just about crossed.

"You managed to hide a goody in there?" Ben said. "I don't think so. I also don't like reaching into places that could have something nasty inside." But he would do it.

Only one finger fitted. He felt around and thought at first there was nothing there. The pad of the finger came to rest on a small, smooth thing that felt metal. Several efforts later, Ben eased a tiny piece of amazingly shiny gold high enough up to grab it with his other hand. He checked the space again but it was definitely empty now.

In his palm rested a gold key no more than an inch long.

24

Sykes answered Ben's telepathic alert immediately… and emerged from his flat looking as sleekly saturnine as ever.

Ben went to meet him. Why hadn't he assumed Sykes would sleep in the flat while his house was occupied? Then he smiled. He hadn't done too much straight thinking the night before.

The two men faced each other. There wasn't a lot of need to talk. Sykes held out his hand and Ben placed the key in his palm.

Sykes turned it over and over again. He looked at the shop and Ben nodded. They needed to get the thing under a microscope so that they could get a good look at it.

"Wait."

Willow's voice stopped Ben, and he turned to see her run down the steps with Marley. Red hair, in two extraordinary shades, and green eyes, also different one from the other, were the only real physical similarities between the sisters, other than their small stature. Marley was much paler than Willow.

"A visual premonition," Willow said, puffing, but with anxiety not fatigue. "Marley explained what I saw." She had changed into jeans and a T-shirt she must have borrowed from Marley.

Sykes's flaring brows rose. "Premonition?"

Willow explained her vision at Sykes's house the night before, while Marley stood by, shifting from foot to foot.

When Sykes didn't answer, Ben dug him with an elbow.

Sykes started. "Yeah," he said. "When you get into the act, you really get into it, Willow. Aren't you the woman who's *normal?*"

"No, dammit. And you don't have to look so pleased about it."

"I got a call from Nat," Ben said. "Can we go inside the shop? I don't think we should risk being overheard."

"You're afraid that monster bird's going to show up," Willow accused. "Who's going to hear us out here?"

No one argued with her, but Marley quickly let them into the gloomy interior of J. Clive Millet.

Behind the counter, Pascal had an office visible through windows on three sides. The four of them hovered outside until they heard footsteps coming down the stairs, and eventually Pascal appeared, swathed in one of his favorite green velvet robes.

"Good idea," Pascal said, to no one in particular, obviously knowing exactly what was going on. "If we put the shop lights on we'll have people at the door. Come on into the office." He let them into the unlocked room and turned on a subdued, green glass-shaded lamp on the desk. It shed a narrow but surprisingly bright pool of light on gleaming wood.

Leather and mahogany suggested a smoking room.

Pascal would never willingly put smoke in his body, but he liked the ambience.

"Where's Gray?" he asked. "He's part of this."

"He knows," Marley said. "He's got a deadline on an article so he's working here today. He'll come down if we need him, otherwise I'll fill him in later."

Marley glanced surreptitiously at Willow, who pulled her eyebrows together.

Ben wondered what they were up to.

"Show me," Pascal said, flipping a folded jewelry display pad open on top of the desk. He moved its white velvet side squarely under the light.

Sykes put the key there. Pascal took a loupe to his eye and bent over to look closely. He flipped the piece over and stared some more. "Take a look," he said, passing the loupe to Sykes.

"Now we need to find my angel," Willow said after taking her turn.

The only one who didn't look bemused was Ben. He said, "Could be."

"What's the connection?" Sykes said.

"I don't know for sure," Willow said, knowing that wouldn't satisfy her brother or the rest of them. "But there is one. See what it says here on one side of the key? Bella. And on the other, Angelus. *Beautiful* and *angel,* in Latin. The man I saw in my office showed me a picture of a stone angel and said she was very beautiful. Beneath her picture it said Angelus."

"So where the hell is she?" Ben said.

The shop doorbell buzzed. And buzzed.

Willow pursed her lips so Ben wouldn't see her grin. She couldn't help thinking, *saved by the bell.*

She left Pascal's office and let her grin stretch when she saw a Mean 'n Green van pulled partway onto the sidewalk. She had been expecting one of her employees to pick her up, but not quite so quickly.

By the time she opened the door of the van, she wasn't so cheerful. "Rock U.? What are you doing here?"

"You're welcome, girl. Do you think I close up shop and come runnin' to help out any good-lookin' female?"

She winced. "Sorry. I was surprised to see you is all."

"We gotta go now," Rock U. said. "Zinnia said that lady who called from the Brandts sounded like she was losing it."

"Zinnia's staying on top of this. She already spoke to me about it this morning."

Rock U. looked away. "Could be she's worried about business," he said, and avoided Willow's eyes. "She talks a tough line, but I don't think she's got anyone else to pick up the slack if her job goes south."

Why hadn't she thought of that? "I don't want any of them worrying." Willow looked over her shoulder, directly into Ben's assessing eyes. "Okay, Rock. I want you to come in just for a second. Whatever I say, you say, yes, or something similar. No personal opinions or ideas. Got it?"

Even in poor light Rock's tattoos were a shock to the eyes. He shrugged and stepped inside.

"Thank you so much for doing this," Willow said. She had been in Marley's flat when she got the call from Zinnia. Marley had heard everything and made it clear that either she went with Willow to do what she could to help at the Brandts, or Marley would join in with the protests that were bound to come when the family found out about the plan.

"Fabio said he'll catch up with us later," Rock said. He whirled his ever-present hunk of keys and tools on their chain. "Could be he's not keen on going over to that house at all, but I said I'd lend a hand."

"You're a prince," Willow said and kissed his cheek. "What's Fabio afraid of?" she whispered while their faces were close.

"Rabid bats? Voodoo? Disappearing like Chris did? Getting sucked into the case at all? Who knows? He's a good guy."

Willow liked him even more for his defense of Fabio. "Sure he is. It's natural to be nervous around all this."

"Well, you people have had plenty of practice," he said with a smile that sent friendly crinkles from the corners of his eyes. "Me, I never could stay away from the action—any action. Er, we do have an audience, kid. They don't look happy to see me. Who's the dangerous-looking guy?"

"Which one?"

Rock U. raised one corner of his mouth. "The one sitting on the desk. I already know Ben Fortune when I see him."

"The other one is my brother, Sykes. And he is dangerous, but only if he's got a reason not to like you."

"Uh-huh. Okay then, I'm fine. I am so likable it hurts sometimes."

Willow led him to Pascal's office and ushered him inside. "This is my friend, Rock U. He's a tattoo artist."

"Really?" Sykes said, and Willow admired how straight he kept his face.

"His shop is in the building with my offices."

"Yeah," Ben said. "We walked through it to get to you, remember?"

In fact, she had completely forgotten. "That's right. Rock's taking Chris's place on a job for me this morning."

Rock said, "Yes."

Willow looked sideways at him. "I'm really sorry, folks, but I'll have to leave now. I'll try to get back as early as possible."

Marley stood up. "Have they said what they want you to do—exactly?"

"No." And Willow didn't appreciate Marley opening the door to questions, not that Marley did so deliberately.

Willow couldn't avoid looking at Sykes's deep blue, very suspicious eyes. "What is this job that's so important you have to leave in the middle of everything?" He looked significantly at the delicate key on its white velvet bed.

"As much as anything else, it's duty," Willow said. "For some reason, Chloe Brandt trusted me. She wanted me to take over running her home and that isn't a decision you make lightly."

"She seemed to," Ben said neutrally.

Willow ignored him. "Her best friend, Vanity, called Zinnia and asked to get hold of me. Vanity's the model. Zinnia thinks fast so she put her off and contacted me directly herself. Evidently, Vanity was even closer to Chloe than I knew. She's going to pieces and begging me to go over there to manage things in the coming days."

"So now you're a funeral director?" Sykes said.

Willow stared at him, and he had the grace to pull in one corner of his mouth in a rueful way.

"If anyone can help them, you can," Ben said, surprising Willow. "You'll stay with her, Marley?"

"Of course. And no one's talking about arranging a funeral, Sykes—that won't happen anytime soon, will it?"

"Probably not," Sykes said, already back to being cynical.

Ben glanced at Rock U. as if he wished the man would disappear. "We'll be around," he told Willow, with emphasis on *around*.

"You're kidding me," Sykes said. "You're going to let her go back into that house?"

"I can't stop her if she wants to go," Ben said, although Willow wasn't fooled by his innocent expression. She wanted to know his angle.

Pascal had been silent to this point. He stirred. "You really think this is a good idea, Ben? I don't believe you like it any more than I do. If that's true, put your foot down."

Rock U. whistled tunelessly and Ben laughed. "If that means you'd like to see me try stopping Willow from doing what she wants to," Ben said to the man, "I can't oblige. I pick my battles. And I always avoid sure losers."

"Yes," Rock U. said, catching Willow's narrow stare.

"I don't like it that I've got something to prove," Willow said. "It's not the only reason to go in there and do the best job I can, but I'm a pragmatist. Nothing will convince people I'm not part of some sort of killing campaign faster than if it gets around that I am in the Brandt house at Vanity's and Val's request. People don't ask murderers into their homes."

"Mrs. Brandt was killed in that house," Pascal said. He folded his arms over his broad chest. "You may not be allowed back there. Have you thought of that? It's a crime scene. Do you want to be filmed for the news being turned away by the police?"

Willow had already thought of this slant. The risk was worth taking. "Got to go now, folks. Keep a TV on so you don't miss any action." They deserved better from her than sarcasm. "That wasn't funny. Sorry. Please don't worry about us."

Walking away from them wasn't easy. Willow and Marley did it anyway.

Rock didn't interrupt their thoughts, but drove quietly Uptown.

Willow turned the pieces of information they had over, tried to fit them together from different directions.

"Embran," Marley said from behind her. "They aren't giving up."

"How many of them are here?" Willow thought aloud. She remembered Rock was listening and didn't say any more.

"That's what Gray was talking about last night," Marley said. "It's not knowing that makes us vulnerable."

Willow nodded. "I shouldn't have waited so long to be part—"

"You're with us now," Marley said. "And remember, none of this is your fault."

"I'm being used."

"We'll find out why," Marley said.

Willow swallowed, sickened by her next thought: would they find out why she had been singled out before the Embran got what they wanted?

25

"You're sure Marley and Willow are okay?" Gray asked Ben. "I've seen what those things are capable of, and it isn't pretty."

Gray was a very unhappy man at the thought of Marley being closer to any danger than she had to be.

It was lunchtime and they'd just arrived at Café du Monde in the French Market.

"Sykes is on it," Ben said, repeating what Gray already knew. "Nat asked for you and me to come. If we made an excuse to stay away, he'd ask too many questions."

"Let him ask," Gray said belligerently. "Marley's my wife, not his."

"You think this is easier for me?"

Gray sighed and shook his head.

Ben slid his arms forward on the table, picking up powdered sugar as he did so. "I didn't know Café du Monde was a cop hangout," he said, watching tourists laughing and snorting the white sugar from platters of hot beignets all over their clothes. The more they brushed at the powder, the more it spread, and not all of them kept laughing.

"It's not," Gray said. In this light, with one side of his face in sunlight, if Ben concentrated, partially using his third eye, he could see faint signs of the vicious scars showing through from the inside of his cheek, scars from wounds that had all but slashed their way to the outside. "Nat's decided he's invisible here because people he doesn't want to see don't think to look for him in this crowd." He would never have found the almost-hidden scars from Gray's childhood if Willow hadn't explained what had happened and given Ben's powers another challenge.

Willow's ability to see hidden scars and read what they meant was unusual.

A kid in an apron slid cups of café au lait in front of them.

He dropped the check on the table and said something Ben couldn't hear over a sudden riff from a clarinet. Ben handed over a couple of bills. The clarinetist sat just outside the metal fence around the café and a banjo player joined him to swing into "The Darktown Strutters' Ball." The guy on the banjo cranked out the words in a pleasingly rusty crackle.

People sweated slowly by on the sidewalk.

"You want to move somewhere quieter?" Gray bellowed.

Ben saw Nat approaching with Bucky Fist and shook his head. "I like it right where we are, and I guess it does what Nat wants it to do. He's something else. How he manages to look like Mr. Congeniality when he's churning inside, I'll never know."

Conversation paused an instant when Nat swung his wide shoulders through the crowd, his skin shining against his white shirt. When Nat grinned, Ben laughed at the sigh he heard from a teenage girl nearby.

Bucky twirled a chair on one leg, set it down

backward and sat astride. He wore his baseball cap back to front over most of his curling, sandy hair and rolled a toothpick in and out of the gap between his two front teeth. He looked like everybody's idea of the charming-goofy all-American brother.

Gray had filled Ben in on Bucky, who was one of the toughest cops Gray—a former supertough cop himself—had ever met. He pointed out that anything less would become a meal for Nat Archer.

"Hey, man," Nat said, gripping first Gray's, then Ben's hand in a hard thumb hook. "How's it going?"

Sliding into a chair, Nat put both hands flat on the table and leaned in. "We may have something. We just got the news."

Ben breathed out through pursed lips.

"Looks like we got a common thread," Bucky said, serious now.

"We'd like to have your cooperation, Ben." Nat's head didn't move a lot, but Ben figured he knew the position of anyone within ten yards.

"Why?" Ben said.

"Willow was there when Chloe Brandt died. She was questioned then, but I've got more to ask. Some of the things I'm going to say to her—the questions I'll ask—could piss her off. Pissed-off witnesses are a pain in the ass. I'm hoping you can make sure she stays reasonable. I'll be using photographs. That's where I want your help, Gray. You and Marley saw the victims we had a few months ago. Blades thinks there are similarities between those and Mrs. Brandt."

"You've heard from Blades," Gray said. "What did he say?"

"Baker and Green, different weapon from Brandt."

Ben thought about that. "So what does it mean? Two killers or two weapons?"

"Blades thinks two weapons, two killers." Nat said. "Copycat." He let his eyelids droop.

"But you don't," Ben said.

The big shoulders rose a couple of inches and stayed there. "We've got three corpses and the cause of death on all three is heart attack. That's a nice way of saying they were scared to death. With some sort of bat—I don't know if there was any bat—dive-bombing you, you could get frickin' scared. The Green woman lost an eye before her heart quit."

Ben wrinkled his nose. "How come that didn't hit the news?"

"You know why." Nat gave him a straight look. "We won't be talking about it anytime soon. Chloe Brandt's face isn't the only place she was cut."

"Define *cut,*" Ben said.

"Similar to Baker, but not the same," Nat told him. "Baker's are puncture wounds. Jabs. Brandt's got multiple short slash wounds made with a very sharp, chisel-ended weapon. Fairly small weapon. There are welts under the wounds that could have come up before or after she was cut. What's on her face is nothing compared to the ones in her scalp. Most jammed into the skull itself before they were yanked out and the next one was made. Blades says nine of them. The hair was soaked with blood."

"The wounds still didn't kill the victim," Bucky said. "This is all some sick thing about fear."

"Yeah," Nat said. "Her neck was broken, too. My take

is one killer, two weapons—this time around. Tried to make it look as if the brass corners on the daybook did some of the damage to Chloe Brandt. Nothing doing there. Blood on the book, okay, but the wounds don't match the corners, and the corners would be demolished if they'd been used. I don't know why they bothered with it."

"You want coffee?" Gray asked, although his own drink was untouched. Nat looked different to Ben, sharp-featured like a man on the hunt. He'd slipped back into homicide detective mode.

"Nah," Nat shook his head. "We need to go. Now."

Ben drained his cup and stood up. "Where? The morgue?"

"Uptown," Nat said. "Brandt house."

26

Even with all the draperies drawn back from the windows and the sun glittering through spotless glass, the Brandt house felt cold and filled with shadows.

Vanity had met Willow and Marley when they arrived. Val sat out by the pool with Preston Moriarty, and they remained there.

Tomorrow night Val was throwing a party to celebrate his dead wife's life. With the help of Marley, Rock U., and promises from Fabio, and the rest of the staff who would be there later, Willow was in charge of what felt to her like macabre—insane, inappropriate—theater.

A tentative suggestion from Willow that the event might be better in a few days threw Vanity into a tantrum. She raged that if the police had their way her dear Chloe would never be put to rest and this memorial was happening *now*. Willow had backed off at once.

Flitting from one room to another, dodging the police, who had sections of the house still closed off, Vanity talked to herself under her breath. A green Hawaiian-print silk tunic and narrow pants, scarlet patent sandals and matching toe and fingernail polish were, she had explained, what would make Chloe happy.

"Those other women arrived," she said to Willow in the kitchen. "I hope they've brought enough."

She was talking about the Potted Ladies, who were to smother both inside and outside of the Brandt home with flowers. "Don't worry," Willow said gently. "The ladies are really good at what they do."

Willow had spoken with the police on-site and they assured her there should be no problem with entertaining the following evening, but she worried that something could change.

"If necessary, we can keep the party to the grounds and kitchen," Willow said, thinking aloud. Vanity's horrified eyes reminded Willow of what a fragile woman she had on her hands—and in charge of a potentially large event.

"It won't be necessary," Vanity said, breathy. "The police said they'll be out by tonight."

"Or tomorrow," Willow said gently. No point in holding back now.

With a Brandt binder open on the kitchen island, Willow went over lists. Working from Chloe's own computerized records, Marley was using the small office off the foyer to call prospective party guests personally. E-mail had gone out first, but the calls were to appease Vanity. Willow had expected the response to be sparse, and then to deal with frustration from Vanity and, possibly, Val, but so far almost everyone had accepted the invitation.

"Chloe did love parties," Vanity said, turning water on and off in the sink—her hands making airy gestures in between. "I know there's something I'm missing that would make it perfect for her."

Chloe hated parties. You told me that yourself, Vanity. She didn't show up for the last one she gave.

Willow was seriously worried about Vanity, whom she would rather see in bed and sedated. When she wasn't following Willow, telling Rock U. yet again how to erect the garden marquee he was clearly comfortable putting up with the help of the men who had delivered it, or leaning over Marley while she made calls, Vanity stood at a distance from the taped-off foot of the main stairs. Each time she could get close enough, she asked when the last traces of Chloe's blood could be cleaned away.

Abruptly fixating on something in the grounds, Vanity walked out of the sliding doors leading to the terrace. She kept on walking until she reached Val and Preston, who both got up and hugged her.

A movement caught Willow's attention: Marley hovering outside the kitchen door, trying to see who was there.

"You look like a scared rabbit," Willow said. "Vanity's gone outside."

Marley slipped into the room, a sheaf of papers under one arm. "Now she wants costumes," Marley said, her brow furrowed. She gripped the edge of a counter hard with one hand.

"Sit down," Willow said. "You're letting this get to you. My other people will be here just as soon as they can—one of them can make the calls, or I will."

Looking past Willow at a section of blank wall, Marley's frown deepened. She narrowed her eyes and the frown turned very angry.

"What is it?" Willow said, glancing around.

Marley shook her head once and turned her back.

"Costumes. I've got to call everyone back and tell them to come in costume."

"No, you don't," Willow said. "I'll deal with it. Vanity isn't thinking."

"She wants a masquerade ball. Masks. High drama, is what she said." Marley faced Willow again, but her eyes slid off to look in the same direction as before. "That isn't appropriate," she said, barely moving her lips.

"What?" Jumpy, Willow chafed her arms. "Oh, you mean the ball idea? There isn't going to be a ball if I can stop it."

Marley went to the sink and looked out into the grounds where Vanity stood with Preston and Val. The three of them were nodding with evident enthusiasm.

"You want to bet she's not telling them about this incredible idea of hers now?" Marley said. "It's going the extra hundred miles, she says. Shows the level of adoration Chloe's friends had for her. *Adoration* was the word she used."

"Wow. That would probably mean decorating the place to theme."

"Yeah, fake stone balustrades, soaring statues, Greek columns, fainting couches, velvet, gold—you should have heard it." Marley paused for breath. She looked repeatedly at the spot over Willow's left shoulder. "How would anyone do something like that anyway?"

"No problem," Willow said, almost ashamed that the challenge appealed to her. She started mentally lining up the people she'd call for props.

"Get off the counter," Marley said sharply. "Okay, that's it. You're annoying."

Willow's stomach flipped. "What did I do?"

"Not you—*him.*" She put her hands on her hips. "You want to bet on that? Give her a chance. Go on—see what happens."

Bemused, Willow turned around.

She couldn't see anything unusual.

"That's not fair," Marley said. "And don't tell me not to let her hear what I'm saying to you. It's your own fault—I'm not going to let her stand there wondering what's going on. You give our talents a bad name. I'm not asking you to go out of your way—just open up to her. If she can see you, she can see you—why should that be so bad? It's all in the family."

A wavering form, with a human shape that faded in and out, but never became clear, sat cross-legged on the central island.

Willow peered closer, and put a hand over her mouth. "Sykes?"

"He loves being invisible when he communicates with me telepathically," Marley said. "Let him in."

"He's not invisible," Willow pointed out. "Not completely."

"That's because he's letting you sort of see him. I told you she would, Sykes. Have a little faith in your own family, you oaf."

"That's the respect I get," Sykes communicated to Willow. *"I'm here to save your rears from ghouls and goblins and what thanks do I get? Insults, that's all."*

Hearing him like that shook Willow, but not as much as seeing his transparent body behaving like a veil of shifting smoke on the counter.

"Did you hear that?" Marley said in Willow's mind. *"He's here to save us."*

Willow swallowed and kept her mouth shut. *"We can take care of ourselves, you overgrown sprite,"* she thought.

"Wow," came back from Sykes. *"Haven't we told you for years how abnormal you really are? Now maybe you believe us."*

"Those three are coming back," Marley said aloud. "What are we going to tell them if they want their silly masquerade ball?"

"First, Sykes, get lost. If Vanity saw you like that she'd completely lose it. If she hasn't already."

"You and I can see him," Marley said to Willow. *"That's because he wants us to. Don't worry about them."*

Sykes hopped to the floor and disappeared completely.

"Does he do that a lot?" Willow said.

"Whenever I feel like it." Sykes voice was too loud in Willow's head, and she jumped.

Vanity came into the kitchen with Val and Preston. This was the closest Willow had been to Val since she arrived that morning. Preston looked drawn, but Val looked like hell. He seemed to have lost pounds overnight. His face drew back beneath his cheekbones and purple slashes underscored his eyes. His hands moved incessantly from his pockets to his face to be held down beneath his upper arms and back to his pockets.

"Masquerade," Vanity announced, her dark eyes feverishly bright. "Start making those callbacks, Marley. Please, darling. This is going to be completely memorable."

"Okay," Marley said slowly, looking at Willow. "What should I tell them exactly?"

"Masquerade ball," Vanity said promptly.

"It's very short notice," Willow said tentatively.

Vanity ignored her. "And we're going to need a videographer. We'll show it at the funeral just as soon as they release Chloe's body." Bright red spots burned high on Vanity's cheeks. "I can give you names for video people."

"Vanity," Val said faintly. He hadn't shaved, and his beard was many shades darker than the surfer-blond hair. "Are you sure this isn't in really bad taste?"

"Damn, one of them is still sane after all."

Willow really wasn't comfortable with Sykes's disembodied voice. She crossed her arms and tapped a foot.

"What?" Sykes sounded tetchy.

"I was thinking I didn't like your disembodied voice too much, is all." She cleared her throat. *"That's a joke."*

Sykes didn't respond.

Marley chuckled softly behind her hand.

The stares they got from Preston and Val wiped out any banter. Fortunately, Vanity was soaring in the rosy haze of her costume party bubble and hadn't noticed anything different.

"Off you go," Vanity said to Marley. "Willow, the man doing the marquee is impossible. He's rude—that is, he doesn't talk to me. And the tattoos—awful. Get rid of him."

"Sorry," Willow said. "That's Rock U. and he's excellent. Let him get on with what he's doing. I'll have him change the decorations. What do you think about the flowers?"

The Potted Ladies had already transferred galvanized buckets filled with white flowers through a side gate and they were lined up in front of a hedge. They were adding set pieces to the collection—also white.

Vanity tapped her fingernails against her teeth. "I think red."

"Bloody hell," Preston muttered.

"*Appropriate.*" This from Sykes, wherever he was.

"Spray them," Vanity said.

"Leave it to me," Willow told her. "Really, Vanity, don't worry about a thing. As long as you can answer our questions as we go along, you have nothing to worry about. We'll take care of the event and the cleanup."

"Red flowers?" Val said vaguely.

"It's the color of love," Vanity told him, placing a palm against his cheek. "Like your love for darling Chloe."

He nodded.

"I prefer to use theatrical costumiers for these things," Willow said. "I can get Sybil Smith over to talk about what you want to wear," she told Vanity.

"We'll all need costumes. Including the help. Everyone. I want it absolutely perfect. Venetian! That's it, Venetian is what we want. Jesters…"

She rushed from the kitchen, and Willow heard her voice raised all the way to the foyer. Vanity was demanding the attention of whoever was "in charge for the authorities."

Marley cringed. "So it's a Venetian masquerade. I'd better get started with the calls. Do I ask if they need any advice on getting costumes in a hurry? Or say they don't have to be in costume if they don't want to?"

"You don't know our friends," Preston said, slapping Val on the back. "They'll be in costume and they'll knock your socks off. Excuse us. Come on, Val, we'd better stick with Vanity."

"Is she cracking up?" Val said.

"Close," Preston said.

Willow caught the door before it could close behind the two men and followed them out. She also wanted to see what the police were up to. The staircase was going to be integral to Vanity's extravaganza.

"Val," the woman called when she saw him. "Your wedding video. Have that on hand, please. We'll use that as a backdrop to the toast tomorrow evening."

Through the front door walked Nat Archer with the detective whose name Willow didn't remember, and both Gray and Ben.

"Didn't you already do that?" Vanity said to a technician in a white coverall. He was suctioning the stair risers, sucking fibers into a clear bag attached to a powerful vacuum.

"No, ma'am."

They could hear heavy footsteps overhead.

"When are you going to be finished?" Vanity asked.

"Still not sure, ma'am."

"Above your pay grade to know that?" Vanity said, her nose wrinkling. "Who *would* know?"

She finally noticed the four men who had just arrived. "What do you want?" she asked. "You can't just come walking in here."

"You met Detective Fist and me last night and earlier today," Nat said. "We have more questions, ma'am."

"Why?"

"We know more than we did last night," Nat said, frowning.

Vanity stared blankly.

"We can see how things go here, but we may have to ask you to come downtown later. Willow, stay where I can find you."

Ben didn't take his attention from Willow's face. She had to look back at him, and he didn't attempt to hide his longing. And something else. Cautiously, she reached toward his mind to ask what was wrong.

She was shaken when she realized he knew what she wanted, but was shutting her out.

"I have to leave," Vanity said. She turned to Preston. "I need to get over to the agency for an hour. I completely forgot. Could you drive me, darling?"

"Of course." He pulled keys from a pocket in his khaki shorts.

Marley hurried away to the office she had been using, catching Gray's hand and pulling him with her as she went.

"Would you rather come downtown now?" Nat asked Vanity.

"Go on into the sitting room," Val said. He looked worried. "Vanity was Chloe's dearest friend. She's under a lot of stress."

Nat made a sympathetic noise.

"I'm not talking to you now," Vanity said. "It'll have to wait."

"I'm afraid it can't. What I need to ask first is what you were doing around the dance hall on Rampart yesterday."

27

"Why do they want to talk to me?" Vanity said, her voice pleading. She gripped Ben's forearm, and her long nails dug in hard. "Why don't they all go away and leave me to grieve in peace?"

Ben had been introduced to Vanity for the first time right after Chloe's murder, which didn't make them buddies. He had recalled when he met Chloe. She had come to Fortune's to see Poppy about a charity project.

"It's a hard time," he said, patting Vanity's hand. "Best get the formalities out of the way. They're only routine."

"He's not acting like they're routine." Vanity nodded to Nat. She sounded whiny. "If it was, he could wait until we've honored Chloe, couldn't he?"

"Ma'am," Nat said, casting Ben a sympathetic look. "Time is really important in these investigations. Things change fast. The longer we take to go over everything, the less chance we've got of finding anything that could be useful in our investigation."

A flash of brilliant red hair, and a knifelike glare from a pair of greener than green eyes, and Willow put herself in the center of the melee. Her attention was focused on Vanity—when it wasn't pinning Nat or Ben.

"You're grasping at straws," she announced. "And you're deliberately trying to scare Vanity."

Nat's eyebrows shot up and he looked questioningly at Ben.

"Willow?" Ben said, as mildly as he could. "What is it?"

"This isn't a good time to patronize me," she said. "You've made it clear how close you really feel to me. You shut me out. Nat, this doesn't seem like much of a way to run an investigation to me."

Nat looked at her askance. "I'm sure you'll explain what you just said later. Bucky, go ahead and make sure they're ready to monitor the interviews from downtown." He sounded tightly wound, and evidently Willow sensed it, too, because she took a step backward.

"Willow," Ben said urgently. "Over here."

She tried to stand her ground, but he placed an arm around her and walked them rapidly away from the group. "What d'you mean, I shut you out?" he said.

"A little while ago I asked you what was wrong, what was going on, and you ignored me. I felt the wall go up."

He smiled before he could stop himself.

Bad move.

"Don't laugh at me," Willow said. "I'm tired of your family putting me down."

She caught him off guard. He kept his hold on her and waited for her to look at him. He shook his head, nonplussed.

Willow met his eyes and took a very deep breath at the same time. "Why didn't you answer me?"

"Did you signal, Willow?"

"Signal?"

"Do you see how many people are around here? They're all talking, and Marley's putting in comments, to say nothing of Sykes. I know you can't see him, but—"

"I did see him in the kitchen earlier when Marley told him to show himself to me, and he talked to me," she said, sounding defensive and embarrassed at the same time.

"But you started a telepathic conversation with me?"

"I don't know what I did—just the same as before, I guess. You and I have been talking like that more and more. The first day you got back from Kauai you were in the shop when I got there, and I heard you talk to me in my mind."

"I signaled first," he said, realizing she might not understand what he meant. "I signaled but you pretended not to hear." He didn't want to make this difficult for her. "Of course. Whatever happened when you just tried to reach me was a misunderstanding. I didn't hear you, Willow. It's all about concentrating on the mind you're looking for. Then there's confirmation that you've been recognized, and you enter—if everything's okay. It happens almost instantaneously. We just need more practice together."

"Of course."

He saw her decide to let the topic go. Okay for now, but they would have to straighten these things out. "What's the deal over Nat asking Vanity some questions? He told me he wanted to ask you a few more, too—that's why I came." *Careful.* "He mentioned it and I wanted to be here with you."

"How do you know Vanity?" she said.

"I met her right here after Chloe died. That was it."

"Of course." Willow gave a short nod. "And Gray—

why is he here? It feels like a special operations force came to take us all down."

"C'mon." He squeezed her, and they both closed their eyes a moment. "Gray's here because Marley's with you, and he doesn't like her too far out of his sight. That's something I share with him—we can be a bit possessive with the women we— With our women."

Her glance said she knew what he'd almost said. He'd like her to look more pleased about it.

"Do you know what an energy sentient is?" Willow asked.

He made the subject switch fast. "Yeah. Someone who feels energy others don't—and some of them—"

"Translate what the energy is and what it means and why someone has it. Marley thinks that's what I am. One of those. She thinks I have it strongly. If I do, what was I picking up on last night when I saw that horrible thing going after her?"

Ben looked at the others, who were clearly not having a happy conversation. "Did Marley make a suggestion about it?"

Willow hesitated. "I didn't exactly tell her the whole thing."

"What did you leave out?"

"That it was her I saw."

He screwed up his eyes. "Any reason for not telling her that you want to share?"

"I didn't want to frighten her. Visual premonitions, energy sentience, it's feeling real to me and scares me— a lot. Maybe it wasn't Marley I saw. Maybe it was me. It was me when I went outside from the room upstairs after Chloe died. Remember?"

His tightened grip made her gasp. "Don't you know who you saw at Sykes's place? You said you did."

She shook her head, no. "I don't, not for sure."

Ben didn't believe her, but he also didn't blame her for wanting to shield her sister. "Okay. That episode could have been brought on by stress, too. Let's see what Nat and Bucky need from you. Probably nothing much."

"I think it's going to make me mad," she said. "Even madder."

"Willow," Nat said when Ben walked her back. "I'd like you to stand by, please. I'll get to you as soon as I can."

"I'm going to be around, Nat, but not standing anywhere for long. In case you haven't noticed, we're trying to arrange a memorial here."

"Bad timing," he said. "And inappropriate."

"Damn you," Vanity said. "I cleared this with your people, and they said you'd all be out of here today."

"I don't think they did," Nat said. "Are you sure you weren't told they'd be clear by tomorrow—we hope?"

Vanity spun toward Val. "We're working around them until they're gone. And we didn't ask for an opinion about what we choose to do. Did we, Val?"

"No." He rubbed her back. "Please stay calm. Does this have to be done now, Detective?"

"Sir, your wife died under very unusual circumstances last night. This is all perfectly normal procedure. We'll take as little time as we can."

This was awful, Willow thought. They were trying to make a case against Vanity. "Vanity couldn't have done it." She heard her own words, explosive, and the silence that followed. "She couldn't."

They all stared at her.

"Don't pretend you don't know what you're up to, Nat. You've got to have someone to pin these deaths on, and you've got some crazy idea about Vanity."

Ben reached for her, but she shrugged away. She didn't feel too steady on her feet, but she did feel plenty mad. "What's that nasty man's name? Molyneux. The chief of police. He wasn't nice to Marley when she had so much trouble. And then—after all that and everything Gray and Marley did to solve the crime for the cops— they lost the people they caught!"

"Who told you that?" Nat said sharply, his eyes narrowed and furious.

Who had told her? "I…I just know," she said. *Someone had told her.* She frowned at Nat. There was something she was almost remembering. Had Nat told her himself?

"Ben?" Nat stared hard at Ben.

"You don't speak to her like that," Ben said. "I don't know what you're suggesting, but I don't like it."

Vanity leaned against the wall. All color had drained from her face. "Me?" she whispered. "You think I… You think I killed Chloe?"

"I did not say that, ma'am," Nat said, glaring at Willow.

An officer near the stairs cleared his throat and said, "You might want to know the chief's been on TV again, sir. I hear he just got off. He commented about a possible new suspect."

"Shit," Bucky Fist said with feeling. "Molyneux held another press conference? That bastard's tongue needs to be cut out." He cleared his throat and the expression from his face. "You want me to check with the chief before we carry on, Nat?"

If Bucky's face showed little emotion, Nat's had taken on the clear unconcern of a choirboy. "That won't be necessary. This is all in a day's work."

"We'll call off the celebration," Val said. He held Vanity's hand. "It can be done when all this nastiness is cleared away."

"It never will be if we don't go ahead now," Vanity said, her voice rising. "The invitations are out and we're going ahead. We owe this to Chloe."

Willow moved closer to Ben again. "This is out of control," she said quietly.

"You've got that right," he said. "Best to stay quiet and let them work it out."

"Vanity," Willow said, looking only at her friend. "You shouldn't talk to any of these people. Not at all."

Ben muttered something unintelligible under his breath.

From behind them, Willow heard the kitchen door open and turned to see the Potted Ladies sliding buckets of red roses over the tiles with the aid of a cloth runner.

"Not now, please," Willow said.

"Good," Vanity said at the top of her voice. "Wonderful. You're every bit as versatile as Willow says you are. Put them here in the foyer, ladies."

Preston Moriarty, who had appeared comatose, stepped forward and helped with the flowers. Willow didn't hear what he said, but the Potted Ladies disappeared back the way they'd come.

Preston gathered himself visibly. "Let's calm down. Vanity, sometimes we have to put up with being just like everyone else. Follow the rules, dearest, and go answer their little questions."

Nat actually smiled warmly at the man. Bucky was already in the sitting room setting up recording equipment, and Vanity started to follow, very slowly, very reluctantly.

The kitchen door slammed open and banged against the wall this time. Rock U., sans shirt, his multihued and muscular torso glowing with sweat, swept in, his black leather pants clinging even tighter in the heat.

"Are the cops bothering you?" he asked Willow.

She almost laughed. When had she gathered such an army of sympathizers? "I'm fine," she told him.

"They've been spreading the so-called news about Vanity," he said as if the woman weren't standing there. "Apparently, she was at the dance hall and at that bakery shop, too. Billy Baker's."

"This is bloody wonderful," Nat said. "We're going to have to take this downtown."

"Zinnia called me," Rock said. He looked around until he located Vanity. The big breath he took suggested he didn't relish dealing with her. "Zinnia's Willow's office manager. She's somethin' else—a really good woman. And she knows a load of crap when she sees it."

Vanity's lips curled a little, but she struggled to obliterate the disdain. "Does she? That must be useful."

"That chief of police is a publicity hound. He's afraid of losing his job so he's looking for a patsy, and you're it."

Vanity seemed about to have hysterics.

"There, there," Rock U. said, as if she were a sad child. "You've got sensible friends all around you. We'll take care of you."

"Why would Vanity be at some dance hall anyway?" Preston Moriarty said. "When was that supposed to be?"

"The night of the party here," Willow said, remembering her last conversation with Chris, and meeting Vanity for the first time a while later. "You got held up at a shoot, Vanity. You said that."

"Oh, my." Vanity's face cleared a little, but her eyes were troubled. "Of course. I talked to Val and Willow when I arrived. And you, Preston. I got here late and felt so bad because I'd told Chloe I'd watch over things. Not that I needed to with Willow here."

Willow gave a weak smile of thanks.

"The shoot was at the dance hall, not that I knew something awful was happening in the building," Vanity said. "Isn't that the pits? We use all kinds of backdrops. It was one of those funky collections—Saber Song—everyone knows Saber Song's designs. They did a lot of poses on the bar. It went beautifully. Tear-away stuff. Very sexy. It's all about the underwear—what there is of it."

Preston laughed. "It's all about license for public nudity, Vanity, baby. I bet the house was packed."

She glowered at him.

Nat puffed up his cheeks and stared at Willow, then Ben. "Think we could meet for dinner later?"

The invitation struck Willow as bizarre, but she heard Ben agree, and felt him squeeze just above her elbow.

"The marquee's finished, ma'am," Rock said to Vanity. "They need your advice on the swags of red velvet, Willow."

If I can make it until the day after tomorrow, I may not lose my mind. Willow said, "Yes."

"I told the guys from the prop shop the space is big in here, but not that big," Rock said. "They want to know if they can set up the bridge and the palace facades in the garden. The fence is going to have to come down anyway to get everything in, but they'll make sure it all goes back. You won't even know anything was different afterward."

"Thanks," Vanity said stiffly. "Will you be here tomorrow evening?"

"Wouldn't miss it," Rock said, showing all of his strong teeth. "No way would I miss seeing the gondola put into the pool."

28

Sykes avoided his uncle Pascal's probing gaze.

They were behind the shop, in the Court of Angels, and Sykes was doing mental jumping jacks trying to sort out the mess he had made for himself. He should have dealt with it before leaving the Brandt house. Ben was not going to understand that impulsive decision.

Sykes looked at the square of very blue sky over the courtyard. *I multitask really well.* He thought about that one and tried it again: *I multitask really well. I didn't need to stay at the Brandt house to know what's going on there.*

How would that sound to Ben? "I knew you could handle it, Ben, and I could always get there fast. Seriously, I knew you'd rather I got back to Royal Street and tried to figure out what that key is for."

One glance at Pascal and he knew he shouldn't have practiced his speech aloud.

"So that's it?" Pascal said in a voice loaded with disbelief. "One of your sisters is stuck being grilled by the police, so you decided you'd slide out and come back here to play sleuth. You like the idea of working it out on your own, don't you? Why is everything a contest with you?"

"Give me some credit. I got bored hanging around is all."

Pascal didn't look convinced. "You want to find out what that key fits. You've admitted it."

"If it fits anything at all," Sykes said. He'd had a hell of a day and felt reckless. "But okay, I'm guilty. I'm a curious guy—who wouldn't want to figure the thing out?"

His decision to return to the Court of Angels was partly for self-protection—his mind had been about to explode with the inane babbling Uptown—and partly because he couldn't think of anything for long except the key.

"I'd better get over to that house," Pascal said. "Ben must have had a reason for wanting you there. I'll take your place."

Sykes inclined his head and counted slowly and silently to ten before he said, "No, Uncle, that's a lousy idea. There are too many people there already. It's a crowded scene. And I'm still watching and listening." Which he was. "Ben asked me to stay until he got there himself. He's there now." Hey, that was true. Just showed you how the simplest explanation was usually the best.

Pascal and Sykes stood in the planting bed where the little red griffon had hidden so well for a century or so. Sykes doubted they could be seen from the shop and only someone on one of the high balconies around the flats would have a chance to catch sight of them in the dense foliage.

Marley's Winnie and Willow's Mario sat, side by side, like two more conspirators in conference. Winnie kept staring at Mario, whose concentration on the griffon never wavered.

Persuading Pascal to stay in the shop and let Sykes deal with his search on his own had gone nowhere, and now Sykes was *really* frustrated with the audience.

"Anthony isn't happy about all this upheaval," Pascal said. Anthony was his personal trainer. "You know how he worries about my blood pressure."

"Yeah, I do. So let me do the worrying for all of us. It was supposed to be my...job," he finished weakly and bent way forward to look at his feet. Damn his big mouth. He had always avoided showing any bitterness over being usurped by Pascal, but now he had carelessly hurt the man.

Pascal's big hand descended consolingly on Sykes's shoulder, and he breathed more easily again. He was grateful for this understanding uncle.

"You know I think it's garbage, don't you?" Pascal said. "The *curse.* I know all about the old stories, the disasters that happened in Belgium and London, the fear that the family could lose everything here in New Orleans and be forced to move on and start over again. Bunk. We're not in the seventeen hundreds anymore—if it was even relevant then."

Sykes shook his head slowly. "I don't think we should go into that. You're in, I'm out and that's the way it'll stay."

Pascal grumbled to himself. He'd never made any secret of how he resented getting stuck with a responsibility he had never expected to have. "I won't be around forever," he said darkly.

"How do you think the dog figured out where the key was?" Sykes said, mostly to change the subject.

"Who says he did? Dogs dig. They always did, Sykes.

This time a dog happened to find a little key that probably doesn't mean a thing."

Sykes grinned at him. "Very good. Lots of passion there. That dog—" he pointed at Mario "—wouldn't leave this spot until he had Ben digging in the dirt with him and defacing that damn griffon. Explain that away as *dogs dig.*"

Pascal chuckled. "You said you wanted to concentrate on looking for this angel of Willow's."

"Yeah, I did." And he still hoped he'd have the luck to be alone if he found her and, in addition, have a chance to try communicating with the fickle inmates of the courtyard. Ben's accounts of interacting with all these carvings was driving Sykes to extremes. He had started hallucinating about carrying on meaningful dialogue with some loose-lipped, superinformed stone buddies of Ben's, who were just dying—well, maybe it was too late for that—to lead him to the great truths that would clear up any Millet mystery questions for good.

And while they were at it, they could explain the real reason the Embran had singled out the Millets for their deadly attention.

But he wasn't comfortable chatting up the stones with Pascal watching him. Ben was the only one who had ever suggested he could communicate with the angels—something Pascal wouldn't know about.

"You don't want me watching you?" Pascal said, startling Sykes. "I wonder why." There had never been any doubt about Pascal's abilities, but Sykes had just been careless with his shield and that wasn't like him.

"No, you weren't careless," Pascal said, smiling broadly. "You forgot one of those pesky little exceptions to the rules."

Sykes rarely thought about the *rules* at all. "I'm a natural, remember? Completely. I don't have to think about exceptions. I just know my stuff."

"Unless the Mentor decides to intervene," Pascal said, only slightly smug. "I think we can take it that we're in serious trouble, nephew, because you just got opened up to me."

Sykes squinted in the dappled light. "You're telling me the Mentor is pulling strings around here?"

"That's what I said. I couldn't get into that armored mind of yours if you didn't want me to—not without help. The Mentor thinks we should be working together. What else can it mean?"

"Damned if I know."

Pascal scowled. "You heard the proof. For once, do as you're told."

Sykes pretended to be in pain. "Can't," he moaned. "Compliance messes with my mind."

He quit the act as suddenly as he'd started. Bamboo canes clicked lightly together, their leaves rustling. The sound grew a little louder. Mario cocked his head to one side. Winnie got up and turned in rapid, tight circles.

"You're right," Sykes told Pascal. "Something has intervened. I can feel it. What else could it be but the Mentor? Let me hang around out here a bit. I need to think. I'll be in shortly."

Suspicious was a weak word for the expression on Pascal's face. He opened his mouth, and Sykes prepared for argument, but his uncle swept silently past him, snatching up Winnie as he went. Everyone knew Pascal had a very soft spot for the Boston terrier.

Sykes paused, concentrating on first one, then

another angel. "Are you having a nice day?" he said, and checked quickly over his shoulder to make certain he was alone.

He caught sight of two small figures and stooped to see them. *Fairies.* "Do you have anything to say?"

Damn, he was being watched. Hair stood up on the back of his neck and he turned around again.

Mario stared at him—into his eyes—unblinking and without a hint of subservience.

"You're a dog," Sykes said. "What's with you?"

Watched by a dog!

Mario dropped to his stomach and rested his head on his paws. His ears and whiskers wiggled back and forth.

The small compartment in the base of the griffon was shut again. Sykes crouched and pushed it open. It surprised him that it moved easily when it was so old and unused. The sophistication of the action impressed him. As a sculptor he knew the intricacies of working with stone and had never even considered concealing anything inside one of his pieces.

He put a forefinger into the space and felt around. The griffon was made of a red stone, North African, he thought, and the inside had been smoothed. His fingernail caught on a ridge and he scraped at it.

His heart beat harder and faster, and he gradually slid out another key. About an inch long. Minutely inscribed with Bella on one side and Angelus on the other.

Identical?

From his pocket, he took the one Ben had found and put it, side by side, with the second one, then he lay one on top of the other.

Not quite identical. This one had a different configuration in the serrations.

Ben would be pissed he had missed the second one. If he had.

Sykes poked around inside the griffon again, using his fingernails to dig for other treasures. There were none. He put Ben's find in his right pocket, and his own in the left.

He had better not forget what Pascal had said about the Mentor and working together. He stood up. Ben would have to know about the new find, too. But Sykes would rather work on this his own way, in his own time—and without help.

"Sykes, are you out here?"

It was a woman's husky voice, familiar, although he couldn't place it. He'd rather know who she was before he committed himself.

"Oh, there you are." Poppy Fortune batted her way through the bamboo to join him in his supposedly hidden bower. She pulled up when she saw him. "I'm interrupting something. Sorry. I didn't really want to see you anyway."

"Hey, hey." He dodged to cut off her exit. "It's fine. I was…finding the dog."

She glanced at Mario. "You were hiding," she said. "The dog just happened to be here."

He barely stopped himself from gaping. "Why would I be hiding in my own backyard?"

"Because you're up to something secretive, and you don't want anyone else around. It's fine, really. I know how you feel. Happens to me all the time."

Sometimes hanging out with paranormal people could

be a drag—especially when you got so accustomed to them that you forgot they might not be what Willow liked to call "normal." It had never struck him to wonder what Poppy's particular talents might be, but now he knew she probably followed body heat to its source—which would be how she found him—and she was very intuitive. Knowing the Fortunes, that was only scratching the surface of her powers.

Tall and really nicely shaped, Poppy had grown from an angular little girl with eyes too big for her face, into a gorgeous, exotic-looking woman. If he didn't know otherwise, he'd wonder if she was Italian, or Eurasian, maybe. He liked the purple leather vest she wore—laced down the front—over a tight black T-shirt and with equally tight black leggings. The higher on the vest, the more widely the laces parted, to allow for the full breasts she'd developed while he wasn't looking.

Hmm.

She frowned. "What's wrong?" she said.

"Not a thing that I can see," Sykes told her. "I was just thinking we've known each other a long time—sort of. We don't really know each other at all, though, do we?"

Her gaze slid away. "Sometimes you seem very familiar to me. Other times you're a stranger. I figure that's how you like it. Man of mystery."

He started to laugh.

Poppy cut him off. "I came to make a confession, and you won't be laughing by the time I'm finished."

That sobered him. "I don't hear confessions. Not my purview." He thought for a moment. "Did you do something I'm going to regret?"

"That wasn't my intent, but yes."

"Huh." He shook his head. "Do we need to go somewhere for this? We could use my flat." He thought some more. "That probably wouldn't be such a good idea. Can I offer you a step on those stairs over there? We've got plenty of them."

"I just want to get this over with."

He held back a bush for her to pass and followed her into the courtyard. Poppy went to the fountain and sat on the edge. Sykes almost warned her about the spray, but thought better of it. He perched beside her instead.

She remained silent, examining the backs of her elegant hands.

Sykes found himself at peace just waiting for her to be ready to talk.

The little red dog emerged and came to sit at his feet. Sykes scratched his head absently and closed his eyes for a long moment. They felt blurry. When he opened them, he remained utterly still, allowing a pale, iridescent green haze to waver over the scene before him.

Lightly came the suggestion of chatter. It disguised itself in a breeze, but he heard individual voices. They argued and cajoled by turns, and Sykes's nerves swelled with excitement. He breathed deeply and turned his head toward the griffon bed. Again and again he was moved to look in that direction.

Clumps of bamboo bent, curled over almost double and straightened, slowly and gently, to stand erect again.

Mario put his head on Sykes's foot and sighed.

"You are still the one."

A man's voice, deep, with some European accent spoke in his mind. Why did Poppy have to choose now to come here?

"Because she has made a mistake that could have cost us dearly. It will be up to you to decide how to deal with her. Think ahead, Sykes. It will not always be today, although you will remember everything you have seen and experienced. Perhaps Poppy has suffered enough."

Who was it? Was it—

"The Mentor. I am Jude, the one some called Judas, but there were others who went before me. I am their voice, their presence."

What could this…person, want from him?

"Be ready. Be watchful. Support Willow and Ben, for they are at the heart of this episode. You can expect more to come. So much is at stake—your whole world as you know it."

Sykes shivered. He looked at the side of Poppy's face and noted that her eyes were closed, her hands relaxed, as if she slept.

"Here."

Almost afraid to raise his eyes, Sykes did so and saw a man with long, gray-streaked black hair. At his neck white linen gleamed. His black, cutaway coat had tails and he was a handsome figure. That thought came and immediately the notion followed that this was someone familiar.

"Yes, you look like me, but why shouldn't you? We are both Millets and we are two of a kind. Listen for me, but do what you know in your heart must be done. The peril is far greater than they know—your authorities as you call them—so much greater. I will not be far away, Sykes, unless an intervention is too powerful even for me to immediately overcome. But trust. We will fight together, all of us."

He inclined his head, his blue eyes smiling, and the manifestation dissolved.

Gasps, little cries of wonder, blended into a new breeze, and more excited chuckling. And, just as abruptly, all was quiet and still again.

Poppy opened her eyes slowly, looking at him with such concern he almost reached out to touch her.

"I've decided I'll do whatever you say," she told him. Her long hair flowed around her shoulders, so dark it shone with a blue light. "It's about Ben."

"Okay." His attention remained with the Mentor. He hadn't wanted the man to go, and now he wanted him to return.

"I did something I'm ashamed of, and I'm afraid it might never be completely corrected. I love my older brother so much. When we were growing up he was my hero. I went everywhere with him that he would let me go. He's still my hero. I had a very hard time understanding that he grew into a man with a man's needs and desires—and that he could not remain mine. You see, I thought of him as mine."

Sykes smiled at her. He picked up one of her hands and held it between both of his. "Brothers and sisters are often very close. And they stay close. Some things change, but the bonds are still there."

Her eyes filled with tears. "I have broken the bonds with Ben. Once he knows what I did, he will never feel the same about me."

He thought about what she said. "Are you still doing whatever it was?"

"Oh, no!"

Rubbing the back of her hand, he ducked his head

toward her and tried to make her smile at him. He got the faintest tilt of her lips that only served to send huge tears rolling. She quickly brushed them away.

"If this—whatever it is—is behind you now, why mention it to him? Find ways to make up for it." He laughed. "He loves to eat. Make him food."

Poppy laughed a little. "Yes. But I think the damage I did may never really mend. I caused doubt and pain. They ran deeper than you can imagine, and even if they seem to have gone away, they could cause distrust and ruin everything in time."

He shook his head, at a loss.

Poppy turned sideways on the narrow ledge to face him and drew his hands onto her thigh. Her fingers squeezed his. "I was the one who drove Ben and Willow apart," she said. "I told Willow she was too ordinary for him. I said he would get bored with her, and since she's a Millet, he'd be bound to her forever, and forever he would hate being with her, and then he would hate her."

"Why?" He knew the answer, but wanted to hear her say it.

"Because I didn't want to lose him," she said, releasing his hands and crossing her arms tightly. "Willow was always the insecure little one. She insisted she didn't have powers and wouldn't want them anyway. I really didn't think she was suitable for him. But I wanted her out of his life, and I was wrong. It could never be my place to do what I did."

Sykes stood up and looked down on her. He felt cold inside. "And now you think what—as far as the two of them go? You can see they want each other."

"But Willow is a woman. I understand the doubts she

will have. She told me she was setting him free, and no matter what happened in future, she knew they could not be Bonded."

"You believe this new closeness they've found won't last?"

"That's what I'm afraid of. Unless I explain to Ben exactly what I did so he and Willow can put it aside."

The woman looked so utterly miserable that Sykes pitied her, even while he was so angry at the thought of all the misery she had caused.

"Tell me what to do, Sykes," she said. "I did try to tell Ben once, but give me the word and I'll go to him again and make him listen to the truth."

Sykes opened his mouth to respond. He felt the sharp words forming on his tongue and raised his head to calm himself.

Dancing purple mist made up of too many silvery specks to contemplate shifted in front of him, and he saw a page in a book.

The picture was of a carved angel—one that looked similar to some of those in this courtyard. Above the picture was written Bella, and below Angelus.

"She is a very beautiful angel," the Mentor's familiar voice said. *"She was always beautiful, and wise. Until it's time for you to know her, you must find your own wisdom. Trust your convictions."*

Alone again, except for Poppy and her large, dark eyes pleading with him, Sykes wanted to throw himself into finding that statue.

"I'm not telling you whether to come clean with Ben about this, or not to talk to him," he told Poppy. "You'll never be free if you don't make your own decision."

29

Sykes closed the front door of his house behind Nat, who came bearing food.

Watchful, Ben studied the detective's manner, looking for signals that there might be a break in the case.

"Nice place." Nat looked around. He looked even more tired, but he had been working with Vanity for many hours.

"Glad you like it," Sykes said.

Ben and Willow tried not to curl their lips at the smells wafting from a stack of obviously foam boxes in several plastic bags slung from Nat's long fingers.

Sykes steered Nat to the kitchen, where the table had been moved to the middle and six chairs placed around it.

Marley had done the honors laying the table and had even popped outside and cut a couple of bird-of-paradise blooms for the center of the table.

"Is Vanity back at the Brandt house?" Willow asked. After Nat took Vanity downtown, Willow had been left alone with her staff and Marley to work on the Venetian celebration for Chloe.

"Bucky drove her," Nat said.

"We got a lot done," Willow said. "But we'll have to start again early tomorrow." She would have to return in the morning, with as many staff as she could scrape up. Even Zinnia would pitch in tomorrow.

"Ridiculous," Nat muttered, plopping his plastic sacks on the table, apparently unaware that he had knocked dishes and flatware askew in the process. "This beats eating at the precinct and having to watch out for Molyneux."

Gray, as solidly impressive as ever, turned the corners of his mouth down. "Here. There. Foo Foo takeout is Foo Foo takeout. Why someone from Indonesia decides to run a Cantonese restaurant, I'll never figure out." He started unloading the sacks. "But I guess I am glad we're not trying to do this in your office. All I could imagine was Molyneux's face appearing at the door, followed by one of us punching his lights out."

"We couldn't have gone there anyway," Nat said. "This is no joke—I've talked to Blades, and missing persons. As long as the powers that be are determined to hide the truth from the people, we're working semialone. Or I'm working both inside and outside the law would be more accurate. We've got two patterns going on. Three killings and seven other missing people for a grand total of ten victims."

"People go missing all the time," Gray said. "That can't even be all of them for New Orleans in a few days."

"It isn't," Nat agreed. "But these seven have something in common. They are all young, sexy, in great shape—and they appear to be unmarried orphans."

Marley laughed. "You're kidding. How do you figure that out? And what does it matter?"

"It could be eight now," Nat said, ignoring the amusement. "A guy who moonlights as a trainer—at a gym—didn't show up for three clients early this morning, and the gym says he's worked there for two years and never done this before. He didn't go to his regular job. His car's where it always is. No one can reach him."

Her movements were subtle, but Willow's hand went into her purse on one of the chairs.

"Okay," Nat said, eyeing her. "What have you got there?"

She cleared her throat and shook her head. She pulled her hand out of her purse and shrugged.

"Are you carrying?" Nat asked.

"I've got a license." *Damn the man's cheek anyway.*

"What good do you think that thing would be? Do you think guns bother what we're up against?" Ben didn't look happy.

"We don't know if they won't. It's better than nothing."

"We've got a lot more than nothing," Sykes pointed out. "If the Embran didn't think we have something they want, why would they come after us? We have old skills and talents, Willow, very, very old. We are powerful people."

"So you think this is all about these whack jobs wanting the Millet magic?" Nat said.

"Not magic," the rest of them intoned in unison.

"Whatever," Nat said. "I've got a theory and I want to know what the rest of you think about it."

Willow saw the way Ben and Sykes looked at each other. She deliberately concentrated on Ben until he met her eyes. If she had to ask to be recognized, she'd better start practicing.

"*What is it?*" Ben said.

"*You and Sykes are up to something. What's going on?*"

"*Good job. We're about to tell Nat what he's already thinking and we expect him to either be furious that we've stolen his thunder, or relieved. Hope for the best.*"

"You think the Embran intend to take over New Orleans, don't you?" Sykes said to Nat. "You think this is a plan a long time in the making, and now everything's coming together for them. Or they hope it is."

Marley sat down abruptly on one of the old chairs. "That's what I think, too," she said.

"It's some sort of undercover war," Nat said. He shook his head. "Do you have any idea what would happen to me if the force found out the kind of things I'm thinking and saying? I'd never work again. I'd be in a padded cell."

"You're among like-minded friends," Gray said. "I agree with you, too."

Ben stared at Willow. "What we don't know for sure is why you've been picked out as the prime target."

She shivered. "I don't know why."

"It could be because they know you haven't been practicing your powers too long, so they think you're weaker than the rest of us."

Willow tried not to be offended by Sykes's suggestion, but she was. "They'd better not think I'm a pushover. I'm as capable as any of you."

"That's something you won't be testing out," Ben said. He stood close to her. "Understood?"

"You can sort that out between you later," Nat told them. "You're going to want to know why we're putting the three recorded deaths together with a particular group of missing persons."

Willow's stomach dropped.

"I already told you what the seven—or probably eight have in common. But two of them have something really strong."

"Spit it out," Gray said impatiently. He rubbed Marley's shoulders as if he were worried about her.

Sykes stretched and swung his torso from side to side. "Let me guess. More bits of Embran eggs."

Nat ignored him. "Willow, who do you know who moonlights as a trainer at a gym?"

She blinked rapidly before her hands flew to her face. "I didn't think of that. Fabio does."

30

Soft hands on his body, all over his body, brought him out of heavy sleep.

Total darkness obscured his surroundings.

He stretched, lengthened the muscles in his arms and tugged against bonds restricting his wrists.

The hands kept stroking. Starting at his eyelids, the fingers traced his face, hovering over his lips, one nail sliding just inside. "Welcome," a husky female voice said. "You've slept a long time. Are you ready now?"

Ready? "Where am I?"

"Here with me, where you wanted to be, remember? You're so shy and you were looking for someone very special to help you learn all the things you want to know."

Fabio was naked in the blackness and stretched out on a mattress so deep it seemed to suck him in. When he tried to turn, he remembered his wrists were tied—to bars above his head—and discovered his ankles were also bound.

"How old are you?" the woman asked.

"Twenty-eight," he told her, panic starting to flare through the thickness of his dulled consciousness.

She fondled every inch of him, his ribs, the heavy

muscles wrapping around from his biceps, triceps, the deltoids and pecs. He tried to relax. His body was better than good, he knew that. Enough people had told him he should lift competitively, but he didn't like losing, and if he wasn't the best, the shame would send him back into his room and it might be so long before he could make himself come out again.

"Magnificent," she said, cupping one of his buns. And she slithered to settle on top of him. Her body felt lush, her breasts large and the nipples hard.

He jerked his head to the side and ground his teeth together.

"You want to learn how to be with a woman."

"I know how," he said, ashamed that she knew something about him that he had kept secret.

"That's not what you told me before you fell asleep. You said you fantasize about being with a woman who will do anything you want, but you were taught sex was dirty—when you were younger—and you can't fully enjoy a woman."

Since he was the only one who knew all this, he must have told her. It sickened him. He worked so hard to have the people he dealt with see him as a stud, a guy who could have any woman and had lots of them—frequently.

"Relax." Her voice had a purring quality. "I'm not like other women. I don't need you to lead me—I'd rather lead you, teach you. I'll drive you wild and you'll never forget how I did it. I promise you."

All the time she writhed over him, massaged him with her body, brushed her breasts back and forth over his face, his chest and belly, his dick. He didn't have anything to feel second-rate about there.

"Well, well," she said. "You're huge. And your testicles are perfect." She weighed them, probing to feel their structure, and her hands closed around him and pulled rhythmically. "Have you reproduced?"

Fabio couldn't clear his head.

"Do you have children?" she said.

"No."

"Are you sure?"

Hell, maybe he did. Just because getting off took forever didn't mean he had never hit the target. "Not sure. Could be."

She laughed. "Your heart is here." Her mouth opened over his right nipple.

"Other side." Why didn't she just fuck him? He wasn't nervous anymore, and he throbbed like he was going to explode.

Her mouth went to the other side of his chest. "Do... Does everyone have a heart on this side?"

He frowned. "You're weird. Sure they do. I guess."

In response, her mouth replaced her hands on his penis and she worked hard enough to bring him to the brink before lifting her head abruptly.

"Don't stop." He panted.

"Nuisance about having to breathe, isn't it?" she said. "Do you think humans always had to breathe?"

She was really creeping him out now. "What's with you? Are we going to do it, or what?"

Her laugher rose steadily higher. "The drive for sex is so strong for your type."

"My type?" He narrowed his eyes in the complete darkness. "What the hell is my type?"

"It's just a figure of speech. We're playing—it's a

game. Play with me. You and I are going to spend a lot of time together."

For some reason he wasn't so sure he wanted that.

"Tell me about your brain."

"Untie my hands." Caution made him hold his temper. "I want to show you a good time, too."

"And you will, baby, you will. Forebrain, midbrain and hindbrain—I know this. But tell me about these things called hemispheres, the cerebellum—"

"Lady, I'm a bodybuilder, not some guy who cuts up bodies. I don't know shit about brains." And he was scared now.

"A bodybuilder." With her knees, she pushed his thighs apart, not that he needed any persuasion. "And you work with flowers. That's sweet."

"I don't work with flowers," he said. "That's Chris. I'm a master shopper. Anything anyone needs, I can get, and faster than anyone else." It sounded like something a girl would do.

"How useful," she said. "You have a lot of talents."

Funny he'd never thought of himself that way. He felt wide-awake. "What time is it? How long have I been here?" And where was he, when did he get there, why was he there?

"Why do you die?" she asked. He didn't know what to say.

"Do you all die? There must be some element you can use to make others die. Fascinating. I want to learn all about these things."

His belly crawled. "Are you for real?" he asked.

She laughed. "I want to keep you interested for a long time so I'll surprise you with my questions."

Mewling sounds reached him. Like a cat, but not quite. A sheet of fur with spiny struts embedded, settled over his private parts and it jerked. Prickling, like pins, and very sharp, tapped at his belly and the mewling turned into a cracking whine.

He swallowed a scream and tried to yank his arms and legs free. There was no way.

A cry shocked him, like someone in pain. More cracking as if something was stretched wider than it ever should be.

Again he tore at his bonds, twisting his body from side to side. He felt blood running from his wrists. The bars rattled, but didn't give.

Whirring followed, and air rushed over him, tousling his hair, cooling his skin. Small, hard ridges glided the length of his penis. He held still, terrified for what would come next. The whirring intensified, propellerlike, faster and faster, turning on his hardened, bursting flesh. He couldn't control the mounting excitement, the intense roaring in his ears and the fire in his loins.

His hips rose from the mattress and he shrieked. Rods of white heat shot through him and his back arched up, trembled, pumped. Then he emptied, so fast he felt he would choke. At the same time the bonds were released, ripped away. What felt like claws rushed the length of him and, gradually, those big breasts replaced the blanket of fur and bony sinew.

"Just let yourself go," she told him. "I want to kiss you."

Her mouth closed over not just his mouth, but also his nose, and she sucked. At first he held her, rocking, trying to please her with his tongue, but then his arms were too short to surround her, his mouth so small it disappeared inside hers.

He was shrinking!

So quickly he couldn't hold a thought, he got smaller and smaller and all the time she kept sucking at him.

His head was in her mouth and she kept drawing on him. He curled up into a ball, tried to protect the soft parts of his body.

The next sound was a pop. He flew away from her and landed in something grainy, began to sink.

Flailing, throwing his arms in circles and pushing with his legs, he fought to the surface.

A small light came on near him and he looked out through a distorted wall of thick glass.

31

"It's a bit obvious when everyone else leaves and we stay behind...together," Willow said when Sykes had whipped out of the house with the other three. "You'll have to be here since Sykes is using the flat, but I'm going to get back."

"Are you?"

Ben's tone said it all. He didn't believe she had any intention of leaving.

"Be serious. I need to get back and take Mario off Pascal's hands. And try to settle my nerves about tomorrow—if that's possible. It's going to be weird and long."

Ben pulled her into the sitting room and sat on a couch. He patted the seat next to him. "Come be with me."

With her purse in both hands, she moved her weight from one leg to the other.

"Still determined to cart the gun around," he said. "Maybe it's not such a bad idea." He patted the couch again and she went slowly to sit on the edge.

"It's really late, Ben."

"You just said it wasn't that late."

She kept her voice even. "You can't take me prisoner."

Standing beside him and looking down accentuated his penetrating eyes, his high cheekbones and the shine on his long, black hair—worn tied back tonight. "You'd only be a prisoner if you didn't want to stay. But you do know I won't let you leave alone."

"I can't spend the rest of my life handcuffed to you, Ben."

He smiled, and she came close to smiling back.

"This won't last forever," Ben said. "You've heard what Nat had to say. I agree with him. So does Sykes. And Gray and Marley. So does Pascal. You heard what was said earlier. Sykes and I both feel we're close to a crisis. You see how Marley is—almost like she's sick. Her senses are wide-open, and she's getting messages she doesn't like. Then there's Nat. He's got every reason to want to debunk our theories, but he's too smart. And he's got guts."

"I couldn't believe it when Nat said Fabio was missing," Willow said. "Zinnia told me he'd called and said he'd be at the Brandts' later in the day."

"She was covering for him," Ben pointed out. "You can't hold that against her."

"I never would. But I've got to get back to the courtyard. I heard Chris there." She turned toward Ben. "I *saw* him. If I contact Fabio the same way, there won't be any doubt about a connection between the missing."

"Willow, I want us to stay here tonight. We'll go back as soon as it gets light and I feel okay about asking some of the others to help out."

She hugged herself.

He continued, "I honestly believe we've hit it—the Embran want New Orleans, but particularly the French

Quarter, as some sort of kingdom. For some reason it feels right to them—and the Millets are there. You've brought them here. You've been causing them to pop up in different places around the world for centuries. They've followed you and now you're in their nirvana. What we still have to find out is exactly what they want from you."

"We're not running away again," she said, growing angry. "We'll fight."

"Sykes and I decided this was a good place for tonight. You and I have been at the Court the last couple of days, and he'll make it look as if we're there tonight. So far I haven't seen any sign of Embran being psychic. If I'm right, they aren't going to pick up on us here."

"You can't be sure. They found me before—and Marley before that."

"They knew where the Millets were. They knew where to look for you, then. They followed you around."

"They could have come after me tonight."

He caught her chin between his finger and thumb. "They didn't."

She stared at him. "Has Pascal put a shield around me? I know he can do that, and then you can only be seen by those he wants to see you."

Ben's eyebrows rose. "For someone who didn't believe in any powers until a few days ago, you've come a long way."

Ben got up and offered her his hand.

He had her off balance. "What now?" she asked, although she knew and willingly put her hand in his.

They climbed the stairs slowly, never taking their eyes off each other.

Willow wanted to lose herself in him, but she was edgy. "You and Sykes and Nat, I guess, you've decided we're definitely close to a big crisis?"

He nodded. "We can't be sure how many of them may be here by now—and we do know they're ruthless. I know all about the theory that there was just the one around—and his two half-human offspring when Marley got involved. But even if it was true then, seeing evidence of their return proves nothing was solved.

"It doesn't help that no one is talking about what happened to Sidney and Eric Fournier after they were arrested. Then there's Bolivar, Marley's dragon. Poof, and he was gone from the jail. But I can't find out the sequence—what happened and when."

"The killings have been different this time," Willow said. "From one victim to the next. Billy Baker and Surry Green were very similar, but Chloe wasn't."

"In a way it was all the same—they were scared to death, weakened and driven to collapse by horror, but we don't believe they were attacked by the same thing. And we want to know why we haven't found any of these missing people."

Willow thought of Chris and the woman she didn't know, both groveling around among colored granules inside glass and so scared. Without knowing what was planned for them or where they were, she felt helpless. And now there was Fabio—she had to assume he was probably in the same position as the others.

A churning wave of terror gripped her. "What if they can multiply quickly?" She caught at Ben's waist. "There could be… Ben, there could be dozens of them waiting and watching. Hundreds of them."

They reached the top of the stairs.

His expression closed. He gathered her against him, but she knew the answer was yes, and he didn't want to tell her that.

"I will never let anything hurt you, Willow."

"How can you see that bat thing when it shows up?" she asked, not expecting a straight answer.

Ben studied her from beneath half-lowered lids. "Have you ever heard of the Third Eye?"

She frowned and shook her head.

"Some of us have it," Ben said. "A very small number. It allows us to see what others can't see."

"What sort of things?"

He took his time again, and she figured he was deciding how much to say. "Things that want to hide from human sight and things that don't care about human sight because they never consider they'll be detected."

"Like what?"

Shaking his head, he said, "You're relentless. Like those who have passed beyond this life, but haven't entered the next."

"You see ghosts," she said flatly, with a flip of her stomach. "Can you see any now?"

"No," he told her promptly, walking with her toward the bedroom.

"And you would if they were here?"

"I would if they were here and I wanted to see them."

"Oh." Her turn to think. "So they're probably all around us. Sitting over there watching us, talking about us."

"No. They've passed beyond that. Unless we catch their attention for some reason, they don't notice us."

"That's comforting."

"And you feel moods," Ben said. "Sadness, happiness, pain, hope, and then you figure out what caused the moods. That's pretty specialized stuff, Willow."

"I don't feel it all the time."

"That's because you don't work at it," Ben said. "But you will as you learn how valuable your gifts are."

She gave him a skeptical look.

His fingertips, circling on the small of her back, shortened her breath. Closing in, holding him as tightly as she could, she absorbed shock after shock fanning from his touch. When he stiffened, his body hard all over, she let their sensations fuse.

"Morning will come too soon," she told him softly, feeling her resolve slip away. "Lie with me." She was gripped with the sudden conviction that she must make the very best of this night with him.

A sigh shuddered along his length. "Things have changed. If we keep pursuing our Bond, what we feel will intensify and it may be more than we can recover from in a few hours." But he braced his legs apart and trapped her with his thighs.

"Ben, we don't know…. Who knows what time they've got, or what tomorrow's going to bring?"

"No one," he said into her hair, stroking her back from neck to waist and cupping her bottom. He lifted her against his pelvis.

"Can't this—whatever we make of tonight—can't it be because we want to be together? Without thinking about all the heavy stuff family expectations put on us?" If she was aggressive, so be it. She had always been too reticent when it came to showing how she felt about him.

"That's more or less what you said the last time you wanted us to be together without any strings." He raised his chin and looked down on her. "I can't let you go, Willow. Not ever. I can't live without you—I know that now."

She knew it, too. She felt as if she bled inside at the thought of losing him, but she couldn't be sure he wouldn't change over time, and that would be even more unbearable.

"Why did you send me away before?" he asked, his face sad and nakedly honest.

Carefully, on tiptoe, she worked the band out to free his hair and let it fall to his shoulders. "You look like a warrior. I love your hair free. You're a wild man when you're like this."

"Don't change the subject."

For a moment she regarded him seriously. "I can't tell you, Ben. Except that it was out of…love, and fear. And I don't know if I'm over the fear."

He spread one big hand over the side of her cheek and head and turned her face up to his. "Does that mean you do know you're not over the love?"

"I'm not going to lie. I can't stop loving you. I never will—not that it looks as if I'll be around long." She gave a little laugh, but it didn't sound convincing.

Absently, he stripped off the shirt. His broad, muscular shoulders and clearly defined chest shone. What low light did for Ben's body ought to be against the law.

"You ought to be scared of the way you make me feel," she said.

"You don't know danger when it peers into your eyes, do you?" Ben said.

"Don't I? Maybe I like danger."

He took hold of her left arm and pulled her in front of him. When he sank to his knees, she stood over him, and he stopped her from joining him on the floor.

Willow had on white sweats and a pair of Mean 'n Green sneakers. She figured she didn't make a sexy picture.

The way Ben looked at her suggested otherwise. He slid down the zipper on her jacket, starting slowly, but losing his control a little as the front parted and he saw the white cotton bra that was all she wore underneath.

He tossed her jacket aside. Her pants slid easily to her ankles, but then he had to stop and take off her shoes. She held his shoulders, but if the moment might have seemed funny at another time, it didn't now. Her heart beat rapidly and hard, and despite standing in only her bra and panties, she was hotter than ever.

His own feet were already bare and she shucked his jeans fast.

One glance proved foreplay would depend on his control.

Maybe she didn't want him to have any control.

Tossed over his shoulder, Willow couldn't make any plans for moves of her own. Ben deposited her on the mattress, hooked her knees over his shoulders and plunged his mouth into the soft, moist warmth between her thighs. His tongue worked rapidly beneath her panties and flicked over the hard, swollen bud there.

Willow writhed. She heard the noises she made—like a squealing animal.

Ben had a capable tongue, a sexy, talented tongue. In seconds, with his hands covering her breasts, he brought her to pulsing readiness. She crossed her ankles behind his neck. Her mind wouldn't work properly, and she didn't try to change a thing.

Willow's climax tore into her. She broke into a sweat that soaked her body. When she opened her eyes, Ben's face leaned over hers, his eyes searing, flame-blue. His chest rose and fell with great breaths. She couldn't stop her hips from rising and falling, or her breasts from stinging.

Ben flipped Willow to her feet, and she clung to him. "I'm going to fall," she said.

"I won't let you. Willow, say the word and there's still time to stop."

"Are you into torture?" she asked him.

"I don't think I can be... I just don't want to hurt you." He had never looked more desperate. Longing mingled with apprehension. "I couldn't bear it if I did."

She undid her bra and shrugged it off.

Ben's lips and teeth closed over a nipple, and she moaned, couldn't stop herself. From his lips to her flesh and beyond, live shocks tore into her. She heard his panting, and the moan in his throat. In seconds they were both completely naked.

"Wait," she breathed. "Wait, Ben, please."

He pulled back, anxiety deepening the lines around his tensed mouth.

She tried to push him onto the mattress, but there was no moving him until he moved himself, never taking his eyes from hers.

Willow sat beside Ben, slipped her mouth over him. She used her teeth, slid the soft, wet insides of her cheeks along the length of him again and again, held his testicles and squeezed gently.

"Oh, my God," he said through his teeth. "Oh, Willow, please." His face contorted with pain but she didn't feel any guilt. This was the prize they shared, the pain that pleased more than anything any "normal" person could hope for.

Her teeth, digging a little deeper, brought his pelvis against her lips in a frenzy. He squeezed her breasts, ran his hands over as much of her as he could reach.

Grabbing one of her ankles, he pulled her leg between his, then underneath him until they rode, her mound to the hard, insistent parts of him. He stretched her other leg along the length of him and took her toes in his mouth, sucking in rhythm to the beat of his hips.

Then he was inside her, gliding up, penetrating more deeply than she had imagined possible. He seemed to reach her womb. She wanted him to fill her up completely. Her arms fell loose and she splayed them. Ben's muscles, with the power of a releasing crossbow, sent arrows that flamed and scorched their way through her body.

The rush of him inside her, the yell at his release, had her shaking and clinging to him convulsively. Before she could catch her breath, he turned her over, pushed his knees beneath her and massaged her clitoris with his fingers.

How could there be more white-hot sensation already? But there was. And need. Pulling on her knees, he slid her over the bulk of his thigh muscles and entered her again. "Willow," he said, clear and strong. "I love you. You're mine, Willow."

She couldn't form a single word. All that escaped her were jarring little groans with each fresh thud of their joined bodies.

They made love four times with only minutes between each soaring journey to satisfaction, between each provocative wound they lavished on one another.

Belly to belly, Willow collapsed on top of Ben. Their breathing rasped.

Willow trembled. "I wouldn't change it," she whispered.

"I wouldn't even if I could."

"We don't know if there is only one person for each of us," she said, and wanted to cry bitterly just with the thought she hated so much.

"Yes, we do." His firm voice never wavered. "You must accept what is obvious, Willow. Somewhere, somehow, the Millets became creatures no one could bear to experience just once—or twice—or a thousand times."

"But—"

"We've got to sleep, my love. I don't want to, but I'm not sure we'll be able to move for hours as it is." He hugged her, tipped up her chin and kissed her, ran his tongue over the soft insides of her cheeks, along the tender flesh just beyond her lips.

"I feel safe here with you," she said.

"You are," he told her. "I'm not sure we should leave at all."

She smiled against his shoulder. "How long do you think it would be before they found us withered away to nothing?"

He shrugged. "At least a couple of wonderful days— Sheesh, what's that?"

Something cool settled on her back. Ben lifted it away and she rolled over to see.

A page, but not simply of paper the way Willow

thought of it. Parchment curling slightly at the edges and discolored. With her head on his shoulder, Ben used both hands to hold it as flat as he could.

"It's her," Willow said, staring at another drawing of her angel. "Look. What's that?"

Ben lifted his head to see more clearly.

Pale mauve haze formed in the air around them. Gradually it seemed to run down, like watercolor on thin glass. The color turned to purple.

Willow's memory clicked into full gear, and she hauled a coverlet over both of them, huddled even closer to Ben. She wasn't dressed for a visitation.

"The edge of something round and gold," he said. "Do you think she's reaching for it?"

She squinted. The angel's lips were curved in an exquisite smile. "Yes. And something must be holding it up. Two red nails or claws."

"That's what it looks like," he said. "I wish we could see more of it."

Willow sighed. "It's just another drawing. The others haven't helped."

"I won't take up much of your time," a deep, male voice said. *"It is for you to put the pieces together. What of the curse? What do they say about it?"*

Ben's hand had closed on her shoulder. "Jude?" he said.

"We're not sure what the curse is," Willow said. "My parents are trying to find out about it."

The sound the other one made was a clear and derisive snort.

"Can't you tell us?" Willow said.

"Against the rules. You must sort out the truth from

the fabrication and foolishness. Only then will you be strong. In the meantime, keep up the search. Remember what you see in this drawing. How beautiful she is, our Angelus. Beautiful and good. Be patient. The Millets have waited a long time to find the truth and they may have to wait a great deal longer. We shall see."

Willow put her chin forward to study the picture.

Purple thinned to a luminous green, and disappeared. With it, it was as if the parchment had never been in Ben's hands.

She looked at him, but he guided her face into the hollow of his neck and put both arms around her again. "I wonder how long his 'long times' are," he said and shoved himself to sit up, so abruptly, Willow looked all around the room, expecting something awful.

"Oh," Ben said, relaxing. "I could see his eyes looking at us, but it's too dark in that corner. Come on out, Mario, you voyeur. Did you know you'd acquired a voyeur?" he asked Willow.

Mario sat in that shadowy corner. He dropped to lie down and closed his eyes.

Ben and Willow laughed.

"I didn't realize you'd brought him with you," Ben said. "He behaves as if he understands every word we say."

"He's just precocious," Willow said. "I didn't bring him. Sykes must have. He's done it before when he figured I needed all the comfort I could get."

Ben made a face, and Willow kissed him until he flopped onto his back.

"You're all the comfort I need," she told him.

"Thank you." He popped up to kiss her nose. "That's what I wanted to hear."

They both heard a small metallic sound and leaned over to see Mario. On the floor in front of him was another gold key. Sykes had spoken to Ben before Willow left the Brandts and admitted to finding one himself, making three with this one.

32

Ben winced and sucked in a breath. As carefully as he pulled shut the gate leading to the Court of Angels, it still squeaked. In the quiet of early, early morning, the noise sounded like a small explosion.

They had given up on waiting to get back to the Court of Angels. Tired as they were, neither of them could sleep, and Willow insisted she had to see if she could find out what happened to Fabio.

The next sound Ben recognized was Willow's giggling, and he caught her—and Mario—in a bear hug. "Quiet," he whispered. "We don't want anyone to wake up."

"*Me* be quiet?" she whispered back and pressed her face into his chest.

"You're hysterical," he muttered, and gave a muted "Oof" when she poked his ribs.

Lightning flashed repeatedly, and thunder rumbled before the light show faded. In seconds, the sky lit up again.

The phone in his pocket vibrated. "That'll be Sykes, so be really quiet or we'll have him down here with us," he said, and answered. "You got my message?"

He listened while Sykes, sounding a bit miffed, told him he still had the two keys they had found earlier. Ben and Willow had wondered if Mario somehow lifted one of them from Sykes and carried it in his mouth. Ridiculous as it seemed, it had been a possibility.

"Okay," Ben said. "And now there are three. Any more ideas about them?"

"Several," Sykes said. "You want to talk about it now?"

Ben considered the best way out. "It's too late now. Long day coming up."

Sykes cleared his throat. "Are you and Willow— Are you getting close again? I mean, really close."

"Is that any of your business?" Ben smiled, though.

"Could be," Sykes said. "If it has to be."

Ben figured he'd wait to ask for a full explanation of what that meant. "We're fine," he said. "Great. Goodbye," Ben said and hung up and gave Willow a long kiss.

"What was that for?" she said when she could.

He breathed in the scent of her. "Let's do whatever we can out here and get up to your place…to sleep."

"Sure." Still carrying Mario, she held Ben's hand and led him, walking as quietly as they could, into the courtyard. It was fortunate that the bedrooms were at the back of the flats.

"See how it glows?" Ben said in her ear. A luminous shimmer emanated from statue after statue, casting a frothy silver-green into the shrubs.

"No," Willow said. She flinched at more lightning. "Now *that* glows."

"Very clever." He frowned and looked around.

"Okay. I don't know why I'm singled out for all the attention here, but I'll take it. The inmates are muttering. They sound like water bubbling." He paused, listening. "They are agitated and excited—and they're welcoming us."

"Okay." Willow didn't sound convinced. "If you say so."

"Hey, aren't you the one who came here and saw Chris in a bottle? How weird is that?"

She leaned on him. "Less weird all the time. I did see colors, but like watercolors. We can't look for angel clues in the dark, but I can see if I can reach Fabio somehow."

"Sykes told me Marley hears voices."

"She does," Willow said. "When she travels they guide her, but she hasn't traveled since the Embran attack. I think Gray's worried she'll try to do something about the people who are missing now. It's dangerous—she could die if she can't get back to her body."

Ben put an arm around her shoulders. "I don't blame Gray for being nervous."

"Particularly now," Willow said. "She shouldn't travel with the baby."

He stood still. "Marley and Gray are having a baby? I didn't know that."

She gave a frustrated puff. "You make me too comfortable. I tell you things I shouldn't. I don't think they know it yet, either. It's only been a couple of weeks. We shouldn't say anything, okay?"

"Okay, Miss Normal. You get more interesting all the time."

She shrugged. "I just know these things, is all. It's to do with emotions. Marley's are all over the place at the moment, but even more gentle than usual. There's something different there."

"But it doesn't have to be a baby," he pointed out.

"Yes, it does," she said, and closed her mouth firmly.

"I'll take your word for it." He squeezed her tightly and kissed her temple.

"What?" she said. "What did I do to deserve that?"

"Nothing and everything. I just had a pleasant thought, but don't try and get it out of me. You need to start concentrating."

"Do you want children, Ben?" she said, her voice very quiet.

"Maybe." He carried on, leading her deeper into the courtyard. Whispering in her ear again, he said, "Our children." And the difficult thing for him to cope with was that he did want their children. He'd always been the lone one, the single actor with a single mind, but now Willow was his other half, almost the beat of his heart, and he longed for their official Bonding—and even the official ceremony they would go through.

Marley and Gray had a real wedding, too. Gray's dad, Gus, was blamed for that by Gray who insisted it was only to please his old man, but Ben had heard all about the excitement over the event.

He took Mario from Willow. The dog struggled and he put him down. Immediately, the animal scuffled off into the closest undergrowth.

Willow went to the fountain and stood in the light spray beating up. "Do you wish it would rain—really hard? I do." She raised her face to the sky. "Everything's so tense. I just want it to break loose."

"I know what you mean."

"Please go on up. I need to concentrate."

He understood how she felt, but he wasn't leaving her here alone. "I'll go keep an eye on Mario. Then I want to check the locks on the shop doors."

Fortunately, Willow was already thinking of other things or the pathetic excuses wouldn't have flown with her.

Ben knew where to find Mario. He sat among the bamboo that hid his favorite stone griffon. Actually leaning against the statue, the dog looked up at Ben as if he was trying to telegraph some wisdom.

Ben crouched to scratch rough, red fur, but he listened hard for any sound from Willow. He couldn't see her from here. He stood and crept far enough through the bamboo to part the canes and peer out.

She wasn't by the fountain.

Panicked, he stepped out and started forward. Willow stood beside what must once have been the doorway to a storeroom. Concreted shut, Ben never remembered it any other way.

With her face pointed skyward again, her arms were outstretched. When he crept closer behind her, he heard her say, "Can you hear me?" and he kept still.

Willow's eyes closed. She listened to air rushing and touched her face. A warm current blew on her skin. The heavy scent of flowers and rich earth settled around her. A tropical place. That's where she was—not the courtyard with its flashes and the rumblings of a storm—but a tropical garden.

"Fabio?" she said. "Chris? Are you there?"

He hadn't heard her when she saw him before. Once more she was looking at glass, thick and wavy, shiny on the outside, but difficult to see through. She concentrated hard.

Not sand, but pink granules rose several inches inside a bottle.

"You gotta stay with me, man."

Willow's eyes opened. That was Chris's voice again, but this time she didn't see him. The bottle wasn't his.

"Fabio—this is gonna get worse. They're planning something—they gotta be."

"Leave me alone."

This time she recognized Fabio's voice, then she saw the pink granules churn, and a tiny, almost transparent creature emerged. It pushed to the top of the grains and seemed to flop out flat.

"Fabio," she said. "It's me, Willow. Tell me where you are."

"It's got to happen soon, man," Chris said. *"I don't even know how many of us there are. I sleep and when I wake up, there's someone else. They're gathering us all up, I tell you. They're clearing N'awlins. They're taking over."*

"That's fucking ridiculous," Fabio said. *"I had this sex. It was, it was—"*

"Frickin' amazing? Yeah, I know. That's how they're getting their victims."

"So why don't they just kill us?" Fabio said.

"I told you. They want us for something, and we're not goin' to like it."

"So how do we get out?"

"That's the rub," Chris said. *"Even if we make it to the top of these bottles, we can't just break out. I heard two of them talking. We're dehydrated. Dried like pieces of*

fruit leather. But if we let air in we start going back to normal size. If our hands are outside the bottle necks hanging on, they'll swell till they're so big they break the glass. We could lose our hands. Put our heads out and—"

"I get the picture," Fabio said fast. *"So what do we do? Lie down and wait to die?"*

"We've got to come up with a plan, but timing will be everything. We all gotta do the thing together. So far I can't get the rest of them to shut up long enough to make sure they're with us."

"What if they're not? Or they're too scared?"

Chris made a frustrated noise. *"Caroline's in. The three of us will go it alone—I think we've got some time. I think they'll be bringing bunches more of us before anything changes."*

"Chris," Willow cried, "Fabio. Please. Where are you?"

The bottles shivered. Water sprayed them and ran down in rivulets. The scent of flowers grew heavier. She could distinguish gardenias, then jasmine.

First the vision disappeared. The floral scents lingered. She dropped her arms and stepped backward. Rain started to fall, and she welcomed it on her hot face and body. Her own tears joined the rain, and she couldn't hold back her sobs.

"It's okay," Ben said, holding her. His touch was gentle.

"It's not okay." She turned in his arms. "Ben, you and Nat, Sykes and everyone, you're right. New Orleans is being attacked."

33

Throughout the hectic day of preparing for the Brandt event, Willow had felt herself waiting. She had no rational idea of what she expected, but whether it happened tonight or at some other time very soon, the hidden enemy would burst into the open, and the idea of what that could mean terrified her.

Now the bizarre celebration of Chloe Brandt's life had begun.

Minstrels wearing rich green-and-gold-striped tunics and bloomers, their legs encased in green tights, wandered through the grounds of the Brandt house. Full face masks hid their identities. Tassels on green velvet caps swung as they bent over their instruments, strumming medieval sounds. And fantastically costumed guests formed a grand, strolling scene.

"Perhaps masks should always be worn at memorials," Ben said, joining her in his flowing black cloak over tight-fitting dark clothes. A white collar stood high at his neck with a white, austerely tied cravat. His white mask and the hood he wore pulled up disguised him, but not the character he played. Ben was a vampire tonight.

He mesmerized Willow, who looked past the mask

and into his fathomless eyes. "This is a celebration," she reminded him. "Why do you think that about masks?"

"They'll hide all the tears Chloe's dear friends must be shedding. In this group, they'll also hide anything else that could give us a clue to who killed her."

"You really believe the killer is here?"

"I'm sure of it. There's something showy about everything these Embran do. They pretend they want to move about in secret, but what they do is guaranteed to draw attention to them. They're tired of anonymity. Now they want to come out into the daylight—or perhaps the spotlight."

Acid burned in Willow's throat. Ben echoed her own thoughts—and made her even more fearful.

Candles, hundreds of candles flickered from every area of the grounds. Even the pool lights had been turned off and more candles gave an eerie glow that didn't penetrate the surface of the water. Inside the house, frescoes painted on hangings and carefully placed columns added to the medieval picture.

Vanity insisted everyone must be incognito and had sent the costumier to Willow, who detested what felt and looked like a Little Bo Peep outfit. The costumier said it was a seventeenth-century shepherdess rig. A tall white wig itched. A whalebone underskirt added an ungainly sway to every step she took. And a bright blue costume with laced white blouse showed more of her breasts than she ever showed in public. Her mask had the face of a young girl with tiny red lips and for some reason huge "diamond" earrings hung from her ears. A wide red slash painted around her neck didn't make her feel less uncomfortable.

Ben bent close to her. "Did your head get chopped off and sewn back on, or did I do that?" His deep curdling laugh made her shiver. She enjoyed it.

"So much food," Willow said. She had an army of staff on duty. "It's obscene. So far I haven't heard one ode to Chloe or even an, 'I'm sorry she's dead.'"

"But it's a celebration of her life," Ben reminded her.

Skirts of fabulous silver and gold fabric covered exaggerated panniers. Jewels slid into décolletage that overflowed tight bodices. Enormous beribboned wigs, shoes with gilded buckles, sequins, beads, tights and masks were everywhere. Several plague doctors in their black oilskins and linen, carrying staffs and wearing wide-brimmed top hats pulled down over their hook-beaked masks, passed among tricorne hats afloat with ostrich feathers, jesters and carnival magicians.

Othello and Desdemona giggled on their way past with a gaudy Harlequin. A couple in black-and-white were clearly supposed to be Casanova and a conquest. A Napoleon or two, Cyrano de Bergerac and Don Quixote and a sprinkling of devils were all part of the diorama.

Willow had always heard that a Venetian masquerade rivaled Mardi Gras in New Orleans; now she believed it. A gentleman in a close-fitting, black satin tuxedo with a gold cummerbund, cloak and top hat, sidled up to Willow. "Elegant affair, *signorina,*" he said. "Truly inspired."

Willow frowned behind her mask.

"The lady thanks you," Ben said, slipping an arm around her shoulders.

"How do you like my cravat?" the man said, lifting the tails of an intricately tied lace neck affair. "Venetian Gros Point needle lace. Authentic, I assure you."

His mask was again full face, but Willow was getting good at studying eyes. "You are a show-off, Preston," she said. "Will you be talking about Chloe, may we hope?"

"Of course." He sounded completely serious, so serious he didn't remark on Willow recognizing him. "I'll find Val and see what he's thinking about the schedule."

Willow didn't even know which of the parading figures was Val, and she watched Preston go, wondering if he did, either.

A woman in an ivory satin ball gown, also swaying from whalebone petticoats, came toward the center of the foyer. It had been decided to keep the event entirely downstairs. More accurately, the police had refused to release the upstairs yet.

"She looks agitated," Ben said to Willow. "Do you know her?"

"No." Gems glittered all over the woman, who was fluttering—there was no other word for the way she moved—and flapping an ivory fan. She kept swinging her head to look behind, sending ringlets at her neck bobbing wildly.

The candles cast an eerie glow, but they didn't do a lot for making anything easy to see.

"Are you all right?" Willow said to the woman.

"Of course." She tittered. "A little indiscretion in the conservatory is all. These gentlemen can be so forward when they think they're disguised."

Dressed as Cleopatra, Zinnia from Willow's office approached Ben. "Could you help with the gondola?" she asked. Behind her gold mask she rolled her eyes at Willow. "The thing keeps trying to turn over. Our boatman says it needs tying down or something."

Ben said, "Come on," to Willow, and followed.

The woman in ivory stepped in front of Willow to follow a line of revelers toward the kitchen. Willow noticed a long tear in the sleeve of the woman's gorgeous gown and tapped her shoulder. "Was your sleeve torn when you got the costume?" she said. "I hope so or they'll be charging you for it. They're so fussy."

The woman pulled the sleeve to take a look and then she backed into the round table in the foyer. "It doesn't really matter," she said. "But people should watch what kind of pets they keep."

"Pets?" Willow shrugged, mystified.

"They've got a bird in that conservatory. It got all bent out of shape because I was close to his damnable cage. I thought he tried to peck me."

"Hold on," Willow said and hurried the woman into the office, where she produced a roll of tape and cut off a piece. She quickly patched the frayed sleeve edges together. "No one's going to notice anyway, but you'll feel better."

"You noticed."

"I'm a details person." She was, and it could be crazy making.

They parted in the foyer, the woman heading for the kitchen again, Willow too curious about the bird not to take another look.

Some of the couples "celebrating" Chloe's life were lip and body locked in the doorways and alcoves Willow passed. These people had the depth of sidewalk puddles. Their lives had long ago become more rumor than reality. She just didn't like the way they lived.

Even the conservatory hadn't escaped the candles,

although Willow noted that ground lights remained on in various places.

She approached the gilded cage, but stopped on the way. The air was heavy with the scents of rich earth and flowers. Orchids were everywhere, but they weren't known for their aromas. The gardenias and jasmine climbing over the cage were. She thought she smelled honeysuckle, although it didn't seem to belong in here. Willow closed her eyes a moment and breathed in. It was beautiful.

And familiar.

Her eyes snapped open, and she looked at the nearest gardenia bush. This had been what she smelled in the Court of Angels early that morning. Glad of the mask to hide another frown, she walked much more slowly to the cage where the little green bird sat well back on a perch as if unaware of all the noise in the house.

"Are you a bird lover?" a man asked beside her. This was a courtier in lush, dark purple velvet piped with black. The feathers flowing from his tricorne were white enough to look luminous in the odd light.

"Not really," she told him. "This is such a lovely conservatory, though. It makes me want to have one of my own."

He wagged his head. "You mean Marie Antoinette *doesn't* have her own conservatories? I could have sworn I saw them at Versailles. How good of you to wear your best earrings—not that you may think them anything at all."

Marie Antoinette?

Yuck.

"I'm so glad they gave your head back," he said, laughing and indicating the red slash around her neck.

"Why, thank you." She bobbed. Of course, the poor little queen playing in her shepherdess costume. How nice that this was the costume chosen for her—she hated the thought.

The man swept off his hat and made a deep leg, sweeping the feathers in his tricorne across the floor, then wandered away.

Willow stared at the little bird again. She stepped closer to the cage. Its beak wasn't petite the way such a small creature's usually was. The upper part hooked over the lower in a nasty-looking point. Willow raised her brows and thought that it could take a nasty hold on something or someone. That woman had been fortunate that only her sleeve was torn.

For an instant she thought the bird stared at her with eyes as green as his feathers, but bright, sharp, piercing.

She couldn't blame herself for being fanciful tonight and smiled. Actually, she was remarkably sane, considering what they were all going through.

Moving from foot to foot, the bird opened its mouth wide, showing a thick, black tongue. The eyes closed slightly. Hateful, she decided and prepared to move on. If she didn't get outside, Ben would notice her absence and come rushing to the rescue whether she needed it or not.

In one corner of the cage an open-fronted cupboard reached from top to bottom. What looked like supplies for the bird and garden items were lined up on shelves.

Willow was grateful she didn't have to confront the little green monster to reach anything on those shelves. The bird had sidled all the way to the end of its perch, the end closest to Willow, and inclined his head to stare at her some more. Its thick tongue darted from its beak, and she thought she heard a hissing sound.

Time to go.

There were bottles on the shelves in the cage.

She stood like stone, staring at them.

Some had labels. They appeared to contain orchid food of various kinds and colors.

Her heart speeded up to a painful hammering in her throat. Leaning closer, she pressed her mask to the bars and stared at those bottles with their thick, wavy glass and the sandy-looking stuff, or bigger, brighter granules inside.

Gasping, Willow looked over her shoulder, but she was alone now.

Again she leaned her face to the bars and tried not to blink.

At last, in a square bottle with several inches of shockingly turquoise granules inside, she saw a movement.

A tiny, almost transparent but pinkish, shrimplike creature revolved through the medium. She couldn't breathe. Gasping for air, she whispered, "I'm going for help now. Don't do anything," even though she doubted she could be heard.

A vicious crack against her mask all but knocked her backward. She straightened, but not before the bird came at her for a second time, its beak wide-open and its purplish-black tongue flashing through the bars, as long as the body of a garden snake.

34

Where was Sykes? Where were any members of her family who had wangled invitations tonight?

Willow rushed through the house to the gardens as fast as her bustles and bows would allow.

Surrounded by disguised strangers, and some people she must know, but didn't recognize, she searched for help. Specifically she wanted Ben. There was no time for long explanations, and he already knew everything. Relief brought a rush of blood to her face. He stood with Rock, alias the boatman from the gondola that stretched from one end of the pool to the other. It listed toward the cabana side of the pool.

She wanted to call out Ben's name, but ran faster instead, and waved.

He saw her and waved back, indicating the line he held, one end attached to the gondola while he waited for someone to finish driving a hefty stake into the nearby grass with a large mallet. The line was one of three at the stern.

Willow avoided a milling group sharing bottles of champagne. She wondered how long ago they had given up on using glasses. If they weren't careful, they'd end up in the pool and they weren't dressed for swimming.

She saw Ben bend over, his cloak flying out behind him, to thread the line through a hole at the top of the stake. Barrels blocked her path and she dodged around them and some flanking shrubs.

Violent blue light caught her squarely in the eyes.

Willow gasped, threw her hands in front of the mask. Strong hands whipped her around, pulled her against a solid body and forced her into the pool with him.

Flailing, desperately grappling to turn and face her attacker, she sank. The wig dislodged and she managed to tear off the mask. Her feet met the bottom and she tried to push off, stretching toward the surface and the flicker of candlelight above the water.

He held her where she was until she fought mindlessly, threw out her arms and kicked.

Her lungs ached.

She would drown.

Willow struggled not to draw in water. Her nose stung and she winced at bubbling in the bones of her face. With all the strength she had left, she grappled to tear herself free.

The painful blue light gouged at her eyes once more. She couldn't see.

Something hard slapped over her face. A diving mask. There didn't seem to be any tanks, yet she heard sudden hissing before air surged into her punished lungs.

She couldn't tell which way she had to go to get to the top and she still couldn't see properly.

Quiet, she told herself.

Willow let herself bend and crumple. She dropped until her knees met the tiles. The arms had let her go, but she didn't know where that maniac was. He had tried to drown her, then put a mask and air tank on her? There was no way to make sense of any of it. She slitted her eyes, searching for him.

Darkness fell over her and she looked up.

Above her head a shadow spread.

The shadow took shape, coming at her through the water. Wings spread wide, grotesque body gliding; it was the creature that had appeared to her on the night she'd spent with Ben at Sykes's house.

The huge beak snapped open and shut. Flaps of gray tissue waved from pointed ears. A feathered coat lay thick and oily against its sinuous body and balloons of opaque yellow slime slipped free of its beak, slid down its loose, fatty beard of flesh and sank.

It ducked its head and charged. The collision knocked her backward, but immediately the bird creature took her hair in its talons and towed her. Willow shot through the water and felt a force she was helpless to resist dragging on her body as if it would turn her inside out.

Another blast of blue glare made her blind again. She thrashed around and began to spin. Faster and faster, she spun. Her ankles crossed, the bones crushed together by velocity, her shoes long gone.

Nausea brought bile into her throat.

She let her eyes close and wanted only to be quiet. At last she stopped fighting and let herself revolve, like an electric top gone mad.

Her shoulders and the backs of her hands scraped hard surfaces. One last time Willow struggled to open her eyes and looked out through a visor. Streams of bubbles whirled past.

She shot through a chute, its dark sides visible through

churning water. Sucked down and down, she was as helpless as a minnow going over a massive waterfall.

Completely numb, Willow didn't care anymore. Inside her head was quiet, and she slipped into a soft, cold, black space that waited for her.

35

She was not dead.

Splayed facedown on a hard surface, her body ached, and pain burned in her head. Willow did not want to open her eyes. As long as she kept them shut, she wouldn't know where she was, and she didn't want to know.

Above all, she didn't want to think about where she had been.

Images scuttled through her brain, not one of them clear, not one of them staying long enough for her to study. Shapes moving in darkness. Coming closer. Fading away. Angry voices, shrieking. And questions. There had been questions, questions, but she recalled only words, here and there. *"Tell us why. Tell us how."* Even those words began to fade away as if her mind was a computer drive in the pull of a powerful magnet.

Cautiously, she turned on her side, but only to curl into a tight ball.

She slitted her eyes.

Hot darkness all around, not a breath of fresh air. Clammy, almost damp, the surface beneath her was slick. She did not dare to look up.

"The wrong one! She is useless." A pointed face,

wolflike, but with scales rather than fur, had poked close to hers. Its body loomed behind, bent almost double to get down to her level.

It gave out an echoing holler and its body rocked and wobbled. Willow had felt gluey drops spatter her face.

"Not useless," another one said. *"She will serve an important purpose for us."*

The impression faded.

"Ben," she said, longing to see his face, to feel him. Letting her eyes close again, she thought about his voice and all he had told her about communicating with each other. They had done that. She had opened her mind, and they had heard each other without talking.

"Ben," she thought, drawing as much calm about her as she could. *"Find me."*

How hopeless.

Gradually, she became aware of noises. Everywhere, noises. Voices a long way away—and dogs barking.

"Ben!"

"It's okay. Don't move. I'm here."

She lay still, barely breathing for fear she wouldn't hear him again.

He came without sound, or rush of wind or any outward sign of the power and speed of his arrival—until he stroked her arm and she peeked to see him kneeling beside her. She felt his pent-up fear and rage, his struggle to let relief at finding her master his need for vengeance.

"Don't move," he said again, gently touching her, his big hands circling her face and head. "What happened to you? Where have you been?"

"What time is it?" Willow asked.

He kissed her face and rested a cheek against hers,

touched his lips to her neck. "Four in the morning. You've been gone for hours. You were coming toward me by the pool. I only took my eyes off you for a second, but then you were gone. We combed the whole place. Now they're tearing the city apart. Nat's in charge. Can you hear the dogs? They're all over this district. He has every agency out there."

She coughed and he rubbed her back.

"I've got to stop disappearing from that garden," she said in a weak attempt at a joke. "I was taken into the earth—deep beneath it. There was a place, far away, filled with creatures. They were mostly different from each other. Ugly to me. They wanted me to tell them something. I don't remember what. They threatened to kill me."

Ben took a ragged breath, then said, "Can you move your fingers and toes?"

Dutifully, she wiggled both. "Yes." She uncurled her body. "I think everything moves. I know this horrible thing won't end. We've got to make everyone understand they aren't safe anymore. Those beasts, they're going to fight for New Orleans, but that won't be enough. They'll want the world."

He bowed his head. "Yes."

"Where am I?"

He grew still. "You don't know? You're in the cabana at the Brandts'."

"I was sent back here?" she said in wonder, turning her head. She could make out the shapes of furniture and a pale reflection on white walls. "I don't want to be a coward, but I'm so frightened."

"Anyone would be, but I should have been able to keep you safe," he muttered. "I'll never forgive myself for this."

"Ben, it wasn't your fault. But why didn't they kill me? Why did they bring me back?"

He eased her to sit up and lean against him. "Because they want you alive and here," he told her. "They've got plans for you, love, but you aren't alone anymore. What did you mean about being taken deep under the earth?"

She told him about the bright blue light that blinded and stunned her, about being pushed into the pool at the Brandt house and the raptor creature she had seen again. "I don't think it went with me. I didn't see it again." There was the bizarre mask that helped her breathe underwater without the help of air tanks; the powerful pull that dragged her through a hole in the bottom of the pool. She had expected the gush of water all around her to continue, but it dried up when she got there.

"The eggs," she said, startled by a sharp vision. "They had piles of eggs, and they ate what was inside, the shells, as well, and any little bones that fell."

"The eggs again," he said.

"I saw some Embran—I think that one looked like a human all the time."

"God, I hope not," Ben said under his breath. "Mutating is bad enough. But all we need is to have no way to separate some of them from us."

"Wait." She clutched his arms. "The Embran are dying and they say it's our fault." Her headache pummeled her temples again. "They want our world, Ben. They kept saying the answer to getting back their immortality is here. They told me they will take our world, and we'll serve them—and suffer."

She held her head in her hands.

"How many of them are there?" he asked quietly.

"I don't know. A lot, I think." She sat forward and broke into a sweat. "We've got to get to Chris and Fabio! I was coming to tell you about them last night. Help me out of here."

"Not so fast," Ben said. "Take it easy."

Willow scrambled to her feet, and he promptly lifted her into his arms.

"Where are we going?" he said.

"They're in the conservatory, in bottles like I saw in my mind when I was in the courtyard trying to reach them. Or they *were* in the conservatory. Are the police in the house? Who's there? We have to go now."

"Okay. Nat needs to know what's going on. I was with him when you called me. He'll think something nasty happened to me, too."

"Just come with me," she told him. "Remember I told you about a blue light on the wall just before Chloe died and how I thought she looked as if she couldn't see when she fell over the banisters?"

"The light on the wall could have been the laser that was used on you. After you left Chloe she could have been blinded by it." He finished her thought. "You said you couldn't move at first—after the laser hit you. It could be that Chloe didn't scream because she couldn't."

Her feet touched the ground again, inside the kitchen of the Brandt house. Ben had pulled another of his speed moves and this time she was glad, if confused.

"Keep quiet and listen," he said. *"We don't need to speak aloud."*

"No," she agreed, still marveling that he was right. *"Please let's get to the conservatory. I'm afraid those bottles will be gone by now. They look like bottles of*

orchid fertilizer or something. They've got colored granules inside. Ben! There's a little bird in there and it's evil. It's guarding the bottles, I think. I saw it the first time I came here, and it seemed harmless enough then."

"*It probably is.*" Ben laughed. "*I think I can manage a little bird.*"

"*Are there any police here?*" she asked.

"*No. They were pulled once it was obvious you weren't here. I think the house is empty.*"

Rapidly, with Willow behind Ben, where he had put her, they slipped from the kitchen into the corridor beyond. Ben's hand shot back to hold her still. "*Do you hear something?*"

She listened. "*I think so. Raised voices. But they're muffled. Ben, someone's coming through the front door.*"

He flattened his back to the wall, one arm stretched protectively across her body.

They could see into the gloomy hall, but the front door was indistinct. Willow saw shadows shift. A small light at the top of the stairs cast an anemic yellow swath that touched the foyer and the opening to the corridor leading to the conservatory.

"*It's Rock,*" she told Ben, squinting to see.

"*Wait. Don't call out. See where he goes first. We can't be too careful.*"

In his leather pants and muscle shirt, his keys making the faintest sound on the chain tucked into his pocket, Rock crept forward, not looking right or left, but making straight for the conservatory.

"*How does he know to go there? Did he tell you why he couldn't be at the event last night?*"

Willow looked up at Ben in the shadows. She could

make out the long mane of his hair sweeping forward when he leaned to see what he could.

"What do you mean? You talked to him. I saw you. At the gondola—he sent for you, remember?"

"You saw the man who took his place as boatman in a full mask and costume," Ben said. *"But I think Rock's a resourceful man and he's very protective of you. He must have had a good reason to duck out last night."*

At last Rock disappeared. Holding Willow's hand, Ben started forward again. *"I don't suppose you'd agree to go outside and call Nat, tell him you're safe?"*

"No," she told him shortly. *"I'm not leaving you. And we need to do this alone. This is nothing the police can charge into. Soon we're going to have to gather all the power we have between the psi families and work together."*

"I've contacted Pascal and asked him to find Sykes," Ben said. *"Sykes has his shield up, probably to keep Pascal from interfering, but that means I'm shut out, too. Your brother has only got one thing on his mind. You."*

"We need him," Willow said.

"He'll check in and then we'll have him."

Raised voices, jumbled together and angry, came from the direction of the conservatory. A crash, then a shriek of rage speeded Ben and Willow in that direction.

"What are you doing here?" Vanity shouted. "You're that man, Rock, with Willow's crew. None of her people are here anymore. Get out. Now."

"You have made a serious mistake, traitor." It was Rock's raised voice. "Don't you know who I really am?"

Silence followed before Vanity made an enraged noise. "You came here in disguise. How dare you trick me."

"I'm flattered that one look at my real head is all you need to identify me," Rock said. "That saves time. You underestimated me, Vanity. Worse yet, you underestimated our leader. You think we are all fools and you can control us. I have communicated with the Protector. It was he who told me about you. I am to take you back to Safeplace. He has already decided how to make you wish you hadn't made your own plans. You should not have followed me to New Orleans. More than that, you should not have tried to take the place I earned. I was the one who fought for the right to come here for the cause, not you."

"Rock is Embran," Willow thought. *"And so is Vanity."*

Frustrated that she couldn't see inside the conservatory, Willow dropped to her hands and knees and shifted forward, but Ben's hand on the back of her neck held her where she was.

Vanity's strident voice broke in. "The Millets are getting closer to finding the key. We know they have one of them—"

"I also know," Rock interrupted her. "I saw it in their shop. How did you find out about them?"

"The same way you did. I have my spies who let me know what our Protector discusses. If we don't stop these humans, they may find all the keys eventually, and then they will be more difficult to stop. We have to capture their secrets first. We must get those keys and find their precious angel."

Willow started to get up, but Ben stopped her.

"They won't get to their legend," Rock said. "Before they can, we will have overcome them all, and the legend will be in our hands. I believe the answers we're looking for are there. Zibock and I are convinced there is a formula that will restore us. You forget that we have the Millets' ignorance on our side. Thanks to the woman who was with Jude Millet in Belgium, the Embran know what we're up against and what we must have. The Millets are still trying to guess about us. They know nothing, not even the significance of the keys."

"I wish we had those—as many as it will take to reach the angel's secret." Vanity took a noisy breath. She sounded as if she could scarcely breathe. "Still, we don't know how many keys there are. But we are all getting weaker. Who knows how many years we have before we can't fight anymore. There have been too many mistakes made."

"Not by me," Rock said. "Bolivar was too easily distracted. Thirty years he wasted here indulging himself. But I am single-minded. I have done what I was sent to do."

"How did you know I was working to undermine Willow's business and get her here in this house?" Vanity asked.

"Have you forgotten what good friends Willow and I are?" Rock laughed. "And how closely we work? I can read, Vanity. And I have my ways around doors. The information is all there, written down."

"Rock's been there, right where I work, planning against us all the time," Willow said. *"He opened the tattoo parlor within days of my move-in. Ben, he's one of them."*

"Did you kill Chloe Brandt to implicate me?"

He laughed again. "How perceptive of you. And it certainly brought a lot of attention you hated. The Brandts were a clever choice for your purposes. *Dysfunctional* is the word humans use, I think. But I only took moderate pleasure in disposing of the woman. No challenge there. Once I was sure she couldn't make any noise, there wasn't a fight. She tried to cover her face and stood there while I cut her. No challenge at all."

With her hands rolled into fists, Willow looked up at Ben, and he shook his head. *"Don't let anger distract you."*

"So you took Willow Millet to the Protector?" Vanity said. "And now you are golden. Has she given the Protector important information?"

"I can't tell you about it."

Willow nudged Ben. *"He's not going to tell her they didn't get any information from me."*

"We can't be sure Rock knows you're back," Ben said.

The woman hissed with frustration. "What happens to us now?"

Rock's voice became silky and completely unlike that of the man Willow had known. "You will be punished, but you will get another chance. You are resourceful and we need you. Let's go and get our next orders. There has been one change I know of. The Protector has given up on infiltrating mankind with single emissaries. Our numbers on earth will grow faster in future. We will be everywhere among them. First New Orleans, then wherever the Protector decides after that. The humans will be allowed to relax, to grow complacent, but not for long. Our everlasting lives depend on the secrets they are hiding from us."

"They are already searching for the legend. They are

curious about the keys. If they connect the two it will be very dangerous for us," Vanity said.

"Yes," Rock agreed. "But we should return to Safeplace Embran. There are signs we are breaking down, you and I. I have brought us something to help us on our way."

Cracking noises followed, and cooing, like the cries of large doves.

"What are we going to do?" Willow asked.

"Stop them. But it may be even trickier than we expect. There was someone else with Vanity before Rock arrived. We heard another voice. But I'm only hearing Rock and Vanity now. Someone must be hiding in there."

"We can't take them all on by ourselves," Willow said.

"I intend to manage nicely on my own until Sykes and the others get the message."

"I want you to know something." Willow reached for his hand. *"I shouldn't have sent you away. I should have had the confidence to trust your love."*

He crouched beside her. *"You sound as if you're saying goodbye. Nothing is going to happen to either of us."*

"I can't live without you, Ben."

His hug gave her some courage. *"Tell me one thing,"* he said, and his arms shook with emotion. *"Admit we're Bonded forever."*

She felt tears on her face. *"Forever,"* she told him.

Ben stood again, and with his back still to the wall, he slipped to the doorway, took a cautious look into the plant-filled spaces of the conservatory and crouched low. *"Please stay here,"* he said. *"Get outside as soon as you can and call Nat. See who else you can reach. Make sure Nat knows to wait for a signal from me before coming in here."*

She didn't answer, and he didn't wait before leaving her.

36

The Embran, Ben thought, didn't know quite as much as they thought they did. For one thing, they didn't know that with some help from him—and Mario—the Millets already had three keys, not one. The failure to find the right angel frustrated him. He and the others would keep looking, that's all.

"How will the Millets become *complacent* as you suggest with one of their own missing?" Vanity asked. "They will continue searching for Willow."

"And they will find her when Zibock sends her back," Rock said with an unpleasant laugh. "All memory of what she has experienced will be gone by the time she returns to the surface. They will think she has suffered an attack of amnesia and wandered away or some such nonsense, but they will not discover where she has been."

"And she will accept this?"

"In time. She can't change it."

Ben wanted to laugh. He had witnessed Willow's struggles to remember her experiences, but they were getting clearer rather than so distant they showed any sign of disappearing.

He would warn her not to let anyone outside the Millets and Fortunes know the truth yet.

Hidden by plants, Rock and Vanity were at the far end of the long conservatory. Ben launched himself invisibly in the opposite direction, planning to come on them with no warning. In the nanoinstant he took to reach an open closet and slip inside, his other sight caught what hadn't been obvious with human eyes. Under a table draped with a long oilcloth, a man with long blond hair. Absolutely still, his arms wrapped around his shins and his head on his knees, his outline shivered as if he were in the process of, but never quite transforming into something else.

"You're trying to hide something," Rock said, almost growled at Vanity. "Move out of the way. What do you have there?"

"What do you mean?" Vanity said.

"Save it. Get away from the cage. You're hiding something."

"Let's concentrate on what's important." The man beneath the table spoke up suddenly, his voice echoing. He emerged from his hiding place, but Ben didn't recognize him. A tall, elegant man in a brown silk shirt and black pants, he had disturbingly light blue eyes.

He continued to fade slightly, only to return to sharp image. And he sauntered between the tangle of foliage toward the other end of the room.

"Well, if it isn't Vanity's slave." Rock laughed at the man. "Hello, John. I knew you were listening. The same as you've known I've been here in New Orleans all along."

"I thought you were—"

Vanity cut the man off. "Rock, you and I will join forces and do as much as we can now. We can go back to Zibock with enough to make him even more happy than you already have."

"Sure," Rock said. "Why didn't I think of that?"

Ben winced. The answer had come too quickly.

"When will the Millet girl be returned?" Vanity said.

"When I give the signal, Zibock will send her back," Rock said promptly.

Ben smiled to himself. Rock didn't know Willow had been found unsuitable for the Embran's purpose. He also didn't know she was already back and in this very house. Ben wondered about this Zibock's plan. It seemed he was playing Vanity and Rock off against each other.

"Perhaps you should wait until we leave," Vanity said thoughtfully. "I have collected a number of human specimens. We could take them back to Zibock. They may be useful—or not.

"Until Willow returns, the humans will be obsessed with finding her and we'll be safe. Then her return will distract them further. The longer we put off having them concentrate on finding us, the better. They're going to find out something about where we come from eventually."

"They don't have to," Rock said. "And remember we can wipe their memories clean. If any of them get through, we will deal with them."

Only you aren't so good at getting rid of memories yet. In short bursts, zipping from one gap between plant displays to another, Ben worked his way toward the other three.

Using his third eye, he could see them completely.

Rock, in his thick-soled shoes and black leather pants, stood a little apart from the other two. His head was in its human form again. Vanity wore a sleeveless top and tight jeans. John's elegant clothes made them an odd set.

A mark on the back of Vanity's left shoulder made Ben stop breathing. It was a festering burn, and he had little doubt how it had happened. In the moment of battle with the batlike creature in that empty shop, he had used his defensive gift. Vanity was that creature, and she carried his scar no matter what form she took. He smiled at her arrogance in assuming he would have no opportunity to make the connection.

He would never forget how that burn had damaged the source of her invisibility and left one side of her bat body fully revealed to his human eyes. Had she repaired herself at all, he wondered, or was she still only able to squirt the fluid, the source of her shield from ordinary sight, on one side, never to be completely invisible again?

Once more he concentrated his powers solely on searching out Sykes. Still there was no hint of him and Ben ground his teeth together. Without reinforcements, he would have his hands full here.

Vanity spoke in a soft voice unlike her own. "Rock, I have a better idea for us. I'll go to Zibock alone and take my little people. You stay here and keep watch on the Millets."

"You don't decide my actions for me," Rock growled.

He tore the chain from his pocket and his fingers furled around a black cylinder. Instantly, a blue beam shot across Vanity's eyes. She stared into the light, unaffected, and ripped the laser from his hand. "You can't stop me. We know how powerful you are, but there are two of us and only one of you. John, whom I call Servant, not slave, has abilities you know nothing about."

John made an angry noise but subsided.

Ben heard Rock bellow. And Vanity laughed again before the sound changed into a yipping cackle. Ben was certain he knew what was happening.

With three of them and one of him, to let them discover him before he was ready could be suicidal. Ben switched his attention back to the Embran.

He wasn't disappointed. The door to the birdcage stood open and inside, Vanity morphed into the bat that immediately surged to several times the size it had been when he saw it before. Hastily, it wrapped its agile claws around the neck of a bottle, one of a number lined up on shelves of supplies. Ben was sure these must be the containers of orchid food Willow had mentioned. If she was right, there were shrunken people hidden among the bright granules.

Ben saw another movement and his stomach flipped. Willow crept through the entrance to the conservatory and inched toward the group of Embran.

"Willow, stop. Right now. They'll kill you."

He waited. If she heard him, she didn't respond, although he couldn't feel any shield over her mind.

A violent crash brought a scream from Willow. Ben leaped from his hiding place and stopped her from rushing forward. She was no match for his speed or strength, and he held her back easily while the Embran were absorbed in each other.

The bottle Vanity had picked up looked as if it had exploded on the floor. "Catch them," she screamed to John. "I need something to carry them in now." She grabbed another and threw it to John, who put it on the nearest bench. More bottles headed for John, and Ben figured either John had dropped the first one, or Rock had intercepted and smashed it. Brilliant turquoise granules had scattered everywhere.

"Stop it," Willow moaned softly, her eyes wild and searching the floor.

The bat continued to pass bottles. Some John caught, some Rock snatched and immediately smashed. With the last bottle, Rock knocked John out of the way and swept the rest from the bench where they'd been placed. They crashed in heaps of myriad colored granules.

"So much for your plans to impress Zibock," Rock said to Vanity.

She swelled even larger, her eyes glittering with fury.

John's uncontrolled fluctuations ceased. His face became all but featureless while he stretched longer and longer, growing thinner at the same time.

John turned into a red, hard-shelled thing, the elegant clothes gone, more twitching appendages appearing rapidly. He was jointed, like a creature wearing armor.

"Save your time," Vanity hissed at him. "I must go to Zibock alone. Wait here…Servant."

John's dislike for his nickname was evident. His tentacles slapped the cage bars angrily, slipped through, and Vanity's bat bared its sharp teeth to bite, snapping off a piece of tentacle while John howled.

Even more horrifically, Rock's mouth opened wide, wider than should have been possible, and when it started to close, a massive hooked bird's beak replaced the lips. Pointed ears rose on top of the head, ears from which loose skin trailed like gray capes. Slimy feathers and hair sprang over his rapidly bulging body. Swaying with every move, a beard of fat hung beneath the beak. And the wings that had made Willow call this a raptor spread with enough force to knock holes in the walls.

Giving attention to the contents of the smashed jars was out of the question yet. Rock's raptor form swung about, thrashing plants to shreds.

He saw Willow and roared as if in pain when he must have realized she could make a lie of the story he had told Vanity.

"What is she doing here?" The bat made a move to leave the cage, but at that moment, the small, green bird in the cage rose from the end of a perch. It flew at Vanity, stopped as it drew close and whipped its blue-black snakelike tongue around her head. Gasping, she heaved to free herself but the bird's tongue tightened on her.

"Call off your bird, Servant," she gurgled to John, who made a cackling sound and leaped about.

Rock lunged at Willow, his beak snapping. He snatched her up by the shoulders and shook her like a rag doll.

Ben had no choice but to give the creature all of his attention and hope John's malignant bird would keep Vanity busy. John seemed transfixed at the struggle inside the cage.

Grabbing a potting fork from a box of tools, Ben thrust the sharp tines into the part of Rock's belly that had yet to finish its transformation. An insane roar sent shock trembling through the atmosphere. Battling powers clashed.

Sykes appeared beside Ben, taking in the scene quickly. And Pascal was there almost at the same time.

"What took you so long?" Ben said.

"If you had made contact with Nat before wading in here, it wouldn't have taken so long."

"Enough, you two," Pascal ordered, sidling toward the elongated red monster that was John, where he stood before the bat writhing in the birdcage.

Giant talons had replaced Rock's hands, and Willow was clutched in one of them. Back and forth she swung with the wounded beast's stumbling gait. Thick black fluid dribbled out around the fork tines still embedded in its belly.

Sykes pried Willow from the talons, and Ben, focusing on his own fingers, sank them into slimy feathers and fur. Instantly, smoke rose and the acrid reek of burning tissue. Rock howled and cast about, wild and still too strong to be taken down easily.

"Willow," Ben shouted, unable to see where she had landed. "Just answer me."

"I'm okay," she said.

Growing tiny, the bat slid free of the bird's tongue and fell as if dead, only to leap up, its size ballooning again and its needle teeth glinting. It cast around, searching for something.

Before Ben could stop her, Willow threw herself toward the smashed bottles, and he stared, amazed, at figures uncurling to full height—men and women, naked, but obviously too distracted to be concerned with their bodies.

"Heavenly hedonists," Pascal exclaimed, although Ben thought the apparently appropriate description was accidental.

"Get out of the way," Willow ordered the group. "Get back. Chris, Fabio, take them all out of here."

Chris, Fabio and a woman who held Chris's hand, stood their ground, but the rest edged carefully backward.

Ben heard another scream. Willow's. Yanked by the rapidly growing bat, she fell inside the cage. Vanity had taken the key and deftly used her claws to close and lock the door on the inside.

He shot to tear at the bars.

Shrieking with unearthly laughter, Vanity threw Willow to the ground and spread herself on top of her, completely hiding Willow.

Ben strained at the bars and one began to bend outward. "Leave her," he yelled at Vanity. "Get away. Willow?"

Willow didn't answer, and Vanity only swelled larger, her whole, ugly body vibrating while she continued to laugh.

Swaying in front of Pascal and Sykes, John used his tentacles to snap at them, forcing both to engage him. One at either side, they pummeled him, but he kept swinging at them.

With a last huge shout, Vanity rose up, revealing a rapidly changing gelatinous mass. Inside it, Ben saw Willow fighting to escape. She might as well have fought with superglue.

What he saw next took his horror to a new level. Starting at one end, the mass formed itself into a hard, yellowish coat—a shell. Willow was disappearing inside one of their eggs.

"I win," Vanity cried. "I will take her egg to Zibock as a gift."

Rock mumbled from the floor, making no sense.

Soaring, her bat wings flapping, Vanity said, "I will tell him to eat her and live forever."

"You don't know that works," Rock said indistinctly between drooling lips.

"But we must try," she told him, emitting high-pitched clicking noises.

The shell grew larger, overtaking Willow, who lay on her side, fighting with the gluey substance that bound her.

"It will suffocate her," Vanity trilled gleefully. "She is not like one of us. She cannot live without air as we do when we're young."

Stretching one arm as far as it would go, Ben thrust it behind the bar he had bent. Vanity flew at him, her teeth bared. She came too fast and he caught her low belly, concentrated all his energy there, and smoke rose.

His smoldering touch impaled her, and she flapped helplessly, thrashing her head, wailing.

The shell had reached Willow's shoulders. He could see her punching weakly over her head.

Leaping against the cage, he rammed the soles of his shoes into the door and strained, dragging at the bar until he felt it yield more.

"Willow," he shouted. "Stay with me."

Just barely he reached the key and unlocked the cage. Aware of the bat's mewling and flopping, he had no time to consider another attack from that direction.

The egg came together at its narrower end.

"No!" Ben threw himself across the space, hauled the egg toward him and saw a space no bigger than a quarter. "No!"

With all his might he jammed a forefinger through the hole and tore away a chunk of gummy shell. Hard on the outside, it was still soft and sticky inside.

Crazed with fear, he stripped away piece after piece

of shell. The viscous matter adhered to the inside, forming the actual egg, and toward the other end it had started to turn opaque.

He dragged at the stuff that still covered her head, scooped it away from her nose and mouth, panting, aware of choking on his own breath.

Sykes joined him and went to work helping clear Willow's eyes and rake at her face and hair. The other man's ragged breathing, his desperation, joined Ben's.

Willow's eyes were closed and she didn't move.

Pushing Sykes away, Ben turned her onto her back and brought his mouth down over hers, puffing into her mouth and turning his head to watch her chest.

"Ben," she whispered. "I'm not dead."

He caught her up in his arms and shook her, kissed her and shook her, not caring what still clung to her skin. It was already drying and falling away.

Sykes cried out. Vanity found enough energy to land on his back and reach for his ear with one claw.

"You *are* dead," Pascal thundered. Holding a bundle of metal orchid stakes, he cannoned inside the cage, raising a single stake in his right hand. He used it to hook Vanity from Sykes's back and pin her by one wing to the back wall, like an ugly butterfly on a board.

Straining, striking out with the still-free wing, Vanity's bat tried to snare Pascal, but he moved with incredible speed, piercing the second wing with another stake and jamming it to the wall. For good measure he sent several more stakes after the first two.

"Don't kill it," Sykes said. "We need its secrets."

Pascal cast a pitying glance at his nephew. "Naturally."

John in his lobster incarnation settled his tiny eyes on Willow, and he made sinuous movements in her direction, only to be met by Chris and Fabio, who threw themselves at his body and climbed him as if he were a rope. They made it to the head where they drove their fingers into those nasty little eyes.

The creature staggered back and forth, its body undulating in outrageous angles before it fell and the entire group of naked humans climbed on top to hold the thing down.

More footsteps pounded toward the conservatory. As Ben expected, Nat, Bucky Fist and Gray ran in while uniformed cops ground to a halt outside.

Ben wouldn't let Willow go. He held her and watched for the moment when he would have no choice but to join the melee. Sykes snagged a stake from Pascal and the two of them fell to stabbing the still-writhing Rock.

Nat, Bucky and Gray flew into the middle of everything, and Ben almost laughed at the sight of Bucky slamming handcuffs on Rock's talons, talons that withered before the eye. When the talons disappeared altogether, the handcuffs proved just as helpful since they were securely attached to Rock's wrists.

He convulsed, and the horrible creature that was the real Rock rolled on his back and lay still while he was bound. "I need eggs," he whispered.

Ben turned to the Vanity-bat attached to the wall inside the birdcage. It heaved and swelled, first in one direction, then another, like some deep-sea jelly creature blobbing along the bottom. Pascal kept watch while Nat stalked closer to the cage.

"Bolivar didn't get away until after he was arrested."

Ben recognized Gray's voice, Gray who had been there when Bolivar was arrested, as Ben had not.

"We can try to do better this time," Ben told Gray. *"Bring that sack now."*

Snatching up a burlap sack, Sykes entered the cage neck and neck with Gray. Together with Pascal they covered Vanity with the sack and worked her free of the wall while leaving the stakes through her wings. She fell heavily into the bottom of the sack. Lumps and bumps poked at the inside as she struggled to get free. Ben and Pascal slapped lengths of duct tape around the sack until it was completely covered.

"That's him," the woman with Chris cried out. She pointed at John who was transforming back to his elegantly dressed form. Already his blond hair had appeared. "He's the one who did it to me. He put me in a champagne glass, then in a bottle and left me there."

As if struck, John grew completely still. Then, first blurring and melting, he changed shape, growing shorter, stockier and eventually, becoming Val Brandt.

Ben stared, but it was Willow who confronted the man. "You were with them all along. You helped lure me to your house. Was Chloe one of you, too?"

Val laughed. "Poor, weak Chloe. She never knew that I took over her Val's body."

37

Rays of golden sunshine penetrated the Court of Angels.

The Millets, Marley and Gray Fisher and the Fortunes gathered near the fountain—all but Poppy Fortune, who had left New Orleans the night before, headed for her parents' retreat house in California.

Ben kept Willow close to his side. "I want to get out of here," he murmured to her.

Her immediate smile was all the response he needed.

"We've got one or two things to get through first," Sykes said, smirking.

"We all know about your out-of-this-world hearing," Willow told him. "But you do have to compete with Ben all the time, don't you? It's pointless because…well, it's pointless is all."

"Pointless," Ben echoed, squeezing her shoulders.

The smirk on Sykes's face didn't waver.

"That's enough, children," Pascal said, but he looked pleased with himself. "This is serious. No horsing around."

"How sure are we that Nat has those three in custody?" Gray asked.

A pause settled in. After taking time only to shower

and change, most of them were exhausted, if relieved, but they knew what stretched ahead and it wasn't pretty.

"They're in restraints," Pascal said finally. "Inside cells."

"What if they morph into something else?" Gray said.

"They don't pass through walls as far as we know," Marley put in.

Liam and Ethan Fortune stood a little apart. They had been brought up to speed by the others, but the fresh concern over what New Orleans and its people faced was obvious. "Couldn't they be put in tanks?" Liam said. "Where they could be watched all the time? They aren't invincible and we're going to know more about them."

"They can't help themselves," Ben said. "They've set a course and it isn't going away. They are slowly dying out. Slowly by their standards is evidently a long, long time by ours, but they aren't ready to give up immortality."

"Finding out the significance of those keys has to be at the top of our list," Willow said. "Especially now we know they definitely have something to do with our missing angel."

"If the Embran have it right," Ben pointed out.

"I think the angel represents a real person," Willow said, and everyone fell silent.

The stands of bamboo rustled and flipped. Winnie chomped noisily on her plastic bone—dinosaur bone as Gray called it. Mario stuck close to Willow and Ben and seemed subdued.

"It doesn't have to represent a real person." Marley sat down abruptly on the edge of the fountain. "Unless it's on a tomb. There aren't any of those around here."

"Not that we've noticed," Sykes said. "I want the connection between our story and the fate of the Embran."

"We may not like it when we get it, but we will get it. We may have to involve people outside the families." Pascal frowned heavily.

"We already have," Ben reminded him. "Nat, Bucky, Blades and who knows how many more have figured out this isn't all a concoction of the psi families. Nat told me the rumors are only getting bigger. And now we have the bunch of people Vanity and John, or Val or whoever he is, assaulted. You can't deny the same story from nine people."

Willow rubbed her knuckles over his back. "You should have heard Chris and Fabio. They are ready to form an army."

"That's not far-fetched. We're going to need an army." Liam Fortune narrowed his eyes and looked into the distance. "I'm hoping for one break. Let it take them a while to get organized again. The powers that be down there don't know what's happened up here as far as we know. The longer it takes them to send some of their monsters to find out, the better."

"Wish they remained monsters," Ben said. "It's when they look like the rest of us that we're in most danger."

"Nat told me Vanity seems stuck in bat form now," Willow told the rest. "And she keeps squirting some sort of fluid over herself from her back. Half of her becomes invisible but not the other half and she throws fits."

Ben decided he'd explain the reason for that later.

The back door to the shop opened and Anthony pushed out a loaded cart. "Are you ready?" he called to Pascal.

"Absolutely. More than ready for some official business."

"We'd better change the subject," Marley said.

"Anthony is my confidant," Pascal said with his nose elevated. "I trust him with anything and he understands everything. He will become very useful."

Pascal's trainer trundled the cart over uneven ground. "This is going to shake up the bubbly," he remarked.

"Can we get a move on?" Ben whispered to Pascal. "I've got things to do."

"Not without the necessary formalities," Pascal told him, but he stopped himself from grinning. "After all, this is a special day, regardless of anything that may have gone before."

Anthony poured champagne and began handing glasses around.

"None for Marley," Willow said. She turned very red and her freckles popped out even more.

She had created a puddle of silence.

Gray sat beside Marley and kissed her until cheers went up. "You keep quiet," he told Willow. "Miss No Talent Who Knows Everything. Seems there's going to be a little person running around here in a few months. But we don't want to talk about it now. This day is for Ben and Willow."

Gray wasn't successful in stopping the whoops, the hugs or the applause until Pascal used a fork on glass to control them all.

"Let's hear the words," he said when he could hear himself again. "Ben and Willow, step up and do it right. Then we can party."

Ben took Willow's hand and they stood in front of

their family members. She wore a long, pale green linen shift and flat sandals. Her hair was still wet, and he had never seen anyone look more stunning. The stirring he felt was no surprise, nor was the current that fused their palms together and sent shocks through his body.

"I know," Willow whispered. "We need to go."

"Get on with it," Pascal said, feigning resignation.

Ben's own nod to the day was a white linen shirt Willow had said she loved. He wore it with blue jeans and sandals.

"Ben and Willow?" Pascal sounded exasperated.

"Okay, okay," Ben said under his breath. "Willow Millet, in keeping with the instructions from your Mentor, I am the best thing that ever happened to you."

Titters built until Pascal clanked the glass again. "That's it," he said. "This isn't a joke."

"It sure isn't," Ben said, feeling a smidgen of remorse for being flip. "Willow and I have loved each other for a long time. We know we are Bonded. And now we want to tell all of you that we will be together forever."

He heard a snuffle and traced it to Marley.

"Willow, will you join me forever?"

"Yes," she said. "I am yours and you are mine. We are Bonded."

"And may you enjoy a long, happy life of pain," Sykes bellowed.

Ignoring the remark, Anthony whipped the cover from a tray of hors d'oeuvres. The smells alone drew a gaggle with outstretched hands.

"Nice how they're congratulating us," Willow said. She stared into his eyes as if she would never look away. "But all I need is you, Ben Fortune."

"Ditto," he said, the color of his eyes growing darker. "Wrap your arms around me and hold on tight."

"Why…Ben, you're up to something."

"You bet, love. Up, up and away."

Epilogue

With her arms still wrapped tightly around Ben, Willow opened her eyes.

Coconut palms, hibiscus blossoms in burning scarlet, orange and gold, ironwood trees and creepers with bright leaves stretching over white sand had replaced the Court of Angels.

Bleached driftwood dotted the shore and beyond that lay the ocean. At first glance she saw ribbons of surf, incandescent under a sun as bright as it had been in New Orleans, but cooled by trade winds here, and water so vivid it appeared pure turquoise, lit from beneath. As she stared, other colors appeared, sapphire, cyan, aquamarine and lapis.

"We're in Kauai, aren't we?" she said. "We just traveled thousands of miles in less than a moment because you decided we would."

"Sort of." He looked a bit sheepish. "I wasn't sure I could take us this far. But we can both swim, so…"

"Not funny, Ben." She felt him watching her face. "You do know you could make a fortune with this trick, don't you?" she said, keeping her eyes trained on his chest. Looking at Ben's chest was no punishment.

"*Trick* isn't a word in my vocabulary," he told her. "Unless you've got some different rules from mine, we don't make money on our powers."

"This is your beach?"

"Mmm. Sometimes it feels as if it is. Hanalei Bay."

"Don't you think we should let the others know where we are?" she said.

He tipped up her chin. "Nope. I told Pascal we would be leaving. That was enough."

The trades blew his hair aside. His neck and jaw were strong and tanned, his eyes the blue of that lapis in the ocean.

"Do you mind that there are…sensations with every touch we share, Ben?"

"I'd mind if there weren't now."

Willow began to unbutton his white shirt—until he stopped her. "I didn't say this was entirely my beach," he said. "We wouldn't want to get carried away."

"Yes, I do." She intended to look serious, but the sudden total absorption he turned on her sent shivers across her skin.

He looked past her and frowned.

"What?" Willow turned around. Behind her, just visible through a break in hibiscus hedges, she could see a green, single-story house with a lanai running along as much as was visible of the building. "That's a pretty place. Is this yours?"

"It's ours," he told her. "It's very island because that's what I like. But if you want something with a lot of glass and everything modern, that's what we'll have instead."

Willow continued to undo his buttons. "Whatever pleases you, pleases me."

"I'll remind you of that. How about what I was looking at, and it wasn't the house? You okay with that?"

She spun around again.

Ben pulled her back against him, and she shivered, closing her eyes to soak him in. "What do you see?"

His chin came to rest on her shoulder. "Are you looking?"

"Of course." She snapped her eyes open to search around. "I don't see anything that isn't beautiful."

"You've always had bent opinions about some things. Staring at us from behind that green rock, the big one. What do you think?"

It took a moment before she realized he was talking about Mario, whose black eyes managed to look as if he'd been beaten regularly and feared he was about to get another whipping.

"Mario!"

The dog raced across the sand and leaped into her arms.

"How did you get here?" she said, rocking him.

"Well, Sykes didn't bring him this time." Ben cleared his throat. "Could it be he made sure he was close enough to get caught up in the moment, shall we say?"

She wrinkled her nose at Mario. "Maybe."

"Come on," he said, lifting her and Mario into his arms. "I've waited long enough. We've got a Bonding to make official."

Willow laughed and kissed his neck again and again until he leaped about. "I think you're electrocuting my throat," he said. "You can put your mysterious little Brussels Griffon on the lanai and tell him to stay there. We have other things to concentrate on."

"My what?"

"I researched him. He's a Brussels Griffon. Purebred. They're show dogs. Or a good specimen would be."

She poked his ribs. "That's weird. Are you sure he's one of those?"

Ben walked with her between poinsettia and bird-of-paradise flowers. "Brussels, Belgium. Been around since the sixteenth century at least. I thought that was strange, too. Quite a coincidence."

He climbed wooden steps, and Willow saw the lanai went all around the house.

"So I found a Brussels Griffon. Big deal."

"You found him?"

"He found me. I want him inside. There's got to be somewhere he can be comfortable—"

"While we're otherwise occupied? You bet."

He slid the screen aside with a finger and walked in through the open front door.

He kissed her then, for so long Willow gulped for breath whenever she had the chance.

"You can see the ocean from these front windows," she gasped when he took a break. "Look at this place. Ben!"

He set her down and she put Mario on the floor. The dog immediately scuttled away behind a couch. The furniture was either made of heavy bamboo and cane with cushions covered in leafy-green fabrics, or Asian, carved and lacquered. Here and there a shiny red piece stood out. And brass bowls, bone carvings and tapa hangings. Loose carpets in beautifully worn and muted colors were perfect on richly shining koa wood floors.

Ben took her by the hand and led her into a bedroom

much the same size as the living room. Again, the view through the windows was of the ocean and beach.

"Come on," he said, still moving. Another door opened onto a small sunken garden of lava rock and ferns. On one side there was a hot tub, steaming gently. And rattan screens covered with flowering vines created a private bower.

Ben shut the door to the bedroom. She had no more time for questions before he pulled her dress over her head and tossed it aside. His shirt and pants followed and he kicked off his shoes.

Excitement curled in Willow's belly. "Ben—"

"Shh." He touched her mouth. "There are things I want. Not just the things you think. More. I want what Marley and Gray have—a marriage like—"

"Shh." It was her turn to break in. "Then we will. I'd like that, too, but I didn't have to have it if you didn't."

He picked up his pants and took a little bag from a pocket. Inside were two simple gold bands. Ben gave the bigger one to her and raised an eyebrow as he held out the small one. Willow gave him her hand, and he slipped on the ring before she put the other band on his finger.

"Tomorrow we'll do the rest of it," he said. "On the beach, maybe. When the light gets mauve?"

Willow thought of the mauve light she had seen in the Court of Angels.

"Sweetheart," Ben said. "Take it from me, the light here gets mauve at certain times of day. And it sparkles. And if we're lucky it'll rain just before we go out there and we'll have rainbows."

She couldn't be nonchalant about the naked man who had just put a ring on her finger. She couldn't look away from his body, tall, straight, powerful and potent.

Her bra and panties made her feel awkward.

"Now," he said, and before she could take another breath he swept her into the hot tub. Immediately, he gripped her waist and raised her partway out of the water. "Your underwear should always be wet and sticking to your skin. Oh, yeah."

Wriggling did her no good. He whipped off the bra then dipped under the warm water to slide her panties down and over her feet. Then he came up sputtering.

"Have you ever made love in a hot tub?" he asked.

"No. Have you?"

He tilted his head as if in deep thought. "Actually, no. I was waiting for you."

"I'm burning up, Ben, and it isn't the water."

Ben tipped her on her back and floated her around the small pool. When she automatically put her hands over her breasts, he moved them away and kissed her in every place that ached for his touch. But when he shifted his mouth to fresh territory, he only left a deeper ache behind. Willow moaned and tried to grab him.

He raised her hips to make a straight path for his tongue, straight to delve into the folds between her legs.

"Stop it!" She writhed.

"You don't mean that," he said and carried on until waves of sweet agony broke over her.

Willow panted and scrambled to get her arms around his neck. "Your turn." But she got nowhere with her attempt to get his feet off the bottom, other than to make him shout with laughter and subdue her as if she were a doll.

"I'll make a deal," he said. "Let me have my way first, then you can see if you can do better."

"Who's the judge of better?" she said, sliding her fingers over his hips, across his belly and grabbing him before he could stop her again. Not that he tried very hard.

But he was ahead of her. In one swift motion, he gathered her legs and wrapped them around his waist. "Well," he said through his teeth. "What are you waiting for?"

Staring into his eyes, Willow put him where they both wanted him to be, and they moved together, first slowly, eyes closed, heads falling on each other's shoulders. Then ever faster, and their cries kept pace with the searing reactions that would always be part of them— their own electrical currents.

The release came, long, raw, filling them up but not enough.

For minutes they hung together. "Don't let me go," Willow whispered. "I'll drown."

He ducked and sipped at her breasts, stood with her legs over his shoulders and made wicked arches of his eyebrows. His mouth closed on that vulnerable place, but first he said, "I love you, Willow. You are mine, so make the best of it." And he carried on to his target.

Willow tossed. "I'm yours, I'm yours," she cried. "I give in. And you're mine. But if we're going to do this forever, you'd better save something for next time."

Ben saved nothing, not then, or the next time. And Willow was his match.

Much later, when the sun set behind the folded, lush green mountains around Hanalei Bay, red, lemon-yellow and purple streaked the sky. They watched rosy chips sparkle along a gold path on the water. But not for long.

* * * * *